# Dun Lady's Jess

by

Doranna Durgin

Star
Ink
Books

This Edition Copyright © 2007 Doranna Durgin and Star Ink Books

5 4 3 2 1

First Printing of the following:
Foreword © 2007 Elizabeth Moon; Introduction © 2007 Doranna Durgin

BSFS Logo, Compton Crook Award, used with permission of the Baltimore Science Fiction Society.

**Published by:** Star Ink Books Published by
Red Deer Press
A Fitzhenry & Whiteside Company
1512, 1800–4 Street S.W.
Calgary, Alberta, Canada T2S 2S5
www.reddeerpress.com

**Acknowledgements:** Financial support provided by the Canada Council, and the Government of Canada through the Book Publishing Industry Development Program (BPIDP).

 Canada Council  Conseil des Arts
for the Arts  du Canada

**Library and Archives Canada Cataloguing in Publication**
Durgin, Doranna
    Dun Lady's Jess / Doranna Durgin.
Originally published: New York, N.Y. : Baen's Book, 1994.
ISBN 978-0-88995-398-7
I. Title.
PS3554.U673D85 2007        813'.6        C2007-903456-X

**Publisher Cataloging-in-Publication Data (U.S)**
Durgin, Doranna.
    Dun Lady's Jess / Doranna Durgin.
Originally published: New York, NY: Baen's Book, 1994.
[295] p. :  cm.
Summary: A blend of adventure, magic, and romance that spans our world and its richly imagined fantasy counterpart. Horse become human, Jess is spirited and intelligent, seeing our world through a unique perspec-tive. Pursued by evil, she must find a way to not only save her rider and both worlds, but also keep who she has become.
ISBN-13: 978-0-88995-398-7  (pbk.)
1. Fantasy. 2. Mystery.  I. Title.
813.6  dc22    PS3554.U673.D487 2007

**Credits:** Editor: Julie E. Czerneda
Bridle Icon: Doranna Durgin
Cover art and design: Kenn Brown and Chris Wren, Mondolithic Studios
Text design: Karen Thomas, Intuitive Design International Inc.
Printed and bound in Canada for Star Ink Books

## DEDICATION

Dedicated to every single person who helped me along the way,

For Leslie and Tusquin, who showed me how it could be,

And especially for Holly, Sue, and Will, who were there at the start.

With shiny bright new thanks to:

Julie Czerneda and Lucienne Diver, both of whom understand.

# FOREWORD

When I first read Doranna Durgin's *Dun Lady's Jess*, back in 1994, I was astonished and delighted. Fantasy had already given us a number of girl-and-horse models, all fairly romantic, reeking with wishful thinking. This was completely different: a serious and successful consideration of what might happen if a horse were transformed into the body of a human, while retaining the essential nature of a horse—the way a horse senses, thinks, moves.

Few stories hinging on the transformation of human into animal or animal into human work as more than curiosities, because most writers can't grasp enough of the animal reality. LeGuin, in the *Earthsea* books, explored some of the possibilities of transformation, but shape-shifting was not the point of those stories—power and the abuse of power— including the abuse of the power to escape through transformation— were. Terry Pratchett, putting a female werewolf in the police department, has handled Angua's transformations to and from her wolf body with sensitivity. The only other horse-human transformation of comparable quality is Judith Tarr's *A Wind in Cairo*, in which a dissolute young man is magically transformed into a horse to teach him a lesson.

*Dun Lady's Jess* is unique. Durgin has created a character who is utterly believable as both horse and horse-in-human-body. The setup is brilliant: the magic that causes the transformation is not in the horse, but external, and the creature that is Dun Lady's Jess must adapt, must find an identity that works in both paradigms. Humans who encounter her, in either body, must also adapt to the reality that created her and that she represents. She cannot be, any longer, just another mare...she cannot be, ever, just another woman.

It's also, of course, a walloping good adventure story, but at the core it's the story of identity and transformation.

*Elizabeth Moon*

Compton Crook and Nebula Award-winning author of *Command Decision* and *The Speed of Dark*

INTRODUCTION

Once upon a time I had a dream.

No, seriously. I dreamt of a man on his horse, carrying important information and running for his life. Running for *their* lives. They triggered a spell and ended up...

Elsewhere. And entirely changed.

So I wrote it, and it became another sort of dream—the one where you're so in love with the story and characters that you want to share. Need to share. Are obsessed about sharing—!

*Jess* sold to the second publisher who saw the manuscript; less than a year later the book was on the shelves. Dream come true? You betcha. And the next spring, when *Jess* won the Compton Crook award for the best "first book" of the year, I realized that what I'd wanted so badly— to find others who feel as I do about Jess and her world—was now a reality.

But as all books eventually do, *Jess* went out of print. Dismayed readers who found books two & three of that series could do no more than haunt used bookstores in search of the first. So then I had another dream: To find an editor who feels the same as I about this story, and who also wanted to see it live again. By then my craft became more mature—the moment a writer stops growing is the moment she falters—but *Jess'* story still called to me above and beyond. I still wanted it told.

Now here I am, years later, and I've found an editor who loves *Jess*, who has offered her a home with Star Ink Books. A home that will allow me to share the story and the people with a whole new group of readers...to share Jess' heart.

Because when you come right down to it, that's what Jess has taught me. While exploring her story, how she reacts to the changes in her life and the people she encounters...while watching her grow from a baffled young woman into someone with destiny...I learned about heart. About having it, and staying true to it. That the lesson applies when it comes writing, to reading...and to life. Having heart is how we grow, how we live lives we're proud of and happy with, and how we fill our lives with people who do the same. And if I ever forget that lesson in the detailed trappings of deadlines and assignments and bills, Jess is—thank goodness—always there to remind me.

This release of *Dun Lady's Jess* is an updated one, which is to say that I've been given the opportunity (nay, privilege!) to wander the manuscript, slyly smoothing off the rough edges of my early prose without changing the story one little bit. I hope you enjoy reading it as much as I've enjoyed revisiting it!

*Doranna Durgin*

# 1

The odor of singed herbs filled the stone stairway, and Carey smiled to himself. He knew that once again, Arlen had immersed himself so deeply in his studies that the outside world eluded him. He reached the wizard's chamber and hooked his hand on the heavy door frame to swing casually into the well-lit room.

Arlen did not notice. His writing table was cleared down to seldom seen wood, and he sat staring intently at the one object gracing its surface. His hair, still full and shaggy despite some gray, fell forward to hide his features: dark, kind eyes and a long nose over a mustache which almost hid his slight overbite.

Carey tapped the thick metal of his courier ring against the stone of the wall, introducing sound into the quiet room. Arlen's head jerked up, then around; when he discovered Carey, his one cocked eyebrow formed an unspoken question.

"You called, remember?" Carey tapped the ring again, which still tingled in summons. With easy familiarity, he moved into the room and pulled up the stool that sat empty before Arlen's spell table. "You've been up here too long. I'll bet you haven't been out since you first sent me out to Sherra's." He reached for the sputtering simmer pot and removed the burning herbs from the frame that held it over its low mage-flame. "Losing track of your fragrance herbs...not a good sign, Arlen."

Arlen leaned back in his chair and raised another eyebrow, offended this time. "I called, all right, but it wasn't to subject myself to a lecture."

"You need one," Carey replied, unperturbed. "If you hadn't kept me so busy running between wizards lately, I'd have made sure you remembered to take care of yourself."

"That's the problem exactly," Arlen said. "That's why I called. I've got another run for you—but this time we need to talk."

Carey abandoned the stool and wandered to one of the four unshuttered windows of the hold's uppermost room. Built along a hillside, the dwelling abandoned any pretense at symmetrical architecture and instead insinuated itself into the nooks and crannies of the steep rocky ground. The result was this five-walled room, of which no wall equaled the length of another. A good place for the creative pursuits of a wizard, Carey had decided long ago. He hung over the window sill to get an unfettered look at the hilly fields and pastures of the area, while the brisk spring air made a pleasant counterpoint to the sunshine on his face. "So talk."

"Carey," Arlen said firmly, "I recognize the habits of your profession don't encourage inactivity. But do you think you could be still for just a few moments, and apply your entire concentration to what I have to say?"

Surprised but unstung by the wizard's admonition, Carey returned to the stool and shook his hair—dark blond instead of gray, but just as shaggy as Arlen's—out of his eyes. "All right," he said. "I'm listening." And then, seeing the smudges of fatigue around Arlen's eyes and fully recognizing their somber expression, he was indeed truly alert to what his friend and employer had to say.

"I've found something new, Carey, something none of us have suspected even existed."

*None of us*—wizards, he meant. Carey nodded. "That explains why you've been sending everything through me instead of popping it around." Magical missives could be intercepted, but a lone rider was most difficult to detect—except through the mundane means of trackers and guesswork. "How dangerous is it?"

Arlen nodded, absently smoothing a frayed spot on his shirt.

"Dangerous all the way around—but wondrous, as well. There are other worlds, Carey. Other dimensions. Other peoples...people who, I might add, don't seem to have any notion we exist."

"Then what's the danger?" Carey frowned.

"At this point, the danger is to them."

Carey shook his head once to show he wasn't following, and Arlen's expression grew intense.

"You know we have checkspells in place to prevent the unauthorized use of dangerous magics. What you may not realize is that the most inherently dangerous moment in the life of any hazardous new spell is the time between when it is discovered and the time the checkspell is in place. There's more than one person in this land who would use this particular knowledge for their own gain—and those other worlds can't know how to deal with a magic they may not possess."

Carey gave a skeptical snort. "I doubt they're as helpless as all that. Besides, what's to gain?"

"Entire worlds." Arlen said with certainty. "As far as I've been able to determine, once a traveler is spelled to one of these worlds, there remains only the thread of a connection between the two places. That gives the person in question all the magic they care to draw on—even in the worlds without magic—with none of the inconveniences of the Council's restraint." Arlen leaned forward, his dark eyes sparking with intensity. "Think past the everyday magics of night glows and cleansing spells, Carey. Think about those things that are used only when one of us without scruples manages to circumvent a checkspell, and how quickly they gain power. The bloody times in Camolen's history."

The skepticism faded; Carey stared at the wizard with widened eyes. "Damn."

Arlen leaned back, taking a deep breath that he released slowly through his long, straight nose. "There's more. These others have developed devices that accomplish some of the same things we can do with magic, including weapons that will work as well in our world as theirs. We've got to get this under control before one of the less conscientious among us figures out what we've got and how to use it. I hope your horses are well rested, Carey, because you're going to be busy."

Carey shrugged sturdy shoulders set atop a wiry frame. "That's what I'm here for."

"True enough." Arlen reached behind to scoop the lone object from the top of his writing desk and held it out to Carey, who rose only long enough to take it. He settled back on the stool and studied the small blue crystal for a moment before glancing back up at Arlen. "It's protection," Arlen said.

"Spellstone?" Carey asked. "Protection from what?" He reached into the neck of his tunic and brought out a heavy silver chain upon which hung several colorful spellstones, and compared the new one to its fellows.

"We've been careful, but—" Arlen shook his head, his lips thinning in annoyance. "Word is out, I'm afraid. At the very least, Calandre knows of the new spell—Calandre, and whoever else she's told. She's been too good for too long. You're bound to be a target, Carey."

Carey set the small crystal carefully on the table, thinking about Arlen's former student. A woman his own age, Calandre had arrived with an enormous amount of talent and not a whit of patience. Her barely scrupulous magical shortcuts had kept her off the Wizard's Council year after year, and as her frustration grew, so did her rationalized, barely sanctioned methods. For several years she had been in her own hold—obtained from an aging wizard under questionable circumstances—and had not bothered to interact with the Council, save for response to the occasional summons. To all appearances, she was operating within the Council guidelines, but.... "What about the shieldstone?" he asked.

"Still holds," Arlen assured him. "As long as you wear the stone, the only magic that affects you will be the spells you release yourself. But you know as well as I that there are other ways."

Unclasping the silver chain, Carey strung the new spellstone and replaced the collection around his neck, looking at Arlen in utter confidence. "No one's going to outrun me."

"Let's pretend that they do," Arlen said, a hint of exasperation in his voice. "That's what this crystal is for. I'm not sure just what effect it'll have—"

Carey looked at him in surprise. "You want me to fool around with an untested spell? I'll rely on my horses, I think."

"Did you hear nothing of what I have said?" Arlen's anger flashed just bright enough to remind Carey who and what his employer was. "You'll be carrying information too crucial to lose! Everything I know of this new spell is in my head, Carey—except for the manuscript you'll be taking to Sherra. In that is everything I know about the new dimensions, and all my explorations into a checkspell. If anyone—and I mean anyone, from the lowest road pirate to the Precinct Guard—tries to take it from you, you invoke that crystal. It will take you to the only place you can't be reached."

Years of working with the wizard as friend and courier alerted Carey to the words that were not said. "Where?" he asked warily, then didn't give Arlen a chance to answer. "To *one of those other worlds.* You're sending me to a place that might not even know magic—how the hell am I supposed to get back?"

"It's a two-fold spell," Arlen said steadily. "It's tied to this world; it'll bring you back when you invoke it again, and reverse any of the results."

"What about the recall? Why don't I just use that in the first place?"

"No! If you're too close to them, and you're running from some-one with magic, they'll tap in and follow you right back here." Arlen sighed at Carey's frustration. "Normally that's not a problem—not with the shielded receiving room in the stable. But we can't take a chance. There we'd be—the manuscript and me, in the same hold with whoever's threatening us both. They'd get it all, and that would leave Sherra with no chance of formulating a checkspell in time to stop the trouble that would inevitably follow."

Carey frowned as the importance of this run—and its dangers—sank in past his protests. "All right, Arlen," he said slowly. "I under-stand." In the silence that followed, he put a hand to his chest, and felt the small lump of crystals. The run to Sherra's was long, a twisting route through thick woods and a deep river gully. Plenty of spots for an ambush.

"I see that you do," Arlen said in relief. "I'm sorry, Carey. I wouldn't choose to put you in this danger, but I need someone I can trust absolutely."

Carey raised his head, a sharp motion that was the preamble of defensiveness for his couriers. Arlen forestalled him with a raised hand. "You're the only one who I *know* will invoke that new crystal," he specified. *Even though it may take you into even worse danger*, unspoken words they both knew.

"I'll take Lady," Carey said, a non-sequitur that spoke of his capitulation, and a claim of Arlen's trust.

"Not the Dun?" Arlen, too, retreated to unspoken words.

Carey shook his head. "The Dun's quick—but her daughter swaps ends so fast it's a wonder she doesn't turn us both inside out."

"Get her ready, then," Arlen said. "I'll be down to see you off."

Lady dropped her weight to her haunches, sliding in the loose dirt of the steep slope where her Carey had guided her. Friction skinned the hide off her hocks as Carey leaned back in the saddle, his hands a lifeline to her mouth in a balance of freedom and support—all the encouragement he could give her. But Lady needed no more encouragement, for Carey was scared. She felt it in the tension of his legs, heard it in his voice. She knew it from the desperate ploy that had sent them down the dangerous slope in the first place.

To the side flashed a sudden falling tangle of arms and legs, hooves and soft yielding flesh, driving her a step closer to equine panic; she lurched to escape from the new threat.

"Easy, Lady," Carey panted as his legs closed against her sides, giving her reassurance and guidance. She took heart and as they gained the bottom of the steep hill she gathered herself and bounded over the intermingled bodies of man and horse. She landed hard, felt Carey take up the reins and lean forward in the saddle. "Go, Lady," he whispered, and her ears flicked back to scoop up his words. She forgot about the tree-dodging chase in the forest, where they'd lost one pursuer to a thick trunk. She forgot about the mad scramble through the knee-high creek; even the dangerous slope disappeared from memory in the depth of her concentration. It was only the here and now, the run, the grunt of exhalation forced from her lungs at every stride she took. Foam dripped from the sides of her mouth and the reins lathered against her dun neck and still Carey whispered in her ear, guiding her as though he knew she lived only in her inner world of effort with no care for what her eyes might see. Then the ground under her hooves turned hard and pebbly, and when Carey asked her for a hard left, she suddenly knew where they were and what he would ask of her next. With rock to her left and only a narrow rim of a path beneath her, she listened to the caress of his legs, the shift of his weight, and pivoted in a rollback that sent her chest and head over empty air, high above the dry river bed they'd paralleled.

"Good job, braveheart." Carey wooed her, his voice harsh in a dry throat. In seconds they met one of their pursuers, and Lady, following the pattern of endless drills, put her nose to the inside of the path and shouldered aside the other horse. Then another—bay flesh that dropped aside with an equine scream of fear—and the path was clear, clear until the narrow foothold widened, to where another man stood his ground on a flaming chestnut horse. He dropped his reins, one arm cocked behind, the other clutching a strained, curving stick.

There was a sudden odd thump just behind her ears and Carey's body shifted wildly, sliding from the saddle, skewing Lady's balance. Her head yanked far to her left with a brutal jerk on the rein, and her body followed. Fear drove her flailing legs but there was no longer any ground beneath them, and they hurtled toward the death waiting in the hard rocky river bed.

*And then the world stopped around them.*

Arrested in mid-air, they were snatched by another force altogether, one that held Lady in a smothering grip and would not yield to her mental thrashing. She no longer felt Carey's failing grip on her black mane, nor his legs slipping off her sweat-darkened sides. Instead, her mind twisted; her body knotted up, disappeared, reformed, and at last abandoned her along with Carey and her senses.

Early spring in the park, and not near warm enough by Dayna's standards. She forged ahead of Eric, who'd been distracted by a small, busy flock of kinglets in the underbrush. When he showed no sign of losing interest, she stopped, put her hands on narrow hips, and called back to him, "Coming? I thought you wanted to get those bluebird boxes checked out."

He uncoiled his lanky body from his crouch, looking at her with the perpetually bemused look he wore. "They'll still be there in another fifteen minutes," he said mildly, pulling at the yellow armband that labeled him a park volunteer. Dayna merely ran a hand through her short, wedged sandy hair and waited for him. "You didn't have to come," he said when he caught up. "If you had other things to do today, you should have done them. You know you don't enjoy this stuff if you have something else on your mind. I do."

"Have something else on your mind?" she responded, distraction so she wouldn't have to admit he was right.

Eric didn't miss a beat. "Know that you don't enjoy. Anyway, you're here now. You might as well appreciate it."

She looked up the significant distance between their heights and made a distinct effort to forget about the laundry piled on her bed, the bills waiting on her desk, the—*no, forget it*. "Okay," she said.

"Saw a weasel here last month," he commented. "You should have heard the chipmunks cursing him out!"

"Give me an example of a chipmunk curse," she challenged him.

"Greedy cheeks!"

"Nut-waster!" Dayna said. "Fox-bait!"

"Good one," Eric applauded. The bright, sharp chirp of the creature in question greeted them from the trees bordering the meadow they approached; a jay echoed with its own harsh warning, and the woods rustled with the movement of small creatures.

"Oops," Dayna said. "I guess we got a little loud."

Eric shook his head, curiosity lighting his features. "Uh-uh. They're leaving the meadow, not running from us." He lengthened his steps and Dayna was forced to a jog. They reached the edge of the meadow together and stopped, listening, watching. The meadow was still in the calm of spring, with short green spikes of grass just reaching through the dead thatch of winter. Three pole-mounted bluebird houses dotted the expanse, which remained as still as the slight breeze allowed. Dayna caught Eric's eye and shrugged.

He lifted one shoulder in reply and left the path to walk the perimeter of the clearing. Dayna fell in behind with a sigh, but he didn't go far before stopping short. "Holy shit," he breathed, and stared into the woods.

"What, *what*?" Dayna asked impatiently, and bumped him with her hip so she could see through the small gap in the brush.

Her jaw dropped—seriously, literally dropped—at the sight of dusky limbs and a tangle of leather equipment. After a moment the details sorted themselves out in her mind and she was able to discern that the limbs belonged to a young woman; the leather was a saddle and its accoutrements. And although her mind raced, it could provide no plausible reason a young woman would be lying in the woods clothed only in a saddle. "Yeah," she said finally. "Holy shit."

At the words, the young woman stirred. With a groan she shook her face free of the oddly colored, ragged hair that had covered it; she opened her eyes and reacted with a strange, frightened *huff* that came from deep within her chest. She pulled herself awkwardly forward, out from beneath the saddle and the lather encrusted blanket, and Eric moved forward to help her.

She saw them for the first time. Her dark eyes widened with fright and her nostrils flared; she lurched to her feet and tried to run, but only got a few steps before she tripped, falling with a grunt.

Eric froze, dismayed, and Dayna tugged his arm. "Let me," she whispered. "There's no telling what she's been through."

Wordlessly, he moved back and crouched down, halving his height. Dayna took a step and said, "It's all right. We'll help you."

The young woman scrabbled backwards, paying more attention to her own clumsiness than to either Dayna or Eric. She looked down at herself and whimpered, and her eyes were huge and terrified. She thrashed to her feet again, just long enough to run headlong into a tree, after which she fell in a tangle of long limbs and curled around herself, trembling too hard to try again.

Dayna exchanged a dismayed glance with Eric; he shook his head. "Maybe she's on something," he said. "I'll go get help."

"No!" Dayna said emphatically. "I'm afraid she might hurt herself, and I can't handle her alone. Wait until we get her calmed down a little, okay?"

He looked at the still quivering huddle of woman and nodded reluctantly. Then he slipped off his loose lightweight jacket and said, "See if you can't get her covered up. She must be cold."

Dayna took the jacket and pushed her way through the twiggy brush between the meadow and the woods. The woman didn't react to her, and Dayna glanced back uncertainly; Eric nodded encouragement.

Another step, no reaction. Dayna quietly made her way closer, then went down on her knees and spoke quietly. "I want to help you," she said, but although those dark eyes were open, they didn't seem to see her. Hesitantly, Dayna stretched out her hand.

"Be careful," Eric whispered.

Dayna nodded without taking her eyes from the withdrawn creature before her. Her unsteady hand brushed the naked shoulder without reaction. "I want to help you," she repeated softly. She stroked the coarsely textured hair, smoothed it in a cautious petting motion. "See, it's all right now." Was it her imagination, or had the trembling abated almost imperceptibly? "Take it easy, now."

The woman stiffened, and Dayna froze, no less flighty than she. "Easy," Dayna repeated experimentally. "Take it easy." To her astonishment, the woman, still huddled in on herself, shifted her weight to lean against Dayna, pressing close.

"Oh, good, Dayna!" Eric rustled in the brush behind her.

"Stay where you are," Dayna warned, her inflection still patterned to sooth. She smoothed back the odd hair and petted and consoled the woman, using the magic word *easy* liberally while she took stock of what they'd had found. Long-limbed and muscled like an athlete, the woman was bruised and scratched, both Achilles tendons scraped raw and bloody. Her body bore no signs of abuse, but she was clammy with dried sweat and exuded an odd musky odor of effort.

Eric rustled behind them again, and Dayna bit her tongue on admonition when the woman didn't react—and when Eric seemed content, from the noises of it, to examine the saddle. "I don't get this," he said, a frown in his voice. "This blanket's soaking wet—smells like horse.

Weird. I don't see any hoof prints.... Maybe there's something in the saddlebags...."

Dayna didn't answer. She kept up her soothing patter of reassuring nonsense and thought, perhaps, that the woman who leaned against her no longer quivered quite as much, was possibly even beginning to relax.

After an excessively long pause, Eric reported, "Not much in here. A hammer, couple of nails, a horseshoe...it doesn't..." he trailed off into pensive silence, then picked up his thought. "These things don't look *right*. Like if I went into a store after them, they wouldn't look like this."

Dayna smiled tightly. "That's useful," she said, keeping her voice low. Her charge was definitely relaxing, unbothered by the conversation. "Isn't there anything that might tell us who she is?"

"Well, there's a packet of papers, but it's sealed."

"Open it," Dayna suggested.

Eric hesitated, then said, "I don't think I can do it without tearing them up. Besides, it looks pretty official, and it's got someone's name on it."

"What's the name?" Dayna said, rolling her eyes. She had no patience for dragging answers out of Eric, a process imposed on her any time he was in deep thought.

After another hesitation, he said, "I don't know. It's in a strange script. I suppose it might not be a *name* at all." After more rustling during which she supposed he was replacing the packet, he sighed heavily. "This just doesn't make any sense. How is she?"

"Better, I think. Maybe good enough so you can leave us, go get some help."

"I've been thinking about that," he told her.

*Uh-oh.* "Eric, this isn't one of your orphaned bunnies to take home and raise," she said sharply. "Something's happened to this woman, and it ought to be reported."

He crawled up beside her and looked into the woman's face. The large dark eyes were only half open, and they noted him without alarm or any apparent care for her nudity in his presence. He took his jacket from where it lay next to Dayna and carefully offered it to her.

Her eyes did open all the way, then, and she drew back from Dayna, only enough to support herself independently. She cocked her head and leaned forward and sniffed the jacket.

Another incredulous glance flashed between Dayna and Eric. "Weird," he whispered, as she drew back again, cocked her head the other way, and brought the other side of her face up to the material. Apparently satisfied, she gave a small huff and sat awkwardly back on her haunches. She took no notice of her completely exposed breasts, but Eric pinked slightly on his high, tightly drawn cheekbones and slowly settled the jacket over her shoulders. She made no move to thread her arms into the sleeves and after a moment, Dayna took her unresisting hand and guided it into the garment. Eric, on her other side, did the same, then fastened the zipper for her. It was an exercise in slow motion that seemed to bother the woman less than it bothered the two of them. She ducked her head down to rub her nose on the inside of her wrist and regarded them patiently, waiting for whatever they might choose to do next.

"Dayna...if we call the police, what's going to happen to *her*?"

"She'll get help," Dayna answered promptly.

"What, they'll put her in some state hospital? Lose her in the system?"

"And what do *you* propose to do, take care of her for the rest of her life? She obviously can't take care of herself."

"You don't know that. I think she deserves a chance to get over whatever shock she's had. Putting her into an impersonal system won't give her that chance," Eric said, a familiar stubborn note creeping into his voice.

"So you just want to walk her out of here, stuff her into your car, and take her home for a few days." Dayna said, sarcasm on high.

He was taken aback only for a moment. "I want to *help* her, Dayna. Don't you?"

Dayna gave an exasperated sigh. "And if we take her home and three days later we discover the police have been looking for her, and that her family's frantic, and that we've done more harm than good?"

Eric rubbed his nose and said frankly, "I know there's a good chance this isn't the right thing to do. But I think it's about even with the chance that taking her to some authority is exactly the *wrong* thing to do."

Dayna said nothing, lost in the surprise that he was anywhere near practical.

"How about this," Eric suggested. "Twenty-four hours of TLC. If she doesn't straighten out by then, well..." He shrugged. "I guess we can call the police."

"Right," Dayna grumbled. "And explain to them why we didn't call earlier."

"Dayna—"

"All right," she interrupted him, looking at the trusting woman before her. There was something about the quality of that trust, especially in contrast with her earlier extreme fear, that made her feel just as Eric did—made her want to take the poor creature home and give her tea and a soft blanket to curl up with. Her mind replaced the tea and blanket with harsh sterile sheets and hospital food, and she knew she'd lost completely. "We'll take her to my place, not yours."

Lady didn't want to move again. That her fall had ended in a gentle thump on fairly soft ground was not so hard to accept; it was almost insignificant beside the other things that flooded her senses. Merely opening her eyes had invited an assault of things outside her experience: colors that hadn't existed, a field of view that was all wrong, and an ability to focus without moving her head to sight in on an object.

Then she'd tried to move. Nothing worked right, her balance was gone, her sense of self skewed. The two strangers had driven away the last remnants of sanity, merely because they, too, were unknowns. She was sinking deep into shock when a quiet voice had used one of her Words. One of Carey's Words. *Easy,* the voice had said, and then gentle hands had petted her, had let her lean and seek the safety of touch. Once she'd trusted the strangers, had believed the Word that meant they would take care of her, the unusual blanket was almost of no consequence. She was used to people who handled her hooves and body, and she was used to complying with their wishes.

But she didn't want to move again. Her body wasn't right yet. She listened to the man and woman quietly argue and became aware it wasn't only her body that was different. Words, words that she'd heard over and over but never assigned any significance to, suddenly fell into patterns. They still had no meaning for her, but she was suddenly aware that they *could*. She flared her nostrils in irritation and tried to understand what had changed, and what had been different before. She became suddenly confused about what she had—or hadn't—been able to comprehend before, and she whimpered, a noise that startled her just as much as her strange new vision.

"Easy," the woman said, and even that was enough to make her wonder how she could still discern this person as a woman, when her sense of smell had diminished so. But the deeply ingrained habit of response to her Words was so strong that she still felt herself relax. *Relax and go along with it, and they'll make everything right again.*

"Come with us," the man suggested. Almost against her will, she moved forward at that word *come*—awkwardly, not sure what to do about the extra length in her hind legs until the man suddenly took her by the front legs and pulled her up to a rear.

Rearing was forbidden. But....

It felt completely natural. They encouraged her, they told her it was good. Haltingly, she walked the few steps to the meadow, then the yards to the hard dirt path. The man walked behind them, the saddle braced against his hip, Carey's saddlebags slung over the worn leather seat. The woman had the blanket and before they'd gone far, she gingerly shook it out and offered to drape the cleanest side around Lady's shoulders. The man's strange blanket came only just below her hips, and Lady was glad to have something else against the chill. Almost by accident, she discovered she could hold the blanket in place with what should have been her front hooves.

Getting into the small metal stall proved to be a little awkward, and when it moved she froze with fear. But by now the woman was more assured in handling her and quickly soothed her, even as Lady herself realized the movement didn't hurt and perhaps there was nothing to fear after all.

Once she reached that point, she was able to recognize that the man controlled the movements of the stall, and that there were many more similar stalls moving all around them. She heaved a big sigh for the perplexity of it all and retreated to her inner world, leaving large unblinking eyes behind. From there she listened to the conversation between the man and woman and let her body sway with the movement of their travel.

When they stopped, she found them sitting before a barn, one of many in a long line. A barn meant food and rest and she willingly followed them into it. Inside, she spent a long time checking it out, approaching its clutter carefully and sniffing with a nose that no longer provided her the information that she needed. She let the blanket drop and discovered that her odd new hooves were sensitive to texture and shape—almost as sensitive as her muzzle should have been. With a variety of snorts and investigative huffing, Lady satisfied her natural curiosity.

After offering her a soft baggy covering for her lower half, the man and woman let her explore. When her curiosity was slaked, the man flopped down on a soft low structure and heaved a big sigh of fatigue. That was a language she could understand and sympathize with. "Dayna," he said, and added something she couldn't understand.

Dayna. That had to be the woman's name; she certainly responded to it. And the man, she was almost sure, was called Eric. Knowing their names made them safer for her, but it wasn't enough to make her as secure as Carey did. She wanted Carey here, wanted him badly, and her throat began an unaccustomed ache.

Dayna said the only thing that could have distracted her. "Are you hungry?"

Lady's whole body straightened in attention. She knew all the variations of words that had to do with food, and she went right up to Dayna and watched her with expectant eyes.

Both Dayna and Eric laughed, and then, when they were seated around a round platform and Lady tried to suck up the liquid offered her in a stupidly long cylinder and it went up her nose, they laughed again; after clearing her nose, she felt a strange bubbling in her chest and it turned irrepressible and came out in a funny little laugh of her own.

And then she stopped short, and dropped the liquid, and froze in fear, hardly noticing as the drink dribbled over the edge of the platform and onto the soft material that now covered her strong dusky legs. It was that laugh, coming from her own changed body, that suddenly allowed her to understand.

*She had turned into one of Carey's kind.* With trembling fingers, she felt for her long, refined muzzle and discovered only a flat face with a ridiculously small nose. There were none of the sensitive whiskers on which she relied so much. Unable to believe or accept, she reached for Dayna—but the smaller woman stiffened, for the first time showing signs of her own fear.

Eric's gentle word relaxed her and Dayna allowed Lady to touch her face, while one hand almost frantically compared the feel of her own. And then the ache came back to her throat, and she whimpered, and, suddenly, she was crying, not knowing what it was, but only that she couldn't help herself.

# 2

When Lady woke, it was dark and she was on a soft bed. Even as she knew it, she realized the ability to recognize this structure as a bed—as much a bed as her own straw-strewn stall—was not a concept her equine self could have handled. But she was through crying for now, and her current concentration was on something much more urgent, for her bladder was as full as it ever got. She stood and moved quietly out of the room.

In the midst of her tears of the evening before, they had tried to lure her up the stepped hill to further depths of the barn, but she'd have none of it. As far as she knew they were up there now, asleep. She walked through the food area to the back door, which posed no problems to a clever horse who'd been able to outwit many a latch with only her lips and who now had hands. She went outside and fumbled with the soft material around her lean hips, heaving a sigh of relief when she could finally crouch and relieve herself. Then she crept back to the warmth inside, suddenly all-too-aware of the soreness from her wild run, and crawled back into the bed.

After that she slept lightly, in the manner of her kind. Her mind raced with unaccustomed notions, and the throat-ache crept up on her almost unawares. This time her response to it was anger, an emotion she was well acquainted with. She was angry to be here, and angry at whatever had caused it to happen. She wanted to find Carey and go home. By morning she knew she must learn to communicate with Dayna and Eric; she'd even practiced quiet words with her newly flexible mouth and lips. For a horse that was a large chunk of thinking and when Dayna ventured down from the upper level, Lady was already as tired as she'd been the day before.

She got out of her bed with an involuntary groan, finding that the last quiet hours of the night had tied her abused muscles into knots. The scrapes on her lower legs were stuck to the soft material and every motion tugged at them. Reacting to the prickle as to fly bites, she stomped one leg several quick times, then repeated it with the other, freeing the scabs. Dayna frowned at her but Lady was through, having accomplished her goal. Soon, she was sure, Dayna or Eric would treat the wounds, as Carey would have in their place.

She followed Dayna into the food area, attuned to her growling stomach. As puny as it was, her nose picked up the scent of apple; she found a bowl of fruit she hadn't noticed the evening before. As Dayna went about the arcane business of preparing food Lady didn't recognize, she helped herself to an apple and, mindful of her changed chewing apparatus, carefully nibbled at it.

Yesterday Dayna had seldom spoken directly to her, other than her efforts to comfort. Now she kept up a running patter and often looked at Lady, looking for a response. Lady gave her the only one she had. "Dayna," she said proudly, if awkwardly.

Dayna dropped the implement she was using to mix eggs and looked at her with widened eyes. "*Dayna?*"

Lady thought it had been quite clear, so she repeated herself with some impatience. "Dayna."

Eric chose that moment to wander in, and, unlike Dayna, he was clearly slow to wake up. While Dayna was in new blankets, a fuzzy shapeless thing with a girth, Eric wore what he'd had on the day before. His hair was a mess and even as he wandered to the big box with the cold air, he gave a huge yawn. Dayna tugged at his arm and spoke quickly, almost sharply; Eric turned to give Lady an interested appraisal.

She could tell he wanted to hear her new word as well. With some dignity she said, "Dayna. Eric."

His eyebrows rose into the unkempt mess of his bangs. "Dayna," he said, touching Dayna. "Eric," he added, touching his own chest. And then he put his hand on her own arm.

Her own name was one she'd known all along. Delighted, she said carefully, "Dun Lady's Jess."

"Dun Lady's Jess?" Dayna repeated in perplexity. *I can't believe I really brought this woman to my home.* "That's not a *name.*"

"She seems to think it is." Eric grinned at the pride in their new friend's face. "She seems to think it's quite a good one, in fact."

Dayna regarded the woman thoughtfully. "I wonder what language she speaks. She's got a terrible accent—though that explains why she hasn't said anything until now."

"She sounds more like someone who's never spoken, not someone who speaks French or German or something," Eric said almost absently, taking the spatula from Dayna's unresisting hand to give the eggs a stir. "These are almost done. Is she having any?"

"Who knows." Dayna shrugged, irritated by Eric's characteristic refusal to deal with the important aspects of any given issue. She left the egg-serving to him and touched the table, naming it for...Dun Lady's Jess.

"Table," the woman obediently repeated. Still nibbling the apple, she followed Dayna around the room with her eyes, repeating the items Dayna named. Her voice was low and throaty and the words came out thickly, somewhat slurred. Until Dayna pulled at her robe.

"Blanket," the woman said with assurance before Dayna had a chance to give it her own name.

Eric set three plates on the table. "You'd think she'd tell us what some of these things are in her own language, if she had one."

"*Blanket?*" Dayna repeated, sitting and taking a fork full of egg without ever taking her eyes from their guest. She plucked at Eric's shirt as he sat, and waited for a response.

"Blanket," the woman nodded. She sniffed carefully at the steam

rising from the scrambled eggs and gave them a skeptical look, checking to see that both Dayna and Eric had eaten of theirs. Ignoring the
fork, she took a tentative sample with her fingers. She didn't quite spit
it out, but Dayna had the impression it was a close thing.

"Maybe she'd prefer cereal," Eric suggested mildly. "Or cantaloupe,
if you've got some."

Without answering, Dayna retrieved a plastic container of sliced
melon mixed with grapes and strawberries, and offered it in place of the
eggs. The woman's eyes widened in unmistakable delight and she
helped herself, chewing each morsel thoroughly before taking another.

"I don't think we're going to get much out of her before this
evening. Not unless we can teach her English in one day," Dayna said
skeptically, returning to her eggs.

Eric was watching Dun Lady's Jess, unaffected by the comment.
"Jess?" he asked.

The woman was slow to respond, but when she realized she was
being addressed, she carefully swallowed and said, "Lady."

"That's not much of a name, not here," Eric said thoughtfully.
"Maybe we'll just call you Jess. You learn enough English, you can set
us straight." He scraped the last of the egg from his plate with a piece
of toast and sat back in his chair. "How about I leave you two alone
long enough to go home and take a shower, change my clothes. Seems
to me she could use some cleaning up, too."

"You got that right," Dayna agreed. "Just keep in mind that I'm
working the hotel's evening shift tonight. We need to come to some
kind of decision about her."

Eric mumbled assent, said, "Bye, Jess. See you later," and dumped
his plate in the sink on the way out.

Dayna looked across the table at Jess and heaved a sigh. "C'mon,
Jess. Let's head for the shower."

She had planned to get things done while Jess cleaned herself up—
dishes, stripping the sheets of the guest bed, maybe even get the laundry sorted and ready to go. She hadn't counted on a Jess who still eyed
the stairs warily, who acted like she'd never seen the inside of a shower
before. Who ran into the door frame in her haste to escape a flushed
toilet. Dayna caught up with her at the head of the stairs and calmed

her, then carefully explained the fixtures of the bathroom. As with everything, once Jess got the hang of it, she proceeded with confidence, but a stumble into the unknown would stop her short. When Dayna finally left her, splashing happily in the tub in lieu of the obviously scary shower, she plumped down on her bed and put her head in her hands. *Good Lord, never mind whether English is her first language— I'd swear this is her first* house.

Still numbly shaking her head, Dayna went to gather her laundry, including the stretched old sweats that had served Jess; they were all Dayna had that might fit the significantly taller, rangy woman, and she'd hardly want to put them back on after she was clean. She stared at the pants for a moment, trying to figure out what she and Eric had stumbled into. For once, it wasn't a matter of convincing her lanky friend that he had—again—left reality behind. *This* time, she wasn't sure what reality was. She thumped down both sets of stairs to the basement and dumped the laundry in the machine, setting the controls with unaccustomed vigor in her frustration.

With the laundry churning away, she ducked into the downstairs shower stall for her own clean-up. When she came out, still toweling her hair dry, Jess waited for her, sporting Dayna's own robe. On Dayna it swirled comfortably around her ankles; it now fell just below Jess' knees. For the first time Dayna realized the extent of the scrapes adorning those legs, and she could have kicked herself for forgetting about them.

Jess didn't bat an eye at the ensuing first aid products. She sat patiently and, it seemed, handed herself unequivocally into Dayna's care. Dayna thought of her cautious reaction to just about everything else she'd seen and added another senseless puzzle piece to her quickly growing collection.

Jess—because for now Lady reluctantly conceded her name to them— spent the day following Dayna around the house, watching the woman at her chores, listening to her identify the objects around her. Words swirled around in her head, mixing with the countless conversations she'd heard in her uncomprehending equine form. After lunch she retreated to her bed—the sofa, it was called—for a short nap, unable to process any more. When she woke, the patterns of the words, past and present, had begun to grow clearer in her mind. Isolated words in smatterings of conversation combined to make sense, in a way that seemed not at all strange to her; she had no similar learning processes to compare it with.

Regardless, she woke with the determination to communicate her wants to Dayna. And what she wanted was Carey.

While she slept, the barn seemed to have undergone some kind of transformation. The random piles of clutter and papers were gone, formerly dusty surfaces shone, and there was a neat collection of blankets in a basket by the stairs. Jess took a careful look around to make sure there were no other, less innocuous changes, then followed the sound of voices to the food room. There she found Dayna amidst an accumulation of neatly sorted papers, waving a small stick at Eric to emphasize her words.

In front of Eric lay Carey's saddlebags. On the floor beside his chair was Jess' saddle and bridle, the crupper and breast band, and the freshly cleaned blanket. Eric tipped his cap back to look up at her and said cheerily, "Hi, Jess. Sit, have something to eat."

Dayna took one look at her and sprang from her chair, interposing herself between Jess and Eric to grab the open edges of Jess' borrowed blanket and overlap them, snugging them securely with the girth.

Eric shook his head in quiet amusement. "She's safe from me, Dayna."

"Fine. But she's got to learn."

"Why wouldn't she know already?" he asked thoughtfully.

Jess only followed the merest outline of the conversation and didn't have the slightest idea what they were talking about learning. At the moment, she didn't care. "Dayna," she pointed. "Eric..." and herself, "Lady." Then she touched the saddlebags, a caress that expressed all her devotion to the man who owned them. "Carey."

"Saddlebags, Jess," Eric said.

"She does that sometimes," Dayna interposed, licking a small square and pressing it onto one of the rectangular papers. "Just like all our clothes are blankets and that—" she pointed to the robe belt, "—is a girth. She might not know English, but she's got a few words she won't budge on."

Jess' phantom tail switched in annoyance. She went through the naming routine again and then tugged at the robe on her arm. "Dayna," she named it.

Dayna gave her a puzzled look. "You know that's not me. That's a robe—or a blanket, if you have to have it your way."

Impatient, Jess snatched the cap from Eric's head. "Eric." The small stick from Dayna's grasp. "Dayna." The saddle and bridle. "Jess." The saddlebags. "Carey."

"What—?" Dayna exploded.

"Wait a minute, wait a minute," Eric said, tumbling over his words so Jess understood none of them. "I think I get it. The robe *belongs* to you, Dayna, and so does the pen. The cap is mine—and the saddlebags belong to someone named Carey?" He directed the last at Jess, who let out a sigh of relief and finally sat. She looked him right in the eye and pointed at herself. "Carey."

"What!" Dayna repeated. Her voice rose considerably.

"Easy, kiddo, now is not the time to push feminist power lingo on her. I think she's really trying to tell us something."

"What, that she belongs to someone named Carey? Slavery's out, in case you hadn't heard."

"Dayna, relax, okay?" He held her gaze until she looked away and nodded, a silent language at which Jess was much more adept. Then he gave Jess his attention. "Jess...you understand us, don't you? A little?"

Jess tried her first nod, a gesture she'd seen many times and finally now understood.

"The saddle and bridle are yours," Eric said slowly, pointing at her. Another nod.

"The saddlebags belong to your friend Carey."

She thought about that a moment. She wasn't sure about *friend*, but..."Carey," she affirmed, drawing the saddlebags closer to herself. Then she reached for the bridle. The metal pieces made the comfortable homey clatter she was used to, and she folded her hand around the double-jointed snaffle to enclose the copper roller that had often entertained her tongue. She looked deliberately at Eric and touched her chest, where the old robe was once again beginning to gap between her breasts. "Carey."

Eric retrieved his cap and thoughtfully jammed it on his head, while Dayna looked first at him and then at Jess before finally exploding out of the chair. "I'm not going to encourage this. The sweats should be dry by now—I'm going to get her dressed."

Jess had snorted and shied at Dayna's sudden movement, but settled quickly. Eric still listened to her, and she dismissed Dayna to give him all her attention. She studied him across the table, her thick hair unheeded where it had settled in her eyes. He was a tall man, rangy but without her own athletic build. His face was a little too spare, but she liked his eyes. They were dark, slightly up-tilted, and nothing but mild. In them were none of the rules that flickered in Dayna's eyes. Jess had been ridden by men whose eyes reflected such self-imposed rules—but not for long. They invariably started a battle for possession of the reins and Carey never let these unyielding riders continue. Jess thought of Carey's hands: give and take, request and thanks. She stared helplessly at Eric, knowing she just didn't have the words to explain.

"Jess," Eric said, nothing more, just the name he'd given her. He'd seen the frustration and loss in her face, and that one word held his own helplessness: the inability to fix things for her. He touched the saddlebags, a curious touch nothing like her own. "If these are Carey's, why is the bridle yours? And the saddle?"

She stared another moment and dredged up what words she could. "Carey...feeds me."

"She takes care of you?" Eric said, seizing gratefully on her effort.

"Yes." Then she frowned and said, tentatively, "He."

"Is he your husband? Uh, brother? Father?" Eric tried, sinking back into their failure of communication when Jess responded to each with a slight shake of her head.

"Were you together in the woods?"

"Running. Yes." She thought of that chase and scowled.

"Where did the saddle come from?"

"Jess."

"I know it's yours. But surely you weren't *running* with that thing."

Jess seemed to grow a little taller where she sat, hearing his apparent understanding. "Yes!"

Baffled, Eric said, "Running with a saddle. With Carey. We found you and the saddle—" he said, looking bemused over the whole image, "—but where's Carey?"

Jess lost her grasp on words, leaning forward with a tremble of intensity. In a flash of insight, Eric said, "You don't know!"

"Yes!" *Please, please, help me find him.*

The unspoken plea was not lost on Eric. "But you want to know, don't you," he asked softly. "Of course you do. What's his last name? We can call a few places, see if he's there."

Jess sat back, defeated. She shook her head and looked down at the bridle in her hands.

Eric put his chin on the heel of his hand and sighed. "No last name. That's going to make it a lot harder. What were you running from?"

Jess heard Dayna come up behind her and stop. She lifted her head, listening for further movement, and returned her attention to Eric when Dayna seemed content where she was. "Men," she explained, and pantomimed the notch and release of the arrow that had hit Carey. "Jess—*I*—run for Carey. Until—" and she repeated the pantomime.

"You ran for him," Eric repeated without comprehension. "You mean you ran with him?"

"No," Jess said confidently. "For him." She flung her head up, and her clean, strong features held her pride. "Fast. Strong. *I*," and she touched her chest again, "run for Carey."

Eric shook his head again. "Sorry, Jess, I just don't understand."

Jess picked up the bridle, splaying the fingers of one hand to spread the crown piece and the other to hold the bit out in front of her. "Horse," she said, clearly, watching his face for comprehension. "Dun Lady's Jess."

Eric stared, first in the bafflement of non-comprehension, then the shock of understanding. "Jess—" he protested, as Dayna cut in from behind.

"That's just great. I don't think there's anything we can do for her,

Eric." Her voice held the finality of judgment, the finality of her rules. Jess' pride drained away, and fear took its place—for in that finality was rejection, and the loss of this safe place.

*I can't believe I let Eric talk me into this pointless little trip.* Jess was probably on the loose from some institution, and the only thing to do was see to her return—and to the return of the saddle, bridle, and saddlebags, which were no doubt stolen.

It could do no harm, he'd argued. Dayna was less sure of that, but somehow here they stood, in the aisle of the Dancing Equine Dressage Center, waiting for Jaime Cabot to finish cooling out her horse so Jess could have a better look around.

"I don't know what good you think this is gonna do," she muttered, once again to Eric, while Jess waited between them and stood very tall, drinking in the scents and sounds of the stable.

Eric, once again, shrugged. "She says she's a horse. This'll give her a chance to see, well, that she can't possibly be."

"If it was that easy, someone would have straightened her out long ago."

Another shrug. "Maybe Jaime can talk some sense into her. Anyway, she knows a lot more about horses than we do."

That was true enough. Jaime competed in the upper echelons of dressage and could swap horse jargon with the best of them. "It's pointless," Dayna intoned, crossing her arms. She leaned against the plank wood wall and stared sourly at Jess' tall straight back. Her choppy hair was more evident from this vantage; although the front strands fell just short of her shoulders, there were also coarse lengths that fell unevenly to the middle of her back. And though Dayna had classified the odd color as similar to dark wet sand, there seemed to be some kind of darkened stripe running through the middle of the unparted mess.

Jaime, a short woman who was dwarfed by a tall young Hanoverian, led the animal to its stall at the far end of the aisle and hauled the heavy stall door closed behind it. She twitched the end of her long dark braid behind her shoulder and came to meet them, looping the lead rope around her hand. "Hey, guys, what's up?" she asked cheerfully.

"We found a friend who's...interested in horses," Eric said, casting Dayna a glance as he spoke up before she had the chance. "Jaime, this is Jess. Think she could look around?"

"Sure," Jaime said. "Just let me turn Silhouette into the ring first." A few minutes was all it took to turn the stalled mare loose in the indoor arena at the end of the aisle. Dayna glanced at her watch, a distinct message to Eric that she was not about to show up late for work because of this futile venture.

Jaime took them on a stall-to-stall tour, telling Jess a little about each of the horses—boarders, competition horses, retirees. Jess was a bundle of curiosity and intensity and movement, greeting each animal with an exchange of puffing breaths—and, for two of the horses, squeals of annoyance. Jaime's expression changed from curious to poker-faced; when they reached the end of the aisle they left Jess leaning on the arena gate, watching Silhouette play, while Jaime led Eric and Dayna to the opposite end of the stable.

"Who the hell is this woman?" Jaime asked bluntly. "She's damned odd."

Eric offered a smile. "Dun Lady's Jess."

Jaime's hazel eyes narrowed. "That's a horse name, not a woman's."

"Exactly," Dayna said, staring hard at Eric. "That's the problem."

"Come on, you two. As long as you brought your little joke here, you might as well let me in on it."

"Both barrels," Dayna warned her. "We found her at Highbanks yesterday. She was naked and scared to death; she had a saddle and bridle with her. She doesn't know much English, or much of anything else for that matter, but she did manage to tell us that she's a horse."

Jaime gave a snort of laughter, but her amusement died away when they didn't laugh along with her. She looked at Eric for confirmation and he gave an apologetic shrug. "Well," Jaime said, her voice too level, "she does have the coloring of a dun."

Dayna was momentarily speechless, until Jaime smirked; she smacked the equestrian on the arm. "Not funny."

Jaime's smile faded only slowly. "What else do you want me to say?"

"We were sort of hoping that just being here would knock some sense back into her." Eric looked over both women's heads to the ring, where Jess now frolicked along with the frisky mare. As if inexorably drawn to the sight, the three silently moved down the aisle.

Unaware of or unconcerned about their presence, Jess played chase with the leggy bay mare, a romp punctuated by abrupt pivots and change of course. Agile and quick, Jess matched the mare move for move, bluffing out her charges and squealing in mock anger when they closed on one another. Dayna's too-small sweats and Eric's too-big shirt did nothing to hide the fluid movement of the body beneath.

"She's definitely an odd one," Jaime murmured. "As close to a horse as anyone I've seen."

"You're not *serious*," Dayna said in horror.

"Just thinking." Jaime nodded at the ring. "Look at her. The color and texture of her hair...she's a dun all right, Dun Lady's Jess. Did you see the way she greeted the other horses?"

"Great. She's been studying up," Dayna said flatly. She squared off to face Eric. "Look. I want to help her as much as you do, but I don't think there's anything we can do. She belongs somewhere where they can take care of her. If you don't call the police, I will. I've got to go to work and I can't fool around with this any longer."

Jaime winced. "I can see you've been in complete agreement on this one."

Eric lowered his voice, earnest as ever. "But Dayna, she's learning all the time! If we just give her a little longer, she'll be able to tell us just what's happened and who she really is."

"We should have called the police in the first place. They'll probably *know* who she is—maybe who Carey is, if he even exists." Dayna shook her head, her voice softening for the first time. "I know you want to help her. So do I. But—" she broke off as Eric's up-tilted eyes widened, and turned around to find that Jess had abandoned her play, and was standing well within earshot. Her eyes were wild and alarmed, and as Dayna took a step forward, hand outstretched in a gesture of reassurance, Jess whirled and sprinted away.

In an instant, Jaime had nimbly hopped the gate to follow her, shouting behind her, "She's not going to stop!" a warning Dayna understood only when she saw Jess crash into the gate at the opposite side of the ring. By the time she'd followed Jaime and Eric over the first gate, Jess was through the other side, the second gate swinging in her wake. "Damn," Dayna panted under her breath, losing ground at every step. She reached the other gate in time to see Jess confront the five foot paddock fence; she gave an enormous leap and dove over it, then seemed stunned when her arms gave way on landing. She managed to untangle herself and was on the run again, with nothing between her path and fields of waist-high corn, when Jaime shouted the word that changed everything.

*"Whoa!"*

Jaime's voice was full of authority; Jess stumbled. No more than a moment's hesitation, it was enough to allow Jaime to close on her, to stand at the paddock fence and speak softly, reassuring her with words Dayna couldn't hear. Eventually Jess climbed back through the fence and Jaime took her hand and held it as they walked together, through the paddock and past Dayna and Eric and into the ring where Silhouette waited, exhilarated and pleased by the excitement. Bemused, Dayna followed, and Eric closed the gate behind them.

Jaime led them into the stable office and seated herself on the short couch, pulling Jess down beside her. Eric perched on the edge of the desk and left the desk chair to Dayna.

"I don't know what's going on here," Jaime said firmly, "but I do know you haven't dealt fairly with Jess."

Dayna felt a scowl form on her face—until she looked at Jess and recognized, with a stab of shame, the betrayal brimming in those dark eyes.

Jaime nodded at her reaction. "If you're going to make decisions about Jess, I think she needs to be in on the conversation, don't you?"

"But she doesn't really understand," Dayna protested feebly.

"No?" Jaime arched an eloquently skeptical eyebrow. "She understood well enough to know you'd washed your hands of her."

"You're right," Eric said suddenly. "Jess, I'm sorry."

She regarded him silently, neither forgiveness or judgment on her face, only doubt.

"Jess," Jaime said matter-of-factly, "Dayna and Eric are concerned about you. They don't know what's happened to you, or why you behave differently than we do, and they're trying to decide how to best help you."

Jess held her breath for a moment and let it out in a deep sigh. "Good girl," Jaime said, and squeezed her hand.

"Did you understand that?" Dayna asked Jess in surprise. At Jess' nod, she added, "You didn't understand us when we found you though, right?"

"No," Jess said, then hesitated, glancing at Jaime, who nodded encouragement. But instead Jess shook her head and brought her knees to her chest, wrapping her arms around them to look at no one, obviously not trusting them enough to try to convey her thoughts.

Eric said softly, "You thought we would help you and we were talking about sending you away. We might be strange to you, but everything else is twice as strange, isn't it?"

Jess nodded mutely.

"All right," Dayna said, finally catching the mood of this forthright conversation. "There are some things we need to know. Have you been sick lately? Been in any kind of a hospital?" Jess shook her head, and her hands crept down to the bony knobs of her ankles to feel the dressings that covered her scrapes. "Have you done something wrong, or against the law?"

A decided shake of her head.

"Where do you come from, then?" Dayna asked in frustration. "Why is everything so strange to you?"

Jess shook her head helplessly. "Send me away...?"

"Jess—" Eric's quiet voice and helpless shrug took the sting out of his words. "We don't how else to help you."

"Carey," Jess said, a heartbreaking plea.

"I know," Eric said.

Late afternoon. With Dayna on her way to work, the others retired briefly to Jaime's house to call around in search of Carey.

"We're calling the places where Carey might be if he was hurt, or if he went for help," Eric explained absently, dialing the first of the emergency numbers listed on the telephone book's inside cover. He perched atop a stool, balancing the white pages on his knee, the phone crammed between his neck and shoulder. Jess sat quietly at the kitchen half-bar while Jaime poked around in the refrigerator, eventually pulling out a plastic soda bottle. Ice, then glasses...she felt Jess' gaze on her as she poured the drinks and pushed them across the bar.

Jaime might have guessed that Jess' eyes would widen at the carbonation, though perhaps the sudden giggle was less predictable. Jess checked to see that Eric's drink was behaving in the same bubbly way and tried a sip, then a swallow. She looked absolutely astonished at the belch that followed; in the background, Eric smirked, but Jaime tried to keep a straight face. "That happens," she said. "But when it does, it's polite to say *excuse me*." In the back of her mind, she was trying not to ascribe any significance to the fact that horses were incapable of belching, that Jess was certainly paying attention to the details if she knew her surprise was appropriate.

"Excuse me," Jess tried dutifully.

Eric hung up the phone with a clunk and reached for his drink. "No one named Carey in any of the hospitals," he said. "At least, none of 'em within 60 miles. I figure that's far enough, if he was on foot like Jess. Was he naked, too, Jess?" he asked straightforwardly.

Jess had one finger held above the surface of the soda, where the carbonation fizz bounced off of it. She put the finger in her mouth and said, "Naked?"

"Like you were when we found you. No clothes." At her continued lack of response he rolled his eyes and said, "No blankets, Jess."

"Blankets, yes," she answered.

"Blankets?" Jaime inquired, and heard the story of the few objects Jess identified on her own. She absorbed it with a thoughtful finger against her lips, then shook her head. "This is...pretty strange." The words she finally settled on were woefully inadequate, but she knew she would find none better. "But as long as we're talking about clothes, my brother's got some things he never wears, and she looks about his size. Let me see if I can't find something better than what she's got on."

But Jess had been distracted, lured to the doorway between kitchen and family room, where the low murmur of a television had caught her sensitive ears. It took Jaime a moment to realize what had attracted her; her ears had sorted out and chosen to ignore the faint babble when she entered the house. To her, it meant only that her younger brother Mark had left the TV on when he'd left the house. To Jess, apparently, it was a wonder.

A Roy Rogers western blazed black-and-white action on the screen, mixing running horses with hopelessly hokey but pleasantly sentimental songs. The hero's horse was faster than anybody else's and Jess watched those chase scenes with complete and rapt attention, on her knees, her weight resting on splayed ankles.

"It's only a story," Eric tried to explain more than once, causing Jaime to wonder how on earth there had remained this soul uncorrupted by even the very thought that somewhere, there existed the play-acted images of television. She and Eric sat on the short couch behind Jess and the afternoon drifted away as the short movie ended and another began; Eric got caught up in the movies and Jaime found herself watching Jess more than the television. It was she who called an end to it, after a chase scene in which a stand-in horse was wire-tripped at the edge of a high cliff to plunge into the river below. She muted the sound with the TV remote and nudged Eric's attention to Jess, who sat pale and shivering.

Eric blinked at the sight. "Jess, it's only a story, remember? People make up a story and film it so we can sit here and watch and *pretend* it's real. But the good part is that we know the guy on that horse didn't really get hurt."

"Horse?" Jess asked unhappily, brows wrinkled in concern.

"The horse?" Eric fumbled, and, when understanding hit, hastily added, "The horse was all right, too. It's just pretend."

Jaime gave him a sharp look, knowing that the movie had been filmed in an era during which the horse's condition would not have been of much concern. But a second look at Jess' distress made her understand Eric's unqualified reassurance. Jess' dark eyes remained touchingly eloquent, as open and candid as a child's—or certain types of honest horses.

Jaime closed her eyes and shook the ridiculous notion out of her thoughts, actually shook her head in emphasis. Then it was Eric's turn to nudge her; he took the remote away and turned the sound back on.

Jaime opened her eyes to a newsbreak featuring a John Doe story. The man had been found wandering Route 23 just north of Columbus; naked, incoherent and violent, he'd been apprehended and sedated, and the search for his identity was on. The newsreel footage showed a middle-aged man with flaming chestnut hair, interspersed with the grainy on-scene video of police officers rounding the man up. Conveniently blurred spots hiding the man's genitals. The officers had had their work cut out for them, for the fellow was agile and fast, long-legged and apparently tireless—according to the report, it had taken an hour and a half to corner him in a drainage ditch.

Jaime found her eyes unaccountably straying from the television to Jess, who was completely lost in the story. In her mind's eye she saw Jess and Silhouette, wheeling, romping, reveling in their exertions.

"Is that Carey?" Eric asked abruptly. A glance at his expression showed that he, too, had made some sort of connection between Jess and John Doe.

But Jess appeared startled at the thought. "No," she said, and pointed to the screen. "Chestnut."

Jaime gave a short laugh. "She's right about that, although most people would consider that guy's hair to be an unusual shade of red. What color is Carey's hair, Jess?"

After a thoughtful moment, Jess shrugged. "Dayna," she offered.

"Sandy blond, like Dayna's," Eric decided.

Jaime shook her head. "I'm not sure I need this, Eric. I wish Dayna could have dealt with it a little better."

"You know Dayna," Eric said. "And this is really the perfect place for Jess to take a few days and sort herself out. Besides, I'm sure she'll be a lot of help around the stable. Unless you have some doubts that she can handle the horses."

Jaime snorted. "Oh, she knows horses all right." She watched Jess in silence for a moment; released from the conversation, Jess was leaning forward, her finger touching the freeze-frame picture of John Doe. Her ill-fitting sweats tugged against her hips and revealed a generous area of lower back. *Very* lower back. Jaime stood up. "Once upon a time, I was hunting up some clothes for her." Back into efficiency mode, she turned off the television and motioned for Jess to follow her upstairs.

A change of clothing meant, of course, that Jess had to face zippers, but the sweatshirt pullover was easy enough. The old denims were a little loose but stayed up without a belt. By then Eric had gone back to the telephone to finish his search for Carey—or Carey's body—and could do no more without actually involving Jess with the police. And that, he told Jaime, he was still reluctant to do—not because they wouldn't honestly try to help her, but because Jess' claims would set them into helping from a different direction: fixing Jess rather than finding Carey.

Jaime felt she had little choice—not to mention plenty of room in the rambling old farmhouse that had housed two generations of the Cabot family and now stood too quiet with only herself and her brother in occupancy. Jess, she said, could stay. She was short of stable help right now, anyway, and if there was only one thing she *knew* about Jess, it was that the woman understood horses. She was even resigned to paying for a pair of shoes for the footloose Jess, not to mention some underwear—but that was before Eric hauled the saddle and saddlebags out of his car, and showed her the pouch of gold.

# 3

"I knew if I told Dayna about it, she'd insist on calling the police." Eric tilted his hand to shift the pile of small square gold pieces. They were crudely stamped in runes that matched the lettering on the sealed document, and there were eleven of them.

Jaime teased a coin off his hand to fall into her own, and held it to reflect the light from the window. "No doubt about that. But just because Carey had this gold, doesn't mean he did anything wrong to get it."

"He had it *and* he was running," Eric corrected. "Jess, you know anything about this stuff?"

She hadn't been paying much attention to them—she'd found her abandoned soda and seemed disappointed that she couldn't coax bubbles out of it. Now she let it be and took the coin Jaime held out. She considered it a moment, and looked at the pouch that lay on the bar. "Carey," she announced.

Eric tipped his head at her. "You mean it belongs to Carey."

Jess nodded.

Jaime looked at the sealed document in Eric's hands. "And that doesn't even give you a clue?"

"Even if I could get it open, I think it's written in some bizarre esoteric language."

"*If* you could get it open?"

He shrugged, sheepishness coming over his tightly drawn features. "This seal...I don't know what it's made of. I can't break it. I tried just prying it off, but the paper—or whatever this stuff is—started to tear. I think if we force it, we're going to destroy it. Maybe it needs some kind of solvent."

"How about *open, sesame?*" Jaime asked wryly. "But there's no point in tearing the thing up. I've got to go into Columbus early next week—I'll take a copy of the words on the front to the OSU language department. If there's someone there who can translate, maybe we'll try a little harder to open it." She looked at Jess. "It would be so much easier if she could just *tell* us the whole story." Abruptly, she held out the pouch, and Eric spilled the gold into it. She cinched the pouch closed with a gesture of finality, and took the remaining piece from Jess, holding it up between them. "I'll wait a few more days, keep an eye on the papers. If nothing shows up, I'll see about selling this. She's got to have clothes, and some personal stuff."

"Selling it?" Eric repeated doubtfully. "Can you do that? Won't they want to know what it is, and where it came from?"

Jaime dismissed his concern. "All a gold trader cares about is how much it's worth. If you're really worried, five minutes and a propane torch would probably get rid of these weird letters. Course, I don't know how this Carey guy is going to feel about us spending his money."

"He shouldn't have left Jess alone," Eric said defensively. "Sell the thing. Get her something really nice."

Jaime spent most of her days in the barn, where Jess was happy enough to clean stalls, feed, and lead the horses to turn-out. She found Jess ever reluctant to speak, although she often caught the woman responding to the horses with some throaty nonverbal comment. Caught up in her own busy schedule, Jaime seldom had time to socialize with the reclusive newcomer, although she was careful to check the newspapers for any mention of a missing woman. She didn't spend significant time with Jess until nearly a week had passed.

With one of her best lesson horses scheduled for minor surgery in Columbus—an hour's drive from the Dancing—Jaime grabbed at opportunity. She wanted a companion for the drive; Jess needed clothes. They dropped the horse off at the university clinic and Jaime made a quick stop at a gold dealer, then dragged Jess—almost literally—into a mall. She outfitted Jess with practical jeans and a variety of men's pullover shirts—a much better fit to her sturdy shoulders than the flimsier woman's versions. It was nothing but utilitarian, and nothing more than what she needed. Choosing footwear turned out to be more of a problem when Jess revealed herself to be fussy about having her feet either handled or confined. Jaime finally convinced her to accept a pair of sneakers, although Jess scorned them once they left the mall. Jaime took a closer look at those tough soles and let her go barefoot as she pleased.

They returned to the university an hour and a half before the surgical procedure was slated to finish. Jaime dropped off the hand-copied characters from saddlebag missive at the Language Department, and they walked the central oval of the vast campus, sightseeing amongst the stately older buildings. Or, rather, Jaime looked at the buildings and Jess reveled in the flat grassy area, jigging ahead, stopping now and then to watch the occasional bandanna-adorned, Frisbee-chasing dog.

Then classes ended and the floodgates opened. Students rushed madly from here to there, intent on covering long distances in as little time as possible. Jess had lagged behind to stare at the massive statue of President William Oxley Thompson in front of the library; now she caught up to Jaime with such haste that she bumped into her.

Startled, Jaime reached out to steady her, and discovered that Jess was wide-eyed, her head thrown back to regard the flow of students around them. She continued to walk almost on Jaime's heels, and finally Jaime stopped, and took Jess' shoulders in her hands. "It's all right, Jess," she said firmly. "In a few minutes they'll be gone. They're just students trying to get from one of these buildings to another. Do you understand?"

"No," Jess said in a small voice. Someone jostled her from behind and she flinched, one leg lifting sharply and then settling in some aborted movement.

"They'll be gone in a minute," Jaime repeated. "See? Watch them.
They came out of these buildings—and even now you can see that
they're all going back inside. Look at them." The mass of moving
bodies hadn't yet decreased, but it was evident that there were more of
them entering buildings than were coming out. "Have you ever been to
school, Jess?"

A quick, short nod stirred thick shaggy hair, but there was hesitation there as well. Eventually she put her thoughts in to words. "Not
like this."

Jaime nodded. "This is one of the largest schools in the country," she
said. "There are quite a few satellite campuses, too." Then she looked
from the finally thinning crowd to Jess' blank expression and laughed
out loud. "That didn't mean a thing to you, did it?"

A small shy grin. "No."

The students continued to part around them like water around a
rock in the middle of a stream, but Jess had relaxed, returning her attention to the statue.

"It wasn't the crowd, was it?" Jaime asked in sudden insight. "It
was the *not understanding*."

Jess' gaze traveled back to hers, her expression a visual question mark.

"Never mind," Jaime said, certain enough that she'd been correct.
"C'mon. Mirror Lake is just down this hill, and there's usually someone nearby selling hot dogs." She glanced at her watch to see that
they'd have enough time to eat, and set off for the lake.

It was a pond, really, so shallow you could see the bottom and man-
made at that. But in the center rose a pleasant, simple fountain, and the
trees and shrubs that circled the area separated it from the campus,
making it into an oasis of peace.

And just over the slight rise on the other side of the pond, Jaime
could see the canopy of the hot dog vendor's cart. "Good," she said
with satisfaction. She pointed out one of the benches by the edge of the
pond, and said, "Wait here. I'll get something for us to eat."

A nod confirmed agreement and Jaime left her, satisfied that Jess'
already apparent fascination with the fountain would keep her occupied.

She bought two hot dogs and an extra bun so they could feed the
few mallards that hung around the pond. But when she turned back, she

almost dropped it all—for Jess was in the middle of the shallow water, stepping carefully, reaching out to touch the cascade. Standing at the edge of the pond was a visibly irate member of campus security; Jaime could hear his loud commands, but Jess was lost in the noise of the water. A particularly angry expression crossed the man's face and he, too, stepped into the water.

"No, wait!" Jaime yelled, juggling hot dogs as she ran back to the pond. If the man heard her, he was too intent to pay any attention. He grabbed Jess from behind, firmly capturing her arms.

Jaime abandoned the hot dogs and sprinted as Jess flew into motion, slamming her foot backwards into the man's shin with amazing force; she twisted and flung herself around with struggles that only increased when they failed. She fell into the rising spray of the fountain and dragged the man with her, and they ended up tussling in the water.

Jaime hit the cold pond without slowing down, pushing through two gawking students on her way. Awkward in the water, she barely stopped in time to keep from piling on top of the wrestling figures. "Jess!" she yelled above the noise of the struggle and the splash of the fountain. "No, Jess—whoa!"

It didn't have the magic of the last time she'd used it; it was the man who realized she was there and trying to help.

"Calm her down before I hurt her!" he bellowed, right before Jess' heel connected with the side of his face. She slithered out of his weakened grasp and floundered through the water.

Jaime knew that look: Jess was on the run again. She lunged directly into Jess' path and flung her arms out wide, not grabbing for her, but making herself large and imposing.

Jess stopped short; she snorted water out of her nose and tossed back the sodden mass of her hair.

"Be easy, Jess," Jaime murmured, not possibly loud enough to be heard over the fountain and the water running off the rising security man—but Jess seemed to respond to it anyway, despite her heaving breath and flared nostrils. She took another step, more deliberate, and put Jaime in between herself and the man, who glared at them both.

"What the hell's she on?" he demanded.

"She's not," Jaime said, forcing calm. "She's just frightened. She didn't know you were there before you touched her."

"She deaf?" he asked gruffly, tempering his anger enough to let Jaime know he considered this a possibility.

"No," Jaime answered slowly, "but she's new to a lot of things." She reached out a careful arm to guide Jess toward the imitation shoreline, and the man took the opportunity to scowl away the spectators, most of whom were satisfied to wander off now that the action was over. When all three of them were out, dripping on the asphalt path that circled the pond, Jaime faced the man squarely and took a deep breath.

"Jess is new to this country," she said, deciding it to be the simplest explanation, as well as her best guess at the truth. "A lot of things are strange to her. She didn't know she was breaking any rules, and she only reacted out of fear when you grabbed her."

"She had plenty of warning," the man growled. "I'm afraid you'll have to come with me."

"She didn't hear you," Jaime said desperately. That much was true, she was sure. When Jess was intent on something new, her whole world seemed to focus down on that object, and she'd more than once failed to respond to Jaime's question or call. "You scared her. Of *course* she resisted—she thought she was being attacked."

Unmoved, the man said, "She shouldn't have been in the water."

"She didn't *know*," Jaime repeated. The determined glint remained in his eye, and she knew Jess was moments away from being saddled with some serious charges. Abruptly she turned to Jess, moved back a step so the young woman was not so much behind her as beside her. "Jess, why did you fight?"

She raised her head, and a stubborn look appeared in her dark eyes. Her reply was slow, hindered by her search for words. "There is no trust for those who grab with no asking." Her precise meaning was unclear but the gist of the words came through well enough.

"You didn't hear him call you to come out of the fountain?"

Jess gave an amused snort. "I am not his. He has no Words for me."

"You see?" Jaime appealed, trying not to shiver. "She just didn't know you were an authority. She wasn't paying any attention to you— so she didn't know you were coming. Wouldn't you act to protect yourself if *you* were grabbed from behind?"

The man rubbed a beefy hand across the back of his neck, his expression reluctant. The side of his face was red where Jess' foot had made contact. "Everybody knows this kind of uniform means police authority," he maintained. "I'm not trying to make trouble for you two, but—"

"Look," Jaime said, swiping the drop of water that trembled on the end of her nose, "the intent wasn't there. Sure, you can pursue this thing, but what you *really* want is to prevent it from happening again, right? And you can do that by letting me explain things to her. Or by doing that yourself, if you want—right here."

He looked down at himself, at the runnels of water that collected at his feet to form a puddle. Then he looked at Jess, who still regarded him with her set-jaw stubbornness. He rested his hands on his bulky equipment belt, his mouth quirked in skeptical indecision. Jaime fervently, silently, hoped that he would back down, for she too had seen the look on Jess' face, and she easily read it for what it was: bull-headed challenge. She would go nowhere with this man, not without a fight.

When the man spoke again, his voice was more composed. "I'm not one of those guys who'll toss his weight around just because he's got it," he conceded. "Although I'm too damned wet to be letting you off easy. What about it, Jess? You understand to stay out of that fountain? You understand that you've got to pay attention to what security police tell you to do?"

"No kicking," Jess said reluctantly. "I broke the rule."

Jaime let out her breath. Somehow, she wasn't quite sure that Jess was agreeing with the man—but it seemed to be the capitulation he was looking for, and she wasn't going to clue him in if he didn't see it for himself.

Defiance, that's what lingered in Jess' gaze. Whoever Carey was, he was the only one with unequivocal Words for Jess.

Compared to the adventure at Mirror Lake, checking on the groggy lesson horse was an anti-climactic event. Jaime left her trailer there, made arrangements to pick the horse up in a few days, and drove Jess back to the Dancing.

The afternoon had been...eye-opening. She was far from amused when she realized that she'd seen subtleties of equine behavior in Jess' actions, for—in the unthinking moments during that debacle with campus security—she'd reacted as if Jess was indeed a horse.

But there were no conclusions to be drawn. Nothing in this situation remotely resembled the realities of Jaime's life. It was just...wait and see. Wait and watch. And while she was willing to give Jess a little more time to find herself and possibly to explain herself, it would be so much better if she didn't attract undue attention before then...

A pair of scissors and five minutes trimmed most of the ragged edges from Jess' wild hair, but couldn't hide the naturally dark streak that ran from forehead to nape—though it led to the discovery that there was nothing Jess liked more than a good grooming—or, rather, that she would sit still forever as long as Jaime was brushing her hair. She also discovered that she could hand Jess a set of brushes, point her at a horse, and count on her to groom until the object of her attentions virtually glowed—unless it was one of the two older mares, neither of whom Jess would deal with in any manner.

Her younger brother, Mark, accepted Jess with the patience of a young man who'd already dealt with every possible manner of horse-crazy girl, and Jess was delighted if he had the time to join her in the spacious back yard for a little one-on-one soccer—which she invariably won by virtue of her speed and agility. It was Mark who kept score; Jess, Jaime noticed, played for the sheer pleasure of the effort.

It was Mark, too, who took Jess on careful forays away from the farm—mostly to the busy Dairy Queen that graced the edge of the nearby one-street mini-town, and to the quiet bar that boasted of near-infamous hot bologna sandwiches.

Jess never seemed to fully trust Dayna, and after each of Dayna's visits, with or without Eric, she would follow Jaime around and solicit reassurance. She was standing at Jaime's elbow in the middle of a lesson when Jaime suddenly realized the problem. "You still think

Dayna might send you away, don't you? Think about those corners, Sandy," she reminded the woman under instruction. "He's falling out behind. Outside leg. Start a serpentine at A—let's see if we can't get him bending a little better."

The non-sequitur didn't seem to bother Jess, whose understanding increased in leaps and bounds. "Yes," she answered. She waved an arm to indicate the world beyond the farm. "All strange. No Carey—no Jaime. Dayna—" and, when words failed her, she stood very straight, scrunched her shoulders slightly, and arranged her features into a hard, implacable expression that immediately drew to Jaime's mind one of Dayna's inflexible moments. She couldn't help but laugh, though she sobered quickly. "Dayna's good people, Jess. It's just sometimes...well, how does the thought of facing that strange world out there," she waved her arm in an imitation of Jess' gesture, "make you feel?"

"Afraid," Jess said without hesitation.

"Right. Anticipate the change of rein at the center line, Sandy—prepare him! Well, Dayna's had some hard times. When she runs up against something that's really unfamiliar—really strange—it frightens her. And she protects herself. Sometimes that makes it seem like she's uncaring, but deep down she cares very much. And you know—sometimes even the caring can be frightening." She let Jess think about it while she watched the team in the ring, frowning over the gelding's unusually crooked position and his refusal to bend around his rider's inside leg. "What's going on with you two? This isn't like you at all."

"I don't know," Sandy said in frustration as she brought her horse down to a walk. The horse, too, wore an expression of frustration and irritation.

Without a word, Jess walked into the ring, across the thick footing of well-mixed dirt and sand and up to the horse, whom Sandy had halted. Jess took the time to greet the horse, gave it a pat, and then carefully but firmly took Sandy's whip out of her hand. "Ride now," she instructed.

Jaime saw an immediate difference in the animal's attitude. It chewed the bit a few times and gave a thoughtful sigh, by which time its entire body relaxed. She looked at Jess standing with whip in hand and frowned. The gelding had never shown any concern over the whip.

Nine times out of ten, the lesson went by without a single flick of the thing. But this time....

"Sandy, is that a new whip?" she asked abruptly, as Sandy started another serpentine with her newly willing horse.

"The other one was too short," Sandy replied distantly, concentrating on her ride. "You know how I sometimes bumped him in the mouth when I used it."

Jess was back; she stood next to Jaime and tickled her arm with the small fuzzy tassel at the end of the whip, removed it, and tickled again, just barely touching her skin.

In a flash Jaime understood. It hadn't been visible to her, this whisper of tassel against horseflesh. "How did you know?" she asked Jess in astonishment.

Jess seemed equally amazed that Jaime should have to ask. "He shouted it."

He had, too, Jaime mused, taking the whip from Jess and contemplating the offending tassel. In every way but words, the horse had communicated his dilemma, and Jess had been the only one able to clearly read him despite Jaime's vast experience. She looked up at Jess, who, oblivious, was watching the much happier pair in the ring. It was just another clue to the who and what of Jess, and Jaime began to wonder where those clues would lead her.

For a while, they led her no further. In addition, there was no mention of Carey, Jess, or gold from any news source, and Jaime relaxed in the belief that she and Eric had been right to keep the gold from Dayna, and to keep Jess out of a system that might have done her more harm than good. Busy with training and instructing, not to mention the business of preparing her two competition horses for the approaching season, Jaime wondered about Jess and her mysteries only in the odd moment.

Jaime got used to the fact that Jess rarely said more than yes or no, that she was easily startled but that when she chose to trust, she gave her complete and utter confidence. It was only when she found Jess asleep in the hay storage, her head pillowed on Carey's saddlebags and dirty tear-smears dried on her face, that she faced truths she'd still been trying to avoid.

Jess didn't belong here. And someone out there was missing her as much as she missed him.

Jaime worried at those truths as she cut the twine on a fresh bale of hay and counted out the flakes for afternoon snack-time. The horses, alerted by the rustling, immediately set up a clamor, each demanding to be fed first. Jess lifted her head and blinked sleepily.

"I'll get them," Jaime said, trying to erase the confused and uncertain look on Jess' face. "Give yourself a few minutes and then check the water buckets, okay?" Jess blinked again and looked at her hands, opening and closing them like she'd never seen them before. Then, as Jaime stacked the flakes of hay into a wheelbarrow and glanced back at her, Jess nodded. She traced a wistful finger along the top flap of a saddlebag and followed Jaime out of the airy shed behind the barn and through the big double doors at the end of the barn aisle.

As Jaime stopped to parcel out hay, Jess passed her, then halted, her head raised in what Jaime had come to recognize as the reaction to an out-of-place noise. Without thinking, Jaime stopped what she was doing, only belatedly realizing how she had come to trust Jess' reactions. It was only an instant later that a man's voice called out from the entrance/tack room.

"Anyone here?"

"Come on in," Jaime answered, her reply barely audible above the indignant protests of the horses as the wheelbarrow no longer progressed down the aisle. "One flake each, remember?" Jaime said, which was all the prompting Jess needed to pick up the job. Jaime brushed ineffectively at the persistent bits of hay on her breeches and met the man in the doorway between the tack room and the aisle.

"Can I help you?" she asked. He wasn't a typical visitor—not a mother with a horse-crazy daughter in tow, or a young professional who had the money but not quite the time to spend on his or her horse. This man was full of visual conflicts, with spiffy new jeans topped by what looked like a well-worn handwoven shirt—and not very clean one at that. The man's dark hair was carefully cut but not much cleaner than the shirt, and his teeth, when he smiled meaninglessly at her, were just plain nasty. She kept a polite distance between them, having no desire to see if his breath was on par with those teeth.

"I'm looking for a horse," he said, eyeing the few curious horses that bothered to peer out at him in between snatches of hay.

"We have several for sale right now," she said. "What kind of horse were you looking for?"

He shook his head. "Not to buy. I lost one a couple weeks back. Looking for her and her gear."

"You lost her tacked up?" Jaime said curiously, wondering about the man's unplaceable accent. "Take a fall?"

"Someone did," he said shortly. "I wondered if I could take a look around."

She had a sudden urge to show him the door, but squelched it, trying to imagine herself in his shoes. "I'd be glad to show you around, but we haven't taken in any strays. There're several private barns in the area, though—have you checked with them?"

"Not yet," he grunted, bringing his attention back inside the tack room, eyeing the gear draped over saddleracks and festooned from wall hooks.

Inexplicably, Jaime felt her own eye drawn to the rack which held the wool coolers, checking to see if any of Jess' saddle was visible from beneath. "I wish I could help you," she said politely, glancing down the aisle to see that Jess had finished distributing the snack, that she was coming back with the empty wheelbarrow. Three stalls away, Jess looked up, got her first good look at the visitor, and froze. She stood very tall, the wheelbarrow forgotten, one leg trembling with the indecision of *run* or *stay*.

The clatter of metal drew Jaime's attention, and she found that the man had invited himself to paw through the tack room; he let her show bridle fall back to the wall with a thunk of the double bit and reached to lift a boarder's saddle off the older saddle that sat beneath.

"Excuse me," she said loudly, striding in to push the saddle back where it belonged. "You aren't welcome to handle my boarder's gear, and yours isn't here. I'd like you to leave now."

He stood back from her, a stubborn look on his face. For a moment she thought he might push the issue, and rebuked herself for not teaching Jess about 9-1-1. Reluctantly, she added, "Tell me what the horse looks like and where to get in touch with you, and I'll let you know if I hear anything."

The offer seemed to be enough. "Ask for Derrick at the LK Hotel," he said. "The gear is a little unusual, looks like a cross between one of your saddles and a western saddle. The horse is a six-year-old dun mare, dark points all around."

Jaime pointedly opened the door for him. "I'll let you know if I hear anything," she said, and ushered him out, leaning on the door after she'd closed it. *Dun mare....*

Jess peeked hesitantly around the edge of the doorway, her expression scared but determined.

*She's been out there since I saw her. She was going to fight for me,* Jaime thought in astonishment. And the sudden realization: *She's seen him before.*

The sound of a car engine and the crunch of tires on gravel told of Derrick's departure as he pulled out of the U-shaped driveway. Jess relaxed a little and came into the room, giving her head an odd little toss. *Dun mare.* Her dark-sand hair fell back around her face, and the blended black swath of her bangs had never seemed so obvious as it fell over her forehead. *Black points.*

# 4

Adding up coincidences, Dayna decided, could drive you mad. It was enough to make you realize that the course of your life was as strange and random as any *Ripley's Believe It Or Not*. There was Eric, whom she'd met through his position as Highbanks Park Volunteer. Though they'd become good friends, they'd certainly never spent this much time together before. And then there was Jaime, whom she'd met through Mark, whom she'd met at work. And of course, Jess—whom she'd met at the park because of Eric, and who was living here with Jaime because she'd met Mark—

She finally stopped herself. The point was, they were all sitting here eating a cook-out dinner. It didn't matter how it'd all come about.

Dayna poured herself another tumbler of ice tea and offered the pitcher to Eric, who shook his head. He, like Jaime, was watching Jess, who was in turn watching a boarder's gelding graze. Mark seemed oblivious to them all as he ate neat soldierly rows of butter-dripping corn. Dayna contemplated taking the last foil-wrapped cob off the grill but then considered the fat in the butter. *Maybe not.* Besides, she didn't want to be distracted from Jaime, who, although she obviously had some purpose behind this impromptu little dinner, had so far confined herself to inane remarks about the food preparation and the weather.

She sighed and looked back to Mark. Like his older sister, he was attractive, with hair and eyes both a lighter shade of brown than hers.

Where she was solid, he was angular, almost too thin. But when he smiled his whole face got in on the act, and Dayna gave one more sigh in a long line of regrets that he couldn't act the age that went along with his birth date. At thirty he was two years older than she—but despite his appealing presence, she was no more than occasionally tempted by the idea of a more serious relationship.

As if to confirm her ruminations, Mark dropped the denuded cob on his paper plate and held his hands out for the old border collie to lick clean. What remained of the butter after that, he left smudged on the seat of his shorts as he got up and headed for Jess.

"He'd better not go for soccer after all he just ate," Dayna warned to his oblivious back.

"He's a big boy," Jaime said absently, reaching for the ice tea and pouring herself a refill while only barely glancing down at her task. Jess was completely absorbed in her own thoughts and showed no sign of noticing Mark's barefoot approach. As the fact became apparent to Mark, he made his advance even cattier, snuck up behind her and tweaked her ribs with a "Gotcha!"

Jess' reaction, immediate and intense, was to lash out with a mulish kick that caught Mark squarely in the shin and knocked his leg out from under him. Eric laughed out loud at the astonished look on Mark's face, but Jaime, Dayna noticed, only became more thoughtful.

"That's the kind of thing that makes me wonder," Jaime said.

"No wondering about it," Dayna responded. "He's never going to grow up."

Jaime gave her a startled look, glanced at Mark, and then dismissed him. "I was talking about Jess."

Dayna said flatly, "Horses have four legs and weigh about a thousand pounds more than Jess."

This time it was Jaime who shook her head, while Eric realized what they were talking about and tuned in to their conversation, bending his long frame around the lawn chair over which he was draped. "Dayna, just pretend, just for a moment, that it might be possible to change animals to people."

"There's no point," Dayna said flatly.

"Sure there is," Eric said. "It'll amuse me." Dayna rolled her eyes at him and Jaime took it as permission to continue.

"I've been watching Jess for a couple weeks now. I'm certain she understands almost everything we say, although she's still not talking much."

Fifty yards in front of them, the object of the conversation was standing before Mark in obvious consternation, her eyes wide in anticipation of retribution for her reflexive kick. Jaime nodded at her. "Look at her now. A well-trained horse, will, if badly startled, kick out like that. And afterward they know they've done wrong, and they have the same expression she does."

"Horses don't have expressions," Dayna said, pure contrariness.

Impatience flashed across Jaime's face. "Body language, Dayna. You *know* what I mean. I see dozens of things that just keep adding up—the way she stands when she's alarmed, the way she pays as much attention to what she hears as most people do to what they see, the way she interacts with my horses...do you know she won't handle JayDee or Leta?" She stated the question in a way that left no doubt as to its significance in her mind, but when Dayna exchanged a glance with Eric she saw he didn't get it, either.

Jaime leaned forward, skewing the plastic gingham cover of the picnic table with her elbows. "Those mares are in their teens. If you were to equate Jess' age into 'horse years,' she'd probably be four or five. And that puts her way down on the pecking order, as far as horses are concerned. It's a rare filly that'll challenge an older mare."

"And you think Jess is the filly," Dayna said in dry amusement.

"A couple days ago, Sandy was working her horse," Jaime said instead of answering. "He was going crooked no matter which direction she took, and they were both getting pretty mad at each other. Then Jess walked right out into the ring, took Sandy's whip, and showed her where the end tassel was tickling the horse. Every time Sandy changed directions, she'd move the whip to her inside hand, and he'd go crooked that way to avoid the tickle."

"So you think Jess can read horses' minds."

"Dayna," Eric said, "you're being an ass. She means that Jess has an extraordinary understanding of horse body language."

In the short silence that followed, they watched Mark get to his feet and reassure Jess. In a moment, she nodded happily and ran for the yard's small outbuilding—no doubt after the soccer ball.

"Okay, so I was being an ass," Dayna said. "What I *should* have said is, what's the point? You're not really trying to convince us she used to be a horse, are you? Or do you think she was raised by them in the wild?"

Jaime gnawed briefly on a cuticle, ignoring the last facetious question. "I don't know," she said. "Except that it all seems pretty odd to me. Jess is so simple—yet so complex. If she's feeling sad, or angry, or happy, she lets you know about it right then—she's amazingly straightforward. At the same time, sometimes I feel like I haven't the slightest idea what's going on in her head."

"I know what you mean," Eric said. "I'd give anything to know who Carey is, and how they got separated."

"That reminds me," Jaime said, sitting up straight. "Today a man came looking for a mare he'd lost—a mare and her tack. I thought for a minute I was going to have trouble with him. And he was looking for a dun."

Dayna scowled even as Eric said, "Dun Lady's Jess!"

"He's staying at the LK." Jaime looked directly at her, uncowed by that scowl. "It'd be interesting to see what else we could find out about him."

"If you think I'm going to use my passkey, think again," Dayna said. "I like my job. I don't want to lose it."

Jaime held her tongue while Mark trotted back and retrieved his sneakers from beside the table. Then she said, "I haven't told Mark yet."

"Meaning...?" Dayna asked suspiciously.

"He has a passkey, too. Who would you rather have poking around, him or you?"

Startled, Dayna had immediate images of Mark in the man's room, carelessly looking through drawers, leaving a dozen and one signs of his presence. When she looked at Jaime, it was with anger and a little bit of respect. "Don't tell him," she said. "I'll do it."

Jess offered the old border collie another scrap of hoof just to see his reaction again. Keg gingerly accepted the treat, looked around to see if anyone was poised for interception, and slunk furtively toward the big double sliding doors. As he exited he scooted abruptly aside, so Jess wasn't surprised when Eric showed up in the doorway. She swept the last of the hoof parings and sharp, used horse shoe nails into the dust pan and dumped it into the garbage while he greeted her. He had an unusual glint in his up-tilted eyes.

"Computers?" she asked, with no notion of what a computer really was—aside from the fact that one sat in Jaime's office, looking sort of like a television—except that Eric usually spent the day dealing with them and should be there now.

"Took off work today," he said. "And I just talked to Jaime—she had the whole day scheduled for the farrier, so she—and you—have the afternoon free. She muttered something about catching up on her record keeping, but *you*—well, you can come with me, if you want."

Her curiosity was immediately piqued; her scalp shifted in the slight way that would have swiveled her ears forward, had they still been proper ears. "Where?"

His face registered satisfaction. "Shopping. For books. I think, and Jaime agrees, that it's important that you learn to read. I'll be the first to admit I don't really understand what's happened to you, or how it'll turn out in the long run—but any way it goes, you'll be better off if you can read."

Jess' memory supplied her, unbidden, an image of Jaime staring at the morning sheaf of paper-that-smudged. And then, of Carey, looking at one of the black-scribbled things that always came with them on a run. Was that "read"? What did it do? "Read?"

"Read," Eric repeated, looking off to the side for an instant of thought. That meant an explanation, for Eric often looked at nothing right before he made something clear to her. Of course, just as often, he looked at nothing for no apparent reason at all. If Dayna caught him at it, she called it *day dreaming*.

"Reading," Eric said, "is a way of listening to someone talk with your eyes."

"*Ears*," Jess scoffed.

"No. Look." Eric drew her over to the board over the grain bin, the green slate-like rectangle that Jess had gotten quite used to without understanding its purpose. He took one of the white sticks that always sat in the tray at the bottom of the board, and brandished it with a flourish. He drew angular lines on the board and said, "That means 'Eric.'" More lines. "And that means Jess. J-E-S-S. Your mouth makes sounds when you talk, and these symbols represent those sounds. So if I stopped by to see you, and you weren't here, I could write—that's what it's called, writing—a message to you on this board. And you could come along hours later, and read it. Like, *sorry I missed you. I'll call you tonight*. So you would wait for my call."

"Those symbols talk to you?" Jess said, so amazed by the concept she couldn't be sure she truly understood. To talk to someone who wasn't even close! "What do those—" she leaned over the grain bin to sweep her long-fingered hand just above the white marks that had already been there "—say?"

Without hesitation, Eric said, "JayDee, one scoop. Windy, one and a half scoops. Silhouette, one scoop."

"Their feed!" Jess pounced on the realization with delight. She'd had to *memorize* the feeding directions. "It tells me how to feed the horses!"

"Right," Eric nodded. "You'll find lots of books that tell you how to do different things. And if someone tells you something and you aren't sure if it's true, sometimes you can read something that lets you know for sure."

"I want to read," Jess said with conviction. "Show me, Eric."

He looked at her, brow lifted in a mixture of surprise and approval. "I don't think I've ever heard you sound so assertive. I didn't know that was hiding inside you, you sly thing."

He was back to words she didn't entirely understand, but she knew well enough how she felt. When she didn't feel strongly about a thing, she was readily willing to acquiesce to someone else's wishes. But when she wasn't concerned for her safety or confused, when she *wanted...*

It wasn't for nothing that the other horses in her pasture conceded to her the best shade tree. She looked at Eric with a confident smile. "I want to read things."

He laughed, and nodded, moving to wipe away the words he'd written.

"No," she said quickly, a hand on his arm. She took the chalk from his unresisting fingers and laboriously copied the as-of-yet meaningless symbols below his examples. "Jess," she announced.

"Look out, world," Eric said, and laughed again.

The first book buying turned out to be an adventure. Jess could hardly believe it when they went into a store with volume after volume lining the walls, crammed into the aisles—even filling a table just outside the store's entrance. She was wildly curious—maybe this world was as confusing for others as it was for her, and everybody needed directions. The explanation that most of the books were stories, just like the television, didn't particularly convince her that her theory was wrong.

"These people know everything in the books already?" she asked Eric of the sales staff. Then she decided her own answer. "Yes. Or they wouldn't be in charge."

Eric shook his head, unable to hide his amusement—both at Jess' notion and the reaction of the cashier. He told the woman, "We're looking for a good first reader."

"I'm going to read," Jess announced.

"Good for you," the woman responded, regaining her composure. "Let me show you some of the books our other adult learners seem to enjoy."

Within a very short time, Eric's arms were full. He had an adult text called *Reading for Tomorrow,* and a variety of young adult books. Jess particularly liked the looks of several books about an orphan named

Anne, whom she fancied might have felt the same as she, arriving at Green Gables unexpected and not particularly wanted. Then she wandered into one of the aisles and found an entire row of books about horses.

"Oh, no. Uh-uh," Eric said, shaking his head before she even looked at him to ask. He shifted his load of books to the crook of one overworked arm and took her hand. "You get through these, and I'll take you in to get a library card. You don't have to pay for *those* books!" He glanced at his watch, bringing her hand up within his as he twisted his wrist. "Besides, we're out of time. We've got another stop to make."

She sensed he would say no more, and didn't ask. She was content enough to trail along, thinking about getting books about horses and seeing just how close they were to being right.

Eric dumped the bag of books into the cargo area of his hatchback and drove further into the small town of Marion, where the roads narrowed and offered a confusing array of one-way streets. Jess clung to her well-developed sense of direction, comforted by the fact that she could always find her way back to Jaime's if she had to. Eric parked in a graveled town lot and led her down the street to a building he called the courthouse. Jess knew it was an important place just by the look of it—steepled, ornate, and based on big slabs of cut white rock.

"What?" she asked Eric, after they'd stood there a moment.

Eric glanced at his watch. "Just about the right time. Jess, do you remember that man we saw on television the first day you were at Jaime's?"

"Roy Rogers," Jess supplied, although she had a flashing memory of a chestnut-headed man eluding those who chased him.

"Well, yes, but I mean the other man. The one who reminded me of you."

"The chestnut," Jess allowed reluctantly. Something about that scene had been hard to face.

"Right. Today, he has to be at this building for an important meeting. I can't help but think you two are connected somehow—you both show up in almost the same spot, almost the same time, and you had a lot in common."

She wanted to deny this, as it made no sense to her—why should she be connected to a man she'd never seen, in this place she didn't belong? But she, too, had seen familiarity in his athletic movement, in the very wildness of his demeanor. She thought again of the chestnut horse that had carried Derrick.

Eric looked down at her, the only one of her friends who was tall enough to do so. "I didn't bring you here to upset you, Jess. Do you want to leave?"

"*He* will be here?"

"Any minute. It was on the back page of the paper this morning, so I thought, why not? He has to go to the courthouse. They're having a hearing to decide whether he can take care of himself, or if the state needs to be his conservator."

Jess made a rude noise at that last gobbledygook, and Eric looked abashed.

"Sorry about that," he said. "When someone can't look after himself, the court asks the state to take care of him."

"Then he has to do what...the state...says," Jess surmised. After all, Carey took care of her, and she followed his rules, listened to his Words.

"Right. They'll give him a place to live, food to eat, that sort of thing."

"Rules."

Eric grinned wryly. "Plenty of 'em."

Jess just looked at him, thinking of all the rules she'd encountered here. How to behave—no playing in delightful fountains. How to dress—the shirt part must always be closed, the feet isolated from the messages of the ground. She had the feeling the rules of the state would be stricter, so tight it was impossible not to fight them. At least Carey, with all his Words, sometimes let her choose the path they took; his hands were careful and light on the reins. With the Words at his disposal, he nevertheless *asked* her, gave her decisions and freedom. Didn't he?

Suddenly she couldn't remember all that clearly. At the time what had seemed like requests came through in her new human thoughts as orders, pure and simple. She had seen Jaime ride, day after day. *She isn't allowed to have opinions*, Jaime would say, when Silhouette wasn't pleased to channel her energy into a collected, balanced frame instead of rushing unchecked around the arena.

It was with utter relief that she saw the chestnut. "There," Jess said, pointing at the trio of people approaching from the sidewalk. One was a middle-aged woman, brisk-strided, confident. The second was a police officer, and he loosely held the arm of the third, the reason Jess was there. The man was cleaner, dressed in clothes that didn't quite fit him, and clearly uneasy. Jess read it immediately in his widened eyes, the tilt of his head and the flare of his nostrils. His steps were light on the ground, his body poised to move in any direction.

Incredibly, his companions seemed not to notice his unease—or surely they would have made those that followed them, those with the black chunky objects held before their eyes, move back. In sympathy, Jess took a step forward. She wanted to be able to tell this man that it was all right, that even though this place was strange and hard, the people were trying to take care of him. She didn't feel Eric's hand on her arm as she lifted her head and stood tall, a call of reassurance hesitating in her chest.

He saw her, saw in her the same familiarity she'd seen in him. He called to her, an odd throaty cry strangled by his human voice.

"Here, now," the officer said, not unkindly, as his formerly loose grip clamped tightly down.

Some horses will obligingly accept a lead rope tossed over a fence, while a securely tied knot sends them into a rage. With lightening speed and amazing ease, the man jerked his arm free, his leg flashing out in a kick that took the officer in the side of the knee. The man's cry of agony didn't quite cover the sound of popping ligament and cartilage.

"No!" Jess cried in fear, knowing there was no turning back from that transgression. She ran a few hesitant steps forward, her gaze never losing the man's even when Eric's ready arms closed about her like a cage, gentle but unyielding. The man gave a snort in sudden decision— she was one of *them*—and bolted away from the downed officer and the lady who no longer seemed quite so brisk or confident.

He ran directly into the street, in front of drivers who had no warning and no chance to react, where he hit the grill and then the hood of a diminutive foreign pick-up truck. The thud of impact was inordinately loud in Jess' ears, blocking out all other sounds—including her own screams. The chestnut rolled to a stop against the curb and lay limply, without any sign of the vitality that had so recently pervaded his every action.

And Jess screamed again and again, until Eric turned her around and his restraining arms became comfort, pulling her into his chest where she hid her face as he walked them back to the car.

"What were you *thinking*?" Jaime's voice, strident and demanding, easily made it past the door of Jess' room to her sensitive ears. Eric's reply was lower, but still audible.

"Jaime, we know so little about her, I didn't think we could afford to pass up the chance for answers. Tell me you didn't see a similarity between those two."

"Oh, it was there all right. *Was*," she repeated. "I understand your motives, Eric. But such an uncontrolled situation!"

It was easy for Jess to visualize her friend shaking her head in dismay. Jaime was a strong woman, with strong opinions.

But Eric, for all his mild and amiable moments, had strength of his own, a quiet strength. It came through in his answer, the voice of a man unshaken by another's doubts. "We wouldn't have gotten in to see him without answering a lot of questions. And then maybe it would have been Jess on her way into that courtroom, facing conservatorship."

Jess let her attention wander away from the eavesdropping, which had been more of an attempt to keep away unwelcome images than a desire to listen in. Though she'd calmed a little by the time Eric pulled into the Dancing, she was shaken and shaking, and Jaime had listened to only a few words before guiding Jess into the den. There, sitting together on the couch, she held Jess until the shaking stopped. Afterward she offered her cinnamon apple tea and the comfort of her favorite barn kitten. Only later did it occur to Jess that the strict no-cats-in-the-house rule had been deliberately broken.

Now the tea was gone, and the kitten, although still purring, was all but asleep on Jess' bed. Jess, still victim of an occasional fat and unexpected tear, stared at the head of her bed. Snugged between the mattress and headboard were Carey's saddlebags. At night she could smell the weathered, well-oiled leather; she could touch them and feel the security of the days under his care. She was very well aware that, bereft of Carey upon her arrival here, she could just as well have ended up like the chestnut.

*Carey.* She pulled the saddlebags out and ran a hand over the spare, tooled design, pausing over the scratches acquired on unusually rough rides. Several of the marks were still lighter than the surrounding area, testimony to their newness. Emblematic of the last moments of Jess' old life.

Somehow, no matter how long she stared, she couldn't recall the innocence and security of Dun Lady's Jess. Another tear rolled down her cheek as she considered that maybe she never would—that even finding Carey would be insufficient to render her back into that bold and carefree individual.

Then, with abrupt resolve, she knew she couldn't afford the doubts, not if she was going to function here. Not if she was to have any chance of finding—and helping—Carey. She took a deep breath, returned the saddlebags to their space, and went out past Jaime and Eric to attend to the evening stall clean-out.

The thing was, Dayna told herself—waiting, several days after the picnic, for Derrick to walk by the office unit—that she had already noticed his oddness, the dichotomies in his appearance and manners. Jaime's request poked at the place in herself that was already curious, and gave her an excuse to do something she otherwise never would have allowed.

Unfortunately, the LK was a small hotel, and its twenty-four units each opened to the outdoors. Waiting for Derrick—for that was the only name he'd given, and as he'd paid each of three weeks in advance, the manager was inclined to leave it at that—wasn't as easy as watching for him to come through a lobby. For all she knew he'd left hours ago, while she was sitting on the washing machine to keep it from lurching across the floor during the spin cycle, or when she was behind the ice maker, tightening a loose flange fitting so the casualty zone caused by its small leak would dry.

It was noon before she finally corralled Cindy, the housekeeper, to ask if the room was vacant.

"That Derrick guy's not there, if that's what you mean," Cindy told her. "But I've been meaning to talk to you about him. He never wants me to clean his room—always has the DND sign out. He's let me in a couple of times to do a good thorough cleaning, but I don't like letting the room go. Besides, I know he's registered as a single, but it sure looks to me like both beds're being used."

"That doesn't go over too well with me, either," Dayna frowned, then realized this was the ideal excuse for her excursion. Perfectly legitimate for a concerned employee to inspect the room. And the room was empty.

Dayna thanked the woman, took a deep breath, and snagged her work keys from the hook behind the counter. Then she was out the door and down the walk, her back prickling with the surety that Derrick would come up behind her, somehow knowing her intent. She looked straight ahead, not allowing herself the furtiveness of checking for him—at least, until she reached his unit. Then she couldn't help herself, and she quickly glanced around. Not only was there no sign of Derrick on this still, bright day, but very little else was stirring. The heat of the spring noon had become something to be reckoned with, and Dayna slipped out of it into the dark coolness of Derrick's room.

Ugh. She wrinkled her nose as the full force of the room's odor hit her. The air conditioning unit was set and running—she herself had explained the controls to Derrick upon his arrival—but she took a moment to flick the air supply from "recirculate" to "outside." As her eyes adjusted to the low light, she realized the odor itself was nothing malignant—merely the smell of an unwashed man, well steeped. Or, she saw with a sudden sharp intake of breath, the odor of two men. And one of them was here. Sleeping.

She stood frozen until her aching lungs made her realize she wasn't even breathing. *O.K., Dayna. He slept through your arrival. Just take it easy—no reason to think he'll be roused by a quick strategic retreat.* She squeezed back between the AC unit and the cheap laminated table that graced every room. In this case the table was piled high with gear, much of which looked similar to the stuff they'd found by Jess—except for a small pile of syringes, used and new, and a half empty drug vial. *You're leaving,* she reminded herself as her hand reached out, seemingly by its own volition, and touched the leather of saddlebags, and the quiver beneath. Quiver? Yes, there was the bow, unstrung, leaning into the corner.

The figure in the bed had not stirred, and, in fact, seemed unnaturally still. Come to think of it, he was stretched out in an awkward position. Biting her lower lip, Dayna took a step toward the far bed, cast an anxious glance at the door, and studied the bed from this closer vantage. Maybe because of the low light, or maybe because she simply wasn't expecting to see such a thing, it took her several long moments to decipher the ropes that stretched from one exposed wrist to the headboard.

Without thinking, she moved the rest of the way to the bed and its captive, rounding the other side where the covers fell back and clearly showed her the figure in the bed.

He wasn't a big man—although that still put him a foot or so taller than herself—and he was wiry, muscled but still lean. Long stubble, darker than the unkempt, oily mass of his blond hair, covered the long, clean angles of his face. A crusty mess of a bandage wrapped the bicep of the free arm, and it was tied with a tight sling that rendered it as useless as the other. His lips were dry, his eyelids gluey, and he definitely smelled.

Then the eyes were open, and looking directly at her, the light brows crinkled in disorientation. "Who—" he started, and it came out as more of a croak than a question.

"I work here," she said quietly, as if Derrick could hear her no matter where he was. "Would you like some water?"

He closed his eyes and nodded, and she quickly filled one of the cheap plastic cups provided by the hotel. "Here," she whispered to the eyelids. They flickered open long enough to locate the cup, as he tried to raise his head enough to meet its rim. With only the smallest of inward grimaces, she supported the back of that filthy head, until he turned away from the water to indicate he'd had enough. She was unprepared for the sudden pity she felt for this poor creature; she had the impulse to untie his bonds, to ferret him away from this room.

But no. The real Dayna took over, insisting on explanations and complete understanding. "What's going on here?" she asked, her voice still low.

He swallowed, licked the dry lips. Didn't bother to open his eyes again. "He's given me something...I can't *think*—" His brows lowered, his eyelids spasming, in the painful frustration of the moment. "If he finds Lady...he can't. Can't let him get the spells—" he opened his eyes and stared directly at her, focused for one moment of intense effort. "*Help me.*"

She stared back, impotent. Help him? How? Call the police? He was probably on the wrong side of the law to begin with. Untie him and muscle him out of here? Sure, when she was reincarnated as Arnold Schwarzenegger. Then his words tickled at her awareness. "Lady?"

"Lady," he repeated wearily, his head falling back, his eyes closed again. "Sweet Lady. Ran her heart out for me..."

Oh, God, she couldn't believe it. *Didn't* believe it. But the coincidence was too much to resist. "Jess?" she whispered.

"Lady," he murmured, drifting away from her.

All right. So she didn't know what she'd do with him. Whatever was happening here, it wasn't *right*. She had to start somewhere. She plucked at the tightly tied ropes with nerveless, fumbling fingers, breaking first one, then another of her nails, without ever getting a good hold of the cotton fibers. Another grimace, and she bent over the rope, applying her teeth, getting the first sign of compliance, a spark of hope—

A key fumbled in the deadbolt. With a small squeak, Dayna started upright, staring at the door in panic. Then she dove to the floor and scurried under the empty bed, oh-so-thankful for her diminutive stature and her size 2 frame.

A brief burst of light sliced across her limited field of view; two worn boots passed by and the door closed with a negligent click.

"Stir your bones, Carey," Derrick said, his voice discordantly loud after the hushed tones of Dayna's recent conversation. "If you want something to eat you'll show a little life. You might even get a chance to take a piss."

Carey! The name barely registered against Dayna's fear, but some small part of her did hear it. Heard Carey's mumbling response as well, hoped he had enough wits about him to keep from giving her away. Clenching and unclenching her fists in an attempt to distract herself from almost unbearable terror, Dayna otherwise lay as still as she could be. She listened while Derrick dealt with the bindings that had stymied her, heard the snake of rope against rope and the moan as he hauled Carey upright. It was easy to follow their clumsy progress to the bathroom, not so easy to force her petrified muscles to respond. But she managed to scrabble to the door; trembling so hard she could barely get the doorknob turned, Dayna literally crawled from the room.

Jess watched from the Dancing's tack room window as Eric, more focused than usual, escorted Dayna to the big double sliding doors at the end of the aisle, taking them out of her sight. Jess carefully hung the bridle she'd just cleaned and went to the aisle door to spot them as they entered, staring unabashed at Dayna.

The small woman was always a little stiff; it came along as part of her many rules for self and others. But today she seemed smaller, tighter. And wasn't she supposed to be working today? Wasn't that the reason Mark had the day off?

Jaime was in the indoor ring, doing concentrated work with her high level competition horse, Sabre. Jess knew she wouldn't notice the arrivals, and wouldn't want to be interrupted. She stepped out in the aisle to greet them when they drew near, about to pass without noticing her quiet presence.

"Jess," Eric said, and his voice gave the name more significance than a greeting deserved.

"Eric," she returned, her own voice in the low end of husky and still awkward with the syllables. She looked at Dayna, who, uncharacteristically, allowed Eric's arm around her shoulders, plainly upset. In unthinking honesty, she sought to comfort. She moved close to Dayna, a hug without arms; it was only as an afterthought she added that human facet of the gesture.

She was taken completely by surprise when Dayna began to sob. She didn't hear the grief and pain that usually came with her own tears, but instead a frightened, childlike quality. After only a moment, Dayna's boyish frame ceased its shaking and she drew away from Jess, wiping her reddened eyes with the back of her hand, staring at Jess like she hadn't quite expected to find comfort there.

Eric said quietly, "Dayna had quite a scare this morning."

Jess heard the clop of Sabre's powerful stride and held her questions. Jaime was coming, and she would say anything that needed to be said, would ferret out the last bit of information that mattered. For Jess had no doubt that it would matter, that it was not coincidence that Eric had brought the shaken Dayna here.

Jaime stopped just behind Jess and murmured, "Stand," to the horse. There was a pause, conspicuous in its lack of greeting. Then, "What's going on?"

Jess stepped away, putting her back against the wall to allow Jaime into the group. She reached to retrieve Sabre's discarded halter and held it out as Jaime slipped the gelding's bridle off. Jaime gave him half a granola bar and left him in cross-ties, tugging her gloves off and tucking them into her waistband as she gave them a meaningful, silent question.

"I got into Derrick's room today." Dayna's voice husked into a low whisper.

"He caught you," Jaime said, with a glower on her face that was meant for Derrick.

Dayna nodded, then changed her mind with a quick shake of her head. "I hid under the bed."

"Dayna, *why*? You're an employee—you could have told him you were checking on the plumbing, or the light bulbs, or *anything*."

"I didn't think he'd let me go, knowing what I'd seen," Dayna said, regaining some of her natural asperity. "He had a man in his room, drugged and tied. Hurt. He called him—"

"Carey," Jess breathed.

"Carey," Dayna affirmed.

"Carey!" This last was Jaime, caught completely by surprise. "Did you talk to him?"

"Just a little. He wasn't in very good shape—and what he did say didn't make much sense. He was worried about someone getting hold of...something. I think he said spells."

Jaime frowned. "Did you call the police?"

"I thought you two didn't *want* the police in on this," Dayna said, looking from Jaime to Eric. "So I waited."

"No! No police," Jess said decisively. She had not lost her equine memory, which was as formidable as any elephant's. The uniformed men had done nothing but blunder—taking her unawares in the fountain, scaring the chestnut into his fatal run.

"Okay, okay," Jaime said, holding a hand up for time out. She turned back to her horse and hauled up on the girth billets to free the buckles, tugged the saddle off the gelding's towering back. "Start from the beginning, Dayna. There's no point in arguing over what to do until we understand what's happened."

Jess tossed her head impatiently, but Jaime caught her eye, and she responded to the directive within that gaze. She took a deep breath, blew softly through her nose, and listened.

"I've told you most of it." Dayna shrugged, nearly her usual unreachable self. "This guy was tied to one of the beds. He was dirty and smelly, and had a gross bandage around his arm. I didn't get much from him—I'm pretty sure he was drugged. He was worried about some kind of...well, *spells* is what he said. And he talked about Lady."

Jess stood straight up. "Lady," she murmured.

Dayna scowled slightly. "He didn't say Lady was a horse."

Jess snorted expressively but kept her thoughts to herself.

"Well, he *didn't*. Just said he was worried about someone getting hold of these spells. I was trying to untie him when Derrick came back." A scowl. "Scum."

"I noticed." Jaime checked the heat of Sabre's chest and returned him to his stall. "Jess, do you know what Carey meant when he said 'spells?'"

Jess sifted through memories of the time before, distinct but hard to translate into human terms. She knew Carey was most likely to be concerned about that which they took from Arlen's stable to the other stables—lately, usually Sherra's, a woody, friendly place with the best of grain, the leafiest green hay. And she also knew Arlen could make unexpected things happen, and that Carey referred to these things under the generic name of *spells*. She wasn't sure how Carey could put one of those spells into the saddlebags, but...

"Arlen did spells," she said finally, frowning in concentration, staring at the aisle's rubber mat floor. "He sometimes gave spells to Carey, I think. We took them from one stable to another. We were on a run when men chased us, and then I was here."

They stared at her, offering various expressions of amazement. Finally Eric said, "I had no idea you could speak so well."

"Of course she can," Jaime said brusquely, responding to the uncertain look on Jess' face. "She knows there's no point to talking unless you have something to say."

"What sort of spells did Arlen do?" Eric asked. Dayna stepped away from his arm and wrapped her own arms around her waist, listening without being part of it all. Without believing.

"I—" Jess started, and faltered. It was so difficult to be sure what they might consider a spell. So many of the strangenesses of this place seemed like things Arlen might have done. "He can move things without touching them," she offered tentatively. "He can make his voice come out of nowhere, when he's at a different part of his bar—um, house. Once I saw him stop a fight across the yard. He said words and pointed and the two foals—children—stopped. Tied by hobbles you could not see, I think."

Eric and Jaime exchanged a frown. He said, "Are you thinking—

"That sealed document. With the strange writing. I'm beginning to think there's a reason the OSU language people couldn't ID it."

"I don't like this," Dayna said. "It's beginning to make too much sense." And she tightened her arms around her slight torso and shivered.

"Jess," Eric said thoughtfully, taking obvious stock of her strong, dusky features, "why haven't you told us any of this before?"

Jess laughed, short and sharp, almost a snort. "You call me Jess instead of Lady. You whisper that I am mad. You give me Words: Easy, Jess. It's all right, Jess. When Carey said Words, he never lied to me. If he said, 'easy,' I knew I could trust him to take care of the scaring things. You—you tell me I am not Dun Lady's Jess. You tell me *easy*— but you lie! You have not taken care of anything!"

Eric's brows folded together in dismay. "Jess—" he started, and then couldn't seem to find the words he was looking for. Jaime did better.

"I'm sorry," she said. "It's easier for us to deny what we don't understand than to try to face it."

Jess studied them a moment, her dark-eyed gaze resting longest on Dayna, who shook her head.

"I'm sorry, too," Dayna said. "Because I still won't—can't— accept all of what you say."

Jess took a deep breath that filled the most remote areas of her lungs, and let it trickle audibly between her teeth. "At least *those*," she said, "are true words."

# 5

Jess stared into the fizz of her glass while Jaime finished the inanities involved with pouring drinks for four people. It was all right, she thought, to play with bubbles when she had little else to accomplish. But now, Carey was found. And he needed her. Jess left the bubbles alone.

"When you first got here, you didn't know our language," Eric said, ignoring his own drink. "But you learned it so fast. How'd you do that?"

Jess watched Dayna draw squiggles on the bar with the condensation ring from her glass. Not listening, she concluded. "The words were not new," she said. "Just the meanings."

"Except for a few." He smiled, inner amusement. "*Blanket*. I guess that's not surprising, given the rest of your story."

Dayna seemed to suddenly realize what she was doing, and reached for a paper napkin to wipe up the water lines.

"Tell us what happened, Jess," Jaime said abruptly. "Now that we're ready to listen—and that we have some decisions to make."

So Jess told them, using the words she hadn't been able to find on that first morning at Dayna's small house. She painted for them her unique view of the uneventful morning's ride, of the sudden ambush as they'd entered the patch of woods that was after the grassy scrub and before the deep, dry river bed. With her inner eye on the memory, her body unconsciously following the dip and shove of her narration, she missed the grim look that traveled between Jaime and Eric as she told of knocking two riders to their death. When she told of her own fall, she faltered, and her dark eyes refocused on Jaime's kitchen, and she gave them a puzzled little look. "Maybe Arlen...?"

"You think it was one of his spells," Eric said thoughtfully, reaching an absent hand to capture Dayna's—which had moved to clean up the condensation and little spills from *all* their glasses. She gave an annoyed sigh and sat still, obviously against inclination.

Jess shrugged. "What else besides a spell could change me like this?"

"Are you really listening to yourselves talk?" Dayna asked.

"We're listening," Jaime assured her. "Maybe it's about time."

Jess brought them all back to the subject uppermost on her mind. "Carey."

"Yeah. Right. Carey." Eric frowned gently. "What about this guy Derrick, Jess?"

"He aimed the flying stick at Carey. We were almost upon him when we fell."

Jaime repeated, "Flying stick."

"Arrow," Dayna said without thinking; her own words seem to catch her by surprise. "Derrick had a bow and a full quiver in his room."

Eric grinned indulgently at her. "Pretty helpful for an unbeliever."

Dayna waved him away with a flip of her hand. "I saw them just hours ago, that's all."

Jaime ignored her. "Right. He was chasing you then, and he's got Carey now. And you want him back."

"Damn straight," Jess said emphatically, creating a moment of astonishment in Eric before he burst out laughing.

"Got it from Mark," Jaime said through her own smile. Then she grew serious again. "Jess, the easiest thing to do is report Derrick to the police."

"No!" Jess cried in refusal.

"Sweetie, I know you had a bad time with them once. It was a misunderstanding. But the cops are the ones used to handling this kind of thing."

"Jaime," Eric said slowly. "What will they do, once they free Carey from Derrick?"

"They'll ask questions, that's what," Dayna said with assurance. "They'll want ID. They'll want things to make sense."

"They will believe him no more than you believed me," Jess said, just as assured. "And what will they do then?"

After a moment in which no one offered an answer, Jaime asked, "So then what? What other options do we have? You want to walk in there and take him, ourselves?"

"It doesn't have to be such a big deal," Eric said. "Dayna's still got the key—all we have to do is go in when Derrick the creep is gone. You and I can help him out if Carey's still all drugged up, and Jess can convince him we're okay. And if it doesn't work, we can still call in the big players."

"If Carey happens to think Jess is a horse, he won't exactly recognize her," Dayna pointed out acerbically.

"Carey will know me," Jess said confidently.

Which is how they came to be lurking outside the hotel after dark. Mark was in the office, and had already told them there was no answer at Room 24. They milled uncertainly at the end of the building until Dayna broke away and marched up to the door, more frightened of the anticipation than the action. The others, startled into hesitation, belatedly followed her into the dim unit.

Jess' eyes adjusted quickly to the low illumination, the only source of which was the bathroom light at the back of the room. She found Carey even before the last of them had made it past the threshold, leaving the door open behind them. "Carey," Jess said urgently, kneeling by the ropes that tied his wrist. Jaime slid in beside her and went to work on the knots right away.

His eyes flew open, clear and piercing hazel. They showed no sign of drugs as they rested on Jess without comprehension. Only when he searched the features of those hovering around him and found Dayna did his expression clear. "You were here earlier."

"Yes, and I nearly got caught," Dayna said dryly, flipping the covers back to discover his feet were tied together as well.

"But you came back."

"With reinforcements," Eric said from the foot of the bed, taking an instant away from his vigil of the parking lot to look at Carey. "Eric, Dayna, and Jaime. We're Jess' friends."

"Jess?" Carey asked, wiggling his wrist around in impatience as Jaime swore and dug in her pocket for a pen knife. "You'd better hurry. If he meant to be gone long, he'd have drugged me."

"Great," Dayna muttered. "Hand me that knife."

Jaime finally sawed through the tough rope around Carey's wrist. She folded her little pocketknife and tossed it; it landed with a thump between Carey's knees. He tried to rise far enough to reach it, grunted with failure, and fell back.

"Take it easy," Jaime said. "Looks like you've been this way far too long."

"Jess?" he asked again, eyeing Dayna as she hacked away at the ankle bonds with the inadequate little knife.

"Me," Jess said, touching his arm, wanting to lay her head on his shoulder like she had so many times before, knowing he wouldn't understand that gesture from this human form. "Lady," she added softly.

His head snapped around; he trapped her with that gaze and examined every feature, every facet of the woman who was now Jess. Or of the Lady who was now woman. "Lady," he said, accepting the fact as easily and simply as that. "Good job, Lady." Then he closed his eyes and shook his head. "That crazy wizard," he said wearily. "He didn't warn me half again as much as he should have. And you had no warning at all."

The ropes at his ankles gave way and Dayna chafed some circulation back into the joints through his high, worn boots. "Talk about it later," she said shortly. "Let's get out of here."

Jaime pushed him upright from behind and Eric moved around to discover he was too tall to offer a shoulder to the unsteady captive. Instead he grabbed the back of Carey's belt and let Jaime move in to offer the shoulder. Jess jigged, trying to hold back for them, and Dayna did nearly the same from behind, trying not to run them over.

So it was Jess who, just out of the doorway, ran squarely into Derrick and his slick looking companion.

"Lady, run!" Carey blurted.

It had the effect of all his Words. Jess obeyed without a second thought, evading both grasping pairs of arms with her quickness, long lean legs putting instant distance between them—running hard, full out, not concerned for the darkness and the unfamiliar ground. Noisy hard-soled pursuit spurred her on, and she raced over pavement to the long uncut grass behind the hotel. Small town turned instantly to dairy country and she ran along a barely visible wire fence line, pulling away from her pursuer with every stride. It was breathing space, and it gave her the room for thought—for the realization that hers were the only running-away feet. Jaime, Dayna, Eric—Carey—all were still at Room 24.

Thought took away attention and the dark line of a drainage ditch escaped her notice. She sprawled hard, skipping across the dew-slick grass like a stone across water, finally spinning to a stop against the solidity of a deep-sunk wood fencepost. There she gasped, hearing her pursuer come on, his steps now awkward and irregular with fatigue. And something else: the faint *zzzt zzzt* of an electric fence just above her.

She found the line, a ribbon of wire-woven plastic that ran inside the top tensile wire strand. She recognized it immediately as the same kind of ribbon that discouraged Jaime's horses from leaning on her board fence. And when her eyes fell on the wheel-like bulk that hooked on the tensile wire, she knew it was an insulated reel attached to the end of the ribbon.

She rose and snatched at the reel in the same movement, pulled it back down the way she'd come and stripped the ribbon loose of its guiding insulators. Then she fell back into the wet grass and waited, listening to the extra loud *zzzt* of the line grounding out beside her, hissing in time to her own pulse. She made herself very small, very flat in the tall grass, and, when Derrick's companion stumbled to a stop in front of her, cursing her and searching for her, she made herself lie absolutely still. When he took another step she sprang to her feet, ignoring his first startled exclamation and the second, more heartfelt cry when the initial pulse of electricity hit him.

She looped the line around him once, twice, and had just enough left to hook the reel back to the tensile fence.

Out of his reach.

The curses increased in intensity as he was jolted again, and again, and he realized his predicament. Jess backed away, warily eyeing his jerking silhouette against the starlit country sky. Then she turned and loped back toward the hotel.

In her innermost self, Jess was a prey animal, elegantly suited for running away. She forced every return step against her instincts and all too soon found herself on pavement again, tossing her head in protest against the inner struggle. She moved up to hide against the hotel brick as she stared at the open door of Room 24.

Light flooded out of the room, clearly outlining Derrick's form just inside the door. Way in the back, crowded into the anteroom to the bathroom, were her three friends—and Carey. Derrick's sideways stance and alert posture left no doubt that his attention was trained inward as much as out, and in his hand he held...

He held Jess didn't know what. But he held it like a threat.

Jess slid along the building. Room 16. Room 17. And then she realized she didn't have to be alone, and her next step was a pivot that turned into a sprint.

"Mark!" she cried, bursting through the door to the office unit.

He jumped off the stool behind counter, as startled by her ragged appearance as by her sudden loud entrance. "Geeze, Jess, you knocked ten years off my life! Don't tell me it's gone wrong."

"All wrong," she said, still panting. "Derrick—and another. He still has them! Hurry!"

"No kidding," Mark muttered, following on Jess' heels as she flung herself back out the door. She looked back once to see that he was still there, and took his hand as they jogged down along the bricks together.

The light from the room streamed out onto the walk, Derrick's shadow clearly cast within.

"Jess!" Mark hissed. "You didn't say he had a gun!" But he waved away her puzzled look, murmuring, "Never mind. This isn't going to be so easy. This second guy—is he here, too?"

"Fence," Jess said, pointing toward the pasture, her hands flashing to indicate the tangling as newly learned language deserted her.

He took her arm and drew her back, motioning imperiously with his head when she resisted. Together, quietly, they moved away into the anonymity of the night.

"Now, look," Mark said, his hand still closed around her upper arm, more reassuring than commanding now. "We haven't got much time, if you've just got the other guy tangled up in fence. We're going to pretend I'm him, okay? I'm the other guy, and I've caught you, but I need you to fight like hell—and be noisy about it! I want Derrick's eyes on *you*. Got it?"

"Be noisy," Jess nodded.

"Scream and shriek and curse—all the lung power you've got. When we get there I'm going to turn you loose on him while I go for the gun. Ready?"

It wasn't hard to fight him. It was harder to fight him and *not* successfully break free. Mark's grip grew tighter as she nearly slipped away, and he shoved her along ahead of him, ducking his head. Jess was brilliantly vociferous, letting loose one equine curse after another—attention getters, every one. In the doorway, Derrick's jaw relaxed into a wide grin.

"Atta boy, Ernie," he said. "She's a prize."

Almost close enough to smell him. Close enough so he was beginning to frown, to peer more attentively at the ducking man behind her.

Mark gave her a sudden shove and she pinballed wildly into Derrick's solid form. He automatically reached out to steady and contain her, slow to realize she was no longer trying to get away—

—That she had gone for his face with her teeth, unaware, for the moment, that she lacked the formidable incisors and jaw strength she expected to have.

She merely tore flesh instead of crushing bone.

Derrick yelped; he batted her away and flung her against the door frame, closing in on her dazed form to haul her up and cock his arm back.

"Think twice."

It was Carey's voice and Carey's shaky but resolute arm drawing the bowstring behind a notched arrow.

"Think *hard*." Mark this time, holding the gun like it was an old friend.

Carey glanced at the gun, frowned uncertainly at it, and maintained the tension of the bow string. "Step inside," he said. "Just one step. Then back into the corner behind the table." The head of the arrow followed Derrick's resentful compliance. "Lady, push that table in against him."

Jess responded without second thought, meeting Derrick's gaze with her own anger. She stood back and flicked her head in a wrathful gesture, one Carey seemed to be able to interpret and attribute to his own version of Lady, for he smiled a grim smile.

"Let's get *out* of here!" Dayna burst out, inching along the wall opposite Derrick.

"Let's go," Jaime agreed. She brushed by Eric, picked up Dayna along the way, and grabbed Jess as she passed by. Eric followed, careful to stay out of the path of both arrow and bullet. Then Carey, the arrow still trained on Derrick—and lastly Mark, who slammed the door closed behind him and joined the tail end of the group that hustled for Jaime's pickup.

They moved as a single unit until Carey stumbled and sank to the pavement, his meager supply of energy depleted. Jess was at his side in an instant, her eyes full of worry; Eric looped back and hauled him up, ignoring the warning—*be careful*—on Jess' face. She dogged him to the truck, where Jaime flung up the cap door and down the tailgate, then went for the driver's door. Dayna dove for the passenger side as Eric slid Carey into the pickup bed and folded his own length to fit; Jess pushed in behind them and waited for Mark. Instead, Mark slammed the tailgate up and peeled off for the office unit.

"Mark!" Jaime called, tension riding her voice. "You're not going—"

"I'm on the desk tonight, Jay," Mark called, still backpedaling for the hotel. "Besides, now that you've got Jess' guy clear, I take it you have no objection if the police suddenly get interested in that room?"

"Mark, be careful. This isn't a game!"

"I know that," he said, the scowl clear in his voice. Then it brightened. "Besides, *I've* got the gun!"

Jaime growled something unintelligible and gunned the pickup to life. As they pulled out of the parking lot, sacrificing rubber, Jess imagined she saw a running man outlined against the fence line. Then the view swung with their turn onto the four-lane, and the hotel was out of sight.

And Carey, still panting, barely aware, was here in the truck beside her. Hardly daring to believe, Jess put her hand on his leg, a leg that was so familiar to her side but never to such things as fingers. In some strange way it brought upon her all the depths of despair from the uncontrolled changes in her life, and in this moment that should have been joyous, she found herself crying again.

It was a sober, wrung-out crew that pulled into the giant *U* of Jaime's driveway and disembarked onto the gravel. Carey managed to stay on his feet as they escorted him into the kitchen. He slumped into one of the table chairs and stretched his feet out while Jaime went straight to the bathroom to relieve her aching eyes of her contacts. When she came back in glasses, still in that perceiving-the-world-anew mode that came with the eye wear, she looked around at the group and couldn't help the bubble of laughter that escaped. "Will you look at us? We look like we've been on a 20-mile hike under full gear—and we only left this kitchen an hour and a half ago!"

"I, for one, think we did pretty damn good," Eric announced. "And I'd like something to drink."

"Drink, or *drink*?" Jaime inquired, thinking that her kitchen was fast becoming the ritual place for group drink-and-thinks.

"In-between. A cooler would be nice," he allowed.

"I'll have a screwdriver. A double," Dayna muttered, then shook her head at Jaime's inquiring look. "No, a cooler is fine."

"Coolers all 'round, then," Jaime announced. "Except for Carey, I think. Food is what he needs—how about some scrambled eggs, Carey? And a glass of milk?"

Bemused, Carey nodded.

Jaime reached for the eggs and pointed Eric at the refrigerator. "You're the barkeep," she told him, and turned on the stove. Carey, she noticed, had grown more alert, and was watching every move. "Would you believe," she asked no one in particular, "That I've got a show in two days?"

"If you can handle this, a horse show'll be a piece of cake," Dayna said.

Jaime laughed. "I guess you're right at that." And, with hardly any pause, "Carey, after you've had a meal and a chance to clean up, we've got more questions than you'd want to answer in your whole life. I hope you're up to it."

Carey glanced at Jess. "I'm not surprised," he said wearily. "I haven't seen much of this world, and I know even less about it, but I don't guess you get many like us dropping in."

Dayna's laugh was short and just short of bitter. "I guess not."

Eric scooted the last of the coolers onto the bar and looked thoughtfully at Carey. "Jaime, you got first aid stuff around here somewhere?"

"Um, yeah," she said, stirring eggs. "In the downstairs bathroom linen closet. But it'll wait, Eric. Just have a seat and drink your wine. Take a couple of deep breaths. I think we *all* need it." And while they followed her advice, she finished with the eggs, coming around the bar to slide the plate in front of Carey, and adding a glass of milk before she finally grabbed her own drink and settled down on one of the bar stools.

The silence that settled around them was part awkward, part comfortable. Comfortable to be relaxing, strange mission accomplished, and yet awkward in Dayna's almost sullen, cross-legged posture on her chair, backed into the corner. Threatened, Jaime knew, by what she still couldn't—or wouldn't—understand. And awkward in the way Carey kept looking around, watching them, double-checking Jess—as if he needed to see again that she was there, long and lean and tousle-haired. Jess herself had withdrawn somewhat and looked a little befuddled, like she didn't know how to act around a man whom she'd obviously worshiped as a horse.

Jaime heaved a big sigh and wished that she was indeed at the relative simplicity of the horse show, where all she had to do was remember the patterns of the several different classes her two horses were entered in. Training level, test four. Young Silhouette's first class. *Enter, working trot. Halt at X. Salute.* Her mind quickly fell into the familiar exercise, leaving her as quiet as the rest of them until Carey pushed his plate back and downed the last of the milk.

Jaime roused herself. "Through? Feel better?"

"A little," Carey nodded. "Just now starting to get hungry, now that my stomach's awake."

"Not surprising. Tell you what—you know how to use the shower?" she asked, remembering Dayna's account of the debacle of Jess and the shower monster.

Carey ruefully shook his head. "I saw it in the hotel, but I never got the chance to use it. As I'm sure you can tell."

"I don't think Derrick used it much either," Dayna said dryly.

"Good," Jess said, interposing her first, fierce contribution since their arrival home. "That way we can smell him coming."

Eric choked on an endearing, unmasculine giggle, and even Dayna relaxed for a smile of true amusement. "I'll show him around," Eric offered, holding out a hand to haul Carey to his feet. "Start making a list of those questions, Jaime. We won't be long."

Jaime hung up the phone and stared at it thoughtfully. Jess knew it had been Mark from this end of the conversation, but she, like Dayna and Eric—who'd left Carey to take care of himself in privacy—waited to hear what his news had been.

"He didn't call the police after all," she told them. "Derrick and his friend took off. Mark checked the room and there was nothing left there. He doesn't think Derrick will be back, and neither do I."

"I wouldn't, if I was him," Eric agreed. He rinsed out his wine cooler bottle and added it to the other glass in the bag by the door.

"Mr. Environment," Dayna said. "Always recycle, even in the midst of a crisis."

Taken aback, Eric gave her a puzzled look. "Why are you coming down on *me*?"

Dayna covered her face with her hands and scrubbed her cheeks and eyes. "Never mind. I'm sorry. You know chaos drives me crazy."

Although Eric and Jaime seemed to follow the entire exchange, Jess was left in the dust. But maybe she would have been the first, anyway, to notice Carey coming out of the downstairs guest room, the room where Jess now slept. At the sight of him, something within her relaxed, for he was much more the Carey she was used to seeing— clean-shaven, *clean*, period, his blond hair several shades lighter than it had appeared an hour ago if still too long for conservative society. The fatigue from his ordeal showed clearly in the dark hollows beneath eyes set a trifle too deep, but there was something of his jaunty self-confidence in evidence as well.

"I'm going to have to tell Arlen about that shower business," he said. "There's got to be some kind of spell that would make it work for us, too. More water pressure."

"Arlen," Jaime repeated thoughtfully.

"Jess said something about a man named Arlen," Eric said, then added, "But not much. She really hasn't been able to answer our questions, Carey. That's why we've got so many for you."

Carey rolled back the sleeves of the lightweight shirt Mark had unknowingly contributed to the cause. The pants, too, were too long, for Carey's build had helped to make him the successful courier he was. Not too tall, leanly muscled as opposed to muscle-bound. Now he sat that rider's frame down by the table again, giving Jess a pensive gaze. "I'm surprised she was able to tell you anything," he said. "Considering her point of view."

"Which was?" Dayna prodded, and Jess knew what it was about, knew the others were waiting for the answer as well. They wanted confirmation. They wanted to hear from the lips of someone else, someone who seemed infinitely more worldly, that Dun Lady's Jess was who she claimed to be.

"This some kind of test?" he frowned, sensing the tension that had suddenly diffused the room, pitting Jess defensively against the others. "If it is, maybe you'd better tell me the stakes."

Jaime shook her head. "Not really a test, Carey. The problem is, we're trying to believe in things we—well, that we *don't* believe in. Horses that turn into women. A man named Arlen who makes magic spells. So far, we've been hearing it from Jess—and considering the state she was in when Dayna and Eric found her...let's just say that we're confused. Anything you can do to help clear that up would be great. Other than that, you don't owe us a thing. There's more than enough gold in those saddlebags to take you just about anywhere you want to go."

Dayna's head rose sharply at the mention of the gold, and she gave Eric a look that clearly said *we'll talk about this later*. Eric shrugged, seeming not in the least affected.

Carey sat in a moment of thought, fingering the plain silver band on his little finger. "Which was," he said distinctly, answering Dayna's question of minutes earlier, "Dun Lady's Jess. Best courier mount I've ever trained. Nearly sixteen hands, black points and the prettiest tiger striping on her legs you'd ever care to see." He gave Jess a sudden thoughtful look, and beckoned to her with a single word. "Lady."

Jess responded immediately, went to stand in front of him and then went to her knees when he gestured her down. He didn't appear to notice that Jaime stiffened at his casual commands or that Dayna's jaw had set; with a sure but impersonal touch he tipped Jess' head and pushed her coarse shaggy hair aside. "Lady was branded," he murmured. "I just don't know exactly where the spot would be on this form—"

Jess closed her eyes as he searched her neck and nape. Part of her thrilled to feel Carey's touch again, but there was definitely a part that wasn't sure about it. And there was a part, too, that was decisively aware, for the first time, of his *maleness* as opposed to his Carey-ness. Behind her closed eyes, Jess succumbed to a quandary of opposing feelings, until the only bearable response was, for the moment, to fall back into the relationship that she knew. She was Lady and he was Carey. He had the Words, the hands that groomed and fed her, and the affection that drove her.

"There we go," Carey said softly, his fingers touching the raised tissue of a scar in the hair behind her ear. "Look, if you want to believe."

And they did. Four sets of fingers, in turn, lightly touched her scalp. Four sets of eyes stared at her, and breath gusted lightly down her neck as they all leaned close.

"It's Arlen's brand," Carey said. "It was set magically, which is how he got the detail."

The breath and the stares retreated. Carey let the thick mass of hair fall back into place; Jess opened her eyes and barely had time to relax before his fingers caught her jaw, this time tipped her face up to look at him. While the others absorbed what they'd seen—one more chunk of evidence in the growing assortment—Carey examined her new features. He brushed back her bangs to stare into her dark, slightly-larger-than-normal irises, eyes that gazed trustingly back up into his. He ran his fingers along high, long cheek bones and down the slightly long nose that complimented them so well. Strong jaw, good bones under dusky skin. It was when he lifted her lip to look at her teeth that Jaime spoke, and her voice was distinctly cool.

"She may have been a horse to you, but she's a woman now. While you're in my house, you won't treat her like an object that you *own*."

Carey's hand fell away from Jess' face, but his expression was mildly perplexed. "I think," he said moderately, "that I know her better than you do, considering that I raised her and trained her—but in consideration of your ignorance of magic and its ways, I defer to your wishes."

"Oh? You've seen horses turned to people before?" Jaime asked archly.

Dayna laughed out loud, and startled the rest of them away from the impending argument. "Sorry," she said to their surprised faces. "It just struck me funny. We can't believe she's a horse and he can't believe she's human."

"What does Jess believe?" Eric asked, looking at her.

Jess knew with unwavering confidence that she was completely confused, and her expression must have shown it, for Carey once more reached out to her, this time with a consoling touch.

"Tell us," Jaime said, changing the subject but very little in her tone of voice, "about this special spell of yours."

Carey grew instantly somber. "You said you had my saddle bags. Can I have them?"

Jess rose to her feet and moved quickly into her bedroom, retrieving the bags from between mattress and headboard. There they were safe; there she could nightly smell the oiled leather that reminded her of Carey, Carey and his careful hands adjusting her tack so none of it pinched or rubbed dun horseflesh.

She returned with the saddle bags and held them out to him, not certain if she should sit by him or take her seat again.

"Have a chair, Jess," Jaime said softly.

Jess backed into the seat and Eric's hand fell on her shoulder, quiet and supportive.

Carey took no notice. He dug into the cavernous pockets of the saddle bags and mined the contents, depositing a horseshoe, a handful of nails, and a small hammer onto the table. A light, oiled-canvas slicker followed.

"We haven't taken anything," Jaime told him. But the pouch of gold came next, and she amended, "Well, not quite true. We took one gold piece and cashed it in. Jess needed something to wear."

"You're welcome to *all* the gold if I can get back to Arlen with—" he came up with the sealed document and brandished it with a sigh of relief, "—this."

Eric reached over Jess' shoulder for the document, and Carey surrendered it only after a painfully reluctant pause. "And just what is it?" he asked, looking again at the strange paper and the dark wax that sealed it. Beside the seal were the runes he and Dayna, and then Jaime, had puzzled over. His eyes widened and he glanced from the dark ink to Jess and back.

"Yes," Carey said. "It's the same as the brand. It represents Arlen's name."

"How come you speak English?" Dayna asked abruptly. Eric looked at her in mild surprise while Jaime's eyebrow raised in appreciation of the question.

"Jess didn't," she contributed. "Although she seems to have picked it up pretty damn fast."

Carey suppressed most of his amused laugh. "I'm not surprised at that," he said. "She's been listening to me ever since she was a foal. She had most of the words in her memory—just not all the meanings."

"She knew *blanket* well enough," Dayna muttered.

"*Food* went over pretty big, too," Eric added. "But why English? I know Americans tend to think it should be the universal language, but I don't think this is quite what anybody had in mind."

Carey shrugged. "Magic," he said simply.

# 6

"Magic," Dayna repeated flatly.

Carey ducked his head, scratching the back of his neck in a vaguely embarrassed way. "Unfortunately, I can't tell you exactly how it works."

"Convenient." This, too, a mutter from Dayna.

Carey's head raised sharply, a flash of anger replacing the chagrin. "If I understood magic *that* well, I wouldn't be a courier, would I?"

"Just tell us what you *do* understand," Jaime interposed, shooting a warning glance at Dayna.

Carey's hand went to the neckline of his shirt, flattened against his breastbone as if searching for something, and fell away, empty, to rest on the table. Jess had often seen the small colorful stones he wore hung on a chain, and she wondered where they'd gone and why they were important. He caught her questioning gaze and gave her a nod, a moment of connection.

"I suppose the easiest thing is to tell you why the document is so important." He took a deep breath and appraised their somber, attentive faces. "Until recently, no one in my world suspected that you existed. I suppose we should have wondered—the unscrupulous and just plain stupid magic users traffic with unspeakable monsters every time they figure out a new way to circumvent the checkspells."

"Checkspells," Jaime repeated. "Laws?"

"Oh, we have those, too—but the checkspells deal only with magic. When the Wizard's Council—which is independent of all the little countries in my land—can agree long enough to decide certain magics shouldn't be used, they figure out a checkspell and set it in place. It more or less nullifies that particular spell, if anyone is of a mind to try it anyway."

"Makes sense." Eric thought about it a moment longer, and then nodded to himself. "Sounds like a good system."

Jess listened, entranced, learning about her own land for the first time, and fitting the explanation into a hundred different pieces of memory.

"The tricky part," Carey went on, "is that there's always a gap between the discovery of a new spell and the formation of the checkspell. Normally it's not much of a problem; little spells are discovered every day, and even the ones that could cause potential mischief don't get a lot of attention right away. There's usually enough time to do something about it."

"I'll bet we fit in here *some*where," Dayna said.

He afforded her the barest sideways glance. "Occasionally, someone comes up with a revolutionary new spell that's problematic, and then there's a scramble to keep it classified until it can be evaluated and checked. And that's what I have here. A spell on its way to one of Arlen's associates."

"And one that Derrick wants," Eric concluded.

"Derrick's employer, most likely," Carey said. "Calandre."

"Pretty name," Jess murmured.

"Pity it went to one so foul," Carey said, his expression darkening. "For it was she, Lady, who sent those men to chase us."

Jess closed her eyes and shuddered, finding the memory of that chase all too easily summoned.

"All right," Jaime said, stretching. "So you've got a really nifty spell and Calandre wants it. How'd you end up here? And why hasn't this kind of thing—visitors like you—been going on all along?"

Dayna's light blue eyes narrowed. "Because they haven't known how. Isn't that right, Carey. That precious spell of yours tells them how to get here, and you still don't have any way to keep them off our world. A thousand Derricks could pop in, or maybe even a thousand Calandres. We haven't *got* anything to check magic. What happens when they start summoning their monsters here?"

Eric blinked at her, while a slow smile spread across Jaime's face. "Woman, I like your style," she said. "Sat there behind all that sarcasm and figured it right out, didn't you?"

Carey, too, seemed taken aback. "I thought you were the one who didn't believe me in the first place."

"That doesn't mean I turned my brain off," Dayna said smartly.

"Apparently not." He hesitated, then picked up the thread of her statements. "But you're right. And that's not even considering all the things you have here that *we* couldn't come up with checkspells to stop in Camolen. Guns. Explosives. Machines that poison your air and land. Things that we've never even thought of, because so many of our needs are met by magic. Things that people like Calandre would introduce just to get an edge." His face was grim. "I've learned a lot since I arrived here, even though I spent most the time tied up in that room. Derrick spent a lot of time watching that television thing. And I tell you this—even though Arlen's concern was for your world, I've seen enough to know my world is in just as much danger."

Eric regarded him with a puzzled look. "So what's the problem? You've got your spell, and Derrick's probably in some dark alley, hiding from the police."

"Marion isn't *big* enough to have a dark alley," Dayna objected, a glint of humor finally showing in what had been an entirely too somber face.

Eric rolled his eyes and poked her on the arm. "Smart ass," he murmured, not without affection.

"The problem," Carey said, his hand drifting up to his chest again, "is that Derrick took my spell-stones."

"Is that supposed to make sense?" Dayna asked.

Carey scowled. "I never said this was going to be easy to understand."

"Just do your best," Jaime said patiently. "We're with you so far— Derrick has something you need before you can leave."

"Arlen provides all his couriers with a certain number of spells. By setting them into an object—different kinds of crystals and rock, usually—he gives us something we can take along and use if the ride turns ugly."

"For instance, if someone like Calandre sends someone like Derrick out to chase you down," Eric suggested.

Carey nodded. "Usually it's a recall spell, which would take a courier back to the safety of his employer's dwelling. But Arlen is the only one who fully understands the spells that can cross worlds. He couldn't take the chance that someone after the document would be included in the recall."

"Then Calandre—or whoever—would have both the document and Arlen. It'd be impossible for anyone else to come up with a check-spell," Jaime surmised.

Carey blinked at her. "Exactly. So he set the new spell for me, twice—once to take us away, and once to get us back. But magic is a little tricky—"

Dayna laughed out loud, then covered her mouth as he turned an annoyed gaze on her. "Sorry," she mumbled around her hand, the smile still in her voice.

"—and some of it works on the principles of intent rather than direct instruction; all I knew was that language would be accounted for. I had no idea Lady would be changed like this." He scowled on her account. "I doubt *he* knew—it may even be a glitch in the spell."

"Gives you confidence in the whole procedure, I imagine," Jaime said dryly.

"I still don't get it," Dayna said, resting her chin on her hand, elbow on the table. "In order to use that spell, you'll have to trigger it from here. This world. You know, the one without magic."

"I was *told*," Carey said, his dry voice showing his full awareness of the situation, "that the spell still has some connection to my own world."

Jaime looked at him for a moment, and then rested her gaze on Jess, who sat wide-eyed, beginning at last to understand some of the aspects of her situation. "And if you're wrong?" she asked finally.

He looked at her, facing both Jaime and the circumstances squarely. "Then I live the rest of my life here. Lady stays as she is. And Arlen assigns another courier to the same job, and tries again."

"Does he know we're here?" Jess, finally, began to take an active part in the conversation. "Will he look for us? Will he come for us, and give me back my running, the wind in my face?" She held her hands before her, regarding them with something akin to scorn. "These are not sturdy enough. My face is flat and I have no *whiskers*."

Eric moved around to face her, taking up her hands and enfolding them in his. "Your hands are elegant, Jess, and so is your poor flat face. Jaime's horses will take you on wonderful runs—and you will learn to find the beauty that's still inside you. What about the Jess that speaks, and cries, and plays soccer—do you want to lose her?"

Jess gave a humph. But she let him keep her hands.

Behind him, Carey shook his head. "She is what she is, Eric. That's what I was trying to tell you earlier. Essentially, Lady will always be a horse. Magic can change form, but not essence."

"This means if you want the recall spell, you'll have to deal with Derrick again." Jaime shook her head, a grim gesture.

The edge of Carey's mouth quirked into a wry grin. "That shouldn't be too difficult to arrange. I'm sure he's still looking for me."

"How reassuring." Jaime tucked back dark strands of hair that had escaped her French braid and said, "Look. I've got my own life here. I'm heading into a busy show season, one I can't afford to screw up." She looked up from the thumbnail she'd been contemplating and caught Carey's carefully expressionless face, while Jess made no effort to hide her anxiety. "Relax, you two. I'm just saying that my life's got to go on. I can't arrange it around you while you figure this out. On the other hand, Jess is a real help around the place and I could use her at some of the shows I've got scheduled. So if you don't mind paying for your own groceries, you can stay on for a while."

Carey sat stiffly, his face giving away nothing of his thoughts. After a moment Jaime's expression closed up, too, leaving only the confused hurt of the apparent rejection of her offer.

Carey took belated notice. "No," he said. "It's not...it's..." He took a deep breath, blew it out hard. "I'm not sure you realize the danger," he said. "Derrick is ruthless and he's already found contacts with his seamy counterparts here. If—*when*—he finds me, he won't hesitate to do whatever he has to, to get his hands on that document."

"He can't be any worse than some of the people already here." Jaime sat back watched him, arms crossed, until he nodded a succinct acceptance of her offer.

And Jess thought her head would explode if she tried to think about all these new things for one more minute. "I'm hungry," she announced boldly, and Carey laughed affectionately.

"That's my Lady," he said.

The rest of the evening, Jaime thought—in direct contrast with conversation about magic, wizards, and alternate worlds—had been incredibly mundane. She stared down the barn aisle from within the arena, watching Jess go about the morning cleaning. Carey still slept; after the adrenaline of escape had faded, so had he, and he'd done it in a big way. She wouldn't be surprised if he slept for days.

Sabre walked up behind her and pushed her shoulders with his nose. He knew the routine: a few days before a show, she turned her competition horses into the arena and free-longed them; twice a day, enough to get the kinks out and keep them fresh. But it wasn't any fun, he seemed to say as he nudged her again, unless she played too.

"All right, big guy," she murmured, shoving him away and raising the longe whip to a more attentive position. "Move out, then." With faked annoyance, he shook his head, lay his ears back, and struck out into a reaching trot. After ten minutes of it, he was ready for a good roll, and she left him to himself, tucking the longe whip behind the arena kick boards.

Jess was waiting for her by the arena/aisle gate, the mounded wheelbarrow behind her. She seemed lost in thought, and didn't take her gaze from Sabre until Jaime was at the gate.

"You don't look happy," Jaime observed. "Especially considering we finally found Carey."

Jess shrugged, one of the gestures she'd completely incorporated into her new persona. She looked down at herself, and then at Sabre. "I

am not me," she said, with the look that meant she didn't think she'd
be understood. "Carey is Carey, but I'm....?" Another shrug.

"You're Jess," Jaime said. "And Jess isn't someone who's ever had
to deal with Carey before."

"Yes," Jess said with a small sigh.

"Forget it," Jaime said. "Just go on being Jess. Finish *Reading For
Tomorrow*, keep working with the horses, and go on learning about the
things you do or don't like. Carey's got a lot of decisions to make, and
he's probably not worrying about what you're up to."

Jess looked at Sabre again, and this time brightened a little. "First
show this weekend," she observed. "You still want me to come?"

"You'd better believe it," Jaime said emphatically. "I need someone who takes care of the horses without constant direction, and you
can do that."

Jess nodded and turned back to the wheelbarrow, balancing a
bigger load of old bedding and manure than Jaime had ever dared. The
conversation, Jaime felt, had not entirely appeased the young woman's
worries. She needed what Jaime herself needed: distraction. She
glanced at her watch. She had a lesson scheduled in fifteen minutes, but
beyond that, and the chores of packing the show trunk and horse trailer, her day was dismally short of distractions. "Jess," she called, as Jess
and wheelbarrow were about to disappear out the open double doors,
"Would you like to try riding today?"

It was an impulsive suggestion, and an activity Jess had never
shown any interest in—but perhaps Jess was equally aware of the need
to be *doing*. "Yes," she said simply, and pushed the wheelbarrow out of
sight.

Fifteen minutes into Jess' lesson, Jaime was all but convinced the
whole idea was her biggest mistake of the week. Month, maybe.
Looking the perfect equestrian in a pair of Mark's breeches and
snugged into his expensive but seldom-used riding boots, Jess had

walked into the arena like an instructor's dream: long-legged, straight-backed and leanly athletic. And the illusion had shattered the moment she settled into the saddle.

Somehow, Jaime had expected Jess' intimate knowledge of horses to translate into the reactions of a good rider. Thank goodness she'd put Jess up on her most trustworthy mount anyway. Sunny wandered amiably around the outside track of the arena while Jess sat, stiff and awkward, her hands clenched on reins that hung uselessly along the gelding's neck.

"Whose idea was this?"

Carey. Jaime glanced at him, confirming what she'd thought she'd heard in his voice: the faintest tinge of derision. "It was my idea," she said calmly, returning her full attention to Jess. "Jess, just relax. You *know* Sunny's a great beginner's horse; he knows what he's doing."

"What did you think, that she would be a natural, just because she's a horse herself?" Since that was exactly what Jaime had figured, she bit back the angry denial she wished she could snap at him. What was he doing out of bed, anyway? He looked...fragile, and not ready to face the world. "I had no idea she'd be so frightened," she allowed, taking his appearance into account as she moderated her voice. "Since you seem to know more about it, maybe you have some suggestions that'll help."

Carey shrugged, grimaced, and rubbed his sore arm. "I never would have put her up there," he said. "Not unless she asked me to."

"It didn't take any convincing," Jaime said sourly, not sure how much longer she would be able to take his attitude. "Jess, come on down to this end. We'll put you on a longe line—that way you won't have to worry about guiding him. All you'll have to do for now is sit on him."

But the change brought little improvement; instead, Jaime felt that Carey's presence was making Jess more nervous. She sat so stiffly that Sunny, feeling her unmoving seat bones, began to offer halts, trying to respond to her apparent signals. Finally Jaime said, "Jess, you're not happy with this, are you?"

Jess mutely shook her head, though it was obvious she didn't want to admit her feelings.

"Are you frightened of him?"

"Of Sunny?" Jess blurted in surprise.

"No," Jaime smiled. "I see not. Give me a clue, kiddo—we're going nowhere here."

"If I do the wrong thing," Jess said hesitantly, staring down at the reins in her hands, "then it hurts him."

*Ah.* Jaime glanced at Carey to see if he'd lit on Jess' meaning as clearly as she. He had indeed lifted his chin from where it had rested on his fist atop the gate. "Okay," she told Jess. "I think we can work on that. First of all, I want you to know that as long as you're just sitting up there, moving with him while he walks around in this circle, you're not going to hurt him. Don't worry about what you might be doing tomorrow, or next week, or even ten minutes from now."

Jess eyed her uncertainly, but her fisted hands seemed to relax a little.

"What about it, Carey?" Jaime asked, taking him by surprise. "You ever put a beginner up on Dun Lady's Jess?"

"No," he said without hesitation. "She's not that kind of horse. You've got to be a thinking rider with her."

"Anybody else but you ride her at all?" Jaime persisted—even though the realistic little voice in her head insisted the whole conversation was absurd.

"Sure," he said. "Arlen's always having to contend with people who're politicking him—and every once in a while it suits him to humor them. Since he's got a reputation for one of the best courier fleets in the region, the horses get attention, too." He nodded at Jess. "Lady's a pretty mare, elegant...a little more compact than you might think from what you see of her. Quick, though. She tends to catch the eye. Sometimes they ask to ride her. Sometimes I let them."

It was, Jaime thought, an awful long answer to her question. The answer of a man who was trying to justify himself. Jess, though, was now paying him more attention than she gave Sunny. "They asked for me?" she questioned. "Me? They thought I was a good horse?"

"Thought?" Carey snorted. "You *are* a good horse, Lady."

The turn of the conversation was...far from what she had been looking for. Uneasily, Jaime said, "I was just wondering if she could relate to having a rider who was stiff and tense."

Carey shrugged. At first she thought he wasn't even going to make the effort to search his memory, but then his know-it-all attitude fell away, victim to a pleasant grin. "Hey, Lady, you remember that wizard's son, the one who couldn't even spell a night glow?" At her blank expression he realized, "No, you wouldn't remember that part. Tall, skinny guy, walked like he had a pike stuck up his ass. Sat that way in the saddle, too."

Jess perked up, forgetting her fears and twisting in the saddle so she could see him as she traveled the circle. "I stepped on his foot!" she recalled with just a little too much enthusiasm; Jaime saw her quick double check to see if Carey had noticed the slip.

"You sure did," he agreed, letting it pass if he had.

Jess laughed. "He sat with his feet stuck out like this," she continued, locking her knees and pointing her toes east and west. "He was awful!" Looking down at herself, she laughed again.

Carey's grin broadened; it was hard to hear Jess' laughter and not smile. "He *was* awful."

Jaime smiled for a different reason. Jess, absorbed in amusement, had relaxed. Sunny sighed a huge sigh, one Jess could not fail to feel through the saddle, and was now softly chewing the bit, a contented little gesture. And Jess looked down at him, and then over to Jaime, as understanding dawned.

"*I* was riding like that man," she said. "With a pike up my ass. And now I'm not, and Sunny likes it much better."

"Didn't *you*?" Jaime asked mildly.

She nodded, and then, with a sly smile, asked, "Do you think Sunny will try to step on *my* foot?"

# 7

Carey sat on a low stool by the arena aisle gate, absently kneading his healing arm as he watched one of Jaime's advanced students longeing a lesson horse. The critical nature of his gaze was more due to Jaime's refusal of his own offer to exercise the horses while she was gone than to any slight errors he might have seen in the student's effort. Cathy, her name was, and she seemed to know her way around Jaime's barn pretty well.

The Dancing was a beautiful set-up, Carey had to admit. When it came right down to it, he almost admired Jaime's firm but pleasant refusal of his riding services. She'd pointed out that she'd never seen him ride and she didn't want to fool with it one day before her departure. It was his pride that growled at her response, not his common sense. But it was all tangled up in something that wasn't merely pride, and that was his strong and even fearful conviction that this small group of friends had no concept of what they had taken on—not when it came to Derrick, or to magic in general. Petite Dayna wasn't even thoroughly convinced that Lady was a horse. Was *still* a horse, and not what Jaime seemed to think—once a horse and now human. Association with Arlen had taught Carey that not even magic could change a creature's essential nature.

He nodded to Cathy as she passed by, leading in the horse to exchange it with another. The clothing on this world was certainly something to get used to. Despite a certain level of sophistication lent to it by mage-technology, Camolen had not yet discovered the stretch fabrics which changed bodies from vague shapes under loosely tailored clothing to distinct shapes and movements. He'd had to work hard at nonchalance two days earlier when he'd found Lady wearing those breeches for her first ride. Part of Lady's essential nature was her beauty—and that certainly hadn't changed, not even if she was more exotic than conventional.

He caught himself wondering how she was doing at the horse show.

Behind him, a horse paced briefly in its stall and squealed. *JayDee.* In heat, and announcing it to the world, hoping she could get somebody interested. Just like Lady when she—

Carey gave an internal shudder and cut the thought short—or tried to. He and Jaime had had a short and somewhat awkward conversation in which Jaime mentioned that Jess the woman was not dealing with any kind of monthly cycle, and did he suppose she would stick to her equine cycles? *Probably.* Thank goodness spring had passed with no sign of such an event, for Lady in heat was a...was a...

Was less than demure.

*Stop it! She's not human!* No little wonder he couldn't get his thoughts aimed in the right direction; as long as he sat here looking at horses, how could he expect himself to ponder anything else? Back to the house, he decided, rising and shoving the stool against the wall. He ducked under the cross-ties, gave the horse there an absent pat, and murmured a reply to Cathy's, "See ya," wondering why everyone in this place seemed to use that phrase, regardless of the chance that it might happen.

In the house he found Mark, with whom he'd had little contact so far but whom he judged to be amiable enough. Mark was in the final stages of preparing the boxed ingredients of what he called macaroni and cheese; he looked up from the stove and said, "You want some?"

It smelled good enough. "Sure," Carey allowed. Food in boxes. Hard to figure. But he wasn't spending a lot of effort to get used to this world, despite the purchase of new clothes and his now much shorter hair. He hoped he wouldn't be here long enough to make familiarity a necessity.

Mark dropped two plastic bowls on the table, dumped the macaroni into them, and hooked a chair with his foot, sitting with a thump. "Not the greatest stuff, but I don't do much cooking when Jaime's at one of her shows."

Carey thought it was odd to apologize for offering food and nearly said so. Instead, he said, "I'm grateful you and Jaime are letting us stay. I hope it won't be for long."

"I thought you didn't have a way to get back home," Mark said through a mouthful of macaroni. He swallowed and added, "You really think this Derrick guy'll try to find you?"

"I know he will." Carey tested a cautious bite of the pasta. Not bad. "I suppose he might go home, but I doubt it—Calandre's a pretty tough mistress, and he'd do better to stay in this world than return to Camolen without the spell."

Mark frowned, and spent on obvious moment chewing on words as well as his dinner. "Some of this doesn't make sense to me. I mean, how do things work over there? Who's in charge? Isn't there *some*one who does this James Bond stuff for a living? The feds, the Camolen CIA?"

Carey ignored the unfamiliar references. "There is...but there isn't." He waved off Mark's protest with his fork. "It kind of works like your states, from what I've picked up so far. Camolen isn't one country, it's about two dozen little ones, called precincts. Originally they were just territories held by powerful wizards. For the most part wizards aren't interested in politics...but they tend to attract people looking for power or security."

"And the precincts formed around *them*."

Carey shrugged. "It's part democracy, part inheritance...lander control tends to stay in the family."

"Like the Kennedys." Mark nodded, amused by yet another reference that sailed by Carey.

"Whatever. Even now, though, people tend to think of Anfeald as Arlen's and Siccawei as Sherra's—or Erowah as Calandre's. But each precinct has its own guard, and a Lander Council."

"So who's really in charge?"

"Depends on who you ask." Another shrug. "The wizards that hold us together as Camolen. A long time ago they decided that if they didn't create a council to police one another, they'd tear the land apart. Now people can go to the Lander justice sessions with complaints, and the Landers go to the Wizards." He grinned. "I understand life was pretty interesting before that."

"Spare me," Mark muttered. "It's been interesting enough around here lately."

Carey snorted. "Yeah." He took a deep breath. "Major political squabbling tends to upset the wizards—too distracting—so that helps to keep things quiet. And the landers usually stay out of the wizards' way, unless they're really causing problems."

"Like Calandre."

"She's been pretty good lately—until this. They'll be in on that soon, if they're not already." Carey held out his bowl for seconds when Mark got up to help himself. "But everything rides on that checkspell—and keeping Arlen's spell out of Calandre's hands in the first place. That brings it right back to me. Somehow I've got to get those spell-stones back."

Mark inserted some obviously reluctant reality. "Maybe you're not connected to your magic after all—maybe there's no point to butting heads with Derrick."

"There's only one way to find out, now." It came out much more casually than it felt. Deliberate, that. Because if Mark truly under-stood...

"How's that?" Mark asked, immediately hooked.

"Try Arlen's spell," Carey said matter-of-factly, looking up from the bowl to see Mark's obvious curiosity.

"Can you do that?"

"Probably not. I've never done magic, aside from a few simple spells almost everyone knows."

"Can't hurt to try, I suppose," Mark said, scraping the last of the food from his bowl.

Carey didn't say anything. It could, indeed, hurt to try. If Arlen had been right, and he had some tie to Camolen that let him bring magic into this world, a botched spell could wreak havoc. But if he took it slow....

"Well, whatever you're going to do with that manuscript, I'd find a good hiding place for the thing," Mark advised, dumping his bowl into the sink, along with the other dishes that had accumulated since Lady and Jaime had left.

"Hide it? Why?"

Mark gave him a surprised look. "Because your friend Derrick knows Jaime lives here, that's why."

Carey fought through astonishment, and then anger. How in the nine heavens had Derrick found this place? And how could Jaime have neglected to tell him about it? "Derrick knows..." he said slowly, closing his eyes.

"Jay forget to tell you?" Mark asked. "Yeah, I'll bet she did. She gets like that before a show, and things have been a little...odd around here lately anyway. Old Derrick came by a couple weeks ago—he was checking all the stables around here, looking for Jess. It's hard to believe he wouldn't recognize Jaime when we were at the LK."

"So of course he'd come back here again," Carey muttered, half to himself, suddenly glad he'd stowed Derrick's bow and quiver under the couch he'd been sleeping on. He decided that tonight, he would string it. "He'll probably come as a thief would," he told Mark. "At night, or when no one's home."

"Hey, I know just the place to hide that letter." Mark squirted a liberal amount of thick blue liquid over the dishes as he ran hot water; he ended the task with a flourish and returned the bottle under the sink. "Toss your bowl over here, huh? Might as well get this done before they take over the kitchen." He fielded the bowl that Carey obligingly—and literally—threw to him, and explained, "This is a pretty old house. When they built it, they used a pier foundation—didn't put in a basement, aside from a little storm cellar. Since then the family's been digging it out. There's one wall that's not blocked up yet. It leads right under the front porch crawl space. A guy your size could get in there easy—heck, I'm skinny enough to do it—but Derrick's big enough he probably wouldn't even think about it. We can put the spell inside a couple zip-locks and stash it under there, if you want."

It was just clever enough to suit Carey. Except... "Zip-locks?"

"Yeah, it'll keep the paper dry." Mark glanced over at Carey's skepticism and said, "Never mind, you'll see. Anyway, it'd be easier to do it before dark."

Carey glanced out the window over the sink. Another hour till sunset, maybe. "I want to get a quick look at the spell first," he said. "Just so I can get an idea of what I'm working with." A look he'd been wanting for two impatient days, and that he didn't dare try to take until he felt clear of the fatigue and drugs of his captivity.

"I don't know how you're going to do *that*," Mark called after him as he went to get his saddlebags, also under the couch. "It's sealed pretty well."

It would be, Carey thought, dropping to his knees to fish the saddlebags out, retrieving the bow and quiver while he was at it. Fortunately, the spell that would release those seals happened to be one of the few he knew—although he doubted Arlen realized it. But it was inevitable that a wizard's top courier would pick up something of magic, over the years. And Carey had been with Arlen for...ten years, twelve? Ever since his adolescence. He absently thumbed the courier's ring he still wore.

He pulled the manuscript out of the saddlebags and rested it on his thighs, contemplating the notion of trying it himself—and the possible consequences. Maybe he'd use the indoor arena. He didn't think any pyrotechnics would affect an area larger than that, although the noise might alarm the horses. He ran his fingers along the edge of the thick, creamy vellum and sighed. What a mess. *You're the only one who I know will invoke that crystal*, Arlen had said. Given a second chance, Carey wasn't certain he could be trusted to do it again.

Mark came in the family room, leaned down to look over Carey's shoulder. "See? We thought about getting into it—Jaime was going to take it to OSU, see if they could identify the language, but decided against it when they couldn't do anything with a copy of the letters on the front. But we decided we'd just rip the thing up, so we left it."

Magic, Carey had learned, was little more than a series of mnemonic devices that channeled the user's will, which in turn guided the power of the magic. That was the one problem with magic, and the reason he'd never given any thought to learning more than he already knew—any power that was used in a spell was also channeled through the magic-user's body, and the more potent the spell, the more the power. No, thank you. Fortunately, the spell for releasing Arlen's seal required little power.

And it would tell him if he had any hope at all of employing magic in this world.

With a glance at Mark, Carey closed his eyes and took the deep breath that triggered his own minor level of concentration. His fingers spelled out the short formula, and with a wash of relief greater than he'd expected, he felt the slight tug of magic pass through body and soul. When he opened his eyes, the seal didn't look any different, but it was warm putty to his fingers, and peeled right off the vellum.

Mark, still close over his shoulder, gave a low whistle. "Holy shit—it's for real!"

Carey couldn't keep the satisfaction out of his voice. "It's for real. And it means I can go home."

Well into dark of the next evening , Carey ferried flakes of hay for the horses' bedtime snack—a chore Jaime *did* trust him with—while Mark fumbled around in the dark, hauling in the sacks of grain that should have come in while it was still daylight, but which had been forgotten in a day of fence-mending. They were both tired, and Mark was slow— slow enough that Carey had once checked, and found him listening to the owls in the small patch of woods behind the paddocks.

Carey couldn't blame him.

Keg the dog was at work as well, running his nightly rounds of the property—and the first to alert Carey to trouble, although at the time he was more concerned with his ongoing baling twine skirmish. It took him a moment to recall Mark's warning of the previous day...and by then he'd heard the unmistakable grunts of a fight.

He flung aside the loose twine and ran outside, momentarily blind in the darkness. The dog's barking escalated into fury; Carey followed the noise to the front of the house, and had just made out two struggling figures when a thunderous blast of noise stunned the night. Keg went silent. Through the ringing in his ears, Carey shouted Mark's name.

"Son of a bitch!" Mark yelped in way of an answer, and by then Carey had found his night vision, and could see Mark fighting to keep a larger man partially pinned to the ground. "Get the gun, Carey!"

With no moon, the gun sat invisible on the dark grass; not until a car drove by and its headlights glinted off the steel did Carey see it, and then they all three dove for it at the same time. Carey's hands closed around the warm barrel and he rolled away and up to his knees, brandishing the weapon even though he had no idea how to use it. Three wary figures hesitated as they each deciphered who was who, and then Carey pointed the gun more accurately and advised, "Stand fast, Derrick."

"You don't even know what a gun does," Derrick sneered, nonetheless following instructions.

"I saw enough of that *television* to tell me exactly what it does," Carey said, mostly bluff. "I know what you're after, Derrick, but I don't have the spell anymore."

"You think I'm going to believe that?" Derrick scoffed. "I'll get it, Carey—if not tonight, another day. That spell is the only thing on this world that I care about."

"Life's a bitch," Mark muttered without sympathy.

Carey said bluntly, "I lost it. Lady and I were separated when I fell, and she didn't have any idea how important it was. You want the spell? Fine. Go look in the woods—I already have."

"No," Derrick said, his head shaking, barely visible in the darkness. "It's a good story, but...no. Too convenient. It's here somewhere. As soon as I remembered where I'd seen that woman's face, I knew I'd find it here. And I will."

"Fine." Carey shrugged. "Then I might as well kill you and get it over with."

"Um..." Mark said. "Carey..."

"I don't think so," Derrick said, his voice full of smug certainty. "Your spellstones aren't on me. Without them you've got no way home."

"I wouldn't count on that." But as Carey readjusted his grip on the gun, Derrick spooked; he dove away into the night, running silently on grass until, far down the road, a car started and squealed away on abused tires. Keg gave one last indignant bark and went to Mark, whining anxiously.

"I thought Derrick shot him," Carey said with some relief.

"No, gunfire scares him. He's been hiding." Mark rubbed the dog's ears and stared down the empty road. "That guy's provided us with two guns. I think tomorrow before Jaime gets home, I'll go get some ammo."

Carey thoughtfully hefted the weapon in his hand, then held it out to Mark. "When you do, maybe you should show me how to use them."

Mark gave a single guffaw, and slapped Carey's unsuspecting shoulder. "Bluffed him out, did you? Yeah, I'll show you how to use 'em—once I figure 'em out myself."

# 8

Jess lifted her head as the feel of the road changed; it was well after dark on the day Jaime called Sunday—as if the sun wasn't out the other days of the week, too—and they were just moments from the Dancing. She stretched and yawned hugely, and Jaime moaned, "Oh, don't start," right before she gave in to the yawn Jess had inspired.

"Almost home," Jess said encouragingly.

"Right," Jaime agreed. "Where we have to unload Sabre and Silhouette, and haul in our things—"

"Mark and Carey," Jess interrupted decisively. Her self-confidence had taken a great bound upward this weekend, which she had negotiated without attracting undue attention and without making any errors that left Jaime in the lurch. Armed with a watch and a simple written schedule, she had had the horses tacked up on time, groomed to perfection and ready for several classes each. In between her duties she had plenty of time to wander around the show grounds and soak in the people, their behavior and language. She'd proudly decided that very few of them knew horses as well as Jaime, or for that matter rode as well. And on that score, she decided, she was as well or better equipped to judge than anybody else, even if she was new to this world and this body. She yawned again, big and satisfied, then clapped her hand over her mouth. "Sorry."

"Never mind," Jaime said. "Here we are!"

Suddenly Jess was wide awake, and had somehow managed to forget her distress over being human with Carey.

He and Mark were out in the horseshoe-shaped driveway before the truck had stopped rolling, and she hopped out of the truck to greet them, uncertainties forgotten for the moment. "We did good!" she announced, grabbing both of Mark's arms in her excitement and using him as a human pivot.

"He-ey!" he said, a laughing protest, as she left him to give Carey a snatch of a hug, there only an instant and then gone to one knee to greet Keg.

"We did good, Keg!" she told him, as he solemnly offered his paw.

"Lady, you'll bounce yourself all the way up to the fifth heaven if you aren't careful," Carey said, still looking a little stunned by the hug.

She stopped short, cocking her head a little, the gesture that had evolved from her attempt to prick her ears. "You used to say that to me," she realized. "When I was...when I was...."

"Full of yourself," Carey supplied. "When you ran up to me in the pasture at a full gallop and stopped right up in my face."

"Did you like that? I did."

Carey shook his head, but it was in amused agreement.

"C'mon, guys," Jaime said, climbing stiffly out of the truck. "Horses to unload. Gear to carry in. More excitement than you've had all weekend, I imagine."

Mark laughed out loud, and Carey gave him a grin as the two shared some secret joke.

"What?" Jaime asked blankly.

"Later," Mark said, moving around the back of the trailer to swing the doors open. "It's a short story, but I think you'll want to give it all your attention."

With four sets of hands and legs, the unloading went quickly, and by the time they were finished, so was Jess' burst of energy; Jaime sent her into the house with their suitcases while Mark and Carey moved the truck and she herself put the horses to bed.

Jess dumped her suitcase in her room and Jaime's at the bottom of the stairs, and collapsed on the couch in front of the television Mark had, as usual, left on. She automatically changed the channel to the one of the several stations that often ran nature shows and sat there, grateful to be back and just then realizing she'd come to think of this place as home.

But real *home* was a completely different place, where she was a completely different creature. She closed her eyes and was instantly drawn into memories of running free, of taking Carey from wizard to wizard, feeling the power in her sturdy limbs. Then, relieved to find she could still draw so easily on those memories, she just as quickly left them behind and focused her attention on the strange new object on the coffee table.

It was heavy and metal, and it had a sharp, acrid smell to it. She picked it up and turned it over in her hands, recalling that Mark had named another similar thing a "gun." It was a weapon, she thought, from the way they'd all reacted to it at the hotel, but she couldn't see the threat in it. It wasn't sharp, and it wasn't a good shape for throwing. But it was here, on the coffee table, where it hadn't been before.

With sudden alarm she wondered if Derrick had been here. He was the only one she'd ever seen with one of these things. She sniffed the gun without thinking, but her puny human nose—*so inadequate*—told her nothing more than she already knew. She frowned at it with such intense concentration she didn't realize she was no longer alone.

"Jess!" Mark said, lunging after the gun as just as she grew bold enough to explore its various moving parts. He snatched it from her and she sprang away, eyes wild, ready to bolt.

"Lady," Carey said evenly from behind Mark, command in his voice; she huffed, relaxing back into her more human reactions.

"Why?" she asked pointedly.

"It's dangerous," Mark said, pushing out the middle part of the gun and shaking out the pointed cylinders within. "Jess, we've got two of these things in the house now. I want your promise that you won't touch them."

Why could they touch them but she was not allowed? Though the question instantly came to mind, Jess swallowed that small rebellion and instead asked, "Promise?"

"It's easier to tell you about *breaking* promises," Mark said. "If you tell me you'll never touch this gun, and then you wait until I'm gone and you pick it up, that's breaking a promise."

"It's a Rule," Jess offered uncertainly. "Carey teaches me no kicking, and I don't ever kick. You tell me don't touch, and I don't ever touch. If I say I promise, then I mean I'll follow the Rule."

"That's about right," he said, which *should* have given her a sense of accomplishment for having mastered yet another concept of this perplexing world. Instead she wasn't sure she wanted Mark to have this power over her. She wanted to argue and swish her tail and paw her front hoof against the ground; one bare foot came up and rested briefly on its toes, tapping ever so slightly.

"Mark—" Carey started, looking at that foot, but Jaime's arrival cut the warning short.

She dumped her knapsack by the suitcase at the foot of the stairs, stared at the gun in Mark's hand, and said shortly, "Where'd it come from?"

"Why didn't you tell me Derrick had been here, and would recognize you?" Carey shot back at her.

Stunned at first, Jaime quickly realized the implications of the question. She covered her face with both hands, massaged her temples, and sat gracelessly on the bottom step by the suitcase. "I just didn't think about it," she groaned, pushing loose strands of hair away from her face.

"Well, it turned out okay," Mark said, looking at the gun. "Wonder how he keeps coming up with these things?"

"His little weasel-bait friend Ernie," Carey growled. "Same place he got the drugs he used on me. He found that guy within two days of our arrival here. I guess there are some things our worlds have in common."

"Slimeballs. Great," Jaime said tiredly. "Just what *did* happen?"

Carey shrugged, and no longer seemed interested in making an issue of Jaime's oversight. "He came looking for the spell. He didn't get it."

"We found a great place to hide it, though," Mark said. "Stuck it back in the crawl space under the porch." Then his eyes lit up. "He got it open, Jay, did a spell on that seal and it peeled right off! Magic *does* work here!"

"At least, I can draw on Camolen's magic," Carey allowed.

"You can do spells?" Jess demanded. "You can take us back home?"

Carey looked at her for a long moment, openly studying her. "Is it so awful, being human?"

Jess was just as thoughtful. "No," she said. "But it is hard not being a horse."

Mark put an arm around her shoulders, the unloaded gun dangling casually beside her. "We'd miss you, human *or* horse."

"Can you?" Jaime asked bluntly. "Get yourself home, I mean."

"I doubt it," Carey said. "But I'm going to study the spell anyway. It's better than sitting around waiting for Derrick's next try."

Jess wondered if they'd noticed she hadn't promised not to touch the gun—or suspect that she didn't hold herself to a promise they'd discussed but she'd never actually given. She did, however, decide that the gun must be a dangerous thing; she needed to understand it before she made any final decision about it. Maybe she would decide it *wasn't* something she wanted to handle—but somehow it seemed very important that she come to that conclusion on her own.

Which is why she went with Mark and Carey to the far edge of the paddocks, back by the tree line where they'd earlier hauled some rejected, moldy bales of hay. Armed with a pad of paper, a pencil, and a whole page of words to practice writing, she settled down cross-legged while Mark explained the gun to Carey, and replaced the pointed cylinders he called bullets. As she carefully formed the letters of her name, mentally identifying each one, he held the gun out before him and pulled the trigger.

*Blam!*

Jess and paper exploded into motion. Blank pages fluttered, airborne, while Jess scrabbled away, not waiting to get to her feet before attempting speed.

"Ninth heaven!" Carey said, his voice holding the edge of anger that meant he, too, had been frightened. Then, quickly, he regained his composure and called, "*Jess*," a mixture of command and assurance.

She exerted control over her reflexive flight and stumbled to a stop, spinning to face both the threat and Carey. *It was the gun. It was the gun.* The gun, and not any direct danger. Carey held out his hand and she slowly returned to them, determined to override the equine instinct with human reasoning, although her trembling and uncertain legs weren't quite convinced. She reached Carey and he touched her arm, holding it in a brief but pacifying contact.

"Sorry, Jess," Mark said sheepishly. "Even got Carey with that one."

Carey shook his head. "Even after that night, I wasn't expecting it to be so loud."

"The gun," Jess said faintly, and then cleared her throat and stood a little taller, declaring firmly, "Too loud."

"Yeah," Mark agreed, eyes widening at some sight behind her. "Better get your papers before they blow away."

Jess jerked around, well aware of the havoc the perpetual mid-Ohio winds could cause. She ran after the loose papers, playing a little, rounding them up like a lead mare. By the time she'd gotten them all and found the pencil, Carey was pointing the gun at the target. Clutching her papers, Jess waited for the thunderclap of noise, and couldn't help but flinch when it came. But she didn't run. And when Mark led Carey up to the target, she was right on their heels.

"See?" Mark said, poking his finger into the hole that was there. "That was the first shot. I don't know where yours went," he added somewhat apologetically to Carey.

"I can't believe it moves so fast," Carey said.

"The bullet comes out of the gun, and makes a hole in the paper?" Jess asked, looking closely at the target.

"It makes a hole in whatever's in its way," Mark replied grimly. "Including people."

Maybe this gun wasn't something she wanted to touch, after all. Jess retreated to the long grass and smoothed her paper out on her knee. She watched the two men as she nibbled wood away from the broken pencil point to expose the lead, and went back to work. But she watched and she listened, and letters weren't the only things she learned that afternoon.

Carey checked the clock over the kitchen sink as he rinsed the last of the dinner pots. Not his favorite chore, but he wasn't being picky these days. Everything—his own personal whims and even needs included—was second to returning to Camolen, with the spell safely out of Calandre's greedy little hands. So if Jaime asked him to do dishes, he did dishes. But he'd rather be out in the barn, caring for the horses. Lady would just now be finishing up with their evening meal, while Jaime worked with an advanced student who'd trailered her horse in for the lesson. If he hurried, he'd catch the last half of the hour lesson, and whatever his mixed feelings about being here, he was rabidly interested in Jaime's riding and teaching techniques.

He slung the dish towel over the oven door-handle and hurried out to the barn, past the open hay stall and Lady—and then reversed his tracks and peered in at her. "Lady?" he questioned, unable to figure out why she was on her stomach on the upper level of bales, her arms and head hanging off one end of the prickly mattress, her knees bent and feet bobbing loosely in mid-air over her bottom.

"Kittens," she said, somehow perceiving the meaning behind his inquiry.

He stuck his head into the stall and found there were indeed kittens, young creatures wobbly on their feet, waving unsteady paws after the enticing stalk of hay Lady waved above them.

"I always liked the cats in the barn," she said, almost dreamily. "I was a good horse, wasn't I, Carey?"

"Usually," he said, coming around to her head, crouching to pick up one of the kittens. It batted feebly at his fingers, purring.

The hay stem stopped its twirling, as Lady looked up at him. "What will happen to me when we go home?"

"Happen?" he repeated, not quite understanding.

She wrinkled her nose impatiently. "Will I be Jess, or will I be Lady?"

Oh, that was it. "You're still Lady," he said gently. "You always will be. And when we return home, I'm pretty sure you'll be Lady on four legs again."

"Am I Lady now?" she asked, more of a contradiction than a question. "I make my own rules now. Lady wouldn't."

"Magic can't change what you are." Carey lay a hand on her thick dark sand hair for a moment, then let it drop away. "You'll be fine."

She accepted the caress, but shook her head in disagreement. "I *miss* what I was—but to be Lady again, I would have to give up Jess. And now sometimes I think...I think maybe I would miss Jess."

"And not go on the runs anymore? And what about the courier competitions—do you remember coming along with the Dun Lady when you were a yearling? She took second overall in those games. You were my choice for this year."

"Was I?" she asked with interest. "That would be fun. Is that why you took me down Arlen's stairs last fall? Were we practicing for a strange game?"

Carey blinked at the unexpected question, not eager to admit that somewhat dangerous prank was merely macho silliness. "No," he said, through a cough, "that was just...a learning experience."

"I had a lot of those," Jess said somewhat remorsefully.

Carey smiled, well caught up in memories that revolved around the dun filly he'd raised and trained. "How about that stuffy guy who tried to buy you once—the only courier of some barely wizard, out to get a back-up mount. I'd just started you under saddle, and didn't have any intention of selling you, but..." he shrugged, still crouched down in front of her, watching the memory rather than Lady. "Had to go through the motion, you know, for Arlen. So I let him saddle you up, and you'd stepped on his foot three times before you even got out of the barn cavern. And when he mounted, he dug your ribs with his toe, the clumsy oaf—you went straight up in the air, hopped twice, and took off with him—" and though the memory was still clear, Carey got no further, distracted by Lady's laughter. She'd rolled over on her back and was giggling almost uncontrollably, no doubt remembering the creek in which she'd dumped that unfortunate courier. He found himself smiling, then chuckling, and when she twisted her head around to look at him upside-down, he was lost, and they were both hopelessly caught up in laughter, set off anew each time they caught one another's eye.

When they finally wound down, gasping for breath, suspended in a moment of complete ease with one another, Carey suddenly found himself wanting to reach for her and hold her close, to feel the lithe lines of her body against him. With a shock, he snapped back into proper perspective, where this dynamic creature was a *horse*, and not someone he could ever really call his—not if he wanted to be hers, as well.

His smile faded, and he stood, saying, "I want to see the rest of this lesson." And then he left, but he could feel her puzzled gaze following him out of the stall, and, even though it was impossible, all the way down the aisle to the indoor ring.

It seemed like the learning never stopped. If it wasn't reading and writing, it was new words, or discovering how to go to a nice restaurant and not embarrass herself, or even riding—although now the riding was more like a reward, after both dinner and Jaime's early evening lessons. While Carey sat on the stool and stared with growing frustration at the spell he'd been meant to deliver and now counted on to take them both back to Camolen, Jess spent time on Sunny, making large circles around Jaime while she did stretching and relaxation exercises at the walk, trot, and finally the canter. As Jess' vocabulary and the evenings grew longer, she was given the freedom of the entire ring, while Jaime stood in the middle and called out instructions. Derrick faded into an unpleasant memory, one kept alive mostly by the sound of Carey's target practice.

Although Jess was more than satisfied with the flow of her life, Carey was harder to please. Mark's lunch-time comment that Derrick must have given up and gone home earned him a glare of the highest order, after which Carey stalked out of the kitchen and into the basement to retrieve the spell, which he still secured each and every time he was through studying it.

"If only the job had been done," Jess said somewhat mournfully, looking after him as he passed back through the kitchen on his way outside, into the steady rain of the gray day. "If he could know for sure what has happened at home...."

"Or if he was a wizard instead of a courier," Jaime added with some asperity. "But he's not, Jess. Sooner or later he's going to have to accept that."

"Did you think the same about me, when I wanted to find him?" Jess asked, adding, in case they hadn't gotten it, "I *did* find him."

"True," Mark said. "But that was a little more within reach, Jess." He stood and grabbed the light jacket that hung on his chair. "Well, ladies, I gotta get to work early today—gotta overlap Dayna's shift so we can deal with some paperwork."

Jess watched his breezy exit, but her thoughts were on Carey. "He seems so different," she said wistfully.

"What?" Jaime asked blankly. "Have you started in the middle of a thought, Jess?"

"Carey," Jess said. "I know I saw things...differently before I came here. But not so different as this."

"He's got a lot on his mind," Jaime offered.

Jess shook her head. "I know. He wants to do his job, for Arlen. He wants to get us back home. But I miss him."

Mystified, Jaime asked, "What do you mean, different? How?"

A shrug. "More...open," Jess said, searching for the words that would go along with the man who had cared for her. "Easier. Now he closes his eyes and walks along his trails very fast." She clenched her fists, closing her eyes and putting his most determined expression on her face. Then she looked at Jaime and said, "You would like that other Carey better, I think."

"He's got an awful lot on his mind," Jaime repeated, then sighed. "And I've got an afternoon of lessons to get ready for. Had to get them out of the way early this week, so I can leave early for the show."

"You still want me to stay home?" Jess asked wistfully.

"I'm only taking Sabre," Jaime replied, patiently considering the number of times she'd answered this particular question. "I don't really need a groom, but I *do* need someone here I can trust to exercise the horses. None of the other students can do it this time, and Mark's working this weekend."

Neither of them mentioned Carey. Jaime had seen him ride, had been openly impressed, but had unspoken reservations that Jess could clearly read in her significant silences. It was no wonder, she thought, for Jaime had only seen this one side of her master-now-friend, the headstrong, determined side—not the side that knew how to speak in the diplomatic language a horse could welcome. Jess sighed, loudly.

"Did I mention," Jaime said casually, "that I want you to exercise Sunny *and* Sarah under saddle?"

Jess responded with the ear-perked head tilt that was well part of her now, and Jaime laughed. "You can free-longe the others—Mark'll have time for JayDee, and Leta's owner will be riding this weekend herself, so don't worry about them."

Tossing her thick dun hair, Jess said airily, "I wasn't," but they both knew it was bluff. It didn't matter. She was to ride Sarah, on her own!

"I'm going to get JayDee from turn-out," Jaime said, amused affection still in her voice. "Would you make sure her grooming tote is out where Cindy can find it?"

Jess nodded and picked up both of their lunch plates, but never made it to the sink with them. A blast of thunder reverberated through the barn and house, chasing itself around the spacious confines of the arena until it rumbled into silence. The shatter of the plates on linoleum was lost in the angry sound.

An instant of silence followed; then the clamor of frightened horses rang out from the barn, hooves smashing against solid plank walls to punctuate the shrill screams of terror.

"My Lord!" Jaime gasped. "The horses!" They ran from the house and Jess passed Jaime in the rain, sprinting through the long aisle and into the arena, where she knew—she *knew*—Carey had tried to work magic. Behind her, Jaime ran from stall to stall, peering anxiously at each of her charges and murmuring ineffective reassurances.

Carey was in the center of the ring, sprawled in a twisted, broken-doll pose, face down in the dirt. Jess didn't slow until she reached him and then fell over herself to stop in time, her throat filled with the terrible fear that he was dead. She wanted to grab and shake him but somehow restrained her touch. Instead she gently lay first her hands and then her head against him, lost in the not-knowing of what to do. So still. So limp.

But then he stirred, and groaned, and said, barely audible, "Oh, shit."

"Carey," Jess said breathlessly, straightening to look at him. There were no marks on him, no blood anywhere; as he got himself upright, his legs sprawled before him and his arms propping him from behind, he looked no more than stunned. "Carey, what did you do?"

He squinted at her, shook his head with a tiny, puzzled gesture. "What?" Then his eyes widened, and for the first time Jess saw the thin sheaf of smoldering papers centered in the ring; a quiet line of smoke spiraled up and lost itself in the rafters as they both stared, agog, at what they had fought so hard not to lose. "I didn't—" he started, and frowned, shaking his head again, continuing anyway. "I only wanted to do the very first part," he whispered. "I wasn't really going to try anything...not here, with the horses. I just wanted to feel the magic."

Jess ran a hand down his arm, feeling its intact solidness and, moderately reassured, withdrew to entwine her arms in a self-hug. "Magic," she said, and shivered. "For *Arlen*, Carey."

"I couldn't *not* try, Lady," he said, agonized, staring at the blackened paper. Then his features cleared a little. "I'll bet Arlen set some kind of protection on that thing—it could have been the magic itself that triggered that reaction. It doesn't mean I had the spell wrong."

Jaime appeared at the gate, surveying the arena anxiously—but only until she saw Carey was apparently unharmed. Then the anger blossomed. "We've got a hell of a mess," she said, her voice so tightly controlled that Jess shuddered inside. "If I could kick you all the way back to your damned Camolen, I'd—" she stopped, jaw clenched. "We've got to take care of these horses. I've checked them all—no one's doing any heavy bleeding. Carey, look in all the stalls for glass— every damn window in this building is broken. Jess, get Sabre out of his stall, bring him in here, and talk him down—and check him over, every inch, you hear? I want to know about every ruffled hair on that horse's body. I'm going to call the vet—we've got at least one horse that looks shocky—and then I'm going to take a closer look at the others." She stared at Carey, hard, and shook her head before turning on her heel and stalking away.

"What did she say?" Carey asked, his voice low, his eyes on the spot where Jaime had been. "I can't hear a thing."

"Check all the stalls for glass," Jess said. "She wants you to do that." She scrambled to her feet, fear for the horses overcoming her concern for Carey. She had never seen Jaime so wrathful, and she suddenly dreaded what she might find.

It was hours before the vet left, leaving behind several horses with stitches and two treated for shock. It was longer still before the barn regained any semblance of order. While there was no interior glass to pick up—the windows had blown *out*—there were many minor wounds to inspect and treat; almost every horse had leg injuries, self-inflicted during the panic. Jaime sent Carey inside when she saw his white, strained face, but she had extra help when Cindy arrived for her lesson, saw the chaos, and immediately pitched in to help. They pulled stray shards of glass from the window glazing, cancelled the day's lessons, doctored the horses, and closed the barn up so there would be little or no intrusion from the outside world. Quiet dulcimer music played over the barn's sound system while the distressed horses retreated to their favorite corners and watched, worry-eyed, for anything that looked like another threat. Jess spent the whole time with Sabre, for the big horse was deeply shaken and sent anxious, pealing neighs after her each time she tried to leave.

Finally, late in the afternoon, Cindy left. Jaime walked slowly into the middle of the arena, where Jess sat with Sabre. She kicked the small pile of ash nearby and regarded her anxious champion, quietly offering him a sugar cube. As he nuzzled it, knocked it out of her palm, and ignored it, tears for the whole afternoon finally found their way down her cheek. "God, I wish I could make him understand."

"He understands that you are here to take care of him," Jess said, quietly but firmly.

Jaime searched her eyes for a long moment, then wiped her cheek. "You *know*, don't you? You really know. But you can't tell me what this will do to him. The ego, the edge—the special spark that makes a top level horse like Sabre—it's so fragile."

"He is still himself," Jess said, more of a guess than her last assurance, though she didn't let it through to her face.

"No show this weekend," Jaime said with a little laugh. "No way. You ready to be pampered, big fellow?" she asked, gently slapping his neck. "For the next few days you're going to think you're in heaven. Longeing tomorrow, maybe a light workout day after that."

"Yes," Jess said. "Do the things he likes, that he does best. The passage. He is so proud to do that with you." And, seeing the pain in Jaime's face, she stood, and they quietly held one another.

Carey's voice intruded on their silence. "I'm sorry." His words were hushed, the voice faltering.

Jaime pulled back from Jess and looked at him, nothing more than that, while Carey stood and took the unspoken judgment without protest.

"Do you have any idea of what you might have done to me this afternoon?" she said at last. "Do you know how often a horse like this comes along?"

Carey's eyes flickered to Jess, then he looked down. "I think so."

"Did you see the look on Dr. Miller's face when I told him the barn was hit by lightening? He didn't buy it, and neither will my boarders—all of whom love their horses as much as I love Sabre."

"I know." Just as quiet.

"What do you mean, you *know?* You *don't* know, or you never would have done this."

"I didn't have any idea *this* would happen," Carey said, an edge creeping into his voice.

"You did," Jaime contradicted flatly. "You did, or you wouldn't have come out here to do...whatever you did. Well, we're going to get a few things straight. Frankly, I was—*am*—one word away from booting you out." Her gaze softened, momentarily, as she glanced at Sabre, stroking his neck while he crowded her, seeking solace—and turned into flint when she looked back to Carey. "Jess is the reason you're still here. The only reason. And it's not that I don't want to help you. I just think your judgment sucks, which means I can't trust you."

For a long moment, Carey said nothing. He watched Jaime, gave her the chance to add to what she'd said. And he looked at Jess, his expression becoming a mixture of remorse and wistfulness. "I don't blame you," he said, his gaze still on Jess. "You're right. I let my need to get home become more important than the safety of the horses. I just—" and he stopped, and clenched his fists, his jaw working. Jess' heart went out to him, for she knew he wanted to go home as badly as she'd wanted to find him, and she remembered how much it hurt. It was a bittersweet feeling, this thing that tugged at her, and she didn't completely understand it.

"No more magic," Jaime said firmly. "Not here. Go out to the woods, go stand on top of the Waldo Levy, go out to the middle of Delaware Lake, I don't care. Not near this barn." Then she added, "Not that you have any magic left to do."

Carey snorted. "I've had that thing memorized for a week. I'll keep working at it."

"You can do some work around here, while you're at it. I'm thinking about selling JayDee—she's too temperamental for a lesson horse. But she needs tuning, and she needs to be reminded she doesn't choose when she listens to her rider. You can do that for me, I think."

Carey nodded, almost absently. "All right."

"For now, you can treat us to dinner. Pizza sound good to you, Jess?"

Jess nodded, enthusiastic in her relief. Carey and Jaime...the two people she cared for most in both her worlds. The two people she needed most. Pizza together, after this...it was as normal as two people from different worlds, one of whom had been and still was a horse, could possibly be.

# 9

"Good, Jess!" Jaime said, watching Sunny come up into the bit, moving nice and round beneath his perfectly relaxed rider. "Let's do some walk-trot transitions, every ten strides, and keep him in this frame."

On the other end of the arena, Carey sat on JayDee, working on his own. Jaime had given him a week of lessons, and discovered there were, perhaps not unexpectedly, some similarity in the riding theories of their two worlds—although Carey's interest was naturally in rendering his mounts more agile and responsive in rough territory, not in the highly controlled exercises of the ring. But he had good, giving hands and a remarkable seat, as well as a firm gentleness she would not have credited him with to judge by his sometimes too-confident behavior on the ground. For the first time, she really understood Jess' devotion to him, and she wondered if only the stress of his mission drove him to the edge of intractability. He reminded her of a racehorse with blinkers on, striving madly for his goal with no awareness of the world around him.

She knew it puzzled Jess. She would catch her friend—for Jess had grown into a friend, no longer just a lost soul dependent on Jaime's good will—staring at Carey, looking a bit bewildered—and a bit hurt, for Carey seldom did anything to indicate that he thought of Jess as other than his former courier mount. Stupid man.

Jess rode deep in concentration, using an intuition no one in this world could hope to match. Jaime sighed as she glanced at her watch and discovered she'd run out of time if she wanted to get more grain before the feed store closed. She watched her pupil for another few minutes, enjoying the sight of horse and rider working in simple but complete accord, and she was about to call a halt to it when she noticed Carey walked JayDee on a long rein, his attention on Jess. She had the feeling his slight frown had nothing to do with Jess' riding, and she would have given anything to have read his mind as the frown faded to something...sad, something she couldn't quite identify, before his face closed up again. Now what was that about? "Jess," she called, "you had a really nice ride today. Cool him out on a long rein and then turn him out in the west paddock. I've got to get to the feed store, so you're on your own."

Jess nodded, obviously reluctant to accept the lesson's end. As Jaime stood up from the lawn chair at the arena gate, she glanced back at Carey. He was riding JayDee through some simple lead changes across the ring diagonal, with no sign he had ever been distracted.

"Thanks for coming along, you guys," Eric said cheerfully as he handed Carey a seine net and Lady two buckets. "It'll be a lot easier this way—and more fun, too."

Fun. Carey had never called fishing *fun*, but he supposed it might be if, barring success, you could then pick up a full meal at the grocery store. Only Camolen's larger cities had comparable establishments. In this world—or at least in this part of this world—people were so far removed from the basics of how their natural world worked that he and Lady were about to help Eric catch river creatures for a display in the nature center at Highbanks Metropark, where Eric volunteered. At the very park, in fact, where he and Lady had entered this world.

He caught Lady staring doubtfully ahead as they walked across the very green spring grass of the park lawn, looking at the river, the Olentangy, that awaited them. He could see only a glint of bright sunlight off water, for the river was bordered by a generous band of trees and brush—but Lady had fixed her gaze on it, and he could tell by the stiffening nature of her walk that she was remembering how much she hated putting her feet in a river she didn't know. He couldn't figure out, how, barefooted, clad in a pair of Mark's worn, torn cut-off shorts and a too-short T-shirt, she could still remind him so much of the mare he'd raised and trained. For today's adventure her hair was pulled back and tied off, and from behind it looked like nothing so much as the tail that belonged on Dun Lady's Jess.

They walked the short path through the trees and paused at the edge of the river, where Lady toed the water briefly and stepped back. Eric unrolled his own net. "You guys done this before?"

"*I* have," Carey said, amused.

"Oh, yeah—right." Eric laughed at himself and held the net stretched out between his open arms. "See, Jess, the two of us stand downstream from you, and all you have to do is stir up the river bottom. All the little river goodies get carried right down into our nets. Got it?"

"Stir up the river bottom?" she repeated, clearly uncertain about her role.

"You can hold one of the nets if you want to," Eric offered.

Carey knew that wasn't the problem. He tightened the laces of his sneakers and walked, splashing boldly, out to the middle of the river. The water came up just past his knees, well below the shorts he'd been advised to buy along with the sturdy jeans he appreciated so much, and he stood in the moderate current as casually as possible. "It feels good," he said indifferently, dipping a hand into water that was in fact a little chilly. "Good footing, too."

Eric seemed to sense what he was up to, for he followed Carey into the water and deployed his net. "Half the time all you have to do is stand here, and you get some sort of catch." But he gave Carey a questioning glance, and then looked back at Lady, who had still not committed herself to the water.

"Most horses are afraid of putting their feet somewhere they can't see," Carey told him in a low voice. "Lady's no exception. I was surprised when she agreed to come along."

"She came to be with you," Eric said, as though it were obvious, giving Lady a thoughtful look.

Carey tucked his dripping net under his arm and moved upstream. "We can do it with just the one net," he suggested. "Any time you decide to come in, Lady, we can use the help." And he proceeded, with great fanfare, to kick and shuffle his way through the sand and rock of the river bottom, stirring up great clouds of silt that sluiced through the current channels downstream. Eventually Eric held up a net full of crayfish and hellgrammites and a few flopping minnows.

"Need the bucket," he said, and Carey watched with a smile as Lady, her curiosity overcoming trepidation, moved into the water up to her ankles, dipped the bucket in the river, and held it out to Eric. He splashed over and jiggled the contents of the net into the bucket, sloshing away without a backward glance. Lady set the bucket on one of the plentiful flat rocks and stayed in her safe part of the river.

The second time they came up with an empty net, and Eric suggested, "We need to move upstream a little bit, though...we could try it here with two nets."

Carey looked at his undecided companion, and his mind's eye translated her into a horse hovering at the edge of the deeper water, one hoof pawing the air over the surface. Then he blinked and saw only Lady with her dun/black hair pulled back, her toes curled protectively around the rocks at her feet and a thin line of dusky skin peeking through where the t-shirt fell short of her cut-offs. Carey held out his hand. "C'mon, braveheart," he said, in the same voice that had wooed her into countless rivers.

She took the plunge. Scooting through the water, slipping on the rocks she traversed too quickly, she ended up right at his side, trembling a little at her own boldness.

"Hey, all right, Jess!" Eric hailed her, and she smiled uncertainly at him.

"Good job." Carey slipped an arm around her waist, offering but not forcing the support, and together they kicked up another cloud of silt. Outwardly he was matter-of-fact but inwardly he smiled, and thought there was, perhaps, a little more satisfaction to convincing this free-willed creature than to bluffing one of his horses.

He wasn't surprised when Lady eventually soaked all of them with her enthusiasm. Once she trusted the footing she entered into the game with abandon, and Carey knew that they'd been out there long after Eric had his quota for the nature center aquarium. If Lady noticed that he was discreetly releasing as many creatures as he kept, she pretended not to.

But it was Lady, as engrossed as she was with kicking around the Olentangy River bottom—or Old-and-dingy, as Eric called it—who noticed they had company. Although she'd ignored the occasional hiker who'd stopped to exchange a few words with Eric and his volunteer's armband, this time she flung her head up; her nostrils flared and Carey knew she was laying her ears back. It was a warning...to Derrick.

*Nine hells.* "You must waste a lot of time keeping track of me," he said, so that Eric, who had not been tuned into Lady's signals, jerked his head up from where he bent over one of the buckets, nearly turning it over in his surprise.

"It's not that hard," Derrick said, watching them from the river-bank. "And don't forget, right now you're the only thing I've got on my mind. You and that spell, I mean."

"I figured you'd given up on us," Carey said—though he hadn't, really, despite Derrick's long absence. His gaze skipped over the trees along the river. "Where's your friend Ernie?"

Instead of answering, Derrick said, "Give up? No. Ernie and I have just been busy with one of his projects." Derrick casually nodded back toward the nature center parking lot. "He's back in the car—he prefers pavement under his feet, I think. Besides, I'm not here to make trouble."

Carey did not deign to respond to that one. Of course Derrick was here to make trouble—a point Derrick himself proved by leering at Lady, who was looking less gamine—and more defensively threatening—by the moment. Carey stepped slightly in front of her, a message to both her and Derrick.

"She's done better than my chestnut," Derrick said, idly snapping a twig from one of the sycamore saplings on the river's edge. "That fool didn't take well to a new body. Ran off and left me—and you—in those woods; didn't take him long to run out in front of a car. But your mare, now—she came looking for you." He fingered the fresh pinkness of the healed bite on his cheek. "Why was that, Carey?"

"Go burn," Carey said, a particularly coarse remark almost hidden in his pleasant tone of voice.

Derrick shrugged. "Doesn't matter, I suppose. Just...interesting. But not what I wanted to talk about."

Carey put both end poles of the seine net in one hand and put the other on hip, a bored looking stance. "Yeah, right. You want the spell. Well, I've learned a saying here that seems to fit just right: get real, Derrick."

"I'm not here just to take," Derrick protested. "I've got something I know you want—and *I* want to trade."

Carey snorted. "For my spellstones, right? I don't believe it."

"You want to go home, don't you?" Derrick asked, sounding reasonable.

"And so do you. You're not about to just give up those stones."

"They won't work for me. It reads like an empty stone to me. Maybe you were just lying about them."

Carey shook his head. "I wasn't lying." He was suddenly aware of the chill in the water that rushed past his legs, and he waded to the shore—a less vulnerable position in any case. Now he was close enough to see that Derrick had done well in this world. Probably provisioned, as Carey had been, with the gold that was fairly plentiful in their world but worth a great deal in this one. He'd kept himself clean, his dark hair handsomely styled. He'd even—and Carey confirmed this as Derrick tried out an affable smile on him—gotten his teeth worked on. Probably in the interest of blending in; it made him seem more benign—which Carey knew he definitely was not. "No, I wasn't lying," he repeated, although he hadn't been telling all of the truth, either. "I was hurt and drugged—do you think I *could* have lied to you?" It was just a small matter of not mentioning the correct spell was keyed into his new stone—not the regular onyx recall that Derrick would have tried to trigger.

"No," Derrick said, "I don't think you could have. And that leaves me with a useless path home, and without the spell. You want to go home? You give me the spell, and I'll give you your spellstones. I'll take my chances at getting home—they won't be any worse than they are now."

"You lie!" Lady said, still standing in water up to her knees, toss-ing her head back to once again lay back those non-existent ears. "You would never let us go like that, and be stuck here."

Carey smiled at Derrick, but it was without humor. "Even Lady can see through this one, Derrick," he said. "You keep the spellstones, I'll keep the manuscript." *Maybe only in my head, but it's still mine.*

Derrick shrugged. "I just thought it would be easier this way—for both of us. I'm willing to do it the hard way—though you might not think so much of it."

"You might as well settle in here, Derrick," Carey said, as though he was offering serious advice to a friend. "Don't waste the rest of your life chasing after that spell. It doesn't really matter anyway."

Derrick frowned, for the first time losing the thread of the conver-sation.

"Do you think they're all in stasis back in Camolen?" Carey sent him a look of scorn. "Arlen's already sent another courier and I wouldn't be surprised if the checkspells are in place by now." Meaning none of them would get home unless Arlen, in some fashion, came looking; a recall spell based on magic that had been checked was worth no more than a recall spell in Derrick's pocket.

To his surprise, Derrick laughed. "You're right, at that," he said. "Life goes on in Camolen. But don't forget that Calandre, too, is part of that life. There was a strike set for Arlen's little hole in the hills—it should have gone off about the same time we ran you down."

Carey couldn't help his consternation, and Derrick laughed again. "We've had one of his recall spells for a year, now. You remember that girl who disappeared on her first run?"

Carey remembered well. The young woman had been sent on an easy run with an insignificant message. They'd put her disappearance down to accident, not ambush. But if Calandre had truly engineered her disappearance, and had one of the recall spells that would gain her access to Arlen's little fortress.... "Those recalls go to a shielded hold-ing room," he said; he had the only two-layer recall that would take him within the hold if he made the extra effort to trigger it. "Magic won't get her out of there."

"No, but she can work magic within the room...and stone can be moved." Derrick's slyly pleased expression was suddenly almost unbearable.

Carey mustered his temper. "It could have gone either way," he said, and kept his sudden, deep worry to himself. "Give me the spell-stones and I'll take you back with me—but the manuscript is mine."

Derrick laughed again, well pleased with the overall effect of his negotiations despite his failures. "It was worth this little jaunt just to see you try that one out on me," he said. "Of course the answer is no. But don't worry—I'm sure we'll be talking again soon enough. Until then." He made a brief, courtly obeisance to Lady, and walked back onto the open park lawn.

Carey looked at Lady, and found her shivering in the water. Eric looked no happier. And Carey himself felt the bright sunshine had somehow dimmed.

It was certainly no longer enough to keep him warm.

Jess sat in the hay loft amidst the cutting-season overflow, her body arranged over several levels of bales. She was supposed to be tossing them down into the aisle to be stacked in the stall below her—but she hadn't even started yet.

Not that it mattered. Jaime was riding Sabre, who'd for the most part recovered from his shock, and she wouldn't notice Jess' inactivity for some time yet. And Jess was feeling out of sorts. Some of it, she felt, was due to the shorter days of this world compared to a Camolen day, an observation Carey had recently made. But most of it was her deep distraction with the movie she'd seen the evening before.

There were lots of things about the movie that she loved. The characters' Aussie accents, which helped her to realize that lots of people talked differently, and that her own still-faltering syllables were nothing to be ashamed of. And the tough little mountain horse who raced, without hesitation, over terrain that reminded her of some of her own runs, and who wasn't so different from her own deep dun color. But when the wild stallion had been intimidated and rounded up, she wasn't sure she considered it the happy ending everybody else did. And she was mightily puzzled over the significance of pressing lips together. *Kissing.*

Jess rolled over on her back and wiggled against the hay, letting its scratchy roughness find all the itches between her shoulder blades. Then she lay there, and closed her eyes, and took herself back to the times of running with Arlen's small herd of courier horses. She could pretend that had been freedom, but in reality, she'd belonged to someone. The stallion hadn't; he'd been truly free, and magnificent, and in the end, conquered. And she thought she should feel unhappy about that, but she couldn't quite manage it—because the part about being a horse that her mind most often strayed to, the memories she caressed and savored, were those moments she and Carey had been in such accord that she read his every thought through the mere tension in his muscles. And the stallion, wild, would never know such partnership.

A sigh; a few more wiggles for that one, hard-to-reach spot. Being owned wasn't such a bad thing for a horse, she decided. But she wished Carey would realize she wasn't only Dun Lady's Jess. Not anymore.

Abruptly, she sat and hopped down off the hay, and, with a quick check to make sure Keg wasn't in the aisle below, began shoving bales out of the loft. Ten more minutes had them stacked neatly in the stall, and she meandered out of the barn into the rising temperatures of the early summer morning. Mark's abandoned soccer ball lay in the shade of the house, and she toed it closer, nudging it along in a desultory way as she wound through the obstacles of the picnic table and lawn chairs.

"Too warm for soccer, Jess," Mark yawned from the back doorway. "Geeze, last night's shift was a killer. Had all the guests for a wedding, must've been some kind of biker thing. They really know how to party."

Jess, typically straightforward, asked, "What is kissing for, Mark?"

Mark blinked, did a deliberate double-take. "Whoa, Jess—yeow. You sure you don't want to ask Jaime about that?"

"Jaime is busy," Jess said, pushing blithely onward. "Every time we look at the TV, there are people kissing. Why?"

"Um," Mark said. "Because...it feels good."

"Show me."

He put both hands over his face and drew them down slowly so his eyes peeked over his fingers, full of misgivings. "Well, Jess, that's usually something two people do when they like each other."

Jess frowned. "I do like you."

"In a special way. You know, love, getting married, having a family—two kids and a dog, the whole works."

She did, then, understand a little of what he was driving at. Special, in a way that she'd almost deliberately avoided considering because it was simply too much when added to everything else. "I have to understand," she said slowly. "If Carey takes me home, there will be no more chance to learn. If I have to decide, stay or go, I want to know all the things I'm deciding about."

Mark bit his lip, staring at her, hesitating. "All right, but...Jess, people kiss for a lot of different reasons. Sometimes just because it does feel good, but usually because they love one another. I can show you how it's done, but...it won't be the same."

Jess nodded, and waited, and he closed the short distance between them, gently touched two fingers to the side of her chin, and gave her a soft but definite kiss. He drew back to look at her, and this time it was she who blinked, considering. Warm. Nice. But nothing wonderful. She drew her teeth over her bottom lip where she could still feel the contact, and gave him a quizzical look.

"Didn't make your hair stand on end, huh," he said. "I'm not surprised. It's different when—"

"Do it again," she said abruptly, and, at his raised eyebrows, added a contrite, "Please."

"Again," he repeated, and sighed, but didn't offer any argument. Instead he simply kissed her, tasting slightly of bacon and coffee, lingering, giving her the chance to respond. And she found that she did, that there was some small stirring deep within her, and that there was more pleasure when she kissed him back. She began to understand the point to it, and when Mark stepped back to look at her, she just stared at him, touching her mouth and thinking that a horse's mouth wouldn't do that.

He grinned, and opened his mouth to say something, but snapped it closed along with his eyes as the grin turned into a grimace. Jess only then heard the footsteps she should have noticed long ago, should have swiveled her ears to catch, and to know it was Carey. She suddenly felt as discomfited as Mark looked, although she wasn't sure why. She turned to face Carey as he stopped by the lawn chairs, his hazel eyes dark with anger.

"What in nine hells do you think you're doing?" he snapped, the anger in those eyes turned on Mark, a few unconscious steps taking him all the way up to Jess in a protective posture. "You might as well take advantage of a *child*—"

"I asked him," Jess interrupted, and had to repeat herself to be sure he'd taken it in. "*I asked him*. I wanted to know."

He stared dumbfounded, and, stumbling over the words as though she'd somehow lost her tenuous knack of shaping them, she said, "I see people kiss in the TV stories. I saw *you* kiss women, in the empty stall next to mine. I wanted to *know*, Carey—why does that make you mad?"

Mark cleared his throat, filling in the gap of Carey's flabbergasted silence. "I told her," he explained quietly, "that it was something for people who had special feelings for each other. But there's nothing wrong with getting her first kiss from a friend, Carey. Lighten up. Better that she asks and knows about it before someone *does* try to take advantage of her."

"You could have asked *me*," Carey told her, the storm of anger fading to puzzled hurt.

"I—" she started, stopped short by the utter inability to voice that she *couldn't* have asked him, because that would make it matter too much. And then he had her by both arms, a possessive grip that drew them close, and when he kissed her there was no time for analyzing the feel of having him close—she simply *was*, centered on the pressure of his lips and the fire that made her heart thud almost painfully in her chest. He released her mouth, gave her lips one last gentle nibble nothing like the ardent touch he'd just relinquished, and stared directly into her dark, widened eyes.

"Is that what you wanted to know?" he asked, a rough, low question.

"Yes," she whispered. And he stepped back, deliberately released her arms, gave Mark a hard stare, and left them there.

She watched him go, barely feeling the pat Mark gave her arm. Through the haze of her emotions, she heard him say, "It's all right, Jess," but it *wasn't*—for she suddenly knew that if she followed her newly discovered, very human heart, it would take her to Camolen with Carey—where she would lose it to an equine form.

# 10

"My, you certainly do devour these books," the young librarian said, smiling at Jess. "You haven't been reading very long, if I remember right."

"Not long," Jess agreed, fingering the spine of *The Magician's Nephew*. She could still feel Carey's embrace, still lose herself in all those feelings—all the anguish of knowing the choices she faced if he found a way to take them home. The inner tumult drove her to ride into town with Mark, where he dropped her off at the library. There she could lose herself in the next installment of the Narnia series, leaving reality behind for what seemed like a familiar world.

After all, she saw nothing strange with traveling between worlds and talking to animals.

She retrieved her library card from the woman and smiled her thanks, then took her treasure to the comfortable stuffed chairs in the reading section to linger as long as she could, wrapped up in the adventures of Digory and Polly.

At nine o'clock, one of the librarians apologetically ushered her to the door and locked it behind her. Jaime wouldn't be here until after her last lesson, another 45 minutes. Jess stood in the slight chill of the night air, a warm day gone drizzly, and heaved a sigh for the loss of her refuge. There was nothing to keep her mind away from the changed nature of her need to be with Carey, the odd sweet twist she had never felt before. Perhaps because it was nothing a horse *could* feel. What was the point, then, in returning with him, if she would only lose the very feeling which drove her to be with him?

Except if she didn't, she would be stuck with it and stuck without him, and she had a hunch it would be a hundred times worse than the pain she'd felt when they'd first separated on this world.

There was only a scuff of warning, enough time for her to straighten in alarm, raising her head to cast futilely for scent in the slight breeze. And then a man grabbed her arm from behind, a tight grip that did less to stop her wild defensive reaction than the cold, hard feel of metal at her neck and the biting, newly familiar scent of gunpowder.

"It's been a long wait," Derrick said in her ear, "but I think my luck has changed."

"You leave Carey alone!" Jess demanded, sitting on a torn, dusty couch in an old house behind something Derrick had called the *whyemceeay.*

Derrick exchanged an amused glance with Ernie. "It's *you* that we've got," he said.

"To try to get *him,*" she insisted. She was angry and hard put to sit still, but she was very aware of the gun Derrick now held casually in his lap. At the same time, she had the strangest feeling that although Derrick was not one who could be trusted, she was, in some strange way, safe here—as long as she followed their rules. They'd made it plain enough that the current rule was *sit still.*

"No," Derrick corrected. "To get the *spell.*"

She frowned at him, trying to figure out this bizarre human game, finally shaking her head in exasperation.

"You really *were* his horse, weren't you," Derrick mused, another turn of mood Jess couldn't quite follow. He left the gun on the seat of his shabby chair and approached her, leaning over her, one hand reaching out to control the tilt of her head—though he hesitated at the warning that flashed in her dark eyes.

"Be professional, Derrick," Ernie said, bored amusement in his voice. "This is business, not playtime."

Derrick shot him a dark look. "I'm not paying you to preach. If you believed what I've told you, you'd be a lot more interested in this woman."

"I'm interested in the money you've promised me," Ernie said, bitingly candid. "Although I admit you've provided a little amusement as well. And here I thought my little retreat from the Columbus heat was going to be boring."

Derrick didn't bother to answer; he might not even have been listening as he stared thoughtfully at Jess. Then, watching for her reaction, he said, "I'll call your master in a few minutes. I think he'll trade the spell for you, don't you?"

*Would he? For a woman he considered to still be a horse?* Jess shook her head, feeling stubborn and glad that the true answer was one that could confound him—which it did.

"No?" Derrick said in surprise. "I saw the way he looked at you at the park. Very protective, he is. He'll understand that there's no point in holding on to the spell when he can't get it back to Camolen, anyway."

"Neither can you," Jess pointed out, perplexed and a little suspicious that this obvious fact had escaped him.

"Can't I?" Derrick asked, his expression turning truly smug and making an otherwise attractive face momentarily detestable. "Just because I'm adept with the physical aspects of my role, little mare, doesn't mean I don't have other skills. It's true I could never come up with this spell on my own, but I think I can eventually use it to return home—although, as I told Carey, Calandre will have accomplished her goals through other means by that time."

"If you can not make the spell yourself, you will never get home," Jess said, willing to do almost anything to wipe that look off his face. She well remembered it, through different eyes, from the moment when Derrick had stood in his stirrups and released an arrow at Carey. "The spell is gone."

He laughed. "You *have* learned a lot from your time here. Nice try, but I don't believe you."

She wanted to kick him. "Carey tried to use it and it blew up!"

His amusement died away, his eyes narrowed. "What do you mean, *it blew up*?" Then, as the greater significance hit him, he grabbed her shoulders and asked, "You mean he accessed *magic* from this world?"

She was too startled, too angry, to do anything but fight his touch. She instantly kicked out at him, and would have squirmed from his grasp if he hadn't snatched the hair at the back of her head with an iron grip, forcing her head back, forcing her to stare at him.

"None of that," he hissed. "I can handle a woman as well as a horse, missy—and it can hurt a whole lot more than this."

She stared back through the involuntary tears that smeared her vision, and allowed herself to be a horse again. For that one moment, she let herself feel the acquiescence to rules, to the hold on her head that wasn't so different from her training halter, albeit a more painful one.

Slowly, he released her, never removing his gaze from hers. When she did nothing but sit, not even so much as a toss of the head, he relaxed. Let him take it as submissiveness, instead of the subterfuge she was practicing for the first time. Let him think of her as too much the horse—just as Carey did—while she waited for the right moment to act. With effort, she kept her eyes from shifting to the gun on the chair behind him. Let him forget he had Jess instead of Lady, while he carried a gun that she, too, knew how to use.

And *would* use, with the fierce protectiveness of a mare guarding her own, unhindered by any veneer of civilization she'd acquired in her short time here.

Jaime followed the movement of horse and rider around the ring, nodding in approval, a slight smile on her face. "Good job, Kate! You feel the difference in him when you *push* him up into the bridle?"

"It's hard work!" her student replied, but there was no complaint in her voice as she rode by the aisle gate.

When Kate and her mount cleared the gate, Carey was on the other side, unhooking it and slipping through. Jaime's smile abruptly faded; she felt a growl of annoyance fighting to come out. He knew the rules about interrupting lessons.

But the growl, too, faded, as he walked through the soft footing with long, hurried strides, his face broadcasting a message of trouble while his mouth seemed unable to manage it.

"What on earth has happened?" Jaime asked, trying to keep an eye on Kate as the light lovely trot disintegrated into a rein-tugging match between horse and rider.

"Jess," Carey said.

"She's at the library," Jaime said, annoyance creeping up again. "Walk-trot transitions, Kate. Twenty strides each. From the seat." Then, to Carey, "She wouldn't tell me what upset her today, but she only gets that look on her face when it has to do with you. She's run away from it—and you—and I'll be leaving to get her in fifteen minutes, when this lesson is over." She pointedly turned back to her student, but Carey didn't take the hint.

"Derrick has her," he said.

"*What*?"

"He got her outside the library. He wants to trade her for the spell."

"But—" Jaime started, and couldn't go any further with it. The spell was gone, and they'd never fool Derrick with a fake, not in this world of printer paper and ball point pens. She closed her eyes and took a deep breath, and then called, "Kate, something's come up. I'm very sorry, but I'm going to have to leave. There won't be any charge for the lesson."

"Is everything all right?"

Jaime shook her head, too worried for a professional facade. "It's a long story. Can you get Turner loaded up okay without help?"

"No problem," Kate said. "I hope everything turns out okay."

Not much chance of that. "Thanks. I'll see you next week."

Carey preceded her out of the ring with those same ground-eating strides; Jaime had to jog a few steps before she adjusted to his gait. "What are you going to do?" she asked, as they walked out into the night. Then she'd wished she'd waited, for she couldn't see his face when he stopped and answered, and the ragged quality of his voice was not what she'd expected.

"He's calling back in a few minutes. I'm going to agree to the trade, and then I'm going to go get her. I've already talked to Mark—he wants to go with me."

"So do I," Jaime blurted, her fear for Jess outweighing all sensible factors.

"We've only got two guns," Carey said, his blunt response driving home the danger. "Derrick is sure to be armed, and I wouldn't be surprised if he has his friend with him."

"Give me one of the guns," she said, unswayed. "I may not be very good with it, but the only other thing we've got is Derrick's bow, and I *know* I can't do anything with that."

"That's what Mark said." Carey's voice held a hint of dry humor. "He said you'd want to come. That's the reason I almost didn't tell you—"

"But you needed a ride into town," Jaime supplied.

"Yes." He didn't sound the least bit apologetic. "And I couldn't talk him out of calling Eric, either. He thinks we're going to want someone there waiting with a car. For a fast retreat, which we'll probably need." He started walking again, leading her into the house. "Put a dark shirt on. I'd like you to stay out of sight...surprise reinforcements if needed."

"*You* knew I'd come, too," Jaime said, almost an accusation.

They'd made it to the kitchen; he stopped and looked at her. "I was pretty sure," he said. "You've meant a lot to Jess. I think she means a lot to you, too."

She didn't answer; she didn't think she needed to. But she thought again that she'd missed something significant earlier in the day, because Carey's expression wasn't quite the cool, matter-of-fact determination she'd come to expect from him. It wasn't cool at all.

Mark left the LK reception desk in the hands of a sleepy, curious co-worker and slid into the suddenly crowded front seat of Jaime's pick-up, holding out his hand. Carey placed one of Derrick's guns into it, and then dumped a generous fistful of ammunition into the other hand.

"Dayna's coming too," Mark announced, and Jaime stopped in mid U-turn to lean over the steering wheel and aim a questioning look past Carey. Mark shrugged. "I was surprised, too. But she was over at Eric's place when I called, and she refused to stay behind. Didn't even mention calling the cops."

"No," Carey murmured. "We can't do that."

"We know," Jaime said grimly. "You think if we didn't, we'd be doing this dumb-ass hero act? Good Lord, look at us. We put Clint Eastwood to shame."

"No choice, Jay," Mark said simply, and for a brief moment, she was swept by affection for her brother. And then it faded, and she pulled out of the U-turn and straight into the sparse traffic.

"The YMCA," she muttered. "What a place for a show-down."

"It's as good as any," Mark shrugged.

"He said he'd be in the lower parking lot," Carey told them. "It doesn't mean anything to me."

"Easy," Mark said. "Two lots behind the building, and one's about eight feet lower than the other, has a short drive connecting the two. The lower one's the furthest from the Y, so that gives us a good chance at sneaking Jaime in against the building. Eric's meeting us out front, but I think he should kill his lights and roll down into place between the two parking lot entrances. Once *we* pull in, Derrick's not likely to notice a car coasting dark."

"I still don't know how you think you're going to get Jess away from him," Jaime said, shaking her head as she stopped at the light in front of the courthouse, an impatient foot riding the clutch while she waited out the red.

Carey's voice was full of confidence. "The fake'll throw him for a minute. He never saw the real thing, and Mark said the parking lots aren't well lit. All I need is that minute."

"I don't think," Jaime said quietly, "that Jess will be very happy if you get killed doing this." Despite the silence, she felt that some kind of communication passed between Mark and Carey, and she suddenly realized that Mark knew about whatever had happened earlier in the day.

As if to confirm her thought, Carey said, "I'm not sure she's too happy with me right now, anyway. It doesn't matter. What's important is getting her out of this. I'd give Derrick that damn manuscript, if I had it."

To her surprise, she believed him. But she didn't have any more time to think about it, because the light was green and they were one turn away from the YMCA.

"Dayna can take the car. I want to be out there with you," were Eric's abrupt words of greeting as Jaime double-parked the pick-up beside his little hatchback.

Carey's response was immediate. "No. There'll already be too many people in that parking lot, considering Derrick expects only me."

"Then let me be one of them," Eric insisted.

*No*, Jaime pleaded silently. Not Eric, whose soul was too gentle to mar with the guilt of the potential violence they faced. "Carey—" she started in protest, but he was ahead of her.

"Can you shoot better than Jaime?" he asked.

Eric looked away. "No."

"Then drive for us."

A sigh. "What *exactly* do you want me to do?"

Jaime's attention wandered as Mark relayed their half-formed plan; her hand drifted down to the automatic that lay on the seat beside her leg, glad for it but dreading the notion that she might actually have to use it. Lost in thought, she was surprised to find Mark standing outside her door.

"Hey, Jay, you out in the ozone or what? I'll take the truck from here. You follow the building around and wait next to it until you've spotted Derrick. Then get as close as you can without being seen—that gun won't be accurate from any distance—and keep an eye out for Derrick's pal. He may be pulling the same trick you are."

"Great," Jaime said without enthusiasm.

Mark propped his elbows on the truck door and leaned in the open window. "You don't have to do this," he said quietly. "Eric can handle it, if that's what you want."

Jaime took a deep breath. "No. I'm fine. Just wish I'd thought to change my breeches—Derrick'll probably smell me coming."

Mark snorted, punched her softly on the shoulder. "Keep your head down."

"Yeah." Jaime climbed out of the truck, hesitating on the runner board where she was for once taller than Mark. "Be careful." She gave him a rare, sisterly kiss on the cheek, hefted the gun, and left the pickup behind.

The brick YMCA was bordered by shrubs and small trees, all tempting her to hide while she listened for signs of company. But she was too driven by the fear that the guys would get into trouble before she even made it around to the back, so she moved quickly from shrub to tree and finally to the back corner of the building, where she had a clear view of both parking lots. The only light came from two floodlights on the back of the Y and sporadic yard lights in the run-down housing that pushed up against the parking lot, but it was easy enough to spot Derrick. He stood boldly in the center of the lower lot, visible only from the chest up from Jaime's perspective. Jess stood beside him, a gun shoved against the bottom of her jaw. She waited quietly, and Jaime hoped she had the resources to continue doing so—and then to move when the time was right.

She heard the truck doors slam, one after another, and Mark and Carey walked into the upper lot, looking amazingly casual. Jaime heard the soft tire noise of Eric's darkened car; it stopped at the entrance to the upper lot, unnoticed by the others.

"I told you to come alone," Derrick called. "Alone and unarmed. You didn't do either. Is that all that you care about this pretty little thing?"

Jess twitched in his grip, managed to turn her head enough against the pressure of the gun to look at Derrick; Jaime could well imagine the glare. She took advantage of the confrontation and, crouching, she crept forward, angling left toward the street and intending to get a clear line of fire.

Carey lifted the strung bow in a shrug. "The problem is, I don't trust you. But yeah, I want Lady. I'll give you the spell. It doesn't really matter—you can't get home."

"Yeah, well—I don't trust you either. Especially not since the mare is so insistent the spell's been destroyed by some foolishness on your part."

"*You* are the foolish one," Jess said, her voice barely audible to Jaime. "You come after him again and again. I will kill you when I can."

A chill ran through Jaime as she recognized the utter intent in Jess' voice. She no longer worried if Jess would move when she had to—she worried that she wouldn't wait, wouldn't realize there was more to this than just Mark and Carey. She straightened just enough to reassess the scene before creeping forward again. The sound of her own movement nearly obscured Derrick's laugh. *Good. He thinks he's already won.*

"She's spunky. Too bad I didn't get the chance to ride her myself." Then his voice changed. "The spell, Carey. First put that bow down— no, give it to your friend there. It'll keep his hands full. Then bring the spell here—slowly. As soon as I'm satisfied, I'll let your little filly go."

Jaime eased down to her hands and knees, sinking to the pavement each time Derrick seemed to glance her way. Then she reached the edge of the two lots and went down to her stomach, not ready to go any further.

Carey took the quiver off his shoulder, held it and the bow up so Derrick could see them clearly, and handed them to Mark.

"Hold them out," Derrick said as Mark's hands fell to his sides, and, reluctantly, Mark did so. He and Carey exchanged a quick look before Carey stepped out away from him, holding out the hastily con- cocted fake spell, the other hand palm up in placation. He slid down the short, steep bank between the lots without seeming to notice it was there, and stopped a few feet away from Derrick and Jess.

"C'mon, c'mon, let's see it," Derrick said impatiently, snaking his gun arm around Jess' neck to keep that threat alive while he reached for the paper. Jaime held her breath, waiting for Carey to pick his moment—but it was Jess who moved. As Derrick snatched the bogus spell, Jess twisted her head and sunk her teeth into his hand, exploding into offensive elbows and feet.

Derrick yelped as Jess ducked out of his weakened grip and whirled around, but not to run.

To attack.

Carey reached him first, grabbing at the gun. Seconds passed in a scuffle too close for Jaime to separate them, and she finally jumped to her feet and slid down the bank, stopping with the gun held out in almost steady hands. "Derrick!" she screamed, trying to startle him, succeeding only in startling Carey and giving Derrick the opening to slap his gun across Carey's face.

Carey staggered back, stumbled, fell to his knees. Appalled, Jaime tightened her grip on the gun and shouted in best TV cop fashion, "Drop it!"

It didn't work; he didn't even seem to hear her as he brought his gun to bear on Carey, who was still stunned, wobbly, and trying to get to his feet. *Oh my God I'm going to have to kill him*—but suddenly Jaime didn't think she could.

She never found out. Jess wrested the automatic from her grasp, whirling to shove it against Derrick's chest—and pulling the trigger not once but three times, creating an oddly muffled noise that matched the jerking of Derrick's body. He fell with a peculiar dull thump; Jess stared at the gun in her hand, holding it away from her as if it was carrion, then quite deliberately opening her grip and dropping it to the pavement.

Jaime snatched it up and handed it off to Mark as sprinted over; her brother knelt to check Derrick's body. It was only a moment more before both Eric and Dayna were there, too, and gaping at the man Jess had killed.

But Jess seemed oblivious to all of it. She crouched by Carey, touching his face where the blood ran freely. When he finally responded to her, dazed but reaching out a reassuring arm, she dropped her head into the hollow of his shoulder and kept it there, shivering but silent.

Dayna didn't gape long. Ever practical, she said, "We've got to get out of here. The porch lights just came on all the way down the street."

Carey didn't seem to hear her. He gently disengaged from Jess and made it to Derrick's body without ever making it to his feet, feeling around the man's neck. With a small satisfied sound, he pulled out a chain strung with small stones and crystals. As he sat back, his fingers closing around the gems in possessive relief, he glanced up at Jaime and said, "We can go home now."

"Not if the police get here first," Dayna warned.

"She's right, Carey," Jaime said, reaching for Jess, who was still curled up into a shoulder that was no longer there.

"Not even the police can stop me if I invoke this," Carey said, but he drew himself together and stood, wiping the back of his hand across his face where the blood from his split and puffy brow still ran. He took a deep breath, bent and drew Jess upright. "I'll take Derrick," he said, distracted as he brushed a careful hand over Jess' cheek, clearing away the parking lot grit that had stuck to her tears but leaving traces of his own blood. "That way no one here can get in trouble over him."

Dayna was gathering the guns, wiping them thoroughly on the tail of her shirt. "You won't want these going back with you," she said. "We'll dump 'em in the reservoir. And Carey, I don't want to sound heartless, but if you're going to go, dammit...*go*."

"No," Jaime protested without thinking. "All his gear is at my place, and the gold—"

Carey shook his head. "Dayna's right—"

"We can't stand around arguing about it," Mark said abruptly. "Eric, take this guy's hands; I'll get his feet. We'll throw him in the back of the pick-up and talk about this *somewhere else*."

Eric complied with a swiftness that bespoke his worry—though Jaime had decided they'd already lingered too long, that the police would have arrived if they'd been called. The shots *had* been muffled...

She picked up the bow and quiver Mark had dropped and they all moved in silent procession, led by Eric at the head of Derrick's body. While Mark and Eric manhandled Derrick's body into the truck, Carey removed his arm from Jess' shoulders and swung her around to face him. "Jess...I think you should stay here."

"Here?" Jess repeated, bewildered. "You don't want me?"

"You called her 'Jess,'" Jaime said in a low voice. Not Lady. *Jess.*

Carey spared her only a glance. "Once I told you that you would *always be Lady*—that magic couldn't change the nature of who you were." He stared into her eyes, used his thumb to wipe away the last traces of grit beneath her eye, and then lightly kissed the spot where it'd been. "Maybe *magic* couldn't—but *you* did. There's more to you than there ever was to Lady, and if you come back with me, you're going to lose it all."

"I don't want to leave you," Jess said, her low and occasionally husky voice now thick with new tears. "There is no rule that can make me leave you."

"But, Jess," Carey said, and he sounded stunned, "if you come, you're going to lose *you*."

"Now that is *just too sweet*."

The voice startled them all, and Mark quickly slammed the truck cap door closed while the rest of them searched for the new participant in their little drama.

Jaime closed her eyes in despair when she recognized Derrick's pal Ernie. He leaned casually against a tree beside the parking lot, but there was nothing casual about the silenced gun he had trained on them. "Figured I was out of a payroll when she nailed Derrick," he said, nodding at Jess. "And then I heard you say something about gold. I'm interested. Real interested. In fact, I think I'll want to keep a couple of these ladies with me until one of you gents brings that gold back to me."

"Whatever he was paying you, it was too much," Carey said. "It didn't go too far toward keeping him alive, did it?"

Ernie shrugged, unoffended. "I was watching *her*," he said, tipping the gun at Jaime. "He said he could handle the trade. I guess he was wrong."

"No more than you, if you think we're going to trot off and bring you back gold." Carey's voice was hard, and it suddenly made Jaime consider that his past held the experience that hardened that voice. And though she wanted to protest his reaction, fearful it would simply set Ernie off, a small voice told her to let him handle it.

"Oh, I think you will," Ernie said easily. "You know, it's not true what they say about silencers. They don't really *silence* the gun. It's a popping kind of noise—about the same kind of noise it makes when a bullet hits a kneecap."

Jaime couldn't believe her ears. Where had Derrick *found* this guy in little Marion, Ohio?

"That one, I think," Ernie said, pointing the gun at Jess. "Everyone seems to be so concerned about her. And she's such a pretty thing. Be a shame to see her hobbling around on a leg that doesn't bend any more, don't you think?"

Jess made a sound in her throat that both Jaime and Carey recognized as the threat it was; Carey stepped in front of her. It was meant to restrain and not protect her, but Ernie's false affability vanished. The gun bucked slightly, and Eric yelped as the glass door of the truck cap shattered, spraying him with shards.

"Even if the police *aren't* coming, I don't want to hang around here all night," Ernie said in annoyance. "I want the women to move back into the parking lot, and I want you to go get that gold." His voice rose to an abrupt shout that startled them all. "*Now!*"

Jaime wasn't sure just what happened next, as Dayna took a first hesitant step toward the parking lot. Suddenly they were all moving, and Jess flashed past her but jerked up short as someone swung her around, trading places—the gun popped, there was a cry of pain—and then Jaime was caught in a crushing grip, unable even to call out to the freeze-frame of her friends around her. She was yanked and twisted and wrung out like dirty laundry, then dumped, gasping, onto ground that in no way resembled the parking lot of the YMCA.

# 11

**P**rickly stemmed, low growing plants covered the damp ground. They smelled...spicy. Jaime dared to open her eyes and quickly closed them against bright sunlight. But...

She couldn't hide forever. She rolled over and pushed herself to her knees, opening her eyes once and for all.

Bodies in various states of disarray littered the ground; only Carey, like Jaime, slowly climbed to his feet. He pulled himself up on the tailgate of the pickup, a vehicle that was totally, almost hilariously out of place.

Jaime stumbled over to him, trying to voice some coherent question, when sudden thought gripped her. *Jess.* She whirled, a move turned clumsy with her yet-uncoordinated limbs, and searched the prone figures for one that matched Jess.

Instead, off to the side, she found a dun mare stretched flat on her side and adorned with the rags of what had once been clothes.

"*Jess,*" she whispered, horrified, and turned to Carey. His eyes were closed, but the pain on his face left no question but that he'd seen the mare.

The others were stirring, and Carey's eyes opened, hard again, the pain safely tucked away. He staggered over to Ernie, pulled the gun away, then wobbled a few steps backward so he could take in the whole group at the same time. The surprise and dismay on his face was

Jaime's first clue that there was something else going on here, something she'd missed. Dayna's cry of alarm drew her attention to Eric—to his stillness. Something deep within her twitched in horror.

"Eric!" Dayna cried again, crawling closer to her friend, trying to turn him over. Carey took a few impotent steps forward and then stopped, looking away from the scene that Jaime had not...quite.... The gunshot. She remembered the gunshot, and the cry of pain, and she suddenly dove to help Dayna turn Eric.

There was very little blood. It was Eric's blank eyes and slackly hanging jaw that looked so terribly *dead*, the way his arm flopped to the ground as they turned him. Dayna touched his face, a tentative gesture, and her brief moment of disbelief turned to a flood of grief. She threw herself over him and wailed.

Mark crawled, horrified, to join them. He reached a trembling hand out to confirm that what he saw was real, but didn't quite—couldn't seem to—touch Eric's body. Jaime finally did what no one else seemed capable of, and closed Eric's wide-open eyes.

"Just stay right there on the ground," Carey said harshly, a voice out of synch with their grief, and close enough to the edge of reason that Jaime turned to see what he was talking about. She found Ernie flat on his back on the bare, rocky ground and carefully compliant. But then his mouth opened, and once started, he couldn't seem to stop the words that poured out.

"Where the hell are we, huh? Take me back, man, *take me back!* I won't give you any more trouble, I don't even know you and your damn gold *exist*. Derrick wasn't anything to me—take me back, and I'll make sure nobody ever bothers you, and I mean *no*body. I've got connections—"

"None of 'em will do you any good from here," Carey said coldly, cutting off the panicked rush of words. He wiped the slow trickle of blood from his face, trauma left over from another world. "We can't take you back. I wouldn't if I could. You've killed a friend, and now you're going to get a taste of *this* world's justice."

"Carey—" Jaime started, but when he looked at her, she couldn't do anything but shake her head. She suddenly felt she couldn't stomach any more violence, not even retribution. Carey watched her a

moment, and must have deciphered her unspoken thoughts. He lowered
Ernie's gun so it was no longer a threat.

"Okay, Jaime," he said. "Let him learn to survive here—that's punishment enough. *If* he survives at all." To Ernie, he said, "You got questions? Figure 'em out for yourself. Somewhere else."

Ernie sat, his wild glance going from Carey to Jaime and back
again; he couldn't quite believe any of it yet.

"Go," Carey said, softly dangerous. "Before I change my mind."

Ernie scrabbled to his feet and stumbled away, looking back more
than he looked ahead.

"He'll die out there," Jaime said, more to herself than anyone else.

But Carey shook his head. "He'll survive. His kind always does."
He looked at the huddle of friends, considered them, and finally turned
away to Jess.

Or maybe, Jaime thought, maybe now she was *Lady* again. She tore
herself away from Eric's side, where Mark had gathered Dayna into his
arms, and moved over to Carey and the dun mare, much steadier on her
feet now. Carey crouched to run his hands along the mare's side; she
stirred, flipping her nose off the ground a few times before she gave a
chillingly human groan.

It did what Eric's death couldn't. It drove home all the sorrows of
their situation, and Jaime suddenly found that tears were running down
her face, that a sob choked her throat.

"No," Carey murmured, though she wasn't sure to whom, until he
took her arm and shook it. "Not now, Jaime—help me get her up."

She stared blankly, pulled up the bottom of her shirt to wipe her
face, and blinked at him.

"Remember Sabre after the magic?" he asked, short, clipped words
in a strained voice; he snatched a remnant of Jess' jeans and threw them
aside. "Remember the other horses? They didn't understand, and it was
more than they could take."

*Shock can kill a horse.* Her fears from that day echoed in her mind,
and her tears miraculously vanished. Hands and knees, she moved to
Jess and joined Carey in freeing her from the leftover clothes. Then,
with Carey pushing from behind, she moved to the mare's head and
urged her to get up, starting with pleas and quickly deteriorating into an

absurd tug of war, her hands entwined in the dark, thick mane behind black-tipped ears.

"Maybe this isn't such a good idea," Jaime panted, pausing to read-just her grip. "Maybe we should just give her some quiet, some time to adjust—" she broke off at Carey's unyielding expression.

"No," he said firmly, a denial touched with anger. "I know her. She's got to get up, get moving...get *distracted*." He stared down at the muscled rump before him and gave it a sudden kick.

"Carey!" Jaime gasped, although he'd turned his foot so he was not digging her with his booted toe.

He ignored her. "Get *up*, Lady, burn you! Get *up!*" He punctuated each command with another kick, and the dun stirred; Jaime danced back out of the way and back behind the horse, bending over to add her own, less violent incentive—thumbs over sensitive ribs. Lady gave a grunt of pure annoyance and in one quick heave, was on her feet. She shook herself off and then stood dully, her head drooping so low her nose almost touched the ground. Carey quickly moved to her head, crouching down and touching her forehead with his. "Don't you dare," he whispered to her. "Don't you dare give up, Jess. I know you're in there somewhere. You've got to be." He stood, and gently tugged her head up with her forelock. "Got anything in the back of the truck I can use as a halter?" he asked Jaime, never looking away from his...*horse*.

"Maybe." She heaved a deep breath, suddenly fatigued—suddenly overwhelmed with the realization that they had only begun to tackle their problems. "I'll check."

She was rooting around in the truck, trying not to touch Derrick's body, when Dayna's first shriek rent the air. *What now?* Turning awk-wardly in the confined space, she discovered Mark holding the small woman back, while Dayna, in the strength of her anger, was proving almost impossible to restrain.

"You bastard!" Dayna screamed across the hard, scrubby ground, looking after Ernie. Jaime scooted across the tailgate and hopped to the ground, only then able to see that Ernie lingered at the fringes of a small patch of brushy woods. She ran to Mark's side, grabbing at Dayna's twisted shirt, interposing herself between Ernie and Dayna's fiery wrath—with no effect on Dayna. "You bastard!" she repeated, jerking herself out of Jaime's grasp at the expense of several buttons. "I'll kill you! *You're going to die for this!*"

Suddenly Jaime felt a pressure, as though a transparent force field had traveled through her body and left her behind; she jerked around to look and saw nothing...except Ernie, staggering out of the woods and falling to the ground.

"Stop her!" Carey shouted. "Stop her, Mark!" He left Lady and sprinted toward them, not slowing as he tackled Mark and Dayna together and brought them all to the ground. All except Jaime, who stared first at the tangled mess of her friends and then at Ernie, who had struggled to his feet and disappeared into the woods with no time wasted.

"What was that?" she whispered to the air—Camolen air.

"Magic," Carey panted. "Raw magic."

They regrouped at the tailgate of the truck while Carey, using a halter made of old baling twine, circled Lady around the truck, urging her along until she finally trotted behind him.

"That's my girl," he said, running a hand down her neck as he stopped them by the tailgate. The horse lowered its head and shook vigorously, and then stretched out her head to sniff the truck.

"How much...." Jaime started, and had to clear her throat. "How much of Jess is left, do you think?"

Carey shook his head. "I don't know. I keep hoping she's in there, but...I just don't know enough about magic. Sometimes it's far too thorough. Have you paid attention to your words?"

"Our words?" Mark repeated, as an odd look crossed his face. "Not English," he murmured, looking at Jaime. Not English. And the air was filled with the spice of hot rock and vegetation, and the sunlight was somehow whiter—

"Who cares?" Dayna said dully. "I want to go back home."

Carey looked at the mare for an overlong time. Finally, still looking at the neck he stroked, he said, "I can't get you there. The stone was only keyed for two spells. If you really want to go home, you're going to have to help me find Arlen."

"If he's not already dead," Mark said pointedly.

Carey looked at him then, a sharp glance. "Right," he said. "If he's not already dead."

Jaime scrubbed her hands over her face. "All right, Carey. We need to find Arlen. But *first*, we have to do something with—for—Eric. And you need to tell us something about where we are—in relation to where we're trying to get. Where *is* Arlen's place from here? Where's Calandre, or this Sherra person you've told us you were trying to reach?"

"And why was Dayna able to play around with magic?" Mark inserted, looking at their friend.

"I wasn't *playing*," she muttered darkly. "And you shouldn't have stopped me."

"I didn't stop you because of *him*," Carey asserted, just as darkly. "I stopped you because of what it would have done to *you*. Just ask Jaime. She knows what can happen if you fool around with magic and you don't know what you're doing. That magic could have come lashed right back on you—it could have killed us all."

Dayna's anger dissipated into pale-faced understanding. "Oh."

"I don't understand how she was able to manipulate it in the first place." Jaime frowned, looking at her friend. Dayna, the highly structured? Dayna, the organized and inflexible? Jaime had supposed that magic required great sweeps of imagination and creativity.

Carey shrugged, his attention wandering back to Lady as she investigated Derrick's body, hesitating at the scent of blood on his shirt. "Arlen could tell you, or even Sherra." He looked from the truck to Eric, and then out at the hard, scrubby land around them. "We need to get away from the open ground, get this truck under cover. I think we should dump this guy and put Eric in the truck—and drive it as far from here as we can get."

"Headed *where*?" Jaime asked pointedly. "Look, there's a mileage notebook in the glove box. Why don't you draw us a map or something—anything to give us the lay of the land—and especially which directions we want to avoid." When he seemed about to protest, she added, "We might get separated. We *might* have to fumble around on our own. I'd rather not do it blind."

He shrugged, and handed the thin, tough hay-twine lead to Jaime to hold while he hunched over her little notebook and sketched them a rough map. "We're just over the border from Anfeald—Arlen's domain; that's the direction the truck is pointed now," he said. "You can't make it very far that way driving, though—there's a steep climb that turns into woods at the top. This whole area isn't heavily populated—the bigger cities are northeast of us. Sherra's—Siccawei—is behind the truck—pretty much straight south."

"And in Camolen, in which direction does the sun rise?" Mark asked, his tone so neutral Jaime couldn't tell if he was serious. But Carey took him seriously enough.

"East," he said. "But I'm not sure what the language translation will have done with directions." So he drew a quick compass on the map and labeled the points.

Jaime shook her head when she saw that East and West had flip-flopped, and suddenly had to look away from the perverted map. Somehow that simple difference drove home the fact that she *wasn't* home anymore, and it was almost too much to fathom, never mind *handle*. After a minute she cleared her throat and said, "Good catch, brother. That could have landed us in trouble fast."

"Sherra's is past the dry riverbed—I know it's a gorge here, but it bottoms out to the right, there, and I think you can get the truck over it—unless you don't think the truck'll manage over this ground."

"Drive it till it gets hung up." Jaime shrugged, her moment of overwhelmed disorientation shoved aside for practical matters. "Or goes dry. Though I'm not sure why you're so concerned about the speed. No one knows we're here."

Carey straightened, frowning. "Think in terms of magic, Jaime. Anyone with the least skill felt us arrive."

"Oh," she said. "Ulp." But her light tone was a pure contrast to the dismay she felt.

Carey said dryly, "Right," and pointed back to the map. "Sherra's hold is at the edge of a lake in another huge tract of woods. She's got quite a little village sprung up on the other side of the lake, cleared land and everything there. The paths are clear and you won't have any trouble finding it."

"And Calandre?" Mark asked grimly.

Carey pointed off to the right of Arlen's direction—between Sherra and Arlen. "Erowah is that way."

"Great," Jaime muttered.

"Closer to Arlen than Sherra, but further out," he said. "It's a pretty area, hilly sheep country. The people are good folk." He pushed the map toward them. "Got any questions?"

Jaime looked at the sketchy lines before her, lines that would have meant nothing without the commentary that came with them. "I suppose we can ask, if we lose our way."

"As long as you're sure you know who you're dealing with," Carey reminded them. He looked toward the old river. "I'm thirsty enough to suck on river pebbles, if only there might be some water left in them."

"I wish you hadn't said that," Jaime said ruefully, immediately aware of her own thirst, and the fact that they stood in the noonday sun. A large carrion bird circled overhead to complete the picture nicely.

"That's the same river where Jess—Lady, I mean—and I fell. I suppose she told you about that."

"As best she could," Jaime allowed.

"Let's go," Dayna said abruptly. "I don't want Eric to lie out there any more, and I don't like this place."

"I'm with you," Mark said. He put a hand on Derrick's ankle, hesitated, and then gave a resolute tug. The stiffening body came reluctantly, leaving a trail of clotting blood behind. As Jaime regarded the dumped body with dismay, Dayna crawled in the truck and did her best to wipe the blood up, warning them off with, "Eric's not lying in *this*."

Lady investigated the body with a few impersonal whiffs, then roughly pulled Jaime over to Eric. There she went down the length of his lanky body, nudging, her eyes grown round and anxious. Jaime found her own eyes tearing up again, and gently tugged the lead until Lady followed her back to the truck, where she exchanged a look with Carey. He shrugged, completing the short, silent conversation. How much was Jess, and how much was just wishful thinking on their part?

"You just want to...leave him here?" Jaime asked in a low voice, changing the subject to Derrick and not particularly eager for Dayna to hear. Her glance went up to the bird, where it continued its lazy, spiraling glide in the thermals of the hot riverbed.

"We can't take the time to bury him," he replied in an equally discreet voice, his hazel eyes holding the same faint regret that she felt. "We've been here too long already." Then, as Dayna crawled out on to the tailgate, disdainfully dropping a bloodied rag on Derrick's body, he asked, "Ready?"

She nodded. Carey joined Mark beside Eric, and together they carefully picked him up. Jaime took Dayna's hand and drew her off the tailgate, trying to make some contact with her tightly withdrawn friend—but Dayna's hand felt cool and distant in hers.

Carey closed the tailgate with relief plain on his face. "Let's go," he said. "It'll take them a while to figure out the tire tracks, but once they do, the trail'll be too damn clear."

"You really think they'll be here?" Jaime climbed behind the wheel while Carey squeezed beside the gear shift and Mark filled the other half of the passenger side, Dayna on his lap. No one suggested that there was more room in the back.

"They'll be here," Carey said with assurance. "At the most, they're half a day away. If they're coming from Arlen's, less that half of that. Put this thing in four wheel drive and get it moving, Jaime."

"Right," she muttered. "Wouldn't Chevy just love to base a commercial on this one."

"Jay, you're a nut," her brother said, a brief moment of sibling normalcy that bolstered her spirits. She glanced out the passenger side mirror to see that he had a good grip on the halter lead and that Lady didn't startle too badly when the engine turned over. Then she eased off the clutch, trying to match her pace to the rough ground and Lady's movement. The mare trotted easily along beside the vehicle, and soon Jaime concentrated only on the ground before them.

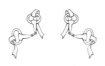

Jaime looked tired, Carey thought. The steering wheel jerked with each twist of the front wheels over rock and bump, and the truck constantly threatened to ground out on the rough terrain. He wanted to offer to spell her—but the truth was, not even Mark was as good as she with the manual transmission. Jaime's hands moved swiftly between the wheel and the stick, and she even managed to downshift from second to first at the same time she slammed them from regular to low four wheel drive, an intricate dance of clutch and two gear shifts that Carey knew he could never imitate—not when most of his experience came from the barn's garden tractor.

But they were making good time. Not better than a mounted party, but certainly faster than if they'd been on foot. Too bad they'd have to abandon the vehicle soon; they'd gone from flat, dusty old riverbed to rocky scrub, and the truck would never make it past the fringes of the woods they now approached.

The Chevy seemed to stick for a moment, then lurched forward. Jaime frowned as she put it in neutral and wiped her sweaty, dusty face on the once-clean hem of her shirt. "Bladder break," she said, cutting the engine. "I've got to check the left front wheel."

They disembarked, slowly stretching their assorted cramps and strains. Carey's legs were so stiff from keeping them out of Jaime's way that he wasn't sure, at first, that they would hold him. Mark dropped Lady's lead and flexed his arm, kneading the bicep, and Dayna headed for the other side of the truck with a taciturn warning that the men had better stay where they were.

"Oh, damn," Jaime groaned from the forbidden side of the truck, giving the tire a token kick. "Flat as they come," she informed the guys. "Got a big spear of rock stuck in it."

"Spare's all right, isn't it?" Mark asked, although he looked far from eager at the prospect of changing it.

"Never mind," Carey said. "The gas is almost gone and we can't go much further than this, anyway. I think we should lay a little false trail with what gas we have left, and go on foot from there."

"Without changing the tire?" Jaime said, aghast. "We'll ruin the wheel!" But before Carey could say anything, she laughed at herself. "Listen to me. As if it matters."

"We couldn't take the time even if it did matter." As Dayna came around the truck, looking self-conscious, Carey looked at the truck cab with resignation and nodded to Mark. "Trade places?"

"Sounds good to me," Mark agreed. "Variety if not relief."

Dayna scowled. "It's not so great from where I sit, either," she said. "I'll bet Carey's knees are just as bony."

That, at least, was a bit of the real Dayna coming to the fore. Mark gave her a big loud kiss on the forehead on his way by, and Carey pulled her into the truck before she could respond.

"Okay, Jay," Mark announced as Carey closed the door and reached out for Lady's halter lead. "We're ready to ramble."

Carey guided Jaime off of the faint road and into rougher territory, where rocks scraped the truck's skid plate with tortured sounds; the wheel rim slid and screeched its way forward. He was forced to drop Lady's lead, but not surprised when she followed along in their trail of her own volition. Lady minus any aspect of Jess would have done that, and this slow pace was—and had been—no real effort for her.

Forty-five minutes later, as they made their way through increasing brush, mowing down small trees and dragging undergrowth, the engine gave a couple of sad coughs and sighed into silence.

"That's that, then," Jaime said, pulling the emergency brake with what looked like the last of her strength. "What now?"

"Out!" Dayna said emphatically, wiggling around to find the door handle. Rather than endure the bouncing, Carey hastily found it for her, helping her out with enough force that she gave a small squeak.

They stretched and groaned while Lady wandered among them, nipping the sweet new growth off twiggy trees. Finally, Carey said, "There's no point in trying to hide this thing. The trail's far too clear."

"I thought that was the whole point," Dayna said. "Lay a false trail, right?"

He grimaced an acknowledgement. "It's hard to break old habits," he said. "But you're right. We'll back-track along it. Do your best not to disturb the ground—these guys won't be stupid."

"Just a minute," Jaime said. "I'm going to look through the truck and make sure there's nothing here we can use." She rooted around in the truck, flipping the seats forward and digging through the accumulation of years. Mark quickly joined her, and a small pile of things grew on the ground.

"I think you're forgetting something," Dayna said firmly, looking squarely at Carey. "We're not just leaving Eric lying in there like that."

Carey steeled himself for a battle. "I don't think we have any choice, Dayna. We can take him out of the truck and find a protected place for him, but we don't have the time to—"

"We *do* have the time!" she snapped. "He's dead and he can't even be buried on his own *world*—you can bet he'll be buried on this one! Until he is, I'm not going anywhere!"

Mark and Jaime abandoned their truck search to listen, and Carey felt frustration well up inside. "You don't seem to take any of this seriously!" he exploded. "You want the truck clean before we put Eric inside. You want a map and a set of the rules before we start out. Can't you understand what I've been trying to tell you since you found me in that hotel? These aren't games! Calandre *will not* hesitate to kill anyone who gets in her way—and she may have already killed one of the most powerful men in Camolen."

Dayna swallowed visibly, but crossed her arms over and stared defiantly at him.

"Damn!" Carey swore, turning away from her, closing his eyes and trying to get a handle on a temper that was just about gone. When he turned back, his eyes were hot and his voice too level. "Listen up. We will find a secluded place for him, and we will cover him with rocks. The moment I see you slacking off, that's it—we're done, even if I have to carry you away from here kicking and screaming. Afterward we'll be marching double time, and we're not going to be able to stop until we reach Sherra's. That's a choice you're making for all of us."

Dayna looked uncertainly at Mark and Jaime, who were visibly alarmed by Carey's frustrated explosion; they, it was obvious, believed him, and had been infected by his urgency. Then she looked away from all of them, and her face crumpled. "He was my friend," she said through a sob. "No one just let me be...*me*, like Eric did."

"All right, Dayna," Jaime said softly.

Mark exhaled a deep breath. "It's not going to be easy. C'mon, Carey, let's get to it. Dayna, find a spot you like and start picking up rocks."

Dayna didn't hesitate. She walked briskly into the thickening brush while Mark went around to the back of the truck and Jaime gathered their booty and dropped it into the empty grain sack that was part of it.

"It's a good thing I never clean this thing out," she muttered, coming around to help the men as she tied the bag closed with another length of hay twine. "We've got a flashlight, a couple of flares, my old jackknife...a fishing lure and some almost tangle-free line—"

"Later, Jay," Mark grunted, trying to handle Eric's stiffened body, his face a stoic mask—or trying to be.

"I found a place!" Dayna announced from a hundred yards away, jumping so that she momentarily appeared above the brush. "Over here! You got it? I'm going to start on the rocks!"

"And work gloves," Jaime said with satisfaction, slapping them down on the lowered tailgate. "I'll take 'em first—you want second dibs, Mark?"

"I'll take them," Carey said, shaking his head when Mark looked at him for the nod to pick up Eric and go. "You've got another job, Jaime. Maybe the hardest one."

"What?" she asked blankly.

"Get on Lady and go," he replied shortly, keeping his voice low. "We've cut our chances in half—hell, to practically nothing—with this foolishness. You've got to tell Sherra we're here. She'll send someone out to meet us, and if they get to us in time, maybe we'll make it after all."

"Me?" Jaime said in total shock. "*You're* the one who knows the spell, Carey. *You're* the one who knows the territory. And you're the one we can't risk, not if we take this as seriously as you're trying to get us to."

He stepped close to her, looking down at her dark brown eyes, guileless, searching his for some sort of answer. Not shrinking from a job they both knew would be just as hard as the burial and march. "Lady knows the way," he said softly. "Just keep the sun on your left, when you can see it."

"But, Carey—"

"If *I* go—if I leave you alone—you're all dead." He closed his eyes at the impossibility of it all and said, "Please, don't argue. You're the

only one besides me who can ride bareback, and whom Lady trusts
enough to obey without a bridle."

"*Jess* trusts me," Jaime said. "We still don't know how much of
her—" but she stopped short at the look on his face and took a deep,
strained breath. *Oh God.* "Okay. I won't waste any more time. Keep the
sun on my left. What else?"

"There are a number of good roads—well, what passes for a good
road in those woods—that will take you there. Head into the sun for
half an hour or so and then put it on your left and go into the woods.
You'll hit a road sooner or later. Don't waste time second-guessing
yourself and blundering around looking for one. Got it?"

"Got it," she said, smiling wanly. "At least I've got my breeches
on."

A small attempt at a joke but he appreciated it anyway. "I'll give
you a leg up," he said, and gave the short whistle that would call Lady
to them.

The first few moments on Lady's back were bizarre. Jaime tried hard
to think of her as just any other first-time horse—in Ohio, not Camolen.
The dun mare, too, had reservations; her ears went back flat, hidden in
the thick mane, and her back humped up under Jaime's seat bones.

"Lady," Carey said sharply, and Lady lowered her head and snorted in what could only be called disgust, nearly jerking the halter twine
out of Jaime's hand. Jaime stroked her neck and gave Carey, then her
brother, one last look.

"Good-bye, Eric," she said, and gave a gentle squeeze of her calves.
It had only then occurred to her that she would miss the important ritual
of formal good-bye, and she felt unanticipated sorrow about it. But
Lady moved forward, a hesitant walk with her head held high and bobbing uncertainly, awkwardly turned to keep one cautious eye on Jaime.

"Straighten out, Lady," Jaime said sternly, using her back and hips
and a squeeze on the halter lead in a half-halt that surprised the mare.

She asked for a trot, twisting her fingers in the long black mane to help her weather the inevitable stumbles from the uneven ground. Lady obliged, but clearly expressed her opinion about the strange situation by making it an uncomfortable, hollow-backed gait.

Another half-halt, ineffective. "Quit!" Jaime snapped, thinking that the ride was going to be torture if she couldn't get more cooperation than this. She grasped a hank of mane and pulled herself up over the tense neck. Speaking right into the mare's ear, she said, "Jess, whatever part of you is left in there knows that this is nonsense. We're not *leaving* Carey, we're trying to *save* him. And you damn well know that I'm not going to do anything to hurt you. I want you to round up and put yourself into a good frame, or I won't have the only sore ass around here!"

The mare stopped short. They were only just out of sight of the truck, and Jaime held her breath, knowing that if Lady chose to wheel around and run back to Carey, there was nothing she could do to stop it. But they just stood there, the black-tipped ears swiveled back at Jaime. Thinking. Then came subtle differences in the body beneath Jaime. The mare's neck lowered, her head adopted a vertical angle, and her back rounded gently into Jaime's seat. Then, without waiting for the request, she moved into a springy trot, picking her way around the dips and bumps in her path.

"Jess," Jaime breathed. *She's still there. Some part of her is really still there.*

Dun Lady's Jess moved steadily onward, having transmuted her human trust into equine acceptance of Jaime's requests. Her sturdy hooves found good footing on the uneven ground, and her muzzle—whiskers and all—twitched at the delightfully intense smells of the world around her—smells which told her of the cool woods long before she and Jaime actually reached them.

Out in the open there had been little sign of travel, but once under the trees they hit a wide, relatively smooth path after only a short while of catching hoof and fetlock in fallen branches and skidding off leaf-hidden rocks. Small birds chittered at them and fluttered away through the underbrush, leaving the woods silent around them.

Dun Lady's Jess knew this path, and knew where they were going. At Jaime's quiet signal, she swung into a smooth, steady canter, glad for the distraction of work.

For some part of this no longer fully equine creature was coming out of the shock of transition and moving into a deeper shock. The thoughts she was trying to process were beyond her, and the emotions she felt far more complex than had ever assailed her before. She was afraid for Carey, trying to comprehend the loss of Eric, and nearly panicked over the fate of a certain human named Jess.

The mare leaned into the thin twine halter, ignoring its bite, and lengthened her strides. No time for the perplexing muddle of human thoughts in a horse's mind. No time for the fear and distress the half-formed thoughts created. Time only for running, running until her breath came harshly in her throat and her muscles burned. Running until Jaime's gentle cues with the biting twine became insistent demands, and Dun Lady's Jess slowed to a fast walk, sweating with far more than the efforts of her ground-eating canter.

"I wish I knew how far this place is," Jaime grumbled, and Lady flicked a quick ear back to listen. "*You* know, I'll bet." She wiped her sweaty face on the hem of her now thoroughly grimy shirt and suggested, "How about a trot, kiddo." Lady moved out without complaint, starting the first in a series of walk-trot-canter cycles that found the path growing almost wide enough to be called a road—but with no sign of their goal.

Or of anybody else, for that matter. Although filled with urgency and a constant harangue from the doubtful inner voice Carey had told her to ignore, Jaime stopped Lady at the small creek that crossed their path and slid off the sweaty-backed mare to splash her own face. She added a couple of quick stretches and then made a clumsy bareback mount, thanking Lady for her rock-steady patience.

Back to the trotting. The spring had gone out of Lady's gait, and Jaime grew spooked as she realized how alone they were. Dark green shadows in mottled sunshine gave her imagination plenty of places to hide bad guys, but it wasn't until she closed her eyes to chase away the illusory threats that she truly ran into trouble.

Voices.

Her eyes flew open as Lady tensed beneath her; together they located a small group of men ahead, just barely within view on the wandering path. One of them must have heard her, for they all turned to look— and then stare—at her.

Maybe she should just trot right by them, give them a nod and nothing else. A stand-offish kind of bluff. It was no business of theirs what she was up to.

They must have read her mind, for they moved apart, and three abreast was all it took to block her way. Lady geared down to a walk of her own accord, and they were close enough so Jaime clearly heard it when one of the men said, "Well, burn my balls! What kind of a woman we got here?"

Suddenly Jaime remembered the strange expression on Carey's face the first several times he'd seen women in form-fitting breeches, and she felt as good as naked. A tiny stiffening of her back brought Lady to a halt a safe distance away.

People. People from another world, and their clothing—pants, soft-soled ankle boots and shirts in an assortment of sleeve lengths and collar styles—was somehow subtly *off*. The colors weren't quite right—too deep a green, an odd iridescent teal...she took a deep breath. *We're not in Kansas anymore...*

What's more, the men were well-armed with knives and short curved swords, all wearing identical, painted leather arm bands—probably enough to tell her whether they were friend or foe, if she'd known what to look for.

They stared at each other for a moment. Finally she hazarded a tired, "You're not just going to let me pass, are you?"

"Depends on who you are and where you're going," one of the men replied promptly.

"My name is Jaime Cabot and I'm going in this direction," she said, just as promptly.

A snort greeted her pronouncement. "Bullshit if I ever heard it."

"That's because," Jaime said, carefully neutral, "I don't suppose it's any of your business. I don't mean anyone harm, and that's enough." She wondered if it might be worth chancing the whole truth. If they were from Sherra's, they might actually help her.

If they weren't, they might kill her.

The third man, the one who'd been silent all this time, finally spoke, and Jaime realized with a start that the tall, sturdy figure was in fact a woman, her lanky figure hidden in her loose sleeveless shirt, her waist obscured by the weapons and equipment on her belt, just like women cops at home. "That's not good enough, not in these times," the woman said. "Especially not with an odd-looking package like your-self." She put a hand on her knife hilt and eyed Jaime pensively. "I don't think we can afford to let you just wander on your way—no matter who you're for. Too many questions about you, woman."

"I'm not trying to make trouble. I just want to get by." And some-how, before she even thought about it, she was startling Lady with abrupt heels. The dun hit a gallop in three strides, and the men jumped out of her way—but not before one of them got a good hold of Jaime's ankle and pulled her right off Lady's slick back.

Jaime landed on the relatively soft form of her assailant and strug-gled to get away from him even as she finished falling, clawing her way across his body. Her fingers found and grasped the hilt of his long knife, but not before someone jerked her head back by the short, thick braid of her hair. She cried out in surprise and pain, a yelp that was echoed behind her as Lady's hoof beats grew loud and close again, sud-denly punctuated by the solid sound of hoof against flesh.

Jaime's head snapped free and she jumped to her feet, whirling to locate all three of them. One was down, clutching a hip, the other was rising, his hand slapping at the empty knife sheath, and the woman was—was behind her! Jaime turned just in time to see the heavy pommel of a huge knife heading for her head, too close to avoid. Then dancing dun horseflesh flashed behind the woman and strong white teeth snatched that knife-wielding shoulder, lifted the woman off the ground, and tossed her effortlessly aside.

Jaime ran to her champion and threw herself astride in a mount she wouldn't have dreamed she could make, and Lady thundered down the path, taking them far away from any feeble foot pursuit. She was still running full tilt when the path abruptly opened into a narrow swath of cleared ground following along a thick log wall.

Jaime almost fell off then, clutching mane and riding air as Lady pivoted to follow the wall without cutting her speed. When they reached the thick path that was clearly a main entrance, Jaime was ready for the equally sharp turn into the gate, and rode it much better—which didn't make any difference in the long run. To Lady's obvious surprise, the gate was closed, and although she reared up in an effort to stop in time, they both crashed hard into the stout wooden structure. A face full of flying black mane swept Jaime into oblivion—but not before her mind's eye flashed her a picture of Carey, Mark, and Dayna, waiting for her help.

# 12

*arey, tired and grim. Dayna with a dirty, tear-stained face going pale with exhaustion—a body pushed to the limit. Stumbling, Mark, catching her, speaking to her, holding a branch out of her way. But where was Jess?*

"Carey!" Jaime called. "Carey, where's Jess?"

*Where's Jess? Where's—*

"You're all right."

It was a calm androgynous voice, a voice that knows it has things under control. Jaime felt immediately better about everything—and then opened her eyes in renewed alarm as she remembered just what "everything" was.

"Carey's out in the woods!" she said, even before she had found the plump, middle-aged woman sitting cross-legged on the ground beside her, wearing a subdued blue split skirt and long tunic. The woman had a cap of thick graying, ash brown hair and remarkably serene brown eyes; she greeted Jaime's statement with a raised eyebrow.

"I thought I just saw him," Jaime started—then faltered, confused. "But...that doesn't make any sense." She was on her back, and aside from the woman, could see little but the trees that towered above her. It suddenly occurred to her that she was still in one piece despite the hard fall she'd taken. Carefully, she rolled to her side, testing to see that everything still worked—but she couldn't find any of the aches and pains that should have been assaulting her after such a hard collision.

She discovered she was just outside the now-open gate, with Lady nowhere in sight. Within the walls there were plenty of people going about their business, casting an occasional curious glance their way but leaving them alone.

"I—I'm afraid I'm confused," she confessed to the woman, looking down at her torn breeches and knowing she hadn't overestimated the seriousness of the fall. *And I know I saw Carey, Dayna, and my brother in the woods.*

"I'm not surprised," the woman nodded; her earrings, two flat teardrops of bright peacock blue, swung with the motion. "Healing a head injury often leaves the patient a little befuddled. It'll pass."

"Healing a head injury," Jaime repeated without comprehension, and decided it was more important to get to the heart of the matter. "I need to talk to Sherra right away. Can you take me to her?"

"Easily." The woman spread her arms. "Here I am, in all my glory."

Jaime blinked, but wasn't taken aback for long. "I'm here for Arlen's courier, Carey."

"Ah, then that *was* one of his duns that you rode in on."

"Lady," Jaime responded immediately. "Where is she? Is she all right?"

"She took the collision with our gate much better than you did, dear. She's with my own head courier right now and wouldn't get better care if she were a princess."

"Carey needs help," Jaime blurted, at once overcome with the complexity of the situation. "He's out in the woods with some friends of mine, and he's got Arlen's spell. They're on foot, and he's sure some of Calandre's men are after them." For a sudden instant she wondered if she'd said the right thing, if this woman might not be Calandre instead, a very clever Calandre. But there was something about those eyes that reassured her....

"I felt him arrive," Sherra nodded, more to herself than to Jaime; then she focused on Jaime again and smiled. "Or should I say I felt you *all* arrive. Please don't worry about him, or your friends. When I felt a spell of such magnitude, I thought it might be Carey; I alerted all my people to watch for him. Now I can tell them he'll be with friends—

and that Calandre's annoying little minions will be snapping at their heels." She stood up and held out a hand for Jaime, who was still dazed enough that she did not question, but reached for the warm, strong grip—and then was glad of it when the world reeled around her.

"Slowly, dear. Head injuries are nothing to fool with, not even with a superb healer such as myself attending the wound."

"That's the second time you've said that," Jaime said, resolutely willing the trees to be still—and relieved when they obeyed. "My head feels fine."

"It *is* fine," Sherra agreed. "Much better than it was half an hour ago."

Jaime frowned. "I don't like the sound of that." She closed her eyes and felt again her friends' struggles, saw their strained faces. "Poor Dayna," she murmured. Then she looked straight at Sherra and deliberately stopped, midway through the gate. "What happened here? To me?"

Sherra eyed her back and said simply, "You and your horse galloped straight into my closed gate. I don't imagine she was expecting that—until recently, it hasn't been closed in years. She was lucky and came away with some bad bruises. You, on the other hand, must have hit the gate headfirst. Your skull was broken and you were well on your way to dying by the time I got here."

"I—*what*?" Jaime couldn't help the gasp that escaped her; something deep within her knew that Sherra spoke the truth.

"You're not going to faint? No? Good. Tell me, do they have magic on your world?"

"No." The word came out strangled, Jaime's mouth on automatic while she tried to assimilate the near death that had passed so quickly she'd all but missed it. Somewhere along the line, perhaps upon learning that some messages still traveled by horseback in Camolen, she had classified Carey's world as less advanced than her own—but now that rather conceited assumption wavered, as she realized she probably would not have survived this fall in Marion.

"I'd like to hear more about it," Sherra said firmly, tugging on Jaime's hand. "But over a cup of tea, dear, not out here where we're blocking the gate."

In a daze, Jaime allowed herself to be escorted into the hold. The first story was mortared stone, but the second was a solid log structure that radiated a homey sturdiness. On a second-story balcony, a woman who was obviously more friend than servant served Jamie and Sherra tea. Jaime found herself staring after the woman, futilely trying to classify what she saw into familiar societal structure.

Her struggle must have been evident. "Everyone's different," Sherra said casually, sipping her tea with a satisfied nod; the purple earrings dipped and danced. "Don't form your opinions of us from what *I* call home. If you were north in Camolen City, you'd find yourself looking out at spell-tamed lands with roads that never rut out and cities that hold tight warrens of people. The wizards are thicker up there, too, and they tend to specialize more tightly—in tall building construction, say, or traffic guides. Down here, we like a little room to ourselves; we take life at a slower pace." A wry expression crossed her face. "Usually."

Jaime glanced around the courtyard. From the balcony where they sat to the flammable nature of the construction, the hold showed very little concession to defense—even the wall didn't seem high enough to discourage anyone with real intent. "Aren't you worried?"

"About Calandre's annoying little minions?" Sherra shook her head. "I have many quiet defenses to resort to. The gate, of course, is the least of it. That troublesome thing and its wall were constructed to keep the livestock in at night, and is closed now only as a reminder to be watchful."

*Oh, yes*—"There was somebody out there—" Jaime blurted, then stopped, suddenly wondering if they might have been, after all, some of Sherra's people.

"You were running from *some*one," Sherra observed with equanimity.

"I don't know who they were," Jaime admitted. "But they got threatening, so I ran. If they were Calandre's...annoying minions, they were awful close to this place."

Sherra shook her head. "Then I doubt they were. We keep a careful watch—and there's no reason for Calandre's people to be handing around quite this close."

"They had armbands," Jaime remembered. "But I didn't really see what was on them."

"Armbands are very popular these days. Don't worry about it, dear." She sat back in her comfortable bentwood chair, and the orange earrings flared against the warm tones of her skin. *But—*

"They were blue!" Jaime exclaimed, and added, lame even to her own ears, "The earrings, I mean. You made them magic, I guess."

"I don't do earrings," Sherra said. "But there's a young woman in Siccawei Village who has a special touch with jewelry." She smiled and fingered one of the teardrops. "But I'd rather hear a little more about you and your world. I have a feeling there won't be much time for such talk once Carey gets here—he'll have so many questions, I won't have a chance for any of my own."

"Carey... is a determined man," Jaime said.

"Determined," Sherra repeated, as if trying the word out; she smiled. "You've come to know him well, I see."

Carey pressed a hand to the stitch in his side and mulishly kept up the pace, spurred by the oppressive prickle of fear that time was running out. He'd stopped looking back at the others half a mile ago, too afraid of the fatigue in Dayna's face. They crashed along through the woods behind him, and he knew there was no point in asking them, one more time, to try to keep the noise down. They were already doing their best.

A movement in the trees ahead brought Carey to an abrupt stop; Dayna floundered into his back and fell, panting, making no attempt to get up. Mark came up beside him and leaned face first against a wide tree, relaxing his whole body against the trunk. "If I sit down, I'll never get up," he muttered, dropping Jaime's sack of goodies by his feet.

Carey gave him a sharp glance to let him know this was no mere rest stop, keeping most of his attention trained ahead, where the movement had not yet repeated itself.

"How close are we?" Mark asked, his voice low and filled with concern as he, too, searched the woods ahead.

"Not close enough," Carey said shortly. There—he'd seen it again, and this time there was no questions. *But how did they get in front of us?*

Horses. He could have kicked himself for not realizing they might try this. Even though they'd probably lost his trail at the pickup, they knew well enough what his destination would be. They hadn't bothered tracking at all, but had merely ridden the established paths until they felt they were between the three fugitives and Sherra's hold, and then backtracked through the woods. Stupid, stupid.

Carey turned back to Dayna and hauled her roughly to her feet, holding her up with a cruel grip. What he really wanted to do was carry her to safety, but what he had to do was something quite different. He ignored the startled look on her face and shook her. "You made the choice," he told her harshly. "Now live with it! We're maybe two miles from Sherra's—" he turned her to the right and kept her that way when she would have twisted back to look at him "—*this* direction. It's not you they want, and there's nothing you can do to help me, so get going and don't stop until you get there!"

"But—" she started, annoyance warring with confusion on her face as she turned back to look at him despite his efforts to keep her pointed correctly.

"But, nothing! Go!"

"Mark...?"

"Go," Mark affirmed, and gave her a tiny little push to show he meant it.

"And you," Carey added.

Mark protested, "I can help!"

"They won't kill me—not outright. You, they'll kill." *Dammit,* go. The movement had coalesced into three distinct figures, heading directly for them.

Mark gave a sly little grin and said, "Carey, old buddy, who taught you to shoot a gun?"

Carey blinked and then looked stupidly at the sack. There were four guns in that sack, minus only a few bullets among them. He hadn't given them a second thought after they'd left the riverside—he was back home, now, where they didn't have such things as guns.

"Me, too," Dayna said in a low voice. "I can't run any longer and you know it. And you know they won't just let me go, either."

Mark released the tie and dumped the sack before Carey could respond. "Don't fire until you see the whites of their eyes," he said calmly.

"As soon as I find out who's side they're on," Carey said, taking the automatic Mark offered him. "Watch." It was a simple spell, one that every good—and long-lived—courier knew. He closed his eyes a moment to slide into the proper concentration, channeling a small rush of magic into the spell that would tell him if they faced friend or foe. When he opened his eyes, those who approached were limned in orange, a quiet effect that quickly faded. "The other side," he stated, glancing at Dayna and Mark to see if they'd seen the effect.

They had, of course—as had the others. One of them raised his hand in a self-confident wave, acknowledging the spell—and reached for an arrow to fit into his bow. Carey raised the automatic and rested it against the side of a tree trunk. Sighting along the barrel, he found the three figures and picked one, waiting just a few more moments while Dayna hesitated beside him and Mark waited to back him up.

*Squeeze.*

The gunshot created an unfathomable assault of sound on a world that had never seen gunpowder. His target faltered and fell, and the other two froze in place, unable to discern the manner of attack. All too quickly they realized there had been no feel of magic and dove for cover; Carey's precious second bullet buried itself in an innocent tree.

"Nice trick," one of them called as their injured comrade struggled to crawl for cover. "But there are more of us coming, and eventually we'll get to you."

Carey turned his back to them, leaning against the same tree that had steadied his hand, his head back, his eyes closed. "If they do get to us," he said, "and we somehow still have bullets left, promise me you'll empty the guns into the ground. Maybe someone'll be able to figure the things out without the powder or bullets, but it'll take them a lot longer." Then he opened his eyes to assess them: Mark, looking unusually grim and determined, no sign of buckling despite an adventure that had started with a kidnapping, encompassed murder, and ended up on a different world. Carey had not realized there was that much strength beneath that easygoing exterior.

But Dayna looked back at him with frightened, red-rimmed blue eyes that clearly showed she had already given all she had—which was more than Carey had expected from her small frame, despite what he'd said when he'd agreed to Eric's burial. She asked, "You think they're telling the truth?"

"Yes," Carey said without hesitation. "They wouldn't stick around if they weren't, not when we've demonstrated how easily we can kill them. And keep your head down—I saw at least one bow, and an arrow can reach us as easily as a bullet can reach them. If they hadn't been so cocky, they'd have had arrows strung before they got within range."

Mark slid behind a tree to the left of Carey, and Dayna sat at Mark's feet, her arms wrapped around her knees, her gun dangling loosely from her hand. Carey exchanged a worried glance with Mark as she began rocking slightly, her eyes closed. They couldn't afford to have her break down, not here, not now.

Then he realized she was muttering to herself, words he divined more by watching her lips than listening to her words. *Goawaygoawaygoway*, she mouthed in a near silent chant. *Goawaygoaway.*

Even though he felt the magic, he didn't really comprehend until it was too late—until the magic flowed steadily through a small tired body with indomitable will. He snapped around to peer beyond his tree.

*They were going away.*

He sent Dayna an incredulous glance, but couldn't take his eyes off the enemy for long. He couldn't see their faces, couldn't discern their expressions, but they were leaving—at first backing away, supporting the injured man between them, and then turning around to depart with even, unresisting strides. *Going away.* Carey looked at Dayna again, and could feel the incredulity on his face, knew he looked like an idiot as Mark stared at the men in confusion.

Carey didn't dare try to explain. Dayna's unremitting concentration was the only thing keeping them safe; he couldn't risk interrupting her. But sooner or later, she was going to run out of concentration—and she didn't know the rules. Burning hells, *he* didn't know the rules, not for magic as pure as this. He watched her silently for what seemed a very long time. Mark followed his lead, crouching silently between Dayna and the tree, still looking out into the woods every few minutes to assure himself the others were gone.

Finally, Carey felt it had gone on long enough—that it was better to ease the magic down before she simply lost her grasp on it. "They're gone," he said quietly. "You did it, Dayna—they're gone."

Her eyes flew open in surprise, and he knew then that she'd had no idea what she was doing, but had simply been herself at the end of her rope. "What?" she asked, as the flow of magic snapped off. Carey winced; he'd been hoping it wouldn't be that sudden, because of the—

*Backlash!*

Mark yipped short-lived astonishment as a flash flood of magic snapped through the woods, flung them to the ground, and left them there, three battered victims of its violent passage.

Jaime had a lengthy chat over Sherra's tea during which Sherra's stout, pleasant husband joined them, and was then shown to a small but breezy room with a narrow rope featherbed where she agreed to rest despite her convictions that worry would keep her staring fretfully at the herb-hung ceiling.

When she woke, she decided there must have been something soporific in the tea—or maybe it came of being healed from a mortal head injury. She peered out the window in search of the sun, and eventually decided the diffuse light meant it was early evening. When she turned back to the interior of the room, she discovered that someone had left her a lightweight tunic and a pair of slacks to replace the distinctly aromatic breeches and polo shirt she still wore. She had to cuff the legs of the pants so they wouldn't drag, but otherwise someone had done an admirable job of sizing them for her. And they were flattering, a bright berry tunic over cream trousers—winter colors that always made her hair look darker and brought out her brown eyes.

*My eyes. My* contacts. She'd be in a fuzzy neverland when she took them out—she shouldn't have slept in them in the first place. She went over to the small mirror that rested above a delicately rose-tinted pitcher and washbasin, and peered to see how red her eyes were.

They weren't.

She took the mirror over to the window and tilted it to catch the light; her dark brown eyes stared solemnly back at her, unsullied by the creeping red veins that always accompanied an inadvertent nap with the contacts. She examined her eyes with her peripheral vision, the *find the contacts* game. She blinked, she squinted, and she frowned, but to no avail. Okay, maybe she'd lost them in the fall. That wouldn't be unusual.

Or it wouldn't be if she didn't still have clear distance vision.

Jaime placed the heels of her hands over her eyes for a moment and then deliberately opened them again, gazing across the courtyard to the trees beyond.

She could see the leaves. The individual leaves, which should have been a blur of muddled greens. *This world has magic*, she chided herself, and wondered how many times she would have to learn that lesson.

Putting it out of her mind—or pretending to—Jaime wandered into the hall and picked one of the several sets of stairs. She ended up in the kitchen, surprising the workers there as much as she surprised herself. It was an odd kitchen, with one big stove that seemed to be wood, and one that seemed to be simply a stone counter with dyed squares on it—although she discovered for herself, by nearly burning a finger, that there was plenty of reason for the big pot there to be boiling.

A moment's observation in this curious, bustling place revealed the person in charge, an aged man called the spellcook. She realized for the first time how deeply Camolen had integrated magic into its society. There were preservation spells, heating spells, baking spells, cleaning spells...and off in the corner she discovered ice forming in stacks of ceramic trays that looked absurdly familiar. Just like Sherra's medicine, it was technology—from pragmatic to sublime—in a different form.

Lesson Number Two. *This world has magic*, she repeated to herself, a chant that was to become familiar of the next few days, even if the world did not.

Finally, she thanked them all for letting her blunder in amongst them and asked to be pointed at the courier barn. They all seemed to know just who she was and were eager to be helpful; each man and woman gave her their own version of the directions she supposed would have been simple enough if she'd only heard them once. She

thanked them profusely and wandered out into the yard with absolutely no idea which way to turn—until she heard Lady's call.

It was an anxious neigh, and it peeled out several times in succes-
sion. Although she had to go around a busy blacksmith's shack and a
chicken cook, Jaime arrived at the barn only moments after Lady began
another round of summons. She circumvented the large barn and found
the dun in one of several small paddocks that backed up against the
stout perimeter wall.

"Lady," she said quietly, and the mare snorted at the sight of her,
not hesitating in pacing that had already worn a visible path along the
border of the paddock. Jaime saw that her right shoulder was indeed
scraped and bruised, but her stride was long and even and unaffected.
"*You* were lucky," she said wryly, and ducked through the rails of the
fence to stand in Lady's path, interrupting the fixated movement.

Lady didn't appreciate the interference and said so with a loud wet
snort as she stopped scant inches away from Jaime, bobbing her head.

"Oh, stop," Jaime said in a *don't be stupid* tone, wiping her cheek.
"He'll get here when he gets here."

"Oh, he's here, all right."

The voice startled her and she whirled, putting her back up against
Lady, who snorted again—this time aggressively, protectively.

The woman held up her hand, and winced. "Don't worry," she said,
rubbing her shoulder appreciatively. I'm not here to make trouble."

Jaime took in the tall, blond figure and had no trouble placing her.
"You were on the path," she said, almost an accusation. "You could
have told me you were Sherra's people—it would have saved us both a
lot of trouble."

The woman shrugged. "We had the armbands on. It didn't occur to
us someone might not know what they meant—all of *Siccawei* knows
what they mean."

"Did you say Carey's here?"

"Him and two others. They from your...*place*, too?" The woman
came up to the paddock fence and leaned on the top rail, frowning at
Lady when the dun snaked her neck out and snapped in a deliberately
rude threat.

Jaime closed her mouth on astonishment and instead gave Lady a reassuring pat. "I'm sorry," she said. "She's been through a lot today."

The woman shrugged, but her expression made it clear she was still waiting for an answer.

"Yes, we came together. The guy is my brother, Mark, and the woman is a friend, Dayna. My name is Jaime," she added as an after-thought, and wished she could have been introducing Eric as well.

"Katrie," the woman said. "It's really true there's no magic on your world?" She sounded as though she didn't believe it.

Jaime laughed. "You know, that's about the same look I had on my face when Carey tried to convince me there *is* magic on yours. But it's true—there's no magic there."

"Huh," Katrie said skeptically.

Jaime couldn't keep the hope from her voice. "Can you take me to Carey?"

She wasn't prepared for Katrie's decisive shake of her head. "We brought him in a fist ago—" she started, stopping at Jaime's expression. "What?"

"A fist?"

"Of course, a fist." Katrie planted one fist on top of another until she pointed directly overhead. "Midday. That's nine fists. Scholars have their tricky clocks for keeping time, but out away from the cities we do it our own way. It's been about one fist since we brought Carey in—and that wasn't any easy chore, I'll tell you."

Jaime's hand stilled against Lady's neck, and she had the uncanny feeling that the dun was suddenly listening, too. It was enough to keep Katrie talking. "Three of them and three of us, and we had to carry them all the way. Sherra's with them, now." Another shrug, this time of dismissal; her job was done.

"*Carry* them? Are they—what—?" The hand gripped and tangled in black strands of mane. *Not all of them. Not them, too.*

"My guess is magic. There wasn't a mark on them—and we'd never have found them if Neron hadn't felt the magic coming from that way. It had to have been big, because he's no sensitive," Katrie said, matter-of-fact.

Lady lifted her head and called out again as Jaime turned away from the woman, suddenly aware that her own nonchalance since crashing the gate was all a cover. How could anyone be nonchalant in a society as alien as this one, when threat and death seemed to be all around her? She wrapped her arms around Lady's dun neck, and the vibrations of the anguished whinnying shook her.

"Here, now." The light touch on her shoulder startled her; she hadn't expected any gentleness from the tough-looking woman who'd stood before her. "Sherra'll put them right."

"It's not just...it's..." Jaime faltered, talking into Lady's neck, overwhelmed by the prospect of finding just a few words to convey everything that needed to be said. Finally she settled for, "We already lost one friend today." *Maybe two*, she thought, as she felt Lady's soft black nose nuzzle gently at her shoulder.

Surprise evident, Katrie said, "What happened?"

Jaime wiped her eyes on the sleeve of the bright tunic and glanced up at the taller woman, receiving her own surprise at the new respect she thought she saw there. Jaime surprised herself again with her blunt question. "Why?"

After a moment, Katrie shrugged. "We're all involved in this story, too. It started here and it's going to end here. And while maybe you'll find a way back home, we'll still *be* here, living with the results of this mess."

Jaime, too, thought a moment, looking at Katrie with her peculiarly acute vision, and seeing a blunt, tough woman who had the depth to come up with that answer.

"Supper'll be on," Katrie said. "I'll show you how it's done here, and you'll have plenty of time to tell me your side of things."

Jaime didn't have to think any longer. "Thanks." She briefly rested her hand on the thick black stripe that traversed Lady's spine. The dun's attention was already elsewhere, and her neck vibrated with a barely voiced call.

"She must have seen them come in." Jaime climbed out through the fence. "She knows he's here somewhere."

"I've seen her here on regular courier runs. She never seemed to care so much then."

"That," said Jaime, "is part of the story."

# 13

Jaime had quite an audience at the meal, a huge buffet complete with hot soapy water in which to wash the copper-veneered wooden platters and utensils—although Jaime now knew they'd be magically cleansed in the kitchen as well, so this was more like rinsing the dishes before they went in the dishwasher. People wandered in and out, keeping the noise level at a loud but pleasant hum, and the food slowly disappeared as Jaime told a tableful of people how she'd met Carey. She did not, however, speak of Jess' involvement, even if it *was* part of the story. Somehow it was too personal and, she decided, not really *her* story, anyway. She simply told Katrie and her friends that Dayna had run into Carey at the hotel. She put Dayna in Jess' place at the YMCA, and did not mention that Carey had memorized the spell—or even that he'd inadvertently destroyed it in the first place. But she told the scrupulous truth when it came to Eric, and the caring person he'd been, and that his death had been stupid and unnecessary. And she told about meeting Katrie on the road, and turned it into a Keystone Cops adventure that even had Katrie smiling.

But she didn't learn the things *she* wanted to know. No one could tell her if her friends would be all right; the best she could do was discover that Sherra had left them in the hands of her students while she recovered from the work she'd done. No one cared to venture a guess about the injuries or the prognosis—although they seemed to think it wouldn't be unusual if Jaime had to wait another day to find out.

Jaime sensed they had some idea of what had gone on, but were simply too discreet to discuss it. They wouldn't even tell her about Arlen, or what Calandre had been up to in Carey's absence—someone always managed to change the subject, or she got a table full of shrugs, and eventually she quit asking. While she quietly fumed over that, she eventually realized they had done no more than she, with her altered version of Carey's adventures, and had to respect them for it.

When the talkfest adjourned, she was told the little room in which she'd napped was hers for the duration, and she returned to it, tried one more time to find her contacts—this time by candlelight, although the halls had been lit with strange spherical glows—and crawled into the soft bed. There she fretted for all of five minutes before sleep kidnapped her thoughts and turned them into a night full of frustrating dreams.

As darkness fell, Sherra's head courier brought Lady into the barn, where she ceased her calling. He stayed with her for a while and offered her some of the choicest hay she'd ever seen, but her mouth was not for eating tonight. And though she knew and liked the dark-skinned man, she did not respond to his gentle words or his grooming. Eventually he left her alone with her thoughts.

For Lady had thoughts. She didn't understand them and she didn't like them, but she had them. She was aware that something of great magnitude had happened to her; every moment of her time as a woman was etched into her excellent equine memory—as memories she couldn't comprehend. Far too many words bounced around in her mind, both the place and object names that she could deal with and the more abstract facets of language that she couldn't. It made her mad, and it frightened her, and more than anything she wanted Carey to return to her and make it stop.

But the very thought of the man who could—who always had—soothed her merely created more torment. She had memories of feelings she didn't understand, and couldn't translate to her equine make-up, and they made her want to crash through the door of her stall and even through the thick wood gate, and to run her fastest through the woods, galloping until her tortured heart gave out.

In sudden frustration she kicked the wall; the solid blow rang throughout the barn and tingled up through her hock. Again she kicked, and again, barely controlled violence that settled into a leg-damaging rhythm. It numbed her mind and distracted her from the unbearable.

"Lady!" It was Morley, the head courier, back again and fumbling at the latch to her stall. Furious at the interruption, she screamed and charged the stall door; he fell back and gaped at her as she resumed kicking the wall. She was lost to herself by the time he ran out of the barn.

Kick, beat. Kick, beat. Kick—Morley was back again, with the same woman who had tended her shoulder. "Lady," the woman crooned, a considerate approach that only earned her the same greeting Morley had received. Only Carey could help Lady now, it had ever been only Carey—except now she couldn't stand the thought of his touch, and it left her nothing.

The woman did not retreat, though Lady bared her teeth and shook her head and rolled her eye. She was...humming. Lady pricked an ear despite herself, then, suddenly aware she'd been thwarted, ran to the back of the stall where she pawed the straw bedding and half-reared, fighting years of training as well as her own frantic passions.

The humming was quite nice, actually. A stray wisp of color ran through Lady's thoughts, startling her; it wasn't a color her eyes could see, although...that other part of her *had* seen such things. She snorted, and suddenly realized that her legs trembled, and that her right hind ached, and that please, please, she just wanted it all to go away and maybe this woman would do that for her. With a deep groan she approached the stall door again, and the woman put a hand to her forehead, ever humming; the soothing blues and greens washed through her mind.

Without quite realizing how it had happened, Lady found herself lying in the stall with the woman beside her. She surrendered herself to those healing forces, and felt the alien part of herself sliding away.

Jaime was furious.

Unfortunately, she had no one at whom to *be* furious—except maybe the well-meaning people who had refused to tell her what was happening with her friends and brother, and who insisted that while they recovered, they were not yet ready to see her. Even then she knew it wasn't really their fault that they weren't quite sure how to deal with a woman from the world without magic. And for her part, she was tired of the constant discoveries—that her bath would have indeed been a warm one if she'd only known there was a spell to trigger and how to do it, that the funny little chime in her head meant someone was look-ing for her and she should return to the great room to meet them, that she could have easily obtained a mouth cleansing spell instead of futile-ly scrubbing her morning mouth with a towel-wrapped finger. *Pah.* She was still spitting out lint.

A ride, she thought, would do her good. Might do Jess—or Lady—good, too. Distract her, perhaps, and give her something on which to concentrate, for the longer hours in the Camolen day seemed solely intended to provide them both with more time to worry. And Jaime was curious to see how a horse whose alter ego was steeped in dressage theory would respond to some focused riding.

When she arrived at the barn—fed, dressed in her clean, mended breeches, and anticipating a good conversation with Carey's horse, she found Lady in the same paddock—but an entirely different animal. Head low, standing in the corner with the weight shifted off her stocked-up right hind, Lady gave her an indifferent glance; the ear she flicked was merely a reflex to rid herself of a fly, nothing more.

"Jaime?"

It was not a voice she knew. Jaime turned to the dark-complex-ioned man who came up behind her and lifted an eyebrow in a polite but not quite welcoming response, unwilling to be distracted from Lady. His confident step faltered.

"Katrie said that was your name—Jaime," he offered in an almost-question. "I'm Morley, head courier here."

"Yes, it's Jaime. What's going on with Lady?"

"That's why I'm here. We're not really sure, and we had hoped you could help us."

"We?"

"Hanni and I. She's our animal handler—um, she specializes in treating animals with magic. I had to call her in for Lady last night."

"What happened?" Jaime tried to keep the demand out of her voice as she quickly turned back to Lady, scrutinizing the dun.

He shook his head. "Burn me if I know. She went crazy last night after I stalled her—started kicking the wall, and then rushed me. She went after Hanni, too, but that woman's a good handler. She got the mare sedated, but couldn't really interpret the problem—although she treated it as best she could."

"Then she was doing the kicking with that back leg," Jaime said, glancing at Morley for confirmation. "Is she still sedated, then? And what did you mean, she *treated* it?"

He shook his head. "The sedation's run its course. I wish Hanni were here—she could explain it a lot better. But she spent a lot of time with Lady and she's sleeping."

"You can't give me *any* idea what she did?" Jaime asked, beginning to feel alarm as she watched a horse who had given her no sign of recognition.

"I know, generally, how they go about working on an unknown like this," Morley said, looking less at ease with Jaime's reaction. "It's about finding the path of most resistance—that's where the problem is. Then they eliminate it."

"Oh my God." Sudden dread clutched her heart. "Jess!" she called sharply, stepping up on the first rail of the fence and leaning far over the top rail. "Jess!"

Morley came up beside, his bafflement palpable.

Jaime ignored him. "Jess! *Please*, Jess, come and talk to me," she pleaded, hearing ominous echoes of Morley's words...*they eliminate it...eliminate it...*

The horse regarded her in an unremarkable way, a mare with lean but pleasing conformation and all the extras that went with being a dun, the black points on ears, muzzle and lower legs, the thick line down her back, and the faint tiger striping on the backs of her legs. It was only Lady who looked back at her, who shook her lowered head so her thick man flapped noisily against her neck, and who looked away to scratch her face against her foreleg.

Beside herself, Jaime turned on Morley. "What have you *done* to her? Get Hanni back here and put her back the way she was, right now!"

Morley took a step back, but was uncowed. "In the first place, *the way she was* was making her crazy. In the second place, this is Carey's horse, not yours, and he'll be the one to make the decisions about her."

"You should have thought of that last night!" Jaime accused him.

"Carey wasn't available and you know it. As far as I'm concerned, Hanni saved that mare's life last night and there'll be no more said about it." His cordial attitude had cooled considerably.

"You don't understand." Desperation set in as she groped for some way to explain it to him, words that would make him understand. She closed her eyes and made a concerted effort to slow her thoughts and choose her words. *Calm and cool, Jaime, that's your rep. Live up to it.*

But she didn't have to.

"Carey." Morley interrupted her thoughts with relief in his voice.

Her eyes flew open to the welcome sight of two figures approaching in two blessedly familiar walks—one loose-jointed, one self-assured. Jaime ran to meet them, grabbing them each for a quick hug that left Mark grinning and Carey surprised.

"You're all right," she said, finding Carey untouched aside from the healing cut on his face and standing back from Mark to scrutinize him, finding pretty much what she always saw in him, right down to his mildly goofy grin. "Aren't you?"

"Just fine," Mark assured her, right before his face distorted in an exaggerated twitch.

She hit him lightly on the arm. "What happened? Where's Dayna?"

"Dayna needs a little more time," Carey said, but his comment was so matter-of-fact that she felt reassured anyway. "I heard you've been nagging the house aids unmercifully—but that none of your questions have been answered. You want some of those answers now?"

"You'd better believe it," Jaime said emphatically. "But I think we've got a problem here."

"Why?" Carey glanced at Morley. "What's going on?"

"It's Jess," Jaime said heavily.

"That's what she's been calling Lady," Morley offered, still back at the paddock fence. "As far as I'm concerned, the problem's solved, but you can decide for yourself."

All three of them joined Morley at the fence and Carey spent a few moments watching the dun. "There's her shoulder, which I've been told happened on the ride in." He looked at Jaime, as if checking out her head.

"I'm fine," she said, which at this point was an absurd lie. "But—"

"I'll tell you what I told her," Morley interrupted. "Last night your mare went into a frenzy in her stall—kicking, which is why her hock is swollen. She was wild, Carey—she came after me, and she meant it. She'd been fussing all afternoon, too, but this—well, I've rarely seen the like. Hanni was in for a calving and she took Lady on. Calmed her, and took care of the upset."

"Jess is gone, Carey," Jaime said in heavy emphasis. "She was there before, you know she was. She knew me, and she listened to me out on the trail—not like a horse would, or even could. She even got me out of a sticky situation with some people who tried to stop me."

"I heard about it." Carey frowned at Lady, who had immediately come over to greet him and was lipping at his outstretched hand.

"I think it was being Jess that upset her so much." Jaime looked away from the oh-so-horsey exchange between Carey and Lady. "And Hanni took care of it, and now I can't see Jess anywhere."

"Who in the Ninth Hell is this Jess?" Morley demanded.

Carey pulled gently on Lady's chin while she made satisfied faces. "When I went to Jaime's world, Lady came with me. Only the magic turned her into a woman, and we called her Jess. Dun Lady's Jess."

Morley stared at him.

"And when we came back, she was Lady again. Only the Jess part of her was still there...." Carey trailed off as Lady removed herself from his range and sniffed a fence post as if it was the only possible reason she came to them in the first place.

"It must have confused the hell out of her," Mark said. "How could a horse deal with a woman's experiences?"

"She couldn't," Morley said firmly. "Maybe your Jess is in there somewhere, maybe not. But I still think Hanni did the right thing—unless you'd rather have lost both of them."

"No," Carey said, barely audible. He turned away from them and looked out on the yard, which was empty of all save a goat that shouldn't have been loose. After a very long moment, he turned back to them. "We've got a lot to catch up on, Jaime. Let's go find a spot in the shade."

"I'm sorry, Carey," Morley offered, genuinely upset at Carey's distraught reaction. "If only I'd known—"

"Don't say it!" Carey turned on him fiercely, stopping Morley's words short even as Jaime realized Morley was really saying, *if she'd told me about it, this could have been prevented.*

"Carey—" she started, but couldn't have gotten any further even if he hadn't broken in.

"Don't even think it," he told her, just as fiercely. "There was no way you could know, just as there was no way Hanni could have suspected what she was doing. It just...happened this way. Maybe," he continued with some difficulty, "maybe it's for the best anyway. Jess...was too vital to have lived the rest of her life trapped in a horse's mind."

"You don't believe that," Jaime said, almost as fiercely as he'd interrupted her. "I know you don't. You tried for two months to convince yourself she was nothing more than a horse in a woman's body, and you couldn't do it. You're not going to be able to convince yourself that—that *this,*" and she gestured widely at Lady, "is for the best, either!"

It was Mark who captured her outstretched hand and used it to pull her into another hug, a slow, cradling hug, resting his cheek on top of her head. "C'mon, Jay," he said. "Let's find that shade."

# 14

When Carey arrived back at the spreading shade tree that was a central part of Sherra's back courtyard, he was armed with three cool herbal teas and ready to get down to business. The part of him that had been so raw and open as he confronted a Lady exorcized of Jess had been closed tightly away, leaving that cold and determined courier who was capable of risking an entire barn full of someone else's horses in order to obtain his goal. A courier who could not take the time to deal with the probable loss of Jess, or even with the horrifying news that every one of his six assistant riders had been killed on the road.

"Mark's told me what happened with Dayna." Jaime greeted him from the carved wooden bench on which she and her brother sat, and accepted the ceramic tumbler he offered her. Carey gave another to Mark and took the bench opposite them, no longer really interested in the immediate past, but reluctantly accepting that Jaime needed to understand what he and Mark already knew. "I can't believe she can manipulate magic so well," she continued. "I haven't the faintest idea how to go about it, myself."

"Neither does she," Carey said wryly. "Or none of us would have spent a day sleeping off the effect of the backlash." But that was not really a response to Jaime's unspoken question, so he sighed and told her what he himself had only recently learned. "Chiara—that's Sherra's most advanced student—asked me a lot about her—what kind of person she was, what kind of habits she had..."

"I told her *inflexible*," Mark put in, adding a quick but fleeting grin to show it wasn't meant to be a criticism. "You know how she is about keeping her own little self-imposed schedules."

"And you were the one person she could never get to pay the least bit of attention to them," Jaime said. "Oil and water, that's you two. But I think I understand what you're getting at...she's got a lot of self-discipline. What we might see as inflexibility can also be called..." and she wrinkled her nose in quick thought, "an ability to channel her energies in an orderly way."

Carey blinked. Damn good thinking there. "Right," he said. "But without the schooling, she put us all in a lot of danger. Of course she got the worst of it—but she'll probably be out and about before this evening."

"I think you're making light of the whole thing," Jaime said evenly. "Sherra was with you for an awful long time, and went straight off to rest. But she took care of my head injury and didn't seem the least bit fazed."

"An...*overdose* of magic like that, pure magical energy...it disrupts the entire body." Carey allowed himself a brief smile as he added, using the benefit of his time in front of the Cabot television set, "Sort of like a phaser on heavy stun. It was damn hard work for her to take three of us and put us to rights again, and I won't lie to you—for Dayna it was a close thing. But she really is all right, and there's no point in dwelling on it."

"Okay," Jaime said, letting go of the topic if not the worry that settled between her brows. "Then tell me what's going on here. Did you learn anything about Arlen? And what about the checkspell—do they have one yet?"

It was then he recognized something of himself in her. For she wanted to go home...but no one on this world would be interested in restoring three people to Marion, Ohio, until the local crisis had passed. She had herself set on that goal, and right now that meant putting aside her feelings about Eric, Jess, and all the strangeness that surrounded her. He glanced at Mark, and wondered what was hidden behind that laid-back expression. Mark, too, wanted to go home...but with Jaime taking the lead, he kept his own counsel.

"No checkspell," Carey said, finally answering Jaime's question. "I dictated the spell to Chiara, but until then, no one but Arlen had a complete version of it."

"Then he's still alive."

"As far as anybody knows." Carey's hand drifted to the spellstones that rested on his chest. "There's a lot of supposition going on."

Jaime shifted in impatience. "Just start at the beginning and give us the whole thing."

Carey shook his head, not in dissent, but rather at the uselessness of it all. "And then what? You think you're going to step right up and solve all our problems?"

She stared at him a moment, her warm features gone cold. "We're here because we took you into our lives. We rate an explanation, dammit! The only thing that's going to make all this bearable is if we know, somehow, that in the end it was all worth it."

Remorse nudged at the walls he had set in place, the tunnel-vision walls he had just seen echoed in Jaime. His quick response came as self-protective, an effort to leave the walls standing. "All *right*, all right." He leaned forward and rested his elbows on his knees, trying to organize recently learned updates. Mark might have heard some of it, if he hadn't been preoccupied with Dayna's condition while Carey grilled Chiara.

"All right," he started again. "About the same time Derrick went after me, Calandre used a stolen recall spell to get into Arlen's stronghold. He had just enough time to blast a warning to Sherra. Calandre cut him off, of course, but at least we know he probably had time to erect the security spell wall to keep her out of his private quarters. So it's possible he's simply waiting out the siege. She's got a surplus of armed men holding the grounds to keep away any chance of rescue—not to mention the forces that are wandering around making trouble in her name."

"He has enough food and water? All this time?"

Carey's inward frown was bigger than the one he let reach his face. "Water, yes, since it's spring and rainy, and he can collect it. Food...I doubt it."

"And magic can't create something from nothing, can it," Jaime said. "Or, at least, you were always saying about Jess that magic couldn't change the essential nature of what she was."

*But I was wrong about Jess.* "Magic affects things. It reveals things. It doesn't create them, or change non-living matter into living matter."

"All of which is a roundabout way to say that Jay is right," Mark said dryly, looking up from his tea. "Which also means that Arlen's probably pretty hungry by now."

"He's not going to be able to keep the security walls up forever," Carey muttered. "Not once he weakens." He flopped back against the bench, his head tilted back so he looked up at the fluffy white clouds above them. *Damn, damn, damn. This gets worse and worse.* Jaime and Mark remained quiet, giving him his thoughts.

"I know how to get to him," Carey said finally, abruptly. "It's fool-hardy, and it'll probably get us both killed, but I do have a way."

"How can you get in there if Calandre can't?" Mark asked reasonably.

You had to know it was there. You had to know how to use it. "Because I've got the only recall that can also be triggered to his private quarters." Carey fingered the stones again, remembering the day he'd been taught the extra nudge of triggering that would take him to Arlen's quarters instead of the stable receiving room—when Arlen had chosen him as head courier. *I'm not a healer, Carey, he'd confessed, but you're going to risk your life for me on a fairly regular basis. If something should happen...well, you use this. I'll do all I can for you.* He'd even used it once before, the day he lost Lady's half-brother. What had he been carrying? Something for Calandre, before she got so ambitious. It hadn't even been all that important, but some burning little wizardlet had thought it would be the key to his own success. Arlen had played the healer well enough on that day.

"Carey?" Jaime prompted. "I think you've wandered off without us."

"Sorry," Carey said absently, thinking about the guns stowed beneath his bed. "Nothing important. Just wondering how long it'll take me to get this rescue launched."

"Absolutely not," Sherra said. Her hand, poised over a platter of sliced venison, withdrew and momentarily tightened into a fist beside her plate. But if she was torn over her decision, there was no other sign. Carey's responsive bristling was anything but subordinate, and Jaime wondered if they were going to get into a brawl over lunch. Sherra's husband, Trent, eyed them watchfully from a few seats down.

After a moment, when Carey's attitude made it obvious he had every intention of charging off on his own despite her verdict, Sherra collected herself. "Our first priority—the same as Arlen's first priority, and you know it—is to find a checkspell."

"That doesn't have anything to do with me," Carey said, not a whit less determined. "You do your job, and I'll do mine. I work for Arlen, if you'll remember."

"It has everything to do with you." Sherra reached for the meat she had abandoned, bringing the conversation back down to a less confrontational mode. Jaime relaxed slightly, and lifted the tumbler of the herbal tea for which she was beginning to acquire a taste. Her eyes never left Carey and Sherra; in her peripheral vision, Mark continued his meal without slacking. *He always could eat through anything.*

Carey shook his head. "Don't stop there, Sherra, not if you're trying to get me to change my mind."

"I'm thinking," she snapped. "I have to say this just right to have any chance at getting through your thick skull."

Jaime coughed, covering laughter, and avoided Carey's quick, suspicious gaze.

"I'm missing something here," Mark said. "Carey told me about your Wizard's Council, and the precinct justice sessions. Why didn't anyone in Erowah manage to warn you guys about Calandre?"

"I've wondered the same thing." Jaime looked over her tumbler and caught Sherra's gaze, raising her eyebrow. "No one *noticed* she was amassing manpower? Magicpower?"

"I watched your television news," Carey said. "Plenty of little governmental overthrows going on. Same thing here. Making quiet alliances with other, lesser wizards wouldn't be all that difficult to accomplish, as long as she didn't make waves in other ways. And she hasn't—until now." He glared at Sherra and came down hard on his next words. "And I want to know what you're going to do about it."

All right," Sherra nodded, apparently having arrived at her strategy. "Given: we're going to need all of the high-caliber wizards at work on a checkspell, and we cannot afford to be distracted. After all, there is a time-limit here—as soon as Arlen can no longer keep up his security, Calandre's people will be on him. She *will* get the spell from him." She nodded to herself, her thick hair stirring with the motion, her eyes on her internal scenario. Then she looked back at Carey and said simply, "Anyway, given that, we cannot afford to have you stirring Calandre up."

"Why?" Mark asked, somehow managing to time an empty mouth with the right moment to insert the question.

"Why?" she repeated, eyebrows raised in surprise. "Carey can tell you that one, if he *thinks* about it."

Carey scowled. "She's got more than ground forces—she's got a cadre of former students. If she throws a temper tantrum, it's going to take magic to counteract her."

"Skilled magic," Sherra asserted. "There are plenty of useful spells around that can be subverted to do harm. Counteracting them would take away from our crucial efforts to get that checkspell."

"But if you rescue Arlen, you won't *need* to race Calandre for the checkspell," Jaime said, puzzled.

"I know it doesn't seem clear cut," Sherra admitted. "But our priority has to be the checkspell. Even if Calandre acquires the spell, we've still got to get a checkspell in place. It might seem like whipping a horse after the race is over, but we can keep the damage to a minimum. If we anger Calandre, we're back where we started in this conversation—diverted from our essential goal."

"So," Mark said, "even though you can't be sure it's not the right thing, the consequences of having it be the *wrong* thing are too great to risk going after Arlen."

"Pay attention to him," Sherra said to Carey, faint humor in her voice. "You could learn from a sensible young man like this."

Carey did not take the gentle reproof well; it struck sparks in his hazel eyes. "*Sensible* is not what Arlen needs! He needs *help*, and I can't sit around here wiggling my toes when I'm the one that can give it to him!"

"Oh, you won't have the time to sit around wiggling your toes," Sherra responded with satisfaction. "I need couriers aplenty to help me coordinate this checkspell business. There's no way, of course, that we're going to spellspeak our information—and there's far too much riding for the people and horses I have left. Even the addition of your mare will be of great help to us."

"Bring the others here," Carey suggested without sympathy.

"And draw us all together in one big target? I don't think so." Sherra shook her head with a wry smile.

"Could you use another rider?" Jaime heard herself saying.

"Jaime, no!" Carey said sharply. "It's too dangerous. Ask Sherra why she's so short on horses and riders in the first place!"

But Sherra was eyeing Jaime with a thoughtful look on her face. "No, it might work, Carey. It's true that I'm short because my people have been injured, but she can take the rides that are close to home, the ones to the less prestigious wizards. We can easily give her a maplight." She paused a moment in thought and then said, "That would certainly free up some of our own riders for the longer runs—the ones out of Siccawei."

Carey looked completely unconvinced. "There's no reason to put her in danger. *More* danger."

"It's my decision, Carey," Jaime said, an edge in her voice.

"And mine," Sherra asserted. "And I think we'll try it, Jaime, with much gratitude. If you feel differently after a few runs, you can always change your mind. We'll still be that much further ahead."

Mark said cheerfully, "I can't ride like Jay can. But I clean a mean stall."

Sherra smiled. "We've no shortage of people qualified for *that* job. But I don't doubt we'll find something to keep you occupied."

The conversation stalled, while Carey picked over his food and a harried man commandeered Sherra's attention with his crowded page of notes. When he left, Carey looked up from the meal he had been pushing around in his plate; his expression had lost its defiance, if none of its determination.

"There's something else," he said. "Another friend of mine needs help."

"That would be Jess?" Sherra asked.

He snorted. "I should have known you'd have heard about that."

"Morley," Sherra provided. "I have no answers for you, Carey. Before Hanni was forced to take action, I could have been more reassuring, but now.... Once we get past some of the details of getting the other wizards here, and have started work on the checkspell, Chiara will investigate the situation."

Jaime half expected another argument, but instead Carey nodded. "It's more than I expected," he said. "Thank you."

"Don't bother—not until Chiara's managed to find time. There's no predicting what's ahead of us, Carey. Assuming that our world will fall back into place just as it's always been is a mistake." Sherra got up from the bench seat and gathered her dishes, looking at Jaime and Mark. "I'm glad we had the chance to lunch together. If I don't have the time to speak with you at length in the near future, please don't take it amiss."

"Of course not," Jaime said, as Mark chimed in with, "Heck, no." Jaime watched as Sherra took her utensils to the wash tub and cleaned them, and suddenly realized how much she admired this woman; she seemed to be as expert with people as she was with magic.

Carey had given up on the pretense of eating; he clicked his tongue, luring one of the several rangy dogs that wandered the room. The animal cleaned his plate with big eager swipes of his tongue while Mark and Jaime kept their silence, letting Carey choose the path of their conversation.

"Hey, guys." The voice behind her was quiet, a little uncertain, a little embarrassed.

"Dayna!" Mark and Jaime chorused, twisting to see her. She was dressed in a simply cut shift that reached to mid-calf, a deep sky blue that echoed the color of her eyes and contrasted with black lines of piping along the seams and hems. Like her own borrowed clothing, Jaime thought—simple but not without style. Dayna herself looked drawn but steady on her feet, if somewhat unsure of her reception.

Jaime and Mark wasted no time scooting away from one another, leaving room for Dayna in an unspoken invitation to sit. Unencumbered by food, she climbed over the bench and sat, quietly offering, "I already ate upstairs."

"Are you all right? You look pretty good. In fact, you look too much like a certain Dayna I know who doesn't believe in magic," Jaime teased.

"Just because it's here doesn't mean I have to like it," Dayna said, her fine brows drawn together.

"Ow." Jaime winced.

Dayna twisted the material of a long sweeping sleeve, and muttered, "Sorry. It's not you I'm mad at."

"Who *are* you mad at?" Mark asked.

Dayna looked like she was about to burst with anger and frustration, and it took her a moment to get her words together. "They say I have to learn magic!"

"*Who* says?" Mark glanced at Carey, who shrugged.

"Sherra. Her students. All the wizards here. I told them I didn't want anything to do with it."

Carey replaced his well-licked plate on the table and scrutinized Dayna. "The ability to channel strong magic is a rare thing, Dayna. You should explore it while you have the chance."

"I don't want to explore it. I don't even want to be here. What I *want* is to go home." Fierce words, determined face under its short wedge of rumpled sandy hair.

"We all want to go home," Jaime told her. "They have other things to worry about."

"They have the time to force me to learn magic!"

Carey looked straight at her, and without sympathy, said, "They've seen what an untaught magic user can wreak on this world. If they insist that you learn the basics, then that's what you have to. Even if they lock you in a room and force feed it down your throat."

Dayna flushed in angry recollection. "That's exactly what *they* said."

"Then maybe you should think about it," Jaime said gently. "It'll keep your mind off going home. That's why I volunteered to ride courier."

"And I still don't like it," Carey said. "But as long as Sherra's said yes, let's go talk to Morley. I want to make sure he understands the kind of assignments you get."

"I can take care of myself," Jaime said, gathering her dishes as she got up from the table. "I'm not a kamikaze, no matter what you might think."

Carey gave her look of clear skepticism, but Mark just grinned. "Have fun, Jay."

"Oh, go clean a stable," she told him, and gave him a sisterly pinch on the arm.

Lady flicked her tail at a fly and found herself—yet one more time—mildly surprised when thick black hair actually brushed her side in response. It was not something she understood, this surprise, just as she failed to understand why feeling out the world with her whiskers was such a preoccupation, or why she occasionally expected to see something else with her eyes.

Given too much time to concentrate on such physical vagaries, Lady became as irritable as during her springtime heat. Her courier runs with Jaime were a blessed relief.

She didn't know why this new person was riding her; she missed Carey's wooing voice in her ear. Jaime's praise, although welcome, did nothing to fill that silent space. And her touch was nothing like Carey's. Light, almost evanescent, it lacked his firmness, yet somehow managed to be just as reassuring. And, as Lady had discovered, the sensitivity of Jaime's touch was not an indication of weakness. Balking for balking's sake warranted a swift and potent reaction, and Lady soon gave up on the subtle little tricks she liked to pull with anyone but Carey.

Besides, the work they did together quickly captured her complete attention. Jaime showed her how to extend herself, lengthening trot strides with power and suspension. She learned how to collect those same strides into an equally powered and elegant gait, building on the careful basics that had made her a balanced and responsive courier mount. Half-passes from one side of the road to the other let her play with diagonal movement, crossing her legs forward and sideways until she snorted with something that kept wanting to be pleased laughter.

Sometimes, it was almost enough to drive away the nagging feeling that something—some unique and important part of her—was missing.

# 15

Extended trot—now!

Jaime fed energy into Lady's dun sides and captured it in the reins, pushing the mare into big bold strides of extension. *Not too many...stop it while she's still successful...*and quietly she brought the mare back down into a good working trot, gently slapping the side of the sweat-darkened neck, ruffling the thick dark mane up and down Lady's crest. There would be no more dressage on today's run; the days of constant work were wearing the edge off the energy of a horse Jaime had found to be nearly tireless. Lady snorted, dipped her head to take advantage of the rein Jaime fed out, and trotted on in an even rhythm before easing down to a walk.

For Jaime the courier runs meant time for dressage—and they meant opportunities to think. Out on runs that rarely took more than half the day coming and going, she was usually back in time to pitch in at the village. The previous week she had helped with dredging stronghold wells—not all of which were in constant use, but all of which would have to flow freely to provide clean water to community under siege. This week it was the tedious process of mowing and gathering the first cutting of hay—although it had been interesting to watch the students come out and place mold-retardant spells on the fodder, a spell she deeply coveted for her own Ohio hay.

After that she thought to wonder how many other subtle ways

magic was at work in this community, where mechanical technology had never advanced past swords and plowshares because magical technology took care of so many necessities. She became caught up in the strangeness of the culture and diverted by the uses of everyday magic. She had even had some success with the glowspells and no longer needed a candle in the room she shared with Dayna—although the feel of using magic was uncomfortable for her, rather like an unreachable tickle in the back of her throat.

If it was a tickle to Jaime, magic was a gall to Dayna, who was learning in spite of herself. Withdrawn and unwilling, Dayna attended the daily work of Chiara and several of Sherra's other students, all of whom had had their lessons suspended for the duration. And although they were now trusted with the commonplace magics that helped to run the stronghold, the students obviously felt a little left out of the pivotal checkspell work, and were glad to immerse themselves in the new if unwilling project of Dayna. Jaime smiled at the thought of her petite friend wielding magic with competence.

Mark applied himself in the only area he felt he could be of use—stronghold and village defense. Though the weaponsmaster continued to drill Mark, it quickly become plain that close confrontation would not come naturally to her brother, with or without weapons. But youthful Boy Scout experience in archery had unexpected benefit, and he spent several hours a day in practice.

Jaime only hoped that he'd never have occasion to use his new skills.

Beneath her, Lady lowered her head and snorted, bored with the slow pace of their breather. "All right," Jaime told her, checking the ground ahead of them for the maplight. A small, bright pinprick of light, it kept her on the unfamiliar routes scattered near Sherra's stronghold. After only a few runs, Lady had learned to follow the guide too, which gave Jaime a chance to keep an eye on their surroundings. Not that there was much to see in this forested area. There were few families still staying outside the fields surrounding the village; the rare soul she met on the road was invariably aloof and occasionally hostile.

She wasn't sure she blamed them, for she looked upon each of them as a potential enemy herself.

Although she wasn't in any danger, not really. Sometimes her ride had nothing to do with the actual checkspell at all, but was simply the result of curtailed spellspeak. Eventually the wizards would gather to pool their work, but they would work separately for as long as possible rather than collecting to present a tempting target.

Instead, the couriers were exposed in regular travel between wizards. And they rode without the safe retreat of a recall spell. Jaime didn't quite believe a recall spell couldn't be tied to some neutral setting, even though Carey had shaken his head and muttered something about the preparation and maintenance of a recall site when she broached the idea to him. It was hard to understand his dismissal when two couriers had already been badly hurt, and when it seemed like a solution was obvious.

Jaime had to remind herself that beginning students were blithely unaware of the riding theories that seemed so clear to her. With an inward *hmmph* at her self-admonishment, she lifted Lady into a trot, posting in a rhythm that her body knew too well to bother involving her brain. It occurred to her that this job was one she might well be doing for some time, depending on how things went for Camolen.

Two hours out of the stronghold, they verged on the first in a series of grassy knolls with bedrock too close to the surface to allow trees. Jaime's guide veered from the well-used trail and Lady followed, until a small cabin became evident amidst the trees and the guide disappeared like a burst soap bubble. Perched at the top of the hill, it had an abandoned look to it. This was a new route, one Morley had grumbled and assigned to her anyway, and Jaime didn't feel particularly welcomed by the dwelling's starkness. A log cabin should be homey and inviting, not foreboding.

She stopped Lady in the trampled grass before the cabin and dismounted, replacing the bridle with a halter so Lady could pick at the grass, and hobbling her as well. This was the boring part of the run, this waiting for the recipients to digest her messages and frame a reply. Sometimes it even meant sitting around and waiting for the magic-user's return, for all that they knew she would be coming. This one hadn't shown his face yet, which meant he was probably out on some wizardly errand.

She went to the door to knock anyway, dropping the bridle by the side of the entrance—but as she raised her hand, the door swung away. The man who greeted her smiled in a way that made her want to step back, and said, "Play time."

*Play time?* She did take that step, and was about to identify herself when his hand shot out and grabbed her wrist, jerking her inside. She stumbled, caught herself halfway down—and found herself staring into the open, filmy eyes of the dead man on the floor. She gaped at his slashing, mortal wounds, and someone else grabbed her shoulders—literally picking her up off her feet and slamming her against the wall. Air whooped out of her lungs as she hit the wall again, and then again, rag doll limp. Her vision grayed; she gasped for breath and blinked her tearing eyes back into focus, discovering a whiskered face shoved up close to her own. It was an unpleasant, leering face, and she flinched from what she saw there.

"Surprise," he said. "You guys are easier to catch all the time."

She wanted to say something daring, something to show she wasn't terrified. Instead she found herself mute, capable only of the whimper that trickled past her throat.

"The message?" the man asked, tightening his hold, hitching her a few more inches up the wall, moving a few inches closer.

"Saddlebags," Jaime finally managed to whisper, after he dug his fingers deeply into the flesh of her arms. He looked away long enough to nod at someone she hadn't yet seen, and she took the opportunity to get some impression of the place, something more than the door, the dead man, and the wall behind her back. She discovered the dwelling completely trashed. A woman sifted through the contents of a cluttered table, frowning in an unsatisfied way.

"For your sake," the man said, letting her slide down a little so her feet took most of her weight again, "I hope we find a copy of the spell in those saddlebags. Not all these stupid little pet wizards can have it memorized already."

"I don't know what's in the message," Jaime ventured, knowing the spell *wasn't*. She tried not to think of the consequences, although the dead man gave her a pretty good idea. Then again, death was probably the easiest of what was waiting for her. No Amnesty International on Camolen.

"It's not here!" a matter-of-fact voice called from the front yard. "D'you know of any other stable that runs duns besides Arlen's?"

"Lots of duns to be had," grumbled the whiskered man, dragging Jaime over to the door in such an absent way she knew immediately that he counted her as no possible threat at all. In the doorway he paused and added, "but not that quality."

The man who'd greeted her was standing by Lady's head; did that mean there were only the three of them? As if that made a difference. "Looks a lot like that mare we found in Arlen's barn—you know, the one that dumb shit Gandy run to death."

Whiskers stared at Lady, his eyes narrowing as he nodded slightly. "She does at that. I think maybe we'll bring this one with us. Calandre might find some use in her."

The other man snickered unpleasantly. "Yeah, like maybe Arlen'll be more cooperative if he doesn't want to see you hurt, courier."

Jaime opened her mouth to say that Arlen didn't even know her— but they wouldn't believe it. She wanted to spit at the man, and fought the unfamiliar desire to rake her work-shortened nails across his face. Instead she looked at the ground and took a slow, deep breath, guessing that subservient cooperation was the most likely to leave her unbrutalized.

The woman came out of the house, stuffing a sheaf of papers into the leather container that looked like nothing more than an executive briefcase; neither it nor her expression fit well with her pert-nosed features and soft blonde hair. "I'm through here," she said brusquely. "It was a waste of effort. The man had nothing."

"One less wizard on their side," Whiskers said reasonably. "Gerrant, go get the horses." Gerrant looked up from the hobbles he'd just taken off, hesitant, and Whisker's grip on Jaime's arm tightened with his irritation. "Go *on*—she's not going anywhere."

A grumble and a shrug, and Gerrant left to do as he was told, heading for the woods behind the cabin. Lady stood uncertainly, knowing she was free and that there was tension in the air. *Lady.* A haltered horse galloping home alone would cause a fuss much sooner than any slowly dawning understanding that the newest courier was more than just slow on her unfamiliar route.

So much for subservient cooperation.

A quick glance at Whiskers confirmed his distraction; he'd turned his attention to the woman, watching her set a spell at the cabin's door.

Jaime took a deep breath and tore loose from his grasp, scooping up the bridle, sprinting for Lady. In the back of her mind she hoped to mount and make a run for it, but Lady went jigging away at the sudden movement—and at the man lunging for Jaime. Just as his grasp plucked at her shirt, Jaime swung the bridle reins in a big circle, a resounding slap against tense bunched in Lady's rump. The mare bolted.

If only she ran to the closeness of Sherra's, and didn't head instead to Arlen's—

A rough tackle slammed Jaime to the dirt, crushed by Whiskers' weight on top of her. He trapped her between his knees, jerked her around to face him, and hit her hard. Pain shot through her head as it bounced off hard ground, and through her face as he hit her again and again and—

"Stop it." The voice was cold and derisive and held aloof disdain. The onslaught faltered; Jaime gulped for air and choked on blood, spitting and gasping, as the woman's voice continued, "That's enough. She's not in any shape to run again, and Calandre will want something to work with."

Immediately the man got off her, unable to resist one last jab with his booted toe. "I hope you like riding double, sweetheart."

"She'll ride with me," the woman said, her voice more distant as she moved away. "Now get her to her feet. Gerrant's coming."

He shrugged, and leaned down to haul Jaime up in an almost off-hand way. But he held on to her, and this time she was almost glad for the support. She swiped feebly at the blood running freely from her lips and nose and waited, stupidly dazed, as Gerrant emerged from the woods with three horses in tow. She was so focused on the epicenter of pain in her nose that Whiskers had to shake her arm when it came her turn to mount behind the woman. Zombie-like, she did as she was told, and was soon riding away from Sherra's at a rough trot that jarred her pains with every step.

Carey patted the sweaty black neck before him and urged the horse up the short but exceptionally steep bank they faced. Denied the chance to help Arlen or Jess, he'd taken up his courier work with a vengeance, riding every day and sometimes twice a day. It hadn't taken many such days to wear him down, and that's the way he wanted to keep it. While he was caught up in the aches and cramps of his body, in watching the trails for Calandre's threats and avoiding the pitfalls of rough travel, he actually managed to avoid the *can'ts* that loomed so large in his life.

One of those *can'ts* he'd discovered early on, as he was saddling Lady for his first run. He was tightening the girth in easy stages when he realized he couldn't just mount up. Having given Jess the respect she was due as a woman, he couldn't fall back to that easy partnership they'd had—one in which he was nonetheless master.

He couldn't pretend he'd never kissed her—or that she hadn't kissed him back. Honest in everything, Jess had made no attempt to hide the confusion—and the passions—he created in her.

So in the end it was a good thing Jaime was riding for Sherra, for he doubted Lady would have responded so well to a completely new rider, not with the turmoil she'd been through. Even if he'd never managed to tell Jaime so...he thought she knew anyway.

The black stumbled and Carey gave himself a mental kick. *You're not supposed to be thinking about this.* Frustrated, he turned his attention vigorously back to the run, turning the horse toward another bank in this rough shortcut with a "Hup! Hup!" of encouragement. The black strained upward, Carey returned to work with the grim satisfaction of its distraction.

When he finally reached Sherra's stronghold, he rode into a courtyard of commotion. His first impulse was to ignore it and return to the stable—until he saw the cause of the disturbance.

Lady ran loose in the courtyard, saddle on her back and halter on her head, evading all attempts to capture her. At the moment her would-be wranglers were several young children and a few of the household workers, none of whom had the skill or nerve to bluff Lady out.

Carey closed his eyes and dredged up the composure he would need to deal with an upset Lady, and then dismounted, leaving his own tired mount to stand quietly in place. "Lady," he said loudly, and all heads turned to look at him, including hers. She took one step toward him and then hesitated, allowing him to move up by her shoulder. He stood quietly as she craned her head around and sniffed him with the quick shallow breaths that meant she was taking in his scent. Then, reassured, she allowed him to quietly grasp the halter.

"Where's Jaime?" he demanded, too tired for tact, too concerned to even try.

"The horse came back without her!" one of the children declared as the others nodded. A livestock hand shook his head helplessly and said, "The children came for help when the horse ran in, and now you know as much about it as any of us."

Where had Jaime ridden today? Carey made a quick inspection of Lady and her tack, and found only that the message was missing. He pointed at the oldest child, a girl nearly into adolescence, and gestured her over. "She'll go with you to the stable now, as long as you keep a good grip on that halter. One of you others can take my horse. And tell Morley to meet me in the main room."

Inside the house, he sat at one of the long, empty tables, his mind blank, his gaze distracted by a young man sweeping up the residue of the last meal. All his urgency ran into a wall built of fatigue and frustration...and the helpless feeling that Jaime would be one more friend he was unable to help.

It was Mark who stumbled across him while he waited for Morley. *Jaime's brother.* Just the person he wanted to deal with right now.

No, that wasn't fair. Carey lifted a hand in greeting as Mark sat across from him, laying an unstrung bow across the table next to a quiver of practice arrows.

"You look beat," Mark said, sounding fairly cheerful himself. "But I think I'm finally getting the hang of things around here. If I can only get that glowspell down...but hey, no need to worry about defense with me around. As long as we're attacked by big oval targets with painted weak spots, we got no problem at all."

Carey snorted, unable to resist the good-natured humor. But he shook his head in the end, and murmured, "We *do* have a problem," as he stretched the arm that had been skewered not so long ago, and which stiffened up faster and more thoroughly than the rest of him. "Damn, we've got a problem."

It was a barely audible murmur, but Mark heard it—and heard the unspoken magnitude of concern as well. "What?" he asked, just short of demand.

"Lady's come back without Jaime," Carey said. "I'm waiting for Morley—he'll be able to tell us her route today. And then, someone's going to have to come up with a Ninth-level reason to keep me from riding out after her."

Mark said, slowly and carefully, "It doesn't have to mean anything dire. She's been dumped before, no matter how much she tries to make me forget it."

"She wasn't dumped," Carey clarified. "Lady was wearing her halter. They must have been at their destination, where she should have been hobbled."

"She could have broken free," Mark offered, even as Carey shook his head.

"Something scared her, or she wouldn't have run in like she did, and had half the household chasing after her. She's not a hard catch, normally."

Mark looked down at the bow and arrows before him, fingering the stiff leather of the quiver. "Jaime's all right," he said in a stiff and determined voice, the sturdy adaptability shaken. "She's all right. She's probably on her way back on foot, embarrassed as hell."

"Maybe," Carey acceded, still not believing it. "If only Lady could tell us...if only we could bring back Jess...*damn*, I miss her." *Not now, Carey—one crisis at a time.*

Mark looked up, a sudden alert glance, and Carey turned to see what had caught his attention. Morley. *Good.*

"Morley—" he started, but the man raised his hands to forestall demands and explanations.

"I know, I know," he said. "Lady came back without her rider. I know where she went, and right now a very brave child is daring to interrupt Sherra at work. We'll find Jaime, Carey."

Eric, dead because Carey had dropped into his life. Arlen, waiting for a rescue that wasn't coming. Jess, buried in a place where no one could reach her. "She's not going to stop me this time," he said.

# 16

Sherra never tried. To her consternation and Carey's barely repressed wrath, Morley admitted he'd sent Jaime to Theo's, an accomplished wizard well within the territory Jaime was used to covering. Accomplished enough to draw Calandre's unwanted attention—or focus it on the courier who might be carrying information about the travel spell. By mid-afternoon in an day turned cloudy and dim, Carey rode point—the only experienced horseman in a small group of uneasy riders on well-worn horses.

Despite his heavy exposure to horse sense, Mark had clearly not spent many hours in the saddle. Gacy, the advanced student Sherra had assigned to the investigation, held the reins as though he thought they might attack him. The fourth member of the company was Katrie, the tall blond woman Jaime had come to trust and Carey had therefore chosen as the warrior for the group. Normally he could depend on his own reflexes and training when it came to defense, but these were far from normal times.

He checked back over his shoulder and decided his neophyte riders could take a little speed. "Going to canter!" he called back to them, and asked his sturdy little bay mare for the transition. Morley, he decided, had been acting out of mercy—or guilt—when he gave Carey the bay for this trip; the animal's gaits were as smooth as slow river water. He knew the others wouldn't have it so easy, but he squelched his sympathies and refused to look back until he reached the turnoff to Theo's little homestead. He found pretty much what he expected: the others straggled out behind him, easy prey for any raiding party that might be hanging around. Mark and Gacy were too busy keeping themselves a-horse to care, but Katrie shot him a look of pure ire.

"Making my job pretty damn hard," she growled at him.

He knew; he just hadn't cared, and his shrug told her as much.

"Fine," she said coldly. "But now we're here and we'll do it my way. Hold my horse and keep your ass right here until I say otherwise. I'll be back after I've had a look around." She dismounted, an unfamiliar maneuver that nonetheless displayed the authority of movement Carey associated with skilled warriors.

Carey caught the reins she tossed at him and watched her stride up the lane. When she was out of sight, he leaned back in a weary stretch, while the bay shifted to a lazy, hip-shot stance beneath him. Mark and Gacy had dismounted, and made various disgruntled noises as they experimented with walking again.

"If this is the accepted mode of transportation around here, maybe I'd better take a few lessons from Jay," Mark grumbled, maintaining his dogged personal fiction insistence that Jaime was perfectly all right.

"There are other ways," Carey said. "As long as you know two wizards you trust with a fairly complicated spell, and don't mind the side-effects."

"It's not *that* bad," Gacy protested mildly. He gave his backside a meaningful rub and added, "It's not the only thing with side-effects."

"No kidding," Mark agreed.

Carey tuned them out, going to the blank, tired space he'd been cultivating so assiduously. And then he blinked, because Katrie was standing in front of him with a mixture of annoyance and concern on her face, saying his name for what was apparently not the first time.

"Carey! What Level have you lost yourself on?"

"What'd you find?" Carey asked shortly.

"No indication anyone's there, though there were horses here earlier. I haven't translated any of the sign, yet—so stick to the edge of the trees when we hit the clearing, and tie up. I don't want you messing up what little that hard dry ground has to tell me." She took her reins from

Carey, looped them over her horse's head, and swung into the saddle, leading the way down the short lane while Mark and Gacy still struggled to mount. Soon enough, they reached the small clearing; Carey slipped his halter over the bay's bridle to tie up along the edge.

"There's a bridle lying in front of the cabin," Katrie said, and pointed. "And there's an area to the right and behind the cabin that I want you three to stay away from until I'm through with it."

"But no one's here?" Mark asked, as though he hadn't heard her earlier proclamation.

"No one you know," Katrie said grimly. "And no one alive."

Carey left the bay while the others still fumbled with halters and bridles, jogging to the forlorn jumble of leather and metal by the cabin. It didn't take a second glance to recognize Lady's current bridle. Nearby a series of hoof prints gouged the earth, the sign of a startled and explosive take-off. *Lady*. He left the bridle and skirted the area in deference to Katrie, heading for the cabin and its ajar front door. *No one alive*, she'd said. Since there was no one outside, that meant—

"Carey, no!" Gacy cried as Carey reached across the threshold to push the door—and too late at that. The doorway erupted in a glaring offensive of light and sound and power, enclosing Carey in cacophony. Then the hard ground smacked him between the shoulder blades, hitting him as hard as the magic. As the discordant assault faded away, it was replaced by the slap of running feet and panting breath and anger.

"Ninth level damnation, you should *know* better than that, Carey!" Gacy said from somewhere above his head, as horse sweat-scented fingers caught his chin and probed his neck for a pulse. A groan wormed its way out from deep inside him, and those same fingers patted his cheek gently.

"Is he alive?" Katrie asked, carefully dispassionate, at the same time Mark blurted, "What the hell was that?!"

"Pyrotechnics, I think," Gacy said. "He's stunned, but I think all right." His voice moved further away, paused, and then pronounced, "Whoever got here first left us a childish little gesture."

"You call *that* a childish little gesture?" Mark said, kneeling by Carey. Carey blinked, trying to see past the multi-colored whirls of light that still obscured his vision. He thought about sitting up, but his body didn't respond; in fact, it could barely feel the comforting hand Mark had rested on his arm as he asked, "What happened to those famous checkspells you guys always talk about? How can you let a dangerous spell like that go unchecked?"

Gacy was close again. "Because very similar spells are used in some of our mining operations. We do our best, Mark, but there are certainly available spells that cause havoc if put to other than their intended purpose."

Off to the side, Katrie made a sound of disgust. "There's not much I can figure here, except that there were several horses—three, maybe. All we know for certain is from that bridle—Jaime *was* here. Is it safe to go inside, now, Gacy?"

"It spells out clear," Gacy said absently. "Here, Carey, I'm no healer, but see if this doesn't help."

*Relief.* His vision cleared, the haziness inside his head faded away, and even if his body still showed no inclination to sit up, he at least had the feeling it *could*, if he insisted. And when he heard Gacy's low voice saying, "Poor Theo," he did, indeed, insist. From his back to his knees to his wobbly feet, with Mark steadying him, he dragged himself to the cabin.

Katrie hunkered by a man's disfigured body, staring with disgust at the slashing wounds. "No reason for this kind of brutality," she muttered, glancing up at Carey's arrival. "If this was done by Calandre's people, she's giving them a pretty long rein."

"This isn't Theo's hand," Gacy said from the long worktable he was scrutinizing. Katrie left the body for the table, and Gacy gestured at the neatly sorted papers set aside from the rest of the jumble. "And I don't think it's all here, either."

"How can you tell?" Katrie let her gaze roam the rest of the cabin, too impatient to wait for Gacy's explanation before looking for her own clues.

"For one thing, Theo works—worked—in a state of perpetual clutter. And he's a scribbler, always putting down cryptic little bits and pieces of his spells on paper. Like this." He pulled out a paper from the middle of a stack; the sheet was nearly black with ink scrawlings, illegible notes that took up the entire surface area. Gacy spread the pile out on the table, stared at it a moment, and shook his head. "There's nothing here on the checkspell or the world-travel spell. And there should be."

"That's not too surprising," Katrie said dryly. "We already know a wizard set that spell at the door. No doubt that same person sorted Theo's stuff. Calandre's trying to figure out where we stand."

"And maybe get her hands on Arlen's spell while she's at it," Carey said. "She must be getting frustrated."

"But—what about Jaime?" Mark said. "They must have taken her, but why bother? She can't tell them anything."

Katrie shook her head. "I don't know the answer to that one—but I think we'd better get back to Sherra with what we've learned. There's no telling what else Calandre is up to, if she's decided to go on the offensive within Siccawei."

And Carey hadn't even precipitated things by going after Arlen. The bitter thought made way for the next, a decision that was made before Carey gave it any conscious thought. There was nothing to stop him from using the recall spell now—especially if no one knew he was going to do it. He glanced at Mark and quickly amended the resolution—there *were* people who would support him in this, especially considering that he might just find Jaime at Arlen's stronghold as well.

Katrie cast him a sharp look. "Are you all right for the ride back?"

"I'm all right," Carey said grimly. His thoughts had forged ahead to new goals, to discarding the overwork that had served him so poorly on this day. It was time to renew his resources, to retreat and recover.

And then it would be time to attack.

But when they returned to Sherra's cabin, riding through the steadily falling warm summer rain, some of that new intent must have shown in Carey's face. She waited only long enough to hear the group's report, and then she took his spell stones away and put him in a guest room under house arrest.

Dayna stood with her back to the late afternoon light of the workroom window and watched Chiara, wondering if her assumptions about the friends and enemies of this world had been correct after all. Jaime was kidnapped, Jess had been suppressed into Lady, and Carey was confined in a first floor room—a comfortable enough place, but there was no mistaking its nature. The spell Gacy set at the threshold let others pass, but kept Carey within. And Sherra had appropriated his spell stones.

Insulting. Callous. Not really benign at all. And it set Dayna to thinking how no one had gone after Arlen, how they were willing to sacrifice Jaime, how they hadn't really looked into the confusion that was Dun Lady's Jess.

So now, while Mark pretended even to himself that someone would soon go and fetch Jaime and while Carey slept, repairing the stresses of an overworked body, Dayna considered their options—and what Carey had asked of her.

She'd poked her head in his room before she'd come upstairs, just to make sure he hadn't changed his mind—but hadn't tried to wake him. If he really meant to go through with his kamikaze plan, he'd need all the rest he could get. And it was that kamikaze plan that put her here, designated thief and spy instead of unwilling student. As such, Dayna slid away from the window and along the wall to the cabinet behind Chiara's back.

*The cabinet of magic trinkets*. Right.

Dayna was still amazed at the way magic threaded through this society. Her initial impression of rude and unrefined lifestyles had been replaced by a reality in which those lives were at least as comfortable and secure as her own. There were spells for keeping teeth clean, there were spells for cramps, there were spells to repel mice and vermin. Not everyone could afford them all, of course, but then, there were plenty of places in Ohio where people lived with mice—including Jaime's old farmhouse.

"You're awfully quiet," Chiara said, without looking up from the leather bound spell notebook she carefully inscribed. Dayna froze with her hand on the cupboard door as Chiara frowned at her own notes. "Do you remember what that woman said she needed? Was it a weather forecast for one day, or one week?"

Dayna forced an indifferent reply. "I don't know," she said honestly. "I was looking at some of the sale crystals while you talked." Crystals she had crudely strung together in an approximation of Carey's necklace and that she was just about to—with a quick glance to see that Chiara still puzzled over her list—switch with the real thing. *Can't believe I'm*—and then it was done. Nary a rattle of stone against stone escaped the muffling flannel cloth she used to handle the necklaces, and Dayna stuffed the contraband into the deep pocket of her shift.

"You talked to Carey lately?" Chiara asked unexpectedly.

"No," Dayna squeaked, then cleared her throat. "Not since yesterday. Why?"

Her tutor turned and gave Dayna a quizzical eye. "Are you catching a cold? No? Because I was wondering if he's accepted things, or if he's just getting angrier."

"He's been sleeping," Dayna said, managing to inject a sensible note into her voice. "Besides, it sounds as though Arlen and Jaime have a better chance if Sherra decides it's time to get them, instead of having Carey blundering around." There, a little disinformation, planted—and hopefully not overdone.

"I'm surprised you feel that way," Chiara said, and looked it. "I thought Jaime was a good friend of yours."

"She *is*," Dayna said stoutly. "Which is why I wish you people weren't taking such a damn long time to deal with this."

"If Jaime's headed for Arlen's hold, she won't get there till sometime tomorrow," Chiara assured her, pushing the notebook aside. "Even if a courier can make it here from Arlen's in one day, not everyone can—and Gacy said there were two men plus the wizard woman, and one horse for each. That means Jaime is riding double with one of them."

"How does he know that?" Dayna blurted. Carey certainly didn't.

Chiara wrinkled her nose. "I'm not sure I was supposed to let it slip." She hesitated and allowed, "Gacy ran a spell on the place while Carey was recovering from the door spell blast. The wizard was a woman, and she had two men with her—the ones who actually killed

Theo." Her expression turned grim. "Gacy said they roughed Jaime up a little, but it seemed she'd basically be safe during the trip to Arlen's."

"And no one told us?" Dayna asked incredulously.

Chiara's sensible response made Dayna all the more angry. "Why? Would it have really eased your mind? And Carey's been so...strange since he came back to Camolen. Unpredictable."

Dayna didn't know about that. She felt pretty sure she could predict exactly what Carey was going to do. And she was just as sure that she'd be in on it.

Dayna broke away from Chiara easily, when the woman sat down to review her brief notes about Dun Lady's Jess. She wasted no time in locating Mark, who was learning to fletch arrows, and gave him the nod which meant she'd been successful. He made a more or less graceful exit from his group and together they hurried to Carey's cell, a pleasant little room that offered luxury compared to the courier's quarters.

"You got them," he said with satisfaction as he saw her expression. They easily stepped through the barrier that was keyed only to him, and he closed the door on their secrets. Dayna answered his greeting by pulling her hand from her pocket, letting the stones and chain trickle through her fingers and into his grasp.

"I got something else, too," she told him. "Chiara told me Gacy ran some kind of spell at Theo's. He knows there were three of them, and three horses—so Jaime's riding double with one of them. They," and she nodded at the ceiling, indicating the upper rooms where the wizards and students worked, "figure it'll be tomorrow before they get to Arlen's place."

Carey nodded absently, his eyes narrowed as he worked out the distances for himself. "I'd have to agree with that," he said after a minute. "Good. If we get out of here tonight...riding in darkness, keeping the speed down for you guys...we can make it to a good base mid-day after tomorrow, and I'll trigger the recall from there."

"I don't get it," Mark muttered, shaking his head. At Carey's questioning look, he scowled. "I still can't understand why they took Jaime in the first place."

Dayna hesitated. She'd heard enough discussion in the work rooms to understand that any courier was at risk, considered a possible source of information. She'd also come to understand that Carey's line of dun horses was well known in the area.

And Mark, bless his soul, had as usual assumed that the rest of the world was as straightforward as he. The circuitous reasoning that allowed everyone else to conclude that Jaime had become a bargaining chip still escaped him, and for once she thought maybe his way was the best. "I can't understand it either," she said firmly, startling Carey—with whom she'd already discussed the possible dangers that might await Jaime. She gave him a quick, hard look, and he hid his surprise behind a shrug that said he, too, was at a loss to explain the abduction.

Not quite as naive as all that, for Mark narrowed his eyes, a doubting look that might actually have led to the truth if there hadn't been a knock at the door. Carey dropped the spell stones around his neck and tucked them out of sight, nodding to Dayna; she opened the door.

Sherra waited on the other side, her fine, thick hair in the kind of disarray that meant she'd been pushing it around during deep discussion. Dayna gulped inside, certain that her theft had been discovered—but Sherra had her mind on other things. "You're all here," she said in surprise. "Well, that makes things a little less complicated. Would you like to talk in the great room?"

"What?" Carey snorted. "You think I won't try something stupid?"

Irritation flickered across her face, but she mastered it. "If you're going to come, you'll have to stop sulking—or don't you *want* to know what's been happening?"

"*I* want to know," Mark volunteered. "I want to know if anybody's going to help Jaime."

"Then come along. I don't have much time, and my throat is dry." She gave the confining door spell a dismissive gesture and its flicker faded as she turned away down the hall. Dutifully they followed; they found the great room hollowly empty of its usual bustle and Dayna looked around in distrust.

"Most of them are out making preparations," Sherra said, helping herself to a tumbler of water from a half-full pitcher and sitting down at the closest bench. She stared at the water in an absent instant of concentration and the tumbler frosted up. Dayna's unexpected flicker of envy at the ease of the spellcasting made her blink, but she easily put it aside to concentrate on the conversation at hand—even if her gaze did return to that frosted tumbler a time or two.

Carey rounded the end of the table to sit opposite Sherra and then leaned over the wood, weight on his elbows, impatience on his face. "So things are happening," he said. "Are you going to tease us, or tell us about it?"

"We've decided it's not safe for the other wizards to be out on their own," Sherra said without preamble. "Theo wasn't the only wizard in trouble over these past few days, though no one else was killed. We're not even risking couriers to spread the news. Those who can handle mage-travel are already arriving. The others will be met by armed escort. This little hold was never meant to be a fortress, but it'll be protecting many frightened souls by tonight." She took a sip of water and met Carey's gaze—an even, hazel stare of judgment.

"You kept me here so I wouldn't stir up trouble for everyone else if I went Arlen," he said. "And now you've got trouble anyway, and Arlen is still a prisoner."

"That's right," Sherra said. "It was the decision that seemed most prudent. I'm not going to second-guess it."

"There's more," Mark said suddenly. "You didn't bring us here to tell us it was going to get crowded real soon now."

"No, I didn't." Sherra took a deep breath, and smoothed back some of her ruffled hair with one hand. "As Carey said, we've got the trouble anyway. There's no longer any point in delaying an approach to Arlen's hold. There are already Anfeald fighters gathering—the ones who have survived Calandre's people so far—and we're coordinating with the Lander peacekeepers. We'll be joining them by mage-travel when we're ready—probably late evening, two days from now. Early the next morning, we'll...well, for want of a better word, we'll attack."

"We?" Carey said pointedly.

"We, the wizards who can be spared from the work here," Sherra said, once more meeting his accusing stare with unruffled calm. "Wizards who are capable of mage-travel," she defined further. "We won't be carrying any baggage with us, Carey—that's the way it's got to be."

"*This* baggage happens to know Arlen's domain better than anyone else you can get," Carey responded heatedly. "If you're going to go after Calandre, you're going to need what I know."

"We're not going after Calandre."

"You're not?" Mark blurted in surprise. "Then you've confused the hell out of me."

"There's no point in going after her. She'll have plenty of advance warning—we assume she's intercepting at least half our messages, despite our precautions—and she'll have a retreat set up. We would need many more wizards than we'll have if we wanted to try a quarantine spell."

Dayna frowned. "Then...."

"You're going after Arlen," Carey said, relief showing in his eyes. He closed them briefly, took a deep breath, and sat back. "Even if you're doing it just to keep the spell from her, you're finally going to get him out of there."

Sherra's expression started out as stern and faded to sad; she shook her head. "I'm sorry we've given you cause to think like that. I've already told you she may very well have that world-travel spell already, and is simply trying to delay while she plays with it. She's risked everything for this, you realize. We may not even get our hands on her before we finish cleaning up her mess, but she'll be an outcast, nonetheless, and eventually, she *will* come to justice. But if she's able to run amok in other worlds, she just may get her hands on something that we can't deal with—and then, *she'll* have *us*. If our motivation was simply Calandre, it's still much to our advantage to stay here and work on the checkspell."

"You're going after Arlen," Dayna murmured to herself; it was *meant* to be to herself, though they all looked at her.

"Yes. We no longer have any reason not to try."

"Then let me come," Carey said fiercely. He reached over and intercepted her hand on the way to the cool tumbler, capturing it in a grasp that made her wince. "I can get in there and back out again before any of her guards even know someone's there. Hell, I can use that special recall—" she was shaking her head and his tone grew desperate. "Sherra, what have you got to *lose*? I can get him out!"

"I, too, know my way around that hold, Carey," Sherra said, gently disentangling her fingers. "And I can protect myself against the magic she's likely to throw my way. I can even protect Arlen. But I can't guarantee I can protect all three of us."

"I'm not asking for guarantees!" Carey cried, and slapped his hand down on the table in frustration, turning abruptly away from all of them.

Sherra's obvious sympathy did nothing to melt the resolve in her voice. "I've told you our plans in hopes that it will ease your mind. You'll return to the room for another day—until it's too late for you to rush in on horseback—and then you can join the rest of the locals in preparation for any physical attacks that might come this way. Not an unlikely prospect, given the wizards that will still be here." She shoved her tumbler into the middle of the table and stood, gesturing to the other end of the room where Gacy waited. "Now, I have plenty of work to get done. Gacy will escort you back to the room and reset the spell when you're ready. Wish us luck."

"You'd better believe it," Mark said fervently. He waited only until she was across the room, then gave Carey a little frown of puzzlement. "If it's too hard to magic along people who can help, and they won't get there any sooner anyway, why don't they just *ride* to Arlen's?"

Carey gave a snort of wry laughter. "Because they can't ride!"

Dayna nodded. "If they're good enough to mage-travel, they probably don't bother going long distances any other way."

"They sure don't," Carey agreed. "It's going to be a real surprise when they find out I've gotten there first."

"Do you still think we should do it?" Dayna frowned.

"Hell, yes," Carey responded without hesitation. "Whatever magic Sherra has, she can't duplicate that recall spell. Calandre's sure to have magical barriers in place, and Sherra's only option will be to try to chip a hole in them. The recall isn't going to have to batter its way through, because its origin is within the hold." His confidence faltered, and he scowled faintly. "If I understand it right, that is."

When he looked to Dayna for confirmation, she could only shrug. "I certainly haven't gotten into anything like that," she said. "Ask me for different colors of glow balls, why don't you."

"Well," he said, with renewed determination that dared them to gainsay him, "All I can do is get us set up, and then try it. But if we're going to make it, we've got to go tonight."

"You're forgetting the threshold spell," Dayna reminded him pointedly.

"The stone that keeps magic from acting on me will probably do the trick—it's a handy little stone. And if it doesn't," he smiled, a trifle too airily for her comfort, and she knew what was coming next—"that's where you come in. That spell has an on-off switch—you've seen it work. Surely you can figure out how to flip the switch."

She wondered if he would have spoken so offhandedly about on-off switches if he hadn't spent time on her own world. "Right," she said sourly. *Dayna the unwilling wizard.* The thing was, he was right. She had absorbed that much, whether her tutors realized it or not.

He shrugged. "The details plan themselves after that. We sneak into the stable, saddle up the horses I've already got picked out, and ride out."

"The gate," Mark reminded him.

"I don't think we'll have any problem," Carey asserted. "I doubt the guard's alerted to stop people who are going *out*, especially since Sherra thinks I'll be safely tucked away in that room. Otherwise, well...we'll have to handle it." He picked up Sherra's tumbler and sipped the cool water, pensive but apparently satisfied.

Much more satisfied, in fact, than Dayna herself. She stared at the strong lines of Carey's lean face and into his deep-set eyes, less shadowed than usual in this airy eating hall. "And then we ride for—how long? A day?"

"Day and a half, probably."

"A day and a half, until we reach some nice little spot that you think is a good defensible camp for us to wait in while you zap into Arlen's place and snatch up Arlen and Jaime."

His gaze moved back to her, a certain amount of amusement held therein. "Dayna, relax. I know just where the nice little spot is—and Calandre's people aren't that familiar with the area. It'll be a safe place to get our breath and decide our next move. *That's* going to depend on how much trouble Sherra's forces have stirred up—they'll probably be in the area soon after I get into the hold. We may even be able to count on them for help."

"*May*," Dayna snorted skeptically. At Carey's briefly rolled eyes of frustration, she said, "Don't give me that look—being aware of details is my strength, Chiara said so."

"Children," Mark murmured reprovingly, a comment so out of character that it did indeed shut them both up.

Carey eventually shrugged, a gesture of finality. "We'll make most of it up as we go along, I'm afraid. There's nothing I can do about that—except maybe get some more sleep so I'll be ready for whatever comes our way." He stood, and nodded to Gacy. "At least she stuck me in a room with a good bed," he added wryly, and strode to meet Gacy, his shoulders set with such determination that they would have clearly given him away had Sherra been there to see.

# 17

*It must be broken*, Jaime decided—not for the first time, as her fingers hovered over the bridge of her nose. She'd been breathing through her mouth for three days, barely able to eat the rough meal rations because of her tender mouth and lips. But for all their disregard, the wizard woman and her two cohorts had not offered to hurt her any more, either.

At first Jaime had hoped the woman, Willand, would provide sympathetic support, but she soon realized the woman's motives for stopping the beating at the cabin had nothing to do with *her*. Everything the woman did centered around whether it would improve her status in Calandre's eyes, and she had offered Jaime no favors, no conversation, and no hope. Jaime kept her conversation to nods and one word responses, trying to conceal her origins. *Marion, Ohio*. She had the feeling that information would give her much more attention than she wanted.

The travelers had broken camp extra early this morning, expecting to make Arlen's place by late afternoon. Jaime squinted as they broke out of a thick stretch of woods and into hot bright sunlight, and then, warned only by the shift of Willand's weight, she grabbed the scant security of the saddle cantle just as their horse shifted into a canter. She'd never ridden double before this trip—at least not in the back seat—and she'd discovered it was an entirely different experience, one that often left her mounted only by determination. Willand never bothered to tell her before a gait transition, or when the changeable terrain presented them with dips or fallen trees. Since her pride wouldn't allow her to clutch Willand's waist, Jaime had only the back of the saddle to cling to, and it wasn't always enough.

The prolonged canter took them first by well-tended vegetable gardens, and then a small group of livestock pens, while a craggy hill jutted up in the background and looked over it all. Not until they were slowing down in front of the abrupt hill did Jaime see the straight, man-made lines of Arlen's hold, a structure that melded with the rock and was clearly inside the hill as much as on top of it. Behind the hill, a green panorama of similar miniature mountains thrust up through tended pasture lands.

"Off," Willand said shortly, even as she stopped the horse. "And don't be stupid enough to run. You won't get far."

Jaime slid right off the horse's rump, preferring it to the clumsy process of dismounting without bumping into Willand. Don't be stupid enough to run, indeed, she sniffed internally, and indulged in an uncharacteristic daydream of a shrieking Willand on her runaway horse. As long as she was this close to Arlen, Jaime certainly wasn't going to run without trying to take him along. Especially not while Whiskers—whose real name she refused to remember—was still mounted.

Willand conferred briefly with her companions while Jaime stuck with her nonchalance, then dismounted to take Jaime's arm in a peremptory grip, steering her toward a dark spot at the base of the hill that turned out to be a cave-like doorway. Inside, Jaime shook off the clutching fingers, and Willand accepted the change by not acknowledging it. The rough walls of the entrance corridor soon turned smooth, and coolness enclosed them along with heavy stone. Willand led her briskly up a brief, single flight of steps, then down a hallway, and then up a series of short flights that wound around themselves with hallways branching off at each turn.

An unshuttered window graced the final landing, and Jaime got a glimpse of the gardens as they hurried by. This hall was short, and ended in a guarded door. Willand took her to the only other room off the hall, striding through the doorway with only the barest of pauses to knock.

"Ah, you've returned. What have you discovered?" The question came from a woman who didn't bother to turn around. She was of unimposing stature, a reed-thin woman whose robe fell unimpeded by curves of any sort. Her dark hair, thick and curly to the point of frizz, was winning its battle with the thong tied back at the base of her neck. Jaime was singularly unimpressed and had to remind herself that this was a woman who had the whole of Camolen swaying with the breeze of her whims.

"Nothing on the spell," Willand admitted without hesitation. "A few scribbled pages that looked like checkspell material, but I'm not sure it's worth much. I did bring back something else you might find useful."

At that Calandre turned, still holding the small book she'd been consulting, her carriage totally at odds with the cheerfully asymmetrical room. She turned out to be about Jaime's age—not so old for all the chaos she'd caused, at that. Her eyebrows, fine and set above angular features, rose at the sight of her captive. "Yes?"

"One of Arlen's couriers. She was on a run to Theo's; stumbled right into us. She was on one of Carey's duns, so I thought she might be of some use with Arlen."

Calandre eyed Jaime's face. "It looks like someone has already done some persuading."

"She tried to run," Willand said simply.

Calandre set the book down and carefully marked her place before closing it, and Jaime eyed her warily as the woman approached in a stalk that was all the more intimidating because it was obviously uncalculated. "What's your name?"

"Jaime," Jaime said in her best I'm-not-impressed voice, still trying to figure out the best strategy for staying alive.

"Well, Jaime, did you learn anything?"

"Only that I should have kicked Whisker's balls up to his throat before I ran," Jaime said perversely, knowing better. But Calandre seemed amused rather than annoyed, and Jaime gathered that she simply wasn't worth the effort of anger.

"So," she said. "You were one of the ones who got away. And now you're back again, finally to be of some use to us."

Jaime suddenly realized that Arlen certainly wouldn't have been the only person caught in Calandre's attack. "What happened to the others?" she asked warily.

"You mean the ones who had the courage to stay and fight?" *Unlike you*—unspoken words that stabbed her even though she hadn't even been there. "They died, of course. Very unfortunate; we could have used the leverage before this—in fact, we've been looking for someone like you."

"I wasn't here when you attacked," Jaime said in a low voice, still stinging over the implications in Calandre's words.

"Whatever," Calandre replied, obviously not believing her, and not caring, either. "Let's not waste any more time."

"Do you want her cleaned up before Arlen sees her?" Willand asked.

Calandre eyed Jaime's face and shook her head decisively. "A little dried blood will make our threat more immediate."

Jaime scowled. She'd tried to wash her face off in a stream the day before, but several of the cuts had opened again, and it was true she'd had another nosebleed.

"Try to maintain that expression, if you can," Calandre said lightly. "It will certainly have good effect on Arlen." Her face, all angles and hollow cheeks, held amusement, and Jaime closed her eyes and took a deep breath, reminding herself that this bizarre situation was as real and as serious as anything she'd ever done. It was *real*—and she was no longer Jaime Cabot, accomplished equestrian with her own sort of following, but Jaime Cabot, prisoner of some crazed wizard woman.

A *powerful* crazed wizard woman.

"Come along," Willand said in irritation, and Jaime opened her eyes to discover that Calandre had already gone out into the hall. She gave Willand a haughty look—she dared that much—and preceded her out of the room.

She'd wondered if there would be another disorienting trek through the innards of the stone structure, but Calandre was merely waiting for them at the guarded door. The guard stared curiously at Jaime, but looked quickly away when Calandre glanced at him. She pushed open the door and swept into the room, calling Arlen's name with the air of a long-awaited guest.

The room within was considerably more homey than the workroom, well-lit by the afternoon sun streaming in the window. Although the furnishings were simple and well-used, they had the look of cherished and comfortable things. Faded but still thick rugs covered the floor, books were scattered about with bookmarks trailing out of them, and one special chair seemed entirely devoted to embroidery work, the accouterments of which were spread out on the arms of the chair and the worn leather stool in front of it. A flash of movement caught her eye, and Jaime caught the tip of a cat's white tail as it disappeared under the chair.

"Still hiding from us?" Calandre asked, and Jaime thought she was talking to the cat until she saw that the woman was looking into a second room, her arms folded in front of her in a mannerism that only pressed the dark material against the boniness of her hips and collarbones. "Well, no matter. I've brought a visitor whom I think will interest you. You might even feel like talking."

"I doubt that." Arlen's voice was low and without strength, but still managed a matter-of-fact defiance. Calandre beckoned to Jaime, and she reluctantly moved up to stand in the doorway.

Arlen looked at her without recognition, and with the beginnings of a frown. Desperation led Jaime to offer, "I'm riding for Sherra now. Carey brought me there, and loaned me Lady."

Arlen's expression shifted rapidly through a maze of emotions and slid into deadpan even as Calandre lashed out and slapped Jaime resoundingly across the cheek. Jaime gasped as the blow rekindled all the sharp pains in her nose, and couldn't help the few tears that followed, fatigue and pain and fright bundled up into two trails of saltwater.

Calandre said coldly, "When I want to hear from you, it'll be screams of pain to make this annoying old wizard talk. Until then, keep your helpful little comments to yourself."

Willand offered tentatively, "At least we've confirmed it, Carey *is* back. So they really do have something to build the checkspell on."

Calandre seemed to relax out of her anger. "True enough, little Willand. It seems you brought me back more than you thought. I'll have to remember to question her before she's beyond speech. Unless, of course," she added, turning to Arlen with brows upraised, "you want to skip the torture and give me the spell now?"

Jaime stared at the man, knowing her life hinged on what he might say next—this man who had never met her and could not possibly care about her. He stared back, appraising her, warm brown eyes beneath disheveled long hair and gaunt, unshaven cheeks that were at obvious odds with the mustache that had been cultivated above a slight over-bite. Despite Calandre's words, he was certainly not old, or even past his mid-forties. She wondered if she really saw the tiny nod or only imagined it, and if that was really recognition of a sort in his gaze.

"Come, now, Arlen," Calandre said with a definite trace of irrita-tion. "You're already losing, bit by bit—you've even lost the outer room, and you're stuck in your own bathroom." For the first time, Jaime realized the seat Arlen perched on with such aplomb was a wooden toilet, and that there was a washbasin next to him, and that the brown thing peeking out into her field of view was a fancy wooden tub. "What next, you'll be stuck only on the toilet? Or perhaps you'll try to convert the spell to a personal shield. Very risky in your condition. And of course by then, your courier will be..." she glanced at Jaime, "a very unhappy woman."

"I can see that," Arlen replied acerbically. "You've obviously start-ed in on her already."

Calandre laughed. "Oh, no. I assure you, when my people use someone as leverage, there is no mistaking the results. This is just the side effect of her capture—I told you our little skirmish is spreading out beyond this ugly little stone den of yours."

"You're a disturbed woman, Calandre," Arlen murmured in a curi-ously detached voice.

"I *like* this place," Jaime dared to mutter.

"Yes, dear, you're very loyal," Calandre said. She held her elbows again, regarding Arlen with complete composure. "I might even give you the night to yourself; you can spend the hours looking forward to tomorrow."

*Bitch.* Jaime gave her an even stare, a complete bluff.

"You might not need it," Arlen said. "Give me a few minutes with her. Give me time to see what's been happening. I may decide there's no point in keeping the spell from you anymore."

"Very good. You said that with a straight face."

Arlen shrugged. "What can you lose, Calandre? If you're in luck she'll spend the time pleading with me to help her—as you can see, she's certainly not going to do that while you're here."

"Not today, anyway. However..." she glanced first at Willand and then over her shoulder at the guard. "You searched her for weapons or spell stones?"

Willand nodded with satisfaction. "She had a protection stone, that's all. And a small knife, of course, but Gerrant has that now."

"Well, then." Calandre gave Jaime another hard look. "Beg well, Jaime. Your future depends on it." She turned her back on them and marched out of the room, followed by Willand, who could not help a few doubting, backward glances.

Jaime couldn't believe it. "Just like that?" she asked incredulously.

"Nothing is ever *just like that*," Arlen said. "Now, tell me the things you think I most need to know."

Jaime hesitated. "What if she listens?"

"She can't, not in these rooms. Quickly, now, don't waste what little time we may have!" His tired voice slid into command mode and though it made her prickle, she balked no longer.

"I met Carey on a different world, my world. It's—well, it's too complicated to go into, but we ended up back here—three of us, and Carey and Jess. Carey gave Sherra the spell, and she's got everyone working on a check for it. I've been riding with her couriers to coordinate the whole thing, and I was on a run when Willand and her pals got me." She thought a moment and added reluctantly, "Carey wanted to come get you—he said something about a special recall—but Sherra wouldn't let him. She didn't want to set Calandre off. It looks like Calandre's out causing trouble anyway."

"Jess?" Arlen murmured, taking her news about the lack of forthcoming rescue with a thoughtful nod.

"Lady. The magic turned her into a woman on my world. She's a horse again, though—that's who I was riding. I sent her back to Sherra's, so they should be able to figure out I didn't just lose my way."

"I suppose that's how you got those battle scars. Willand and her errand boys wouldn't have liked that."

Jaime scowled, even though it hurt. "Willand. That woman belongs in a bad beach movie, damn perky little nose of hers. I wish it could feel like *mine* does right now."

"Yes, well...I'm afraid, my dear, that your nose may be the least of it before this is over."

"Is this where I'm supposed to beg?" Jaime asked, suddenly realizing how sick her stomach felt. "I've never done that before, but I think I could get real good at it."

Slowly, reluctantly, he shook his head. "I can be of no help to you. This is more important that either of us, although it must seem particularly unfair to you. At least *I* got myself into this mess. And you must know by now that there is very little chance of rescue from Sherra—not that I blame her. It's the right decision."

*Right.* "What...what do you think they'll do to me?" Jaime asked in a low voice. Something graphic, no doubt, something to make an impression on Arlen. Her imagination took over and ran, presenting her with scenes of torture that came straight from the Inquisition.

"Jaime, don't," Arlen said. "Listen to me. This won't go on for long—it may not happen at all. I haven't eaten in...well, a couple of days, now. I moved preserved rations up here the same day I sent Carey out, but I didn't plan on being closed in this long. I don't get much sleep—the guards all have orders to rouse me. Calandre is right when she says I won't be able to keep this up much longer."

"At least you chose the right room to defend," Jaime commented, trying hard for a lighter atmosphere.

Arlen smiled, a weary looking expression almost hidden in his scruffy beard. "When it first became obvious that no one was going to help—though Sherra did try at first, and Calandre was delighted to tell me Sherra couldn't get through her shields—I tied a second spell in with *my* shield spell. When it finally fails, I will die."

"But—" Jaime said, startled; then her protest died unvoiced, as she realized his genuine acceptance of such a fate. "I keep hearing about Ninth Level this and Ninth Level that, but no one's said anything about God. Do you have a god to pray to, Arlen?"

Arlen shook his head, brow creased, and Jaime suddenly realized that the word *god* had come out in English. "How can you have heaven without—"

"You didn't change his mind, did you?" Calandre said from just inside the big room. "I didn't think you would—but I can be as indulgent as the next person, when I feel like it."

Jaime gave Arlen a searching look, trying to find that which had sustained him through his harrowing imprisonment—something that she could use for herself. He gave her a sad smile, and she said, "I don't think I'll be very good at this, Arlen. Don't hold it against me if I *do* try to change your mind, later."

"No," he said simply. "I won't."

The sudden three-tiered call of a morning owl brought Carey out of his thoughts and he glanced through the deep gray light of dawn to the indistinct figures who followed him through this lightly wooded area. They still panted after the ascent up the steep, shaley hill that loomed over the dry riverbed, but no one's saddle was sneaking backwards, and the horses still looked good.

At first he'd chafed at the way Mark and Dayna slowed him, resenting every extra moment between this one and the one in which he planned to trigger the special recall, but as the miles passed and neither of his neophyte riders ventured a complaint, the uncharitable thoughts faded. They were doing their best, and he'd be foolish to push them so hard that they had nothing left when he needed back-up in the little hollow he'd chosen for their camp.

Their departure had been straightforward, if not as simple as Carey had hoped. With most of the hold occupants busy in the village and many of the foot soldiers escorting slow-moving wizards around, he had casually and without ceremony walked through the threshold spell that was supposed to keep him in the room. The three conspirators had armed themselves with food pilfered from the kitchen and walked quietly to the barn. The horses were snorty and curious about the late night activity but ultimately accepting; the trio left the barn with nary a wayward whinny, and with three of Sherra's precious horses and Lady.

It was the gate that had almost tripped them up. The guard had turned out to be a man new enough to the post that he was still looking for excuses to use his authority, such as it was, and he seemed almost eager for them to create a disturbance.

Katrie had appeared to ease the way for them. Katrie, whom Jaime had first fought, and then gained as a friend—and who knew who Carey was, and where he should have been. Out and about on her own business, she was drawn to the commotion in front of the closed gate. In a brightly stitched, suspiciously rumpled tunic, still hand in hand with a man who was obviously smitten by her, she told the troublesome guard that Carey, his two friends, and his extra horse were known to her and were classed as good folk, not to be harassed. She held Carey's eye while the disgruntled man went to open the heavy gate, and said evenly, "Just bring her back."

For that role in events, Carey had no doubt there would be a price—and that she would face it head on. It was a gift he accepted without guilt or hesitation, and now he wondered if he should have asked her to join them despite the delay it would have caused. Instead, he had two earnest but out-classed and tired friends from another world.

A chorus of trilling birds had joined the morning owl, and Carey gave another look over his shoulder. This was their second dawn of summer-heat travel and about time to call it quits for a few hours, so they would be well rested—or as close to it as they could get—for the final approach to the hollow. Dayna was right behind him on the little smooth-gaited bay Mark had quickly labeled Fahrvegnügan, a name that seemed to amuse Mark and made Dayna give him one of her *grow up* looks. Mark was on a rangy, cold-backed gray who would cheerfully ignore the banging his rider might inflict upon him while just as cheerfully barging through, past and over any obstacles in his path. Carey rode the big black horse he'd come to know fairly well, and following him on a loose lead line was Dun Lady's Jess—the one horse who'd already taken the stairway in the hold.

A shift of his weight and the gelding stopped, patiently mouthing the bit while Carey waited for the others to draw abreast. "We'll hit some thicker woods in half an hour or so," he said, prompting them both to check their watches. "As soon as we do, we'll eat a bite and grab some sleep. After that, it's only another couple hours to the hollow I was talking about. You two holding up all right?"

Mark groaned expressively in response, but Dayna had the same look she'd kept during their interminable run from the pickup truck toward Sherra's—drawn, tired, and not about to admit it. Well, a couple hours sleep would do her some good—and after he'd invoked the recall, she'd have all the time it took him to return to the hollow by horseback. It would have to be enough.

He touched the gelding with his calves and turned toward the distant hollow.

# 18

"You want me to *what?*" Jaime stared at Willand, a blunt and defiant expression.

Willand studied her long fingernails in a posture of boredom. "I'm quite certain you heard me the first time, but I'll repeat it anyway. Take off your clothes."

Jaime looked at Arlen, a request for guidance. He returned a grave countenance, one that told her there would be no easy answers here. They'd had a virtually sleepless night during which they exchanged bits and pieces of their lives with one another, for Calandre had returned only long enough to tell them they would have the benefit of one another's company for the duration—a more convenient arrangement than ferrying Jaime from place to place. The guard's replacement had carried up a breakfast meal that was so good Jaime knew it had to have been solely for Arlen's benefit. She'd tried to refuse it, but he wouldn't let her and she hadn't argued with him; it would have been a pointless gesture to go hungry.

Now she was suddenly afraid that breakfast would stage a reappearance. She vowed she would at least wait until Willand was within range, and clamped her jaw on the taste of bile etching at the back of her tongue.

"You know," Willand said suddenly, shooting her a dangerous look, there and then gone again as she continued to contemplate her manicure, "this can be a lot worse than I had planned. It's up to you."

Jaime's hands strayed to her tunic, nervously smoothing the close-ly woven material and running over the belt-loops of her culturally alien breeches beneath. Another glance at Arlen showed he'd deliber-ately turned his back. She closed her eyes, took a deep breath, and shrugged the tunic over her head, dropping it on top of the knee-high riding boots she'd removed the evening before. Her thin linen camisole offered little coverage, but suddenly she felt very attached to it.

"Oh, be reasonable, Arlen. We knew you'd try this, the *I'm not watching* ploy. Do you think you can not listen as well? You'd better be listening now, because I'm telling you that if you don't pay proper attention, we'll just kill her right now."

*Blonde beach bimbo*, Jaime thought in amazement, wondering how such a thoroughly depraved person could be hidden behind that face, and how she ever could have missed it at first glance.

"You're going to kill her anyway, in the end," Arlen said heavily, still facing away from them. Jaime's hands hesitated by the snap of her breeches, and Willand made an imperious gesture that commanded her to wait until this little discussion was over.

"Maybe we'll kill her, maybe we won't. The point is, unless you participate I'll just do it right now. After all, as long as she's alive, there's some chance you might be able to save her—that's worth play-ing the game, don't you think?"

"I don't play games, Willand, especially not the kind of games Calandre is fond of. But...Jaime, it's up to you." He turned his head ever so slightly, just enough to let her know he was waiting for a reply. "If it helps, you should know that this is no idle threat. They won't bother to keep you alive if you're of no use to them." His voice sound-ed tired, the weariness of someone who has already seen too much.

Great choice, Jaime thought. Die now, or endure torture and then probably die later anyway. Her trembling hands found the fingered the snap at her waist and she said, "I'm sorry, Arlen, but I'm not ready to give up yet." *I'm sorry, but you're going to have to watch this.*

He turned around as the breeches slid past her hips and down to the floor. She stepped out of them and deliberately lay them on top of the tunic, her eyes on Arlen's and finding if she had that compassionate dark gaze to look into, she had the strength to pull the soft linen under-shirt over her head and to wiggle out of her briefs as well. And then she just stood there, looking at him, and gratified to discover there was approval there—not in what she was, the sturdy, well-shaped rider's body she had revealed, but in *who* she was, and in who she'd just chosen to be.

Willand relaxed noticeably, in complete control of them again. In swift, graceful gestures, she touched Jaime's wrists, biceps and ankles, and Jaime's already racing pulse edged into panic as invisible manacles closed around her limbs, trapping her upright at the edge of the thick worn rug; she put her weight against the restraints at her wrists and felt no give at all. She would stand whether she chose to or not. This was *happening*, it was real, it was—

*Agony.* Willand's light touch, tracing lines of fire from the notch of her throat down between her breasts and all the way past her navel. Jaime wrenched away from her, screaming as much from surprise as the pain. Willand's finger lost contact, the pain faded, and Jaime found she was choking on breakfast, gasping and spitting, trying to clear her mouth so she could breath. She had only enough time for the far too brief satisfaction of seeing Willand's fouled dress before that neat, ladylike finger touched her again, and the world disappeared into vision grayed by the force of her screaming as lines of fire traced inti-mate routes across her body.

"Jaime."

She became aware of herself again, of the slightly rough fabric against her hypersensitive skin. Delicate puffs of breath against her eyelids startled her, and the couch stirred with light footfalls of some creature running away. She was, she realized, still unclothed, but at the moment it didn't seem to matter much.

"Jaime." A quiet voice. Tired. Concerned.

Her mouth was dry and tasted vile. "That bitch," she muttered, words that barely made it into actual sound.

Relief and some amusement touched the voice that responded. "So you told her, and more than once."

She was on the couch, that's where, and that meant her clothes were on the floor next to her dangling arm. She groped for them, the arm strangely lifeless, her eyes not quite yet willing to open and face what might be waiting for her. Ah, that felt like her underwear, all right.

"She's gone. I don't think she'll be back for a while. From what I could gather, there are forces moving in around the hold—still some distance out, but obviously readying for approach."

"And suddenly I'm not that important any more," Jaime said resentfully, finally opening her eyes as she sat up and slowly, like a creaky old woman, fumbled to get her underwear over her feet. There was no separate ache or pain to plague her, but a general malaise that gripped each and every part of her body, echoes of the torment Willand had visited upon her. Jaime got herself dressed as far as the tunic, and then just sat there, worn and directionless, trying to evade the forever crystalline memories of her torture.

"Would you like a drink?" Arlen asked.

She glanced at him. He sat on his chosen throne, resting his chin in his palm, and she searched his expression for any taint of judgment or censure at the way she'd reacted to Willand's games. She didn't think she saw any, unless it was a reflection of her own disappointment in herself. She hadn't thought she'd buckle so easily, that she wouldn't have any resistance at all.

"It's a good thing I *didn't* have any secrets they wanted," she said bitterly, self-reproachfully.

"Oh, Jaime, don't start down that road," Arlen said in gentle admonishment. "Why do you think I've locked myself in my own bathroom? It's because I know better than to think I could endure what you've been through and not tell every secret I ever knew. Now, how about that water?"

Water. It suddenly had a blissful sound to it. "You have some I could get to?" she asked hopefully, looking at the faint spell-shimmer around the edges of the bathroom door.

"Rainwater," he said. "It hasn't been strained, but it hasn't killed the cat yet—or me. Check out the window."

That's what had been so delicately sniffing at her face. "A cat," she said. "I probably scared it worse than it scared me."

"If she wasn't a spooky little thing, she'd never have lived through Calandre's invasion," Arlen said. "She'll be back."

Jaime stood on wooden feet, not particularly concerned about her nearly naked lower half. Being watched during torture was a quick road to intimacy, that was for sure. She made it to the window and leaned out. There, on the wide ledge that blended into the rock on the side of the hill, was the cat—a little black and white creature who stared at her with wide eyes, poised to dart away at any sudden move. On the other side of the cat was a small catch basin with a tile pipe that snaked down from the top of the hill, perched to deliver the rain. Outside the bathroom there was a similar arrangement, except the tile ran right into the room.

"Excuse me, kitty," she said with perfect sincerity, expecting the creature to bolt at her voice. But the cat stood and primly raised its tail, stalking away from the basin as though Jaime had said something rude. Jaime reached for the basin's dipper and with only a rudimentary check for dead bugs, drank her fill. It was warm, it had a funny taste of minerals, and it was the most wonderful water in the world. She splashed another dipper on her face and carefully scrubbed her hands over it, removing what she could of dried tears and other residue from the day's activity. Then she turned around and leaned back against the windowsill, groaning, "Oh, I'm so glad that was there."

"So am I," Arlen said as she paced back to the couch and retrieved her breeches. After she had wiggled into them, she took another look at her boots and decided to put them on. If Willand came back, it would take all the longer to undress again. With deliberate movements, she worked the calf-snugging field boots onto each foot, so absorbed in the simple task that when Arlen spoke again, it startled her. "Tell me, Jaime, does your world have people such as Calandre?"

After a moment, she said, "Too many of them. Of course, they don't have magic to play with. They have to make do with guns and bombs and blind political fervor." Jaime returned to the window, this time looking past the ledge. The view was that of the road she'd come in on and bright green spots of garden punctuating dusty paddocks and lighter green pastures, and she stared at it for quite some time as late afternoon slid into early evening. She thought of the comfortable old farmhouse, and of Keg, who was waiting for them to return, and of a barnful of horses that needed to be fed and exercised, and she forced her thoughts in new directions to wonder at how she'd fit so easily into Camolen life. And finally, when she realized her few moments at the window had turned into many more, she turned back to Arlen and asked, "How can so many things be the same, Arlen? How can you have people, and horses, and carrots and tomatoes, along with the Calandres?"

"That," he responded, coming to the limits of his shield so he could see her as he spoke, "is something I'd hoped to be able to look into myself."

Jaime returned to him, and found she had to look up to find his eyes. She said, "Tell me it's worth it, Arlen. Tell me that all of Carey's effort, and Jess' heartbreak, and Eric's death, and my—" and she couldn't go on then, had to look down and work out the tremendous lump that filled her throat. Arlen's voice, as strong and intent as if he *hadn't* spent the last months in isolation, brought her gaze back up again.

"I would obliterate the existence of that spell in a moment, if I could," he said. "I would undo the scores of small decisions that led Calandre down her path, and Carey down the one that led to you. But even magic doesn't have that power...and the only magic I have left is the spell that will trigger my death."

Jaime shuddered. She wished she could reach through his barrier and hold him, just because they both needed it so badly—and because her friend Jess had taught her to act on such impulses when they hit, and not shove them away under the veneer of propriety. Unable to breech the shield, she merely hugged herself, which was more of retreat than a comfort.

"Jaime," he said, and there was such an odd note in his voice that she instantly feared his shield was failing, and that he, therefore, was about to die, but his eyes were focused beyond her, and she jerked around to see what he was looking at.

Nothing. A quick glance showed her his attention had not faltered, and she gave it another try. Then, somewhere between one blink and the next, the empty space in the middle of the chairs was full of dun and black movement, pungent horseflesh, and the startled cry and rush of the guard. The needlework and its chair went tumbling backward, driven by the same flashing black leg that collided with the astonished guard and smashed him back against the wall.

*Carey—recall—don't just stand here gawking* and Jaime rushed in to take Lady's reins, pulling her out of the melee so Carey could concentrate on the panicked gelding. She ended up next to the guard whom she unceremoniously kicked in the stomach with her booted foot, turning his efforts to rise into retching instead. She wrenched his short curved sword away as Lady dragged her backwards, and managed to position herself and the snorting dun in the doorway where the guard could not get past them to run for help—although he was still panting on the floor, and Jaime was amazed how her surge of hope had given her the strength for that kick, pushing her through the aftereffects of Willand's sadism.

The black's hooves beat a nervous tattoo on the floor when Carey finally coerced him into standing in one spot, and the courier turned his attention on the guard and his efforts to crawl inconspicuously away. He put his foot firmly between the man's shoulder blades and shoved him back to the floor. "Stay put," Carey commanded. "We don't want you and we don't care about you—but if we have to worry about you, that'll change."

"She'll kill me," the man groaned indistinctly, his words distorted by the hard stone against his cheek.

"She probably will," Carey agreed coldly. "You'll have your chance to run in a few minutes. Jaime—" he looked at her for the first time, and stopped short, staring at her face; it took obvious effort to refocus his attention. "Where's Arlen?"

"On the toilet," she said without thinking, and then blurted, "I mean—"

A laugh from the small enspelled room cut her off, and Carey turned with relief to the source. "Arlen—stand *still!*" The last was to the gelding, who'd taken advantage of Carey's inattention to jerk him around; Carey gave the reins a retaliatory yank and said, "C'mon, Arlen, we've got to get started. I thought this gelding would be all right for the stairs but I also think I blew his puny mind with the recall."

Then he craned his neck to try to see his friend, and added, "Are you all right? Can you manage?"

"I'll manage," Arlen assured him, although Jaime thought the strength in his voice was a ruse. "But there's the small matter of a death spell that's linked to the shielding on this room. It'll take a minute or two to get it untangled so I can get out of here without triggering my own demise."

Carey rolled his eyes. "*Hurry*," he urged, and turned immediately to Jaime. "Here's the plan, Jay," he told her, talking fast. "Lady's been down these stairs before, and I think the gelding will follow, if he can find his brain before Arlen gets out of the bathroom. We're counting on surprise—they may know someone jumped in here, but they won't be expecting two horses on the top floor of the hold. We're going to do our best to just plow through them. Sherra's got forces gathering a mile or so out, and if they're enough of a distraction, we may just be able to keep on plowing, all the way out. Oh, yeah—this may help." He reached into the black's saddlebags, a bobbing target on restless haunches, and stretched to hand her a gun while the gelding pulled him the other way.

A gun. For a moment Jaime just stared, remembering the things Carey had said about keeping the knowledge of such things from this world. Then she took it, a little ashamed of the relief she felt when its cool metal filled her hand.

"There are five bullets," Carey said evenly, catching her eye to make sure she was really hearing him. "Don't use them unless they can do some good."

She thrust the gun into the deep pocket of her tunic, and then divested the guard of his sword sheath and belt, which she had to wrap twice around her own waist before she could stow the weapon. When she looked up, Arlen was in the room, leaning against the back of the one chair that was still standing.

"Let's go," he said simply.

Carey had only one hand free; he used it to grip Arlen's upper arm in a tight contact that lasted only a second, his face filled with the expression of a thousand words that wouldn't quite make it to his tongue.

"I know, Carey," Arlen said. "I know."

Carey cleared his throat and said, "Mount up. I'll be behind you in a moment; don't worry about handling the horse."

Jaime gathered Lady's reins and swung up into the saddle, feeling a definite wrongness in being mounted up in this room at the uppermost level of a stone hold. The stirrups were adjusted for Carey and too long for her; she slung them crossways in front of her to keep them from banging around and looked to Carey. He was just settling himself behind Arlen on the gelding—a much stouter horse than Lady even if he had left his brains somewhere else, as evidenced by his continued capers. Carey reached around Arlen to take the reins, supporting his friend with the cage of his arms.

Then there were voices and footsteps in the stairwell, and Carey nodded to her. "Plow through 'em," he repeated grimly.

Desperately wishing for the feel of the gun but not daring only one hand on the reins, Jaime gave Lady a firm and sudden squeeze that sent the dun into a startled bold trot down the hall. A strong, double half-halt to gather the dun's haunches beneath her, to take her into the turn of the stairs balanced and paying absolute attention, and they were doing it, they were lurching and slithering down stairs too narrow for hooves to find good purchase, making 180° turns in virtual pirouettes while the black followed, sloppily, with much snorted objection and Carey's blistering commentary—"That was my *knee*, burn you!"—a commotion loud enough that it almost overwhelmed the startled oath of the young wizard coming to check on Carey's magical shout of arrival.

"Guards!" the man cried down the stairwell, frantically trying to get out of the way. Jaime rode him down without a second thought, feeling Lady's slight stumble over top of him, thinking only of the fact that there were others still below. With a raw shout of encouragement, she urged the dun mare downward, trying not to think about what would meet them when they got there.

# 19

Lady felt the soft flesh beneath her hooves and quailed inside, ever fearful of uneven footing. She remembered the stairs with Carey—but she remembered them at a much slower pace, and the speed to which Jaime urged her on brought out the sweat of fear on her neck, lathered with the rub of the reins. "Come, Lady," Jaime said, a firm encouragement not at all like Carey's wooing tone. But Lady gathered herself to it, and ignored the slips and twists of her feet against carved stone until they were finally on level ground.

The black surged ahead of her then, clearing the way with his bulk and scattering men and women like poorly stacked wood. Jaime abandoned her tightly controlled riding and turned Lady's head loose, offering one solid thump of her legs to release the speed that waited. Lady knew the way from here, knew how the hall opened up into the stable that was built at the bottom of the hill. She crowded up against the black's hindquarters, ignoring the tightly tucked tail of his protest.

Behind them the shouting grew, and a wild arrow clattered against the ceiling above them, scaring Jaime and Lady both so that their balance of *togetherness* was lost and Lady's leg skidded out in front of her; Jaime clutched mane and left the reins alone and Lady caught herself, feeling the wrongness in her leg and forgetting it just as quickly as they came to the closed stable door and she slid right into the gelding. Her head knocked Carey out of the saddle and he grabbed it on the way

down, using her to control his fall. He landed on his feet, lurching for
the door and slamming it aside to leave nothing before them but an
empty road. The black wasted no time, bounding forward like a racer
at the start while Arlen clutched his mane and fumbled for the reins, an
insignificant passenger on the back of power and fear.

"Carey!" Jaime shouted, extending her hand, sticking her foot out
while she pulled hard at Lady's mane to keep her seat. Carey grabbed
her hand and used the foot for a step, settling down on Lady's loins.

"Go," he shouted, as sharp fire raked across Lady's thigh, an arrow
skimming through her flesh. She bolted forward, trying to adjust to the
extra weight and floundering awkwardly while missiles flew around
them and two pairs of legs both tried to steady her and urge her on.
Then she caught her stride, and the shouts fell away behind them along
with the arrows.

The black should have been too far ahead to catch, but he loomed
suddenly in her vision, and Jaime's hands quivered their uncertainty
through to the bit as the three men blocking their way became clear.
With great effort Lady abandoned her speed, and when Carey slid off
to the side of her rump, she stopped short, confused. He stood beside
her, his feet planted wide and his hands out straight in front of him,
holding an acrid smell that suddenly exploded.

Lady exploded, too, rearing and coming out of it ready to bolt;
Jaime caught her with a rein that doubled her back in a tight circle, a
circle she rabbited around while Carey stood steadily, his arms jerking
up in synchronization with his noise. Then he ran for the gelding, who
stood trembling and riveted, refusing to move even after Carey was up
and kicking. Jaime released the rein and Lady shot out in front of them,
waking the gelding and leading him away from bedlam at her top speed.

After a moment Jaime steadied her to a more deliberate pace, and
the gelding drew aside them. Carey motioned for Jaime to follow and
took the gelding off the road, guiding them first through plowed garden
land and then into sparse woods, where they hit a path Lady knew. She
followed its contours with confidence, losing some of her alarm and
running now for Carey and Jaime, and running because she could and
her spirit swelled when she was asked to do so, even when it was along
a path that was meant for an even trot, even as her muscles took the fire

from her lungs and held it into themselves. In front of her, the gelding floundered, unfamiliar with the path and burdened by two. Jaime shouted ahead and Carey only shook his head, moving as close to the edge of the path as he could get, and yelling back over his shoulder, "*Run*, Lady!"

Her ears flicked up and Lady took the lead in the failing daylight, guiding them over deadfalls, splashing shallow creek water high with her passage, settling into a steady pace—her sense of self-preservation lost to her courage. When she topped the shallow rise and found two men with shiny blades blocking the way to the tiny clearing in the rock-walled basin beyond, Lady never faltered, but charged by them, ignoring Jaime's cry and thundering down between rock formations to the hollow, where she fought with Jaime over stopping.

People rushed at them; Lady vaguely recognized Dayna and Mark and ignored their fuss and holler of greeting, the way they bumped her as Jaime slid off her back to embrace them, her own stumble as she suddenly felt her lameness. She struggled to make sense of this wrongness in her front leg; it mixed with anger at being hampered and she tried to jerk the reins away from Jaime, utterly unappeased by the soothing noises everyone suddenly made at her.

"*Down*, Lady," Carey said, one of her Words but not one she was willing to obey, not now, and she thrashed at the end of the reins—finding in the mindless struggle a relief from the stresses that had driven her there, too full of the run to react any other way. Dragging Jaime with her, she careened off one of the jutting rock formations, landing wrong on the leg that suddenly betrayed her, taking her down with its failure.

Instantly, Carey was on her, sitting on her neck up close to her head; so encumbered, she was helpless to rise. She flailed angrily about, her legs scrabbling for purchase they couldn't find. Carey stayed with her, murmuring desperate pleas until at last she needed breath and lay still, her lungs heaving, her body momentarily stilled, and her brain reaching for that small numb corner that lured her with its understanding of things human.

"By all the hells," Carey said wearily, kneeling on Lady's neck. "Horses can be so *stupid* sometimes."

"It's just the same spirit that got her here," Jaime snapped. She rubbed the stinging on her thigh and looked down, astonished, when her hand smeared across warm slickness. That last man with his sword, she realized in amazement, and had a brief disagreement with her body about fainting when she saw the surgically neat edges of the shallow wound—and just as quickly decided it was a hundred times better than Willand's way.

"Back off!" Mark yelled suddenly, staring up at one of the schist outcrops that surrounded them. "Be patient, why don't you? We're not going anywhere!" The audacity of the demand either struck a chord or was simply confusing; the blond head that had crept up to survey them withdrew, but Mark stepped back next to one of the hollow's few trees to stand watch, leaving the refugees to Dayna. "They showed up right after you left, Carey. They've been harassing us ever since—figured we were up to something, I guess."

"They can see most of this hollow from up there," Carey told him, rubbing his face against the fabric of his sleeve, clearing the sweat that dripped despite the chill of advancing darkness. As one, they looked around the level-floored basin, a refuge that had suddenly become a stage. Except for the few trees that had somehow found a roothold in the rocky ground, there was no cover, and the vertical rock walls, though varied in length and filled with insignificant nooks and crannies, offered no quiet escapes. Carey nodded at the indented finger of space behind him, a niche that might have been a cave if the angled overhang of rock hadn't found ground so quickly. "Most of this hollow, that is, except for this back corner, where I am. To see this, they have to come out on that point, where they're just as vulnerable as we are." In unspoken accord, Jaime, Arlen, and Dayna moved in behind him, out of sight, cautious of Lady's apparent acquiescence. Arlen sat down on the rocky ground with a sudden thump, looking as dazed and half-crazed as the mare.

"What now?" Dayna asked impatiently. "I told you we'd get to these little details sooner or later."

"I don't know," Carey admitted candidly. "I'd hoped to run across some sign of Sherra's people by now. But I don't even know what direction to look."

"I don't know, either, but they're here," Jaime offered. "Arlen said— Arlen!"

Arlen was tipping, tipping over, and Jaime lunged for him just in time to soften his landing. "He needs something to eat," she said with worry.

"We brought—" Dayna started, then flattened herself against the rock wall behind them, eyes wide at the re-emergence of Lady's spirit. The small pocket in which they stood seemed suddenly like a trap as Lady fought Carey's weight on her neck, throwing him off and into the other three, bringing them all tumbling down. Jaime helped push Carey to his feet and he dove in after the reins even as Lady was on her way up; they battled each other, and Jaime tried to protect Arlen, cringing each time Lady's injured leg hit stone.

"She'll ruin herself!" Jaime shouted at him, harsh and desperate— and then thinking only of the dark looming bulk of Lady as the struggle grew precariously close.

"Stop it!" Dayna screamed at them, shoved up against the rock. Eyes closed tight, hands clenched into fists at her sides, she shouted it again. "Stop it! You're not a stupid horse, you're Jess! You're Jess!"

Omigod, Jaime thought, feeling the stir of magic. She knew, suddenly, what Dayna was trying to do, and she knew she should stop it, knew it was too much magic for the unwilling neophyte wizard to handle, and that Arlen, although he was stirring, was not focused enough to be of help.

But the part of her that longed for Jess' safety kept her still, crouched over Arlen, eyes riveted on Lady as she flung Carey into a tree and then had to battle the leverage he gained by taking a half-wrap of the reins around its trunk. It was a strange montage of flying hooves and whipping mane, of the thick feel of magic, of Carey's shouted protests and equine grunts of effort and anger that suddenly turned into a human cry of fear and pain. Carey flew backwards, the empty bridle smacking him on the chest as he landed hard. Unmindful of the impact, he immediately got to his knees and crawled to the dazed creature before him: Jess, tangled in a dun horse's gear, disoriented and bewildered, whimpering quietly in the sudden silence. Magic still swirled thick in the air, poised to strike if Dayna lost control, but it was a danger Jaime shoved far back in her mind as she watched Carey take Jess into his arms and whisper reassurance into the tangled fall of hair that covered most of her face. For that moment the world was still, letting them focus on the return of one lost. And then its dangers closed back around them, fast and furious.

One look at Dayna and Jaime's hand clutched Arlen's bony shoulder, shaking him a little as she directed his attention to Dayna. "Never mind the fainting, Arlen—help Dayna let go of the magic!" And then she left him, knowing that if the magic backlashed, it backlashed, and there was nothing more she could do about it. She headed for the open, and the saddles of the two horses that stood hobbled in the center of the hollow. They weren't far, and those blankets would be much drier than the one Lady had been wearing until a moment before. Single-minded in purpose, Jaime jumped at Mark's cry of warning, heard the twang of his bowstring, and ran, snatching the blanket up with such speed that she was halfway back to the safe area before she heard the sickening thump of deadweight meat and bone hitting the ground behind her.

"You dumb son of a bitch!" Mark hollered, half to the dead man and half to his quickly retreating friend. "Leave us alone!"

"Come out where I can see you, then," the remaining fighter yelled back. "I won't hurt you. I just want to keep an eye on you!"

"Go fry!" Mark fired back, a mild curse he'd picked up since his arrival in Camolen.

By then Jaime was back in the pocket, where the magic swirled its thickest but seemed, she thought, less than it had been. She handed the blanket to Carey—dropped it on him, actually, and then dropped herself to the ground as well, suddenly feeling dazed and lightheaded, and thinking in abrupt revelation that her baby brother had just killed a man. She sat with her head between her knees for the moments that the magic took to fade away, and then reached a little further inside herself, finding, somehow, the strength for practicalities. Arlen's loud and relieved sigh was, for the moment, the only sound in the magic-shocked air.

Jaime lifted her head and discovered that the late evening light had finished slipping away, completely shadowing Carey's eyes; she could gain no clues from them. "How is she?" she asked, taking a quick look around to see that Dayna and Arlen sat quietly against the rock wall behind them, and finding the flash of Mark's wristwatch in the moonlight out in the center of the hollow. The black gelding had joined the two tied horses and waited with his head hanging, the reins trailing, for someone to care for him.

"All right, I think," Carey responded. "Confused. Worn out and shook up, like the rest of us. I don't know about that leg—arm—yet."

The dark huddle of blanket stirred, and with characteristic candidness, Jess said, "My arm hurts and I'm sitting on a stone. But I don't want Carey to stop holding me."

Carey gave a short laugh, one that was tinged with emotion—the disbelieving relief of a man who can't really comprehend he's gotten something he wanted so very badly. "Jess, braveheart, I've got a stone under my butt as well. If I promise you can spend the entire night in these tired arms, can we move?"

Jaime didn't hear a reply, but there must have been one; Carey kissed the disheveled hair that covered Jess' forehead and slowly unkinked his body to stand, carefully helping Jess to her feet and tucking the blanket around her when it threatened to slide off her shoulders.

"Clothes," Jaime said. "You need something to wear." Gruesomely, her mind latched on to the thought of the dead man, and then wouldn't let go. "I'll get something," she offered, and pulled herself to her feet, suddenly beset by all the pains her body owed her, the slashed thigh and the worn muscles and even the incredible ache from the afternoon's session with Willand. She stifled a useless groan and moved off to the distasteful task of disrobing a body, hoping at least some of the clothes would fit.

"Details," Dayna said, a still small figure against the lighter colored rock. "Food. The horses. And then there's the small matter of getting out of here before that guy gets reinforcements."

"Run away," Mark's voice agreed, softly but wholeheartedly.

Jaime struggled with the man's shirt, trying to work uncooperative arms through the sleeves as she pulled it over his head; she finally realized the arrow pinned the material to one of the arms, and she almost broke it off before it occurred to her that they might need all the ammunition they could get in order to make it out of the hollow. She gave it a pull, surprised by the resistance.

In the end she had to brace her feet against the limb and put her weight against it, and the arm finally let go of the arrow with a wet sound. By then Dayna was up and moving slowly among the horses, tying the black gelding, pulling off his saddle and letting it lay where it fell as she sloshed water into her hand for him. They finished their separate tasks and met in the middle of the hollow, Jaime's arms as full of clothes as Dayna's were with saddlebags, and together they stumbled back to the small sanctuary against the rock. Mark, moving quietly, met them there.

"I don't think he'll bother with us until daylight," he said. "Hell, he'll see us if we try to leave—what else does he have to care about?" Then his teeth flashed a brief smile against the darkness. "Hey, Jess, welcome back."

"Yes," she said.

Wordlessly, Jaime handed Mark his arrow. Then she turned to Jess, who had moved, with Carey, to the back of the pocket. "C'mon, Jess, let's see what we can do with these."

Jess dropped the blanket and stepped forward; Carey groaned and put his hand over his eyes, while Dayna said, "Jess, I thought we told you—"

"Oh," she said, looking down at herself. "That's right. No breasts. Well, don't look, then."

Arlen snorted, a tired but amused sound. "So this is the woman you found inside The Dun's daughter. Beguiling."

"How—" Carey started, then said, "Ah. Jaime told you. You were together long enough for that, then. You'll have to tell me what you two've been up to, Arlen."

Jaime stopped short, a cold feeling freezing her hands as they shook out the shirt for Jess. "Nothing, Carey. We had a few minutes to chat, that's all. Can you get your sore arm through this, Jess?" Carefully she threaded the sleeves over Jess' upstretched arms and pulled the shirt—a long, unhemmed, coarsely woven garment—down into place. "No underwear, I'm afraid," she said brusquely, holding out the trousers for Jess to step into, "And though I managed to get the boots off, I don't think they'll fit. Of course, you never were much of one for footwear."

Awkward silence followed Jaime's abruptness and she filled it with activity, taking the laces of the baggy trousers from Jess' one-handed fumbling and tying them tightly over the curve of her hip. But Jaime's thoughts were far from the task, and all she cared about was what Arlen might say next.

"I've only been completely out of food for a day," Arlen said, "but it's been lean for a lot longer. Do you think we could get at some of that food? I, for one, will think better on a full stomach."

"Who wants to think?" Dayna cried. "Give that black horse a minute to rest and then Mark said it best—*run away*."

"How?" Carey said, his voice ragged with honesty. "We've got three tired horses and six people, at least one of whom doesn't have the strength to even mount up. The roads will be crawling with Calandre's people—we can't outrun them or outfight them. But they're not familiar with this area—aside from that guy up there, no one knows this little place exists. Hell, he doesn't even have any idea who we are—just that we don't belong. And if he could call for reinforcements, he'd have done it by now. You'd have felt that, Dayna."

There was a long silence. "Details," Dayna said heavily. She set the saddlebags down next to Arlen, and her voice turned resolute. "Don't eat too much, you'll only throw up. Do you think we could have a fire, Carey? If we're really out of sight?"

"It'll make it harder to move around out there," Carey said readily, but he still looked at Jaime. Even without clearly seeing his face she knew he hadn't been sidetracked. He would no doubt make his request of Arlen again later; eventually, he would learn about the torture. Maybe by then Jaime would be ready to talk about it.

Maybe.

"I, for one, could use a cheerful little fire," Mark said. "We can always put it out if we feel like taking a walk. Anyone got a match?"

Carey snorted. "Magic, Mark. Even I know this one."

"You sure can call up a lot of spells for a courier who doesn't know anything about magic," Mark said.

"It's not calling up the magic that's so hard," Arlen said. "It's controlling it."

"Amen," Dayna said wearily. "Make us a fire, Carey, and let's eat."

# 20

Jess stared into the night, sleepless. Exhausted and sleepless. The others slept—except for Mark, who did his best to keep watch although even the still slightly befuddled Jess could see that he was hardly less fatigued than the others. The blue-cast moon had set and the hollow settled into a darkness deep enough to hide everything but the darker bits of blackness of the horses against rock.

Jess thought about that moon, about how tonight was the first time she'd seen it with eyes that could appreciate the subtleties of its icy light. But such thoughts were shattered into irrevocable fragments—*again*—by the pain in her arm. Try as she might, she'd been unable to decipher the events since her return here to Camolen, to the equine shape she had both treasured and feared. She tried to make sense of Eric's death and couldn't; she tried to fit together the pieces of where they were and where they were trying to get...and couldn't. Hard enough without shards of pain fragmenting her thoughts; impossible with them.

She remembered the first wrong step, way back on the stairs. And then all she could remember was the running, and the strength and speed that were hers—and that she'd refused to give up when the leg gave out here in the hollow. She knew it had been dangerous to fight like she had, but she still felt a deep little piece of that fight left in her, an anger at events that were none of her doing.

She hadn't thanked Dayna for bringing her back—not only from her natural form, but from the dark corner of her mind where the human part of her had been coaxed into hiding. She remembered being soothed into that corner, and she shuddered to think that this Jess part of her could have been lost forever.

"You're awake?" Carey asked softly, one arm moving up to touch her where she lay curled up against his chest.

"Did Jaime ever tell you about Ruffian?" Jess said by way of reply, not moving, still savoring the feel of human touch against human senses—no, of *Carey's* touch—and not willing to pull away to look up at him. She could feel the frown of his body language.

"No," he said. "A horse?"

"A great runner. She hurt her leg, just like me. And she didn't want to quit..."

"Like you," Carey supplied.

"And they killed her," Jess said finally. "Because she was only hurting herself. She was making it worse." She waited a long moment, her mind filled with the effort of that struggle, and the human hindsight that told her she had, indeed, only worsened her injury. Then she said hesitantly, "Would you have—"

"No!" Carey recoiled from her, and grabbed her upper arms, pulling her upright, his face only inches from hers while she stared at him with widened eyes. "No, Jess, never! You're not just some race-horse. You're not just Lady anymore. Don't ever doubt that, just because I was too stupid to see it when I first...met you."

Something about the way he looked at her, the intensity in his voice, satisfied that deep longing that had started in Marion, Ohio and lay cocooned within Lady ever since. "Damn straight," she whispered. She settled back down against his shoulder, and it seemed ever so natural to nuzzle his neck in an equine flirt, nipping gently at the angle of his jaw. He shivered as he closed his arm around her, holding her tightly against him. Very tight. And for the moment, whatever else was happening around them, Jess found she was completely content.

Satisfaction brought her sleep, but she was drawn back into awareness by a sound so slight it woke no one else. Puzzled, she listened, searching the breeze in the trees for the other noise that hadn't quite belonged to the sounds of the night. There, by the horses, a definite snuffle. Protecting her arm, Jess slid away from Carey and moved hesitantly into the darkness. She stopped with her hand on the rump of the little bay and said, "Jaime."

A short muffled laugh, no humor in it. "How'd you know it was me?"

"Who else would come to the horses?" Jess asked simply. She hitched at the pants that were bagged around her hips again, and moved to where Jaime sat at the horses' heads, by the small cluster of trees that served as pickets. "Jaime, why are you crying? Are you scared?"

"No," Jaime said. "Well, I *am* scared, but...no."

"I want to make it better," Jess said, thinking that in all the difficult times she'd spent with Jaime, the only tears she'd seen had been quiet and few. Not like this at all.

"Oh, Jess," Jaime said, with a sigh that signaled her shaking head. "I wish you could." After a pause, she asked, "How's your arm? I think that you—Lady—blew something in your knee, so it must be your wrist, now."

Even Jess could recognize an evasion that bald. "It hurts. Won't you talk to me?"

"Talking isn't going to make this go away," Jaime said bitterly, but she relented enough to add, "I was just thinking. About Eric, for one."

Jess tried once again to make sense of the jumbled memories that surround the return to Camolen, and the change from Jess to Lady. "I know...he is dead. Not why."

"He's dead because Derrick's slick friend is trigger-happy," Jaime said, more bitterness. "And...because of who he was. Do you remember going for that slimeball? Right before Carey invoked the stone?"

"No," Jess said, shaking her head in the darkness. "I remember fighting Derrick. I remember...killing him."

"After that, that guy Ernie had us in a pretty bad spot. And things got confusing, everybody was moving, and Eric pulled you back out of the way when Ernie would have shot you. And," she swallowed audibly, "Ernie shot *him*. Damn, I wish I'd let Carey shoot that bastard. I wish Carey had let Dayna kill him with the magic—even if it *had* backlashed on us all!"

Jess was stunned. "Eric was killed because he helped me?"

"Eric was killed," Jaime corrected her fiercely, "because Ernie is an egg-sucking son-of-a-bitch who probably pisses in his own Cheerios every morning."

Jess blinked.

"It's funny," Jaime continued unprompted. "So much has happened since that night. We thought we'd lost you, for one. And I've been so worried about what's happening at home. I mean, surely one of my boarders realized we'd gone missing before the horses missed too many meals. Surely..."

"Yes," Jess said firmly.

"And up until now, I've handled it all just fine. Which is to say I haven't handled it at all, but sometimes you've got to put that kind of stuff aside, until there's a better time to deal with it."

Jess allowed, "I have a hard time doing that."

"But suddenly I can't get away from it. I was so happy to see you, and then suddenly I was so sad about everything else... I just...couldn't..."

Jess found Jaime's hand in the darkness, but it pulled out of her grasp.

"No," Jaime said, fighting for control. "If you comfort me I'll lose it. I'll wake everyone up, and then they'll want explanations and Arlen will tell them—" she cut herself off, leaving a palpable, empty silence between them.

"Tell them *what?*" Jess asked, suddenly aware that this unspoken thing was the key. Threat trickled into her voice. "Jaime, I will yell so loud..."

"Jess—"

"*No.*"

There was a big sigh from the darkness, the sound of Jaime shifting position on the hard ground. One of the horses lowered its head to whuff softly at Jess' head and then at the still-damp clamminess of the dead man's blood on her shirt, but Jess ignored it. And waited.

"Something happened today," Jaime said, finally, reluctantly, her voice very far away even though it came from a spot not two feet from Jess' ears. "Willand—that's the blond wizard who was at the cabin—"

"I remember."

"Willand didn't treat me very well. She...she hurt me. She was trying to force Arlen into giving up the spell. She hurt me a lot."

Jess couldn't think of anything to say. The concept of such behavior had never occurred to her, but with understanding came a cold, cold anger. "You—everyone—treat me like I have to be protected," she said. "Like you think I won't understand the answers to the questions I ask, and that you have to watch out for me. But the next time I see Willand, it will not be me who needs protection."

A hesitation, and Jaime said, "I believe you, Jess. But it won't help me if you turn into another Eric—good-hearted and dead. And nothing can help, I think, except maybe time."

They said for a moment in the darkness, while Jess thought about this woman who was her friend, and with whom she'd shared all her human hours—and many more under saddle. "I liked it when you taught me dressage," she said suddenly. "I wish...I wish this part of me had been there, too. Someday, Jaime, will you teach me more? If the Lady part of me and the Jess part of me are ever in the same place at the same time?"

"Yes, Jess," Jaime choked. "Yes, I'll teach you dressage. But...*this* is between you and me, Jess, okay? When I'm ready for the others to know, I'll tell them. But I have to deal with it before I can deal with *them* dealing with it."

"That was confusing," Jess told her. "But I won't tell anyone." Stiffly, she got to her feet and walked away, her bare feet feeling out ground grown chill with the night. She found Carey and sat as close as she could without touching him, unwilling to disturb his sleep again.

Jess dozed through the remaining hours of the night until the earliest dawn, when Mark woke from his valiant but futile effort at night watch and crept among the others, quietly waking them. In a few moments they gathered together in the haven of the rock formations, all a little chilled, all a lot sore.

Jess was no exception. The sharp pain just below her knee reminded her that an arrow had raked across dun flesh in Arlen's stable. Her wrist throbbed unceasingly and she held it carefully against her stomach, trying to shield it from the occasional shiver that ran up her stiff frame. Arlen actually looked better than he had the night before—not surprising considering he'd probably just had his best night's sleep since the siege. Jaime looked plainly awful—her eyes reddened, surrounded by the black circles from her broken nose. The slash in her breeches was crusted with dried blood and accented by her awkward limp.

Carey looked at them all and said, "It's time to make some decisions."

"It doesn't look to me like there's much to decide," Dayna said glumly. "Unless we somehow just walk right past that guy up there."

"There's a lot more involved here than just *that guy up there*," Carey said. "Believe me, if we wanted to, we'd find a way past him. Things are no different than last night—we can't travel as a group, not with Calandre's people looking for us, *and* stirred up because of Sherra. I'd really hoped to find Sherra's people more of a presence—one we could count on."

"Just like last night," Jaime said. "We're safer here."

"Unless someone misses *him* and starts looking," Mark said dryly, nodding up at the rocky point.

Arlen nodded absent agreement. "Tell me, Carey, where does Sherra stand?"

"They don't have a checkspell yet, not unless they came up with it in the last day or so. She was working with the other wizards on it, not making a play for you because she didn't want to stir Calandre up."

"Quite right," Arlen said.

"I can't believe you really feel that way," Dayna said, scorn and challenge mixed into her voice.

"I've certainly had plenty of time to think about it," Arlen said in gentle reproof. "It was much wiser for Sherra to put all her efforts into the checkspell than to start trouble by mounting a rescue once her first attempt failed." He looked around the little group and a mildly startled expression crossed his face. "I think introduction might be in order, Carey."

Carey laughed shortly as the others, also, realized they'd never really met Arlen, nor he them—even though their lives had been tied together for months now. "I think we might have time for that. This is Mark, Jaime's brother. He's been training with the archers and fighters since we got back. You can depend on him in a pinch, Arlen." Mark looked a little surprised but lifted a hand for a waggle of a hello wave. "This is Dayna—she's from the other world, too. She started using magic almost the moment we got here. One of Sherra's students has been working with her."

Arlen lifted an eyebrow. "You've just started and you called down the magnitude of magic I helped you calm last night?"

Dayna looked at the ground, seeming as small as she ever did, but then her head came up and there was no apology in her eyes. "I'd do it again."

Arlen nodded. "All right, " he said. "As long as you realize the danger you created, and the risk you created for your friends."

"We had a little brush with backlash already," Carey said ruefully. "And I, for one, am grateful for the chance she took this time."

"For me," Jess said. She looked at Arlen, finding it satisfying to view him from her human eyes. He was as tall as she, and didn't look nearly as old as he had in her brief glimpse of him the evening before. Although he was still gaunt, she nonetheless found the arched nose from her early memories, and the warm, honest eyes. She thought his hint of an overbite was kind of cute. "Dun Lady's Jess," she named herself.

"Yes," he said. "And the most magical thing to come of this whole adventure. I owe my life to your bravery last night, Jess. I'm sorry you were hurt."

"I was not the only one," Jess said, and Jaime gave her a sharp look, but no one else saw anything amiss. Their scars were all clearly visible, from Jaime's sword cut to Mark's saddle-sore gait. "And do not leave out Eric, Carey."

"You mentioned that name," Arlen said to Jaime.

Dayna looked away, but she was the one who spoke. "A friend," she said. "One of Calandre's little goons came to Ohio with Carey, and he caused enough trouble that one of us was killed."

"Eric was the first to believe me," Jess said, and grief prickled at her eyes. Another misery to carry along with her wrist.

Carey took a deep breath and filled the pained silence. "We can't just sit here. Right now there's only one man up there, but that won't last. This is our best chance to make a move."

In puzzled protest, Jaime said, "But we've already agreed—"

"Not all of us," Carey said, and held up his hand to forestall further objection. "I've been thinking about this all night, on and off. Listen. As far as that guy knows, there are five of us and four horses. They must have felt the magic—that's probably what our dead friend over there was trying to check on—but they couldn't see anything. If all of us but Jess were out in the open, our guy would think he was watching all of us. He'd feel pretty secure."

"Yeah, but there's still only one way out of here, and it's past him," Mark said.

"But if we had him distracted," Jaime started slowly.

Dayna shifted, and said hesitantly, "There's that thing I did in the woods..."

Mark winced. "I'm not sure that's a good idea, Dayna."

"No," Carey said. "It's a *great* idea."

"Magic," Arlen said. "Maybe you'd better let me in on it. But first, I need to make something clear—you can't count on me for any spells. For one thing, Calandre knows my touch and can locate us through any magic I do. For another—well, I simply haven't got it in me."

"I was afraid of that," Carey said heavily. He leaned back against the rocky wall and gave Arlen a succinct explanation of Dayna's first successful spell. "This would have to be something much more subtle. About the level of a glowspell, where there just isn't enough magic gathered to create a backlash."

"It wouldn't be enough to keep him away," Arlen said. "But as a distraction I think it would be perfect. A go-away spell. Why didn't I ever think of that one?"

"It takes desperation," Dayna said, but she responded shyly to Arlen's approval.

"That's our distraction, then," Carey said, and looked at Jess. "That puts a lot on Jess."

"Me?" Jess said in surprise, having failed to anticipate Carey's plan.

He nodded reluctantly. "If you're willing to do it," he said. "Here's the way I see it, start to finish: we need to eat what food is left and see to our immediate needs. There's a spring back under the rocks, not a fast-flowing one, but it ought to do if we're careful. Jaime, especially, needs to clean out that cut, and the horses need to be watered. We may not get the chance to take care of those things once we start trouble." He nodded at the exit. "And Arlen, if you can, Jess will need a finder. Something like the maplight," he explained to Jaime, glancing at Mark and Dayna to see that they understood the reference—"only tuned in to a person—this time Sherra—instead of a place. And then it gets simple. While Dayna hits that guy with her go-away, with all of us in plain sight, Jess makes a run for it. She should take him completely by surprise, be past him before he even figures out he should stop her."

"I can do that," Jess said, believing it.

"Might not be that easy, braveheart," Carey told her. "There will be others out there besides our one little fighter. You may have to get by them."

"I can manage the finder," Arlen said, "but it's a risk."

Carey looked grim. "Just as dangerous to have someone blundering around out there with no direction. Run into the wrong side, or get backtracked, and we're all caught—unless you can send Sherra a quick call for help, directly?"

"That would blaze a trail so bright Calandre would be blind to miss it. If Sherra's not in a position to respond immediately...well, let's just get a start on the business end of eating and taking care of ourselves. We can make final decisions when we get there."

"That means you have to stay back here," Carey warned Jess.

"But I have to go to the bathroom," she responded plaintively, looking at the other end of the hollow, which had been honored as the latrine location.

"Hurry then," Carey said with a smile. "It's amazing all the little practical things that get in the way of a good plan," he bemoaned to no one in particular as Jess scurried out of the sheltered pocket into the monotone light of dawn, and someone else chimed in with next dibs.

When Jess returned, Carey was attending to the tedious business of watering the horses, filling one of the waterskins at the spring and trickling water into Dayna's cupped hands while the thirsty animals noisily sucked it up. Arlen nibbled at a hunk of bread, very stale if the amount of chewing he was doing was any measure. Jaime sat quietly and let Mark tend to her leg; he gave her suspicious little glances when he thought she wasn't looking and Jess knew he suspected she was holding out on something.

Jess joined Arlen next to the saddlebags and poked through them, finally discovering a peach that hadn't been too badly bruised. She nibbled at it as Arlen gnawed his bread, and then almost shyly offered him a bite.

"No," he said, "I left it for you. You're the one who's going to need the strength. All we have to do is sit around and wait."

"You hope," Jess said, with her usual perspicaciousness. "*I* think we are lucky it was so close to dark when we got here last night. Otherwise that man's friend would have gone for help instead of trying to spy on us. And maybe others will come for him anyway."

"Maybe they will," Arlen allowed. Then he reached out and touched a length of her dun hair, retreating almost immediately despite her lack of protest. She looked at him curiously.

"You're a first, that's all," he said. "More than one wizard has fooled around with shape shifting, from human to bird or dog or something more exotic—and usually to their own woe. But no one has ever thought of finding the human potential in an animal."

She stared at him with a little frown. "Is that good, or bad?"

"Why, neither, I suppose—although once word of this gets around we'll probably have to create some sort of checkspell so innocent animals aren't torn from their natural shapes for the sake of experimentation. I imagine it was quite a traumatic experience."

"It was hard," she admitted. "But my friends helped me, even before they believed me. Now I can help them."

"It seems to me you've already paid your dues in this little drama," Arlen said. He took a gulp from a waterskin and dribbled water down his tunic on the way. "Never could use these things," he grumbled. Then, "Eat, Jess. Here comes Carey, and I wouldn't be surprised if he was ready to move. Full day is almost here, and I don't think we can afford to waste any more time."

"I did not think this was a waste of time," Jess said with another frown. "I think it is good to meet with the man whose stable I have lived in all my life."

Arlen smiled. "Maybe so," he said, and stepped out just far enough that he could be seen from the point.

Carey stopped in front of Jess and said, "We need to wrap your arm before you go out. You about ready?"

"Yes," she said, looking at the dead man's boots as Carey dropped them on the ground. A strip of material trailed from his hand, the same color as Dayna's overlong tunic. He sat next to her and held the boot up next to her arm for measure, then applied his knife to it.

"I want you to take the gray," he told her, his phrasing awkward as he muscled the knife through thick leather uppers. "He's the best rested, and he's strong, and he's got heart. Either that or he's too stupid to be afraid of the things he should be; I haven't decided yet."

Jess scraped the last of the peach flesh from the stone pit with her teeth, and set it on the ground next to her, holding out her arm when Carey gestured for it. He carefully lay the leather against the swollen and bruised limb, but she gasped with surprise and pain when he wrapped the tunic strip tightly around it.

"I'm sorry," he said, looking at it but not backing off. "You can't be worrying about banging it around when you're on this run. We've got to protect it."

She nodded, blinking hard and fast.

He finished the chore, looking almost as relieved as she felt that it was over, and ran an apologetic hand down her shoulder. "Let's hope that was the worst part of the whole run. Now, if Arlen will produce a finder for you, I'll get Dayna started on her spell—if nothing else, maybe the magics will mingle and hide your trace," he said to Arlen. He squeezed Jess' arm and told her, "The finder will take you to Sherra if you follow it, and it won't fade until you get there. Just get her back here, anyway you can. I don't think she'll be hard to convince—just be Jess. Oh—and here." He removed his chain of spellstones and lowered them over Jess' head. "There's only one there that's important now—the shieldstone. It'll keep anyone from directly working magic on you. Don't get cocky, though, because a quick-witted wizard will still find ways to hurt you."

Jess nodded; it seemed simple enough. Looking down at her newly inflexible wrist, she was suddenly ready to go.

"Finder," Arlen said. He caught Dayna's eye. The small woman sat cross-legged in front of Mark, looking fragile and uncertain—but when she finally nodded, there was determination in her face. Arlen waited for Carey to join them and start a conversation that was far too loud and unnatural—*here we all are, out in the open, not up to anything at all*— but one that easily created a rustle of notice up on the point. Then he closed his eyes, holding one hand out palm up; moments later he opened them again, just as a gentle greenish light bloomed into existence. With the other hand he touched Jess on the shoulder, and the light left him to hover several yards in front of her.

"The auto club would love this one," Mark said, interrupting an inane conversation on horse-training ethics that he'd obviously not been following in the first place.

"Right," Jaime teased gently. "No more men refusing to admit they're lost."

Mark grinned. "Good riding, Jess," he said, dropping a hand on Dayna's shoulder. Dayna opened her eyes and shrugged; in her face was a dawning of wonder at what she'd been able to do. The rustle of the guard was conspicuously gone. Carey strode over to hold the saddled gray while Jess mounted, an unnecessary gesture she allowed him without completely understanding. When she was settled, he closed his hand around hers on the reins.

"Come back to me, Jess," he said. "Be careful enough that you can come back to me."

"Damn straight," she said positively. And she pointed the horse at the rock-walled corridor, startling him with her heels.

Their departure rated zero for form; the gray flung his head up and lit out in a stiff, angry canter-turned-gallop, topping the final rise at high speed and encountering nothing more than the angry shouts of belated discovery. Crouched over the whipping salt and pepper mane, her arms following the exaggerated motion of the gray's effort, Jess suddenly wondered about the consequences of her escape to those in the hollow. A ringing gunshot followed her thoughts, barely heard above the hoof beats of her run; she abruptly sat back, pulled the gray up, turned him back the way they'd come—and then as abruptly halted, wanting to go back and ride down the man who was threatening her own but not daring to do it.

The gray pranced in angry impatience, throwing in a borderline buck. She ran a hand down his tense neck and quietly turned him away from the hollow again, still reluctant but in the end willing to do as she'd been asked. If she went back to help them and failed, their one chance would be wasted for nothing. When the gray relaxed enough to lower his head and snort in frustrated acceptance of his situation, she again asked him for a canter.

# 21

Jess knew these trails. She'd been on them as soon as she was old enough to pony-lead beside her mother, following Carey on short, quiet trips while she learned her first lessons, her first Words. And though the little finder glow moved alongside her in a mute, frustrated attempt to get her to turn right, she ignored the first two opportunities, going on instead to a main intersection further ahead. There, she had five different paths to choose from, and she was able to pick the one that most closely matched the glow's indication.

Carey had said there would be people trying to stop her, so she wasn't surprised when the gray pricked his ears and sent out an almost inaudible greeting, his neck stretched high and his body quivering with the forced exhalation of his call. She startled him out of the next, inevitably louder effort by jumping off his back and hauling him back around, swapping ends so she could run him behind the best cover she could find, a barely adequate combination of brush and tree. She clamped her hand over his nose, and had only just noticed that the glow was out in the middle of the trail when the increasing noise of multiple hoof beats made a change of position impossible; a dozen cantering riders plowed right by it, swallowing it in their midst and then spitting it out again in the dust of their passage. They never even glanced her way; Jess had only enough time to see that they were battle worn, sporting blood and bandages and a trophy stringer of armbands. The trophy colors, she realized, were from Sherra's people. She stared after the group and wondered if the woman with the calm voice and pleasant hands had fallen to Calandre's people already.

It was only a moment's dilemma, that tug to go back and help her friends. Then she led the gray onto the trail and mounted and the glow moved out before her, encouraging her onward. Two more furtive dashes into the woods kept her clear of similar self-involved fighters, but it was during a quiet canter along a relatively uncomplicated section of travel that she encountered her first real opposition.

The woman seemed to come from the trees, landing on the trail in front of Jess and startling her so there was no time for thought, only the instinctive effort to stop before she ran the challenger over. And while Jess' eyes were still wide with surprise, the woman had a bow raised and aimed at her.

"What's your business here?" she asked, calm but clearly a demand.

Jess merely stared, caught in a tangle of thoughts, trying to judge which side this woman was on.

"Snappy comebacks will get you nowhere," the woman said with a humorless smile. "Off the horse, then. Whatever you want, you're not cleared for this area, and you'll get no further." Then, when Jess still hesitated, the leftover smile vanished. "Do it now, or die. You don't seem to be particularly well-suited to this game, girl, so quit trying to play it."

"But I can't tell who you're with!" Jess blurted.

"It doesn't really matter, does it?" the woman responded, looking not at all strained as she continued to hold the bowstring taut, her humorless smile back. "Get off the horse. Maybe I'll give you a few answers."

*Run*, Jess thought, but realized she had little chance of surviving any sudden move. Slowly, she dismounted, feeling awkward under the scrutiny of this woman. "I need to see Sherra," she offered, standing beside the gray. "If you're an enemy, try to kill me. If you are not, let me go on. My friends need help."

The woman grunted. "Plenty of people need help." She lowered the bow with this apparent declaration of alliance. "I'm not here to kill you, but that doesn't mean you can go on. You'll be coming with me, to a place where you'll be out of the way until we're ready to deal with you."

Jess tossed her head with an impatient snort. "I have to talk to—"

"Just like everyone else," the woman said shortly. "Everybody thinks their problems are worse than anybody else's, and if you all got through, the important work would never get done. You're not going to see her, and you're not going to ride off on your own. So walk that hell-fried creature in front of me—unless you want to end up like *that* fellow."

She nodded at the woods beside her, and for the first time Jess noticed the limp, raggedly shod feet poking out of the undergrowth. She looked back at the woman's bow, where an arrow still rested loosely against string and stave, and the sentry gave a short laugh. "He was on the other side, as it happens, but I'm in no mood to fool around with you so don't push it. And just so you know—you go further than this without an escort and you'll be shot without warning by the next sentry. That finder isn't going to get you anywhere but the hells."

Momentarily out of alternatives, Jess tilted her head in the human laying-back-of-ears and walked before the woman, taking a newly worn path through the woods with the gray beside her and the finder futilely trying to catch her attention along the way. She'd go to their out of the way place, for now. And then she could wait and hope someone would listen to her, or she could break away and try to reach Sherra— or she could return to Carey.

She didn't think she would make it to Sherra—none of them had counted on heavy security around the wizard. And she didn't have the feeling anyone was going to listen to her.

*Carey.*

They quickly reached an area where the trees thinned to leave room for a narrow, shallow river. The air was thick with the spicy smell of crushed vegetation. There was only one other horse, being watered by a tall, thin man at the river; a disgruntled looking group, men all, were more or less sitting around a fire and its large hanging cook pot of something that smelled good. Jess' stomach growled, telling her the peach had not been enough, although she was far too angry to put food in her stomach.

"Go get yourself something to eat, then. Someone'll take your horse—can't have you getting ideas about making a run for it—and listen to your story. You may even make it to Sherra."

Jess' fingers tightened around the reins. She could not let them have the horse, not let them take away her chance to return to Carey if she failed here. "I can't wait for someone else to listen. *You* listen. I am here from Carey and Arlen, and I need help for them."

"What, you think I came into this world yesterday? Arlen's hold is under siege and he's trapped inside. Now tie your horse and eat or not as you please, but quit wasting my time." She turned to go.

"No," Jess insisted. "Arlen is free of his hold. Carey and I got him out. He said to tell you I am Dun Lady's Jess, and you would believe me."

"Dun Lady's Jess," the woman repeated blankly, as the others stirred with interest at the fuss Jess was creating.

"His horse. I—"

But the woman slapped her forehead in an exaggerated gesture and said, "Heavens abandon me, I've snagged a crazy." Then she pointed, a distinctly commanding gesture, at the fire. "Get over there. And give me those reins—and *shut up*." This last as Jess opened her mouth in protest, and then came an outstretched hand, ready for the reins.

Jess stared at the woman, caught in indecision, her head lifted as she again laid back her mental ears—a sign that would have kept the woman from crowding had she been the least familiar with it. But she wasn't, and she did crowd Jess and Jess' vacillation lost out to deeply ingrained reaction. Her leg flashed a fierce kick that sent the woman tumbling, astonished and unable to take weight on her leg when she tried to rise. Jess was already mounting, pulling herself up with an arm that erupted in pain, charging through the low-ceilinged path with her body held tight against the horse. There were shouts behind her, and a brief flurry of cheers from the other captives.

*Freedom!* Jess rode hard, retracing her path back to the rock hollow at top speed until she nearly ran up on the heels of a rough-looking pair on the wrong side. She dropped back into caution and a slow jog, taking the first turning she could.

And that was when the man caught up with her.

As soon as Carey heard the enemy's angry shout he knew Jess was out and away. He headed for their protected corner, hauling Dayna along with him while Mark and Jaime quickly followed. An arrow struck at the edge of the pocket on their heels, and then Carey saw the man bellying up on the point of the exposed rock. He pulled the awkward bulk of the automatic from the top of his boot and used its last bullet, a miss that nonetheless scared—*terrified*—the man into panicked retreat.

"He's not likely to come back after that," Mark said with satisfaction.

"No, but he's not going to leave, either," Carey said. "And now there's someone else on Calandre's side who's seen the gun and is alive to tell about it."

"It was still a good choice," Jaime said firmly. "Mark wouldn't have gotten to his bow before that guy had a chance to take good aim on us. Anyway, he wasn't close enough to really see anything—"

"And neither were those first men Dayna chased away," Mark said. "They'll just think it was a loud spell."

"A very loud spell," Dayna added, putting a finger inside her ear to pop it.

"And one which I would like to see," Arlen said.

As one, they realized he was not privy to all the secrets Carey had warned to keep from this world. And suddenly things were awkward, and Carey, looking at the gun in his hand, pulled up his tunic to shove the thing in his pants, neatly covering it again until he could find some place to stash it. "I'm sorry," he said at the surprised look on Arlen's face. "There are things no one here should know about. And they won't, not if I can help it. We've got enough trouble with people like Calandre without giving her more to work with."

"Well," Arlen said into the awkwardness, "that's certainly true enough. I'll have to accept your judgment on this one, Carey."

Carey nodded, grateful, but the incident had given him something to think about. While they would all certainly do their best to remain alive and free, he knew it was indeed possible their ragged little group would be killed before Jess came back with help—if she managed to come back with help at all. He had to make sure the guns would not be found.

For what seemed like hours, he scoured their small retreat, and finally found a place he deemed secure. On his belly, inched into the very back of the low overhand behind the spring, he found a crevice in which to tuck the guns. The one without bullets was of no use to them anymore, and he left it there. When he crawled out, covered with moss and streaked with slimy mud, he said to Dayna, "Whatever happens, Calandre can't get her hands on these—she can't even know they exist—and that means we can't risk using them against her. If anything happens to me, I want you to take the other guns to the back of this cave and shove them down the crack in the rock there. You'll fit most easily. After you, it's up to Jaime, and then Mark, though it'll be a squeeze."

"Gotcha," Mark mumbled unhappily, as reluctant as any of them to admit that things might come to that point.

Jaime shushed them suddenly, rudely enough to prickle sibling rivalry, and Mark opened his mouth for what would probably have been an equally rude sibling response. But Arlen came up beside Jaime and looked, as she did, up at the point of rock. Mark subsided into quiet attention.

"Magic," Arlen told her. "You didn't hear anything, you felt it. Calandre's magic." He glanced back at Carey, who had gone stiff and still, momentarily captured by dread. "I warned you this could happen, especially with Calandre scouring the area for any sign of me."

"Maybe," Dayna said hesitantly, "maybe Sherra felt it too, then."

"If Calandre's smart, which she is, she's trying to maintain the illusion that I'm still at the hold, and is defending it against any physical or magical attack Sherra might launch. And that's certainly what Sherra's doing—putting all her effort into breaking down that resistance. Not keeping her wizardly ears open for such small ripples as creating a finder might cause."

"She's here, then." Jaime said, barely audible. "And she probably has Willand with her."

"We'll do our best to keep things from coming to that," Arlen told her, a cryptic response, and Carey exchanged a look with Mark, sharing an awareness that there was more to the story of Jaime's capture than they knew.

Even as Carey came to the further conclusion that it was a subject for another time, a figure stalked to the end of the point and stood, arrogantly confident, staring down at them. Reed-thin, dressed in a dark ankle-length shift, the woman's equally dark hair fell around her shoulders like a crinkly cloud. Around her, the air seemed to crinkle as well.

Carey felt a brief wash of Arlen's magic and recognized the slight optical effect of the wizard's shielding. Arlen gave him a grim look. "I don't have the strength to protect you all. I have to keep—"

"The spell away from her. We know," Jaime finished for him, as though she'd been there before. Mark had raised his bow—but he took a second look at the shielding effects and at the slight shake of Carey's head, and lowered it again with a resigned expression.

"Get the guns, Dayna," Carey said quietly through his teeth, wishing he'd had the nerve to dispose of them all when he'd had the chance. But no, he'd had to hang onto that one chance of survival. "I can't do it, she'll be watching me. Get them and shove them so far down that crack they'll never come out."

"All right," Dayna said, her voice quivering slightly despite her obvious effort to sound calm. "A diversion would be nice."

"Calandre," Arlen said, stepping forward. "I hadn't expected the pleasure of seeing you again so soon."

She made a rude noise. "Nonsense. Although it *was* considerate of you to put out a signpost for me. A little stupid, actually."

"It still seems to have taken you a while to get here," Arlen said. "That spell means, incidentally, that help is on its way."

Behind them, Dayna picked up the saddlebags and headed to the spring, quiet and deliberate.

"Nice of you to mention it," Calandre said. "And you, little person, you can stop right where you are. I don't know what you're up to, but I'm sure I don't want it to happen."

Carey closed his eyes in despair. This hollow as a place to hole up, the finder spell for Jess, keeping the guns for what small advantage they might create...bad decisions, all. His next choices had better be the right ones, because he was running out of room to bumble around in.

When he opened his eyes he discovered that Calandre was no longer alone. Another woman stood beside her, a voluptuous woman whose features edged too close to cuteness to be called beautiful. Her blond hair was bound in some intricate manner, and when she looked down on them, her face held more triumph—or anticipation?—even than Calandre's.

"Willand," Jaime groaned.

"I expect you know what I want," Calandre said, crossing her arms as she shifted into a hip-shot stance that did more than anything to show just how little she regarded them as a threat. "And you already know how far I'll go to get it."

"You must be getting desperate," Arlen said. "All your cards are on the table and you'll never be free again—not unless you can get some advantage with that spell. Your little schemes are falling down around you, woman. It's only a matter of time now."

Nettled, she straightened to glare down at him, nostrils flared, hands on hips. And then she gave a sudden laugh, shook back her hair, and said, "Nice try, Arlen. What you said has some truth to it, but I have no intention of losing ground to misplaced temper. Let me see if I can sum up the situation here." She took a dramatic pause, one finger resting on her chin. "You're down there, we're up here, and you're not likely to invite us down—at least not until you run out of arrows. Of course, I can arrange for that to happen fairly quickly, if I've a mind to. On the other hand, Arlen, you obviously haven't had enough time to gain the strength to shield this hollow—or even the small area it would take to cover the five of you. While I, of course, am well-rested and just brimming with magic."

"I doubt that," Arlen said dryly. "Not if you're maintaining that shield on my hold."

"I am," she told him coolly, "but I have plenty of help. Willand is not my only promising student."

"I'm going to learn quite a bit today, I think," Willand said with a lazy smile that she aimed at Jaime.

"I don't know how," Carey muttered. "When you're that full of yourself, there isn't room for anything else." He hadn't intended for her to hear, but suspected from her sudden sour look that she had.

"Are we all through hissing and spitting at one another?" Calandre asked. "Because I really do want that spell. And I can make things quite miserable for your friends until I get it."

"Can she?" Mark asked Arlen.

"We'll hope Jess gets back soon," Arlen said tightly. "Very soon."

Carey knew that tone, that expression. His mouth went one swallow drier, his stomach a gulp sicker.

"Let me show you," Calandre offered to Mark. "I don't want you thinking about going for your bow, anyway."

The dull snapping sounds were clearly audible, perhaps even amplified for effect. Mark yelped, a sound of surprise more than distress, as his leg went out from under him. But his groan of, "Oh, shit," as he clutched his arm and bent over that leg was nothing but pain.

"Mark," Jaime breathed, her own obvious fears abandoned as she dashed to her brother's side.

"Broken," he told her. "Both of them. Damn."

Crouching next to him with one hand on his shoulder, she looked up at Calandre. "You *coward*!"

Calandre merely sat where she had stood, seemingly unaffected by Jaime or her anger. "Do you understand yet? I can't get at Arlen, but I can reach *you*. Makes you wonder, doesn't it, how long he can stand to watch this?" Her finger moved up to her chin again, this time to tap it in a show of contemplation. "I'm going to let you think about this for a minute," she said. "But not much longer. It's a boring game once people stop screaming and start dying."

"Arlen!" Dayna glared up at him, the saddlebags forgotten in her hand. "How can she do something like that? Why isn't there a checkspell on this kind of magic?"

"Yeah, Arlen," Mark said through gritted teeth, "why the hell isn't there a checkspell on this kind of magic?"

"Because *this kind of magic* is the most elemental form of kinetic magic," Arlen said grimly. "It doesn't even take much effort. It's used every day for a host of mundane things—just like everything else she twists to use against others."

"Yes, *but*—" Calandre protested from above, "you've got to have a good imagination. Those without a truly creative spirit would never think of this one, for instance—unless you want to give up that spell now?"

For a moment Carey wondered if that simply wouldn't be the easiest thing. Surely Sherra's people were close to a checkspell, if they hadn't arrived at it yet. Surely there wasn't enough time for Calandre to cause any real trouble with the world-travel spell. Such a tempting thought, just give her the spell and then walk away from this hollow unharmed—

Except that no matter what they did, Arlen was too much of a threat to her. He'd never be allowed to walk away. And, by default, Carey and the others were doomed as well.

"No takers, hmm? Well, I can't say I'm surprised. So, let's see— Willand, dear, keep an eye on things for me. This is going to take a bit of concentration. I enjoy the fine detail work, don't you, Arlen?" She crossed her legs and closed her eyes while the four of them exchanged glances of dread and wondered who it would be this time.

In another moment Carey felt the fine tinglings of threshold pain running along his arms and shoulders, flowing down to encase his torso...running along the lines of his bones to thigh and shin. He looked at his outstretched hand, but there was no outward sign of the effect. He glanced to her and found he was being watched—him alone. None of the others, then.

*Good.*

"A little closer to home, Arlen," Calandre said. "Higher stakes."

"Carey?" Arlen asked, sending a swift look of alarm and concern.

"I don't know what it is." Carey shuddered as the tingling turned to a burn, overworked muscle on overload. "Except that it's going to hurt."

"Quite a lot, I should think, depending on how good my control was," Calandre said. "If I got clumsy, he won't last as long. The idea is to keep the major organs out of the process for as long as possible."

"Arlen..." Carey said, finding that his legs would no longer hold him up; inner flames engulfed them. "Arlen..."

"Carey!" Arlen just missed breaking Carey's mostly gentle collapse to the ground. "Damn you, Calandre! What spell is this?"

"Something fiendishly clever, I assure you," she replied, satisfaction coating her voice. "A variation on the spell used to make compost."

"*What!*" Dayna and Jaime cried in tandem. Jaime's voice came from beside her brother, but Dayna was at Carey's feet, holding his ankles against the quivering in his legs. "Arlen, what does that *mean*?" she demanded. "She's not...not turning him into...into—"

"No," Arlen said heavily. "We have a common little household spell that's used to speed the breakdown of garbage material. It acts on the smallest units in the material, destroying their structure—"

"She's breaking down every cell in his body?" Dayna asked in horror.

"Major organs last," Calandre called down. "I want Arlen to have a little time to think about this. I'm not sure how reversible this spell is—the healing arts are obviously not my specialty—but I can stop the process, if I've a reason."

*No*, Carey thought. Arlen couldn't give up the spell, not when it would be for nothing. She was going to kill them all in the end. He tried to say it out loud, and all that came out was a gurgling sort of groan that didn't even make sense to him.

# 22

J ess stared hard at the man who rode up behind her, thinking she knew him from someplace—and someplace other than the little detention area they'd both just left. She said, irritated for both herself and his horse, "If you let him drink too much before you came after me, he's going to colic," and tossed her head as she asked for a little more energy in the gray's trot. The man didn't have any apparent weapons, and she had no intention of stopping now; they were nearly to the five-road intersection.

He didn't respond, other than to keep pace with her, drawing nearly even with her and mumbling to himself—and then giving her an annoyed stare. "Now that should have worked," he muttered, then addressed her directly. "Listen here, woman, I want to talk to you. Slow down a little, will you? I can barely ride when I'm *not* trying to make intelligent conversation."

She took another look and saw this was certainly true. Good. A nudge and the gray snorted, pushing his nose out a little as he put another notch of effort into the gait—one that she easily posted and one that bounced the man mercilessly.

"You're Jess, aren't you?" he said, his voice bouncing along with his bottom, and punctuated with an "Ouch!" as he came down on the saddle wrong. His horse's tail lashed in annoyance and Jess had the impression the tall man was about to get dumped. It *had* been her intention, but....

"Jess. Yes," she said, not quite ready to slow the pace. "I told that woman so."

"There aren't very many of us who know Carey personally," the man said desperately. "There are fewer who know his dun mare has also been a woman."

Cautiously, Jess slowed to a walk, moving as far away from him as she could—but she needn't have worried. The man was too involved in regaining his precarious seat and easing his saddle sores to even think about grabbing at her. "But you do," she said. "Know about me, I mean."

"I do. I was there when we discovered Jaime had been taken," he said. "My name is Gacy."

Another moment's scrutiny brought her the memory. "I saw you at Sherra's when I came back without Jaime," she said. "You were getting ready to ride out."

"Right," he said ruefully, "and I wasn't any better at it then, either."

"My friends are trapped by one of Calandre's men," Jess said. "Arlen is with them. He has used magic—"

"For this poor pitiful finder that's trying to get you to turn around?" Gacy asked, and Jess twisted to find the glow trailing her, faithfully pointing out the direction to Sherra.

"Yes. I was supposed to bring back help. Carey said they would believe me."

"We've been extremely careful with Sherra," Gacy said. "She's our best chance of getting through this mess, and we couldn't chance that Calandre would send some unmagical threat her way."

"I don't care about the *why*. I want help for my friends," Jess said. "And now I think I'm the only help they're going to get." Briefly, she wished for her own swift legs instead of those belonging to this stolid gray. She gathered the reins, preparing to canter, and he hastened to do the same.

"Don't lose me, Jess. Once we're there I can send for help. It might draw Calandre but I can hold her off for a little while."

His mumbled, "*I think*," was, she decided, not meant to be heard.

Gacy did his best to keep the pace she set, a fast pace that was not kind to either the riders or their horses. He always fell behind when she was trotting, though, and as the distance to the hollow decreased, so did

Jess' patience. They were midway between the big intersection and the hollow when Gacy, at that point barely within hearing distance, called her with a breathless shout. With much irritation, she stopped the big gray, who was finally reaching his limits. She turned in the saddle to demand why the wizard had stopped her, when she felt it, too.

It was a sensation similar to those that hit her when she was changing from Lady to Jess, but this time it didn't snatch her, it buffeted mildly around her. When Gacy was close enough to hear her normal speaking voice, she asked, "What is that? Is it magic?"

"It's magic, all right, of a hefty sort," he said. "And it's Calandre's. If I had to guess, Jess—"

"She's already there!" Jess cried in alarm, pushing the gelding into a canter before she'd even finished speaking.

"Jess, no!" Gacy yelled after her, hopelessly out-ridden. "Don't just run up on her! Jess!" he hollered, growing fainter. "Be careful!"

She'd be careful, all right. There was no point in running headlong into the hollow so she needed her own rescue. She nursed the idea of running headlong into Calandre instead—but in the end, prompted by the fast-fading gray, she dismounted a quarter mile from the hollow. She tied the horse by the side of the trail, a message of sorts to Gacy, and walked quietly up to the hollow entrance—her phantom tail twitching, her feet a little confused by the impulse to prance nervously.

Jess crouched behind a thick, waxy-leafed shrub and looked out onto the point, the only weak spot for the protective little pocket in the rock-walled basin. Their guard was there, leaning against a tree off to the side—a tired posture that conveyed his relief at handing the reins over to his superior. On the point sat a relaxed-looking woman whom Jess did not recognize, and who she thought was Calandre. And standing next to her—

*Willand*. She instantly recalled the way this same figure had stood in the doorway of the wizard's cabin, and she remembered, too, the things this woman had done to Jaime. Her head went up, ears back. Both women were close enough to the edge of the point that she easily saw herself—an internal image that had four legs—pushing them over the edge. She also saw herself going with them, but the landing wouldn't be too hard if she used Willand as a pillow. She relished the image a

moment and set it aside—and even though no others came immediately to mind, she couldn't bring herself to just *sit* behind the protective
shrub.

Jess moved carefully away from her cover and toward the two
women, trying hard to acquire a *sneak* that was not in her body's vocabulary. She still felt their magic, not as intense but still active, and she
heard Arlen's shout carry up from the hollow, a cry of alarm that sound-
ed very much like Carey's name. She crept toward her goal—a difficult, silent stalk that struggled against both her equine *run from danger*
and an angry mare's desire to trample the ones who threatened her own.
She closed in on them, gathering herself for a rush, when a new feel of
magic flooded the air. Jess dropped to the ground as both women
whirled to look behind her, at the spot where Gacy stood.

"Shield, Willand!" Calandre snapped, and yet a third taste of magic
washed the air as the faint sparkling expanded from Calandre's body to
wall the point and the hollow—with Jess included.

"Too late," Gacy said, making no attempt to get any closer. "I just
called Sherra—she'll be here any minute."

"*Any minute* will be too late for Carey," Calandre said mockingly,
a comment that clutched at Jess' heart. "And there's nothing to keep me
here when I feel them coming, is there?" She looked back down into
the hollow. "Meanwhile, you still have a chance to save this man, Arlen."

*Save Carey. Avenge Jaime.* The thoughts crowded Jess' common
sense, urging her to action; she twitched with the impatience of it, and
suddenly Calandre focused on her.

"What is this?" she asked, frowning, flipping a stray bit of magic
at Jess that slid past without touching her. "She's protected!"

"That's the one who got away," the man said, straightening unwill-
ingly from his observer's slouch. "I'll take care of her."

Jess rose, a coiled, ready spring. She tried to center her thoughts, to
make them sensible, to stop the heat of anger; in failure, she exploded
into motion, a sprint with such speed it took the man completely by surprise and barely left Willand time to realize it was she who was under
attack and not her mistress. Jess slammed the blond woman down
against the roots of a tree, and the shield instantly dissolved. Dazed,
Willand tried to claw her way right up Jess, and Jess grabbed her, using

Willand's own momentum to hurl her into Calandre. Next to her, a stone exploded, showering her with fragments.

A larger rock blew up in front of her and Jess ducked behind her own arms, but only until the air was clear enough for her to dive through; she landed on Calandre's thin frame and fastened both hands around the woman's neck, so close to that angular countenance that the wild disarray of Calandre's dark crinkly hair mixed with Jess' coarse dun strands. A small sharp-edged rock bounced off her shoulder and her injured wrist screamed at the effort—but those were distant pains, not to be heeded.

"Let Carey go," Jess hissed at Calandre, staring into black eyes and flexing her hands over a neck so thin-skinned she could feel the rings of cartilage there. Calandre's fingers tore at Jess' wrists, then clawed at her face, her concentration too shattered to engender magical assault—though there was magic flowing all around them, uncontrolled magic, dangerous magic.

"I can't stop the spell if you're choking me," Calandre gasped hoarsely. Then, in the blink of hesitation she'd created, she snatched at Jess' oversized tunic, ripping the chain of spellstones away. She smiled, a ghastly expression on a face turning dark, and though her words were choked, they were still deadly. "I can't stop the spell anyway, pathetic child. Join Carey in death!" And she turned the wild magic at Jess.

Jess gasped at the onslaught, unprepared for the way it called to the Lady in her. She reeled between the divided comprehension of two different creatures, vaguely aware that Calandre pried her hands away, that Willand was screaming and tugging at her shoulders, that Carey was dying and the woman responsible was about to get away and that she was *two different minds, two different bodies, the same soul...tearing itself apart to be all things at once—*

*Carey is dying—*

Something within her hardened. What she could not do for her own sake, she found she could do out of fury and passion for another. *I am Jess*, she told herself, the thought choking through the chaos inside her. Squeezing her eyes closed, she thought hard about her clever human hands, the things they could feel and the strength they held. Base animal instinct, *kill or be killed*, joined with outrage and centered in on retribution; Jess lost track of what was happening around her, focusing only on keeping herself where she was, *who* she was.

Then, suddenly, there was no ground beneath her knees, no Calandre between them. Her hands were empty—but they were still hands—and the breeze on her face meant she was moving. Only then did she feel the grip under her arms and her knees and realize she was being carried, by whom and to where unknown. Her eyes snapped open and she jerked against the hands that held her, nearly wrenching herself free.

"Deep-fried hells, woman, I almost dropped you!" snapped a voice in her ear as the hands grappled to reestablish their hold.

"Where—" she started, twisting again, but this time only to look about herself. It was a strange perspective, but she managed to recognize the path into the hollow. "Put me down!"

"I don't think so," he said. She tilted her head to look back at him, a view of an unfamiliar, upside-down face. "We've been told to carry you down here and that's what we're going to do—you can do as you please once you're out of our care."

She did not fight them; as confused as she was about just what had and was happening, she sensed no harm in these two—and this was where she wanted to go, anyway. She endured the undignified journey with impatience, until they gained the hollow and gently tipped her up to her feet, making sure she was steady before they actually released her.

She gave them not another thought, but stumbled hastily to the back pocket of the hollow where everyone else congregated, and where she somehow knew Carey must be. Mark limped out from the huddled activity and caught her shoulders, spinning her around with her momentum. "Jess..." he said, warning and regret, not even letting her turn to look for Carey.

"Let me go to him," she said, words that wavered between a demand and a request for reassurance.

"They don't know if they can save him," he told her, brutal truth. "They've got specialized healers here, and they got the process stopped, but there was a lot of damage done."

This was nonsense to Jess, who had not seen Calandre's spell in process. The extra people, she assumed, were Sherra's, and that they were trying to help was enough to know for now—never mind when they arrived, or how long they'd been here. She tugged away from Mark and pushed through the people in the rocky niche where she and Arlen had shared a meal only that morning. "Carey," she said, breathlessly, looking for him, searching a crowded scene of strangers and friends. She was surprised to see Calandre, alive, lying on a horse blanket and looking little more than a fragile collection of limbs. Her gaze skipped from the defeated wizard to Jaime's sudden realization that she was there, to Arlen's bent, concerned visage to—"Oh," she said, a small sound with no force behind it.

Step by slow step she walked to the spot where Carey lay, Sherra at his head and a stranger by his feet, both deep in concentration. Magic flowed strongly throughout the hollow in small, myriad voices of controlled and gentle force, but it grew more concentrated as she went to Carey, kneeling next to him in a peculiar, slow motion fashion that kept what she saw from being quite as real.

Livid bruises etched pathways in his skin; his body twitched and trembled in odd jerky motions. Blood trickled from his mouth and nose and filled the whites of his eyes. She did not think he could see but she leaned over him anyway, and her hair fell forward to brush across his chin.

"Jess?" he said, barely intelligible, more hopeful than educated in the guess.

"Yes," she whispered, her hand hovering above his, but afraid to touch him, afraid that she would hurt him more.

"Good job, Jess," he said, words that faded in and out, jerking along with his body. "Good job."

Jess sat back on her heels, eyes closed, head bowed, fully aware of all the things he was trying to cram into the two Words that were so familiar to the both of them. A touch on her shoulder drew her gaze upward, into Arlen's.

"Come, Jess," he said. "Let these two do their work."

Slowly she got to her feet, following him away with more than one backward glance. And when they had reached the picket line, she found that she, too, had been followed, that Jaime, Dayna—still clutching the saddlebags—and Mark hesitated at a polite distance, waiting for an invitation. Arlen lifted his head, only half a nod, but all that it took.

"Someone please tell me what is happening. Has happened," she stumbled, and then gave up and demanded, "*Tell me,*" looking at Arlen, and then around at the bustle that had filled the hollow in the few moments—it *had* been only a few moments, hadn't it?—since she'd confronted Calandre on the point. She looked at her hands, which still had the feel of Calandre's throat beneath them, and gave Arlen a frown that conveyed all her disorientation and confusion.

"I'm not sure any one person has all the details figured out yet," Arlen said, "but I'll try. Help arrived while you were dealing with Calandre. A significant amount of help, actually. They pulled you off of Calandre and brought her down here with Carey, where the mage-medics have been working on both of them."

"Why?" Jess said bluntly. "Why stop me? Why heal her?"

Arlen shook his head. "Because that is who we are," he said. "Just because she has not earned such mercy doesn't mean we won't give it to her. She'll receive all the punishment she's earned, but death is not part of that judgment."

Jess looked at her bare feet. "You think I was wrong."

Arlen laughed right out loud, a short sound with genuine humor. "Jess! You were fighting for your life—*our* lives! You destroyed Willand's shield, you kept Calandre so busy she couldn't launch her wizard war when Sherra answered Gacy's call. No one is suggesting you made the wrong choice."

"Killing was right for her," Jess murmured, mostly meant to be heard, raising her head the same way Lady would have fought an unnecessary tug on the halter. "She teaches people to be cruel."

"She won't have the opportunity any longer," Arlen said with satisfaction. "The mage-medics have stopped the swelling in her throat, but they seem to think there's been serious damage to her voice. She won't be teaching anyone—and she'll never be permitted to work magic again."

"And Willand?" Jess asked, looking at Jaime. Jaime steadily met her gaze, but neither Mark nor Dayna reacted. *They don't know yet.*

"Willand will be presented to the Council, which will pass judgment on her." He looked at Jaime. "We might need witnesses."

"I'm sure you'll find them ready when the time comes," Jaime said, neatly ending further conversation on the subject.

Jess asked, not to be denied, "Why is Carey so sick?"

"Because breaking my bones wasn't enough entertainment for her," Mark said bitterly, a tone Jess was not used to hearing in his voice. She looked at him, her eyes widening, but found no obvious injuries— although he *had* been limping. He gave her a half-hearted grin. "Arlen stuck me back together as soon as Sherra's people pulled you off Calandre."

"Bones are the easiest," Arlen said. "Although as Mark would readily tell you, he has some healing left to do on his own. There wasn't time to do a thorough job."

"I'm not complaining," Mark said.

"*Carey*," Jess insisted.

Silence greeted her request, until Jaime said, "Calandre used a spell on him, Jess, an awful spell."

"She said she couldn't stop it," Jess recalled in alarm, then looked at Mark. "But you said it was stopped—"

"She lied," Arlen said flatly. "Any wizard as skilled as Calandre knows how to stop what she's started. She was just trying to upset you so she could get away from you."

"But if the spell is stopped, why isn't Carey all right?" Why was he lying between two wizards, fighting for his life?

Arlen shook his head, weariness and sorrow suddenly settling in his eyes. "The spell did a lot of damage. It's a race to see if they can patch him together before it kills him. Frankly, Jess, I'm surprised he's still alive. I think you need to be prepared—"

"No!" Jess said, surprising even herself with her vehemence. Carey was the one link that tied together her different lives, the person who had loved her before and come to love her after. She wasn't sure she could handle the upheaval of a yet another new life—human here in Camolen—without his steady and familiar hand to guide her.

Life as a horse, at least, was something she knew, and something she did well. Something she could continue to do well even without Carey. Dun Lady's Jess would eventually grow accustomed to a new rider, but she thought that Jess the woman would always feel the same sharp grief she felt right now. "Arlen," she blurted, "if Carey dies I want you to change me back to Lady."

"*What?*" Mark jerked to attention; Dayna's lips thinned and Jaime just stared at her.

"I wouldn't want that on my conscience, Jess," Arlen told her gently. "I know how much Carey means to you—no, I take that back. I only know what a good team you make, and...what I saw of you together last night. But I've also seen how courageous you are. You can do this, Jess. On your own."

Jaime's reaction had built into anger. "I can't believe I heard you say that," she told Jess. "You are your own woman—you don't need Carey holding your hand."

"But I *want* him to hold my hand," Jess said, flaring into her own anger; up went her head again. "I have always been Lady, and Lady never hurt like this! *I want Arlen to change me back if Carey dies.*"

Arlen reached into the pocket of his tunic and withdrew the broken chain of Carey's spell stones. "I can't do that for you, Jess. Or, rather, I won't. There are enough heavy things on my shoulders right now. But I can put a spell on the stone that once held the world travel spell. It should do the trick—but it won't work if you have any doubts about changing back. Magic requires a certain sincerity of belief and intent."

"Arlen, no!" Jaime said angrily, before Jess could accept the offer. "You can't give her the means—not when she's grieving!"

"It's her choice, Jaime," Arlen said flatly. "And it won't work unless even the deepest part of her wants it to."

"Do that," Jess said. "Put the spell in the stone. I can make it work." *Do it now, before you change your mind.*

Arlen suddenly looked as tired as he had the evening before, when he'd passed out beside a raging dun mare. "No interruptions, please," he cautioned.

"No problem," Jaime said, her anger still blazing. "I'm not going to watch you do this to her."

Dayna gave him a cold look. "I'm learning more about magic all the time." She followed Jaime away. Mark looked between Arlen and Jess...not happy, not passing judgment. "There are a lot of people who'd miss you, Jess," he said. "And no way for you to tell anyone if you wanted to come out again."

Jess looked at the cluster of people that hid the wounded from her. "I know," she said sadly. In the silence that fell after those words, Arlen slid one of the stones off the chain and cradled it in his palm. Jess felt a brief surge of magic, and then he held it out to her. *That easy?* After a blink of a hesitation, she took it, feeling the leftover warmth of Arlen's hand as though it were that hand she held and not the stone. She had not expected it to be so comforting to hold the thing.

But it was. And now she had her escape, and she would keep it with her until she knew if Carey would live or die...until she knew if this part of her would die with him.

# 23

Jess braced her back against the saddle and the little bay called Fahrvegnügan halted, giving her a perfect view of Arlen's hold—a spot that had taken almost an hour to reach at a reasonable pace, unlike their frantic escape of the evening before. The area wasn't secured yet and the air was full of magic, muffled by distance. There were physical skirmishes as well, as Sherra's forces ferreted out the last of Calandre's people. The fighting meant the area wasn't a safe one, but Jess felt far removed from their struggles, and unthreatened by them.

She stood in the very same place where Carey had shot three men, scaring her other self into the hottest version of Lady. Hot and ready to run, never mind that her knee was no longer whole. She looked down at her encased wrist—for it was a minor injury in the eyes of the overtaxed mage-medics, something that could be tended later—and suddenly wondered what would happen to Lady if she changed back with the injury. She still remembered the anger and panic she'd felt at that disability, but it had been at the end of an exhilarating and frightening run. Maybe she would be able to handle it better now.

On impulse she dismounted and flipped the reins over Fahrvegnügan's head, feeling the sudden urge of a good run in her legs, here by the pastures in which she'd so often gamboled. With Fahrvegnügan's reins clutched unnoticed in her hand and the horse's hoof beats filling the void where her own should have been, Jess ran.

Her bare feet pounded against the hard dirt road, feeling out ground that was so familiar she raised her head and half closed her eyes, drinking in the wind of her run and exulting in the way it whipped through her thick dun...mane. Gulping breath, strong flexing muscles, nostrils wide to the wind—*this* is what she'd been born to do.

Jess and the mildly confused bay mare flashed through the gate of the fall pasture at full speed. The pasture ranged out into the rolling hills behind Arlen's hold, encompassing a creek and a small stand of trees; the dirt path beneath her feet turned to the prickle of newly cut hay, evidence of everyday life going on despite Calandre. She ran to the trees without slowing, ignoring the growing ache of muscles that had been overused the day before. This was her pasture, her life.

*Her world.*

At the trees she stopped and whirled back around, her chest heaving; she looked out on an intimately familiar vista she'd never seen through these eyes. She looked at the ground at her feet, the permanent dust hollow from so many years of being trodden on and packed down by horses seeking shade and a good roll.

*A good roll.* She pulled the bay's bridle off so she could pick grass and dropped to the ground to wiggle in the dirt, concentrating on first one shoulder blade and then the other and finally lying with her arms and legs sprawled out and all the itches in her back satisfied—still panting, still filled with the run. Not the best roll she'd ever had but not bad for a human.

Magic murmured around her, leftover efforts of the skirmishes not far away. She ignored it. Staring into the interlaced branches above her head, Jess tried to turn her thoughts to the reason she'd come here, to the decision of Lady versus Jess. Instead her inner eye was commandeered by flashes of memory—a foal's memory, her first trip out to this place, and—a short time later—being sequestered here during the process of weaning, having the growth of the first cutting hay grass all to herself. She had weathered that occasion with no ill-effects, and was annoyed when a stray thought suggested she could wean herself from Carey just as well. *I don't want to,* she told herself stubbornly. *There is nothing wrong with wanting to be what I've always been. What I really am.*

*But you* like *Jess*, the little thought suggested, and she sat up with a frown. She knew, and had to admit to herself, that this was true. But it was just as true that she wasn't sure if this *being human* was worth it. There was so much pain involved; she was exhausted by the whole thing. In her mind's eye a strong young dun yearling chased another rudely crowding adolescent horse away from the creek, then turned the moment into a romp. She felt again the power in her limbs, the swell of equine delight at her own invincibility—the run and sliding stop, pivot and chase, rear to tower over the ground, her head shaking in mock menace and eye flashing white.

A hand descended on her shoulder, a touch that should have startled her but somehow slid into her awareness so gently that she came back to herself quietly, undisturbed.

"Jess."

A hoarse but wonderfully familiar voice. She stiffened, trembling a little.

A hand, not too steady, brushed against her back. "Been rolling again, I see."

"Yes," she managed, and slowly turned around to the reception of Carey's somewhat rueful grin. His face was pale, his eyes still terribly shot with blood, his skin still marked with just slightly less livid bruising. "Are you...all right?"

He sat down beside her, his movements that of an aged and aching man. "If you mean *am I well*...no, I'm afraid not." He nodded to the side and she discovered Arlen standing by Fahrvegnügan, waiting with no sign of impatience. She looked back to Carey and he added, "If you mean am I going to die—well, hopefully the answer to that is *no*, too. I bullied my way here—but I didn't take the long way, like you did. They were against even that, but...I had to talk to you." He took her hand, and they sat together for a moment. Then he said, "I understand you're not sure you want to stay with us."

"I—" she started, until she caught his eye, and found all her concentration going into her hand as it reached up to touch his cheek, ever so carefully in case it might hurt him. "No," she said. "I'm not sure. I mean, I'm not sure, without you."

He shook his head. "Not good, Jess. Everybody's got their own life.

You can't build yours around mine."

"I thought you—I thought—" she withdrew her hand, and frowned at it.

"That's not what this is about. This is about *you*."

"Arlen gave me a spell," she said, distracted and wrestling with his words, wondering if she'd misinterpreted his human actions along the path of this very long journey. "He put it on your stone, and gave it to me, so I could make my own decisions about who I want to be." She touched the stone beneath the fabric of the poorly fitting, bloodstained tunic, and pulled it out.

"He *what?*" Carey said, his tone more puzzled than angered, not like Jaime's at all. "Jess, that's the stone that had the world travel spell on it."

"Yes," she agreed, as puzzled as he by this reaction. She pulled the thong of the stone from her neck, shaking her hair free of it, and held it out for him. He, in turn, held it up to Arlen, who shrugged in a gesture visible even from a distance. Jess frowned at them both. "What's wrong?"

"Nothing," he said, as though he'd suddenly made up his mind about something. He gave the stone back, to her surprise. In response he said, "It *is* your choice."

Slowly she looped the stone back around her neck, more convinced than ever that she would never understand unfathomable human ways.

"Jess," he said slowly, "You can't just be some extension of me. Maybe that was okay for you as Lady, but it doesn't work with people, not if they really want to be happy. If you stay here, and stay Jess, you're going to have to figure out who you are, apart from me or anyone else."

That made too much sense; she didn't want to listen to it just then. "When you look at me now," Jess said, a sudden spark of challenge in her voice, "who is it you like? Lady, who you know, and who listens to your Words, or Jess, who doesn't?" *Because she's her own person*, added the surprised little voice.

"Not that simple," he said, and sighed. "Lady and Jess have a lot in common, and it's not easy to separate those things. Why do you think it was so hard for me to accept you in this form? The way I felt about you...it didn't seem right to feel that way about a horse."

"You *do* love me," Jess said, hesitant at first, but in watching his face she grew confident. "Real human love, like in the TV stories."

"No, Jess," he said, smiling. "Those are just pretend. *This* is real." And he slid his fingers through her dun hair and rested his hand at the back of her neck and tenderly kissed the high point of each cheekbone as she closed her eyes and drank in the thrill it gave her. Lady had never felt just such a thrill. Maybe Jess deserved a little more of a chance.

"Now," he said, resting the side of his face against hers, "I'm not dead but I've been pretty damn close and I think I may pass out. So do you think we can forget about the spellstone and get back to our friends?"

"Damn straight," Jess said. Then, growing more thoughtful as she carefully helped him to his feet, she wondered out loud, "But do you suppose Arlen could let me be Lady every once in a while, just because I want to?"

Carey laughed, a pained sound, and said, "I imagine that can be arranged."

Mark looked out the window—one of the few windows in Arlen's hold—and said, "So what if they don't believe us at home? They can't prove otherwise."

Jaime sat in a rocking chair, the cat on her lap, and lightly traced the lines of the bandage beneath her trousers. The mage-medics could have easily cared for the scratch, but had requested that she see their unmagicked counterparts unless the small wound became a problem. She had willingly agreed; it was obvious that they had their hands full of injured parties from both sides of the fighting. They had, at least, healed the break in her nose, although the kind young man who'd done it had apologetically explained to her that the natural healing had started slightly crooked, and that he would have to break it again if she wanted it straight. She had declined without regret.

She regarded Mark without responding to him. He, too, had been left to finish healing on his own, and still moved carefully—as though he were afraid his bones would give out on him without warning.

She couldn't blame him. Carey, too, continued to struggle, and was visited daily by medics both magical and not, who monitored the progress of healing from a perverted spell they had not previously encountered. Dayna sat cross-legged on the bed and it was she who broke the silence. "Don't get your story set in stone," she said. "I'm not sure I'm going back with you."

"You're not?" Mark blurted, and the cat leaped out of Jaime's lap at her start of surprise.

"No...I don't think so." She picked at the hem of her trousers, which were slightly too long, as usual. "I don't expect you guys to understand—I'm not sure I do. I mean, at first I hated the whole idea of doing magic. But...I guess I've seen it do some good. I guess *I've* done some good with it. And I think it's something I could *be* good at. Really good."

"That's the truth," Mark said, putting his back to the window and crossing his arms. "It's not something you'll get the chance to try out back home."

"Right. And...if it turns out I hate it, I can always come on home. If you guys are willing to take care of some details with the house, that is."

"Better make a list," Jaime said, somewhat wearily. "And we have to remember to leave you out of our little story—which is thin enough as it is. Kidnapped, taken to Zaleski State Forest in southern Ohio, held for a month or so, during which time Eric is killed, and we escape after killing the bad guys. They'll never find any evidence to back that up, because there isn't any. That's not real life, that's a TV movie of the week."

"There isn't any evidence that we're lying, either," Mark insisted. "Ernie's got a history, I think, and they'll know he's been out of sight. The hardest part will be getting to Zaleski without leaving a trail, and then staggering convincingly out of the woods."

No. The hardest part would be going back to life as usual, and pretending she had not been changed by the things that had happened to her here.

"Besides," Dayna offered, sounding as tired as Jaime of this process, "No one's thought of anything better."

That was the crux of it. No one had.

"When do we leave, then?" Jaime asked. "We could go anytime we wanted, I think. In fact, now that they have the checkspell, I'll bet a lot of wizards are anxious for us to leave before it's actually in place. Afterwards it'll probably take an act of Congress."

"Right," Mark snorted. "It's nice to see bureaucracy is universal."

Jaime stood. "I'm going to take a walk," she said, suddenly overwhelmed with the reality of the good-byes she faced. "If I see Arlen, I'll tell him we're ready to go."

"Yeah," Mark agreed, sounding as wistful as she felt. "We're ready to go."

# 24

As natural as it Jaime found it to head for horses, she was not surprised to discover Carey, a kindred spirit of sorts, trying to organize his thoughts in their company. As she wandered toward the pasture on the other side of the gardens, she heard sounds of work from the round training pen set in the flat ground between the huge garden plots, and she detoured to find Carey riding a dun horse there. This dun was dark, almost brown, and his black points were nearly lost in the depth of his coat—but there was something about the set of his neck and head that reminded her of something...or someone.

Carey caught her staring, and halted next to her. "Jess' brother," he said. "A good steady fellow, but not up to the treatment he got from Calandre's people. I have a lot of retraining to do." He stared grimly off onto nowhere and said, "He's better off than his—and Jess'—half-sister. They rode her to death."

It was his first reference to the destruction Calandre's people had wrought. As far as Jaime knew, he had not yet dealt with the massive loss of his friends and comrades, the couriers he had managed for Arlen. She opened her mouth to say something about them, but hesitated, and instead said, "I'm sorry. Are you up to this yet?"

He gave her a sharp look, but it faded into a rueful shrug that admitted the question was a valid one. "Not just yet." He moved the horse into a walk, and rode figure-eights as he talked with her—gentle, concentrated movements at a good working pace. "Trying to get his confidence back," he told her.

Jaime forbore from mentioning it didn't look like he could handle anything more than a walk, anyway. His movements still had the look of effort about them, and from afar she would have guessed he was an old man with arthritic joints and aching muscles.

"We're gearing up to leave," she said suddenly, plunging into the subject without getting her toes wet first. "We think we have the kidnap story worked out pretty well."

"I still don't quite understand that angle," Carey said, his voice slightly distant as he took the horse through the change of rein from one circle to the other. "People are kidnapped here, too, but it's usually for money, or at least lust."

Jaime shrugged. "A lot of people think if you've got valuable horses, you've got money. The truth is, you've spent your money on the valuable horses. Anyway, it's the best we could come up with. Nothing less is going to explain my disappearance, not with a barn full of those horses left on their own." She leaned against the rails of the round pen. "If you've got any better ideas, I'm open to them."

"Don't go back," Carey said simply.

"No," Jaime responded without hesitation. She'd already been through this discussion with herself. "My life is there, Carey. I've enjoyed a number of things about your world, but it's not who and what I want to be. You've got Dayna, though, I think. I just hope...I hope we can visit. I hope this doesn't have to be good-bye for ever."

"No such luck," Carey said, and brought the dark gelding to a halt again, asking him to bring his nose around to touch each booted foot in a final exercise of flexion and obedience and then dismounting— slowly, creakily. "I'm sure Arlen will be doing research on your world in person—and there'll be judgments that need your testimony. It's not all *that* hard to suspend the checkspell—it's getting the whole Council to make up their minds to do it that takes so long."

Jaime found her expression going cold at the thought of Willand, at the realization that her struggles with the aftermath of Willand's torture were really just beginning—that she wasn't going to be able to run away from them. She forced her attention back to Carey and discovered he was staring at her, aware of her reaction and wanting to know—to help, even. But what she had told Jess was still true—she wasn't prepared to share her experience until she had come to terms with it.

"Jess has been pestering Arlen," Carey said with a grin, quite obviously changing the subject. "She really does want to visit you and ride dressage under you *and* me. Arlen told her that because the magic originates on this world, she can pull an occasional switch between Jess and Lady, but on Earth she has to choose between one or the other. I don't think she's quite come to terms with that." He sobered a little. "She's had three offers of work, good positions—two as couriers and one as a trainer for one of the outfits in Camolen City that run public courier stables. Don't ask me how they heard about her way up there."

"She's unique," Jaime said. "Word's bound to get around. What's she going to do?"

Carey loosened the gelding's girth and ran the stirrups up on his saddle, the same slightly odd saddle design as the one still sitting in Jaime's tack room. "I don't know," he said, and she heard a little wistfulness in his voice. "I told her she had to be her own person, and live her own life, that just staying with me wasn't enough for her. Now I'm a little worried that she listened to me."

"Wherever she goes, her heart will always be with you," Jaime said, and then grinned. "Wasn't that the hokiest thing you've ever heard?"

Carey snorted an agreement, but she thought she saw gratitude in his expression. "She'll be here for Arlen until he—*I*—can get his fleet up and running again. We've only found one of my couriers, and she's so full of guilt over surviving that she's not really functioning yet. We've got one of Sherra's people on loan, but Jess is taking the brunt of it."

And thriving, Jaime knew, for she'd seen Jess the evening before, tired but happy and on her way to see Carey. Her arm was completely healed, done by Sherra herself—who fully understood that the limb had to mend well enough to function as a weight-bearing leg for Lady. "Does she still have that awful spellstone Arlen made for her?" she asked with a frown.

Carey's reaction was completely unexpected: he laughed. Jaime's frown turned into a suspicious look. "You must know something I don't."

"Like the fact that a stone can't be re-used for a different spell?" Carey asked.

"But—what...? He told Jess—"

"I know what he told Jess. But Arlen would never give her the spell she asked for—he just didn't waste time arguing with her. He set a very simple alert spell into the wire around the stone, something that would tell him if she tried to trigger it. If you recall, he *did* tell her the thing wouldn't work unless she *really* wanted it to. If she did try to use it, she'd just think its failure was her own fault."

"He might have let me know," Jaime grumbled, not really as annoyed as she let herself sound. What a relief to know Arlen had not actually acceded to Jess' desperate request; she had had to fight a terrible disappointment when she'd believed it of him.

She turned to look at the hold, the top of which was just visible over the very high corn that grew between her and it. There were still too many things she wanted the answers to, like how come the corn here tasted so like the corn at home, and why were there horses and cats and even—she slapped her arm—mosquitoes here. She wanted to get to know Arlen better, when there wasn't a force shield between them and lives at stake.

She realized that they'd been standing together in silence for many moments, and she glanced at Carey to find him in thought as deep as her own. Probably full of his own questions.

"Come on," he said, catching her glance. "If you don't mind my slow going, I'll walk you back to the hold and we'll go find Arlen. He'll take you home."

*In the Midwest America dressage show circuit, the competitors come to know one another and their horses. Jaime Cabot and her horse Sabre are in the thick of it, although there is speculation aplenty over her recent strange disappearance from competition, a disappearance that lasted nearly half a year when all was said and done.*

*But the real conjecture is over the people who now occasionally travel with Jaime—the tall mustached gentleman who escorts her, and the horse and rider who compete in the intermediate levels. The dun mare is of completely unknown lineage and lacks the power of a truly great dressage mount, but she and her rider often take their classes anyway, carrying the hearts of judges and spectators alike with the gestalt of their partnership and the expressive spirit in the eyes of Dun Lady's Jess.*